The Regency

LORDS & LADIES
COLLECTION

*Two Glittering Regency
Love Affairs*

Honour's Bride
by Gayle Wilson
&
The Rebel
by Georgina Devon

The Regency

Lords & Ladies
COLLECTION

The Regency

LORDS & LADIES
COLLECTION

Gayle Wilson &
Georgina Devon

MILLS & BOON®

*First published in Great Britain 2006 by
Harlequin Mills & Boon Limited,
Eton House, 18-24 Paradise Road, Richmond, Surrey TW9 1SR*

THE REGENCY LORDS & LADIES COLLECTION
© Harlequin Books S.A. 2006

The publisher acknowledges the copyright holders of the
individual works as follows:

Honour's Bride © Mona Gay Thomas 1998
The Rebel © Alison J Hentges 2001

ISBN-13: 978 0 263 85108 3
ISBN-10: 0 263 85108 7

138-1006

*Printed and bound in Spain
by Litografia Rosés S.A., Barcelona*

Honour's Bride
by
Gayle Wilson

Gayle Wilson is an award-winning author who has written almost thirty novels and novellas for Mills & Boon® and Silhouette®. A former English and world history teacher of gifted students, she writes historical fiction set in the English Regency period and contemporary romantic suspense. Gayle still lives in Alabama, where she was born, with her husband of over thirty years and an ever-growing menagerie of beloved pets. She has one son, who is also a teacher of gifted students. Gayle loves to hear from readers.

For Sandra,
The very best example of two wonderful relationships in life, being both my dear friend and my kinsman.

Prologue

London, 1808

"You, sir, are a blackguard and a rogue," the earl of Ryde said softly. "A charming scoundrel, by all accounts, but a scoundrel nonetheless."

Never before had his father subjected him to such a scathing dissection of his character. Of course, never before had he killed a man, Lord St. John acknowledged ruefully. But there were mitigating circumstances behind that death, none of which his father was taking into consideration.

Kit's well-shaped lips tightened, as they had for the last fifteen minutes, over a defense of his actions which he longed to make. Even if he attempted a justification of what he'd done, he knew from bitter experience that nothing would prevent the rest of his father's tirade. Once Ryde reached the point of openly expressing his anger, which happened infrequently, then nothing could deter him. That was a reality Kit had had ample cause to understand through the years.

"More importantly," his father went on, "you continue to bring dishonor to this family. You may enjoy wallowing in the mud of public censure, but I will no longer allow you to drag the Montgomery name there with you. We have endured more than enough of your scandals,'' the earl said softly. ''Far more than enough.''

Throughout this exchange, in actuality an encounter too one-sided to be classified as exchange, the earl's voice had been filled with contempt and cutting in its sarcasm, but it had never risen. The guiding principle of the earl of Ryde's life had always been control, which was why, of course, his relationship with his younger son was so volatile.

Kit Montgomery, Lord St. John, was almost a throwback, far more attuned to the exploits of his warrior ancestors than to the man before whom he stood today. Yet, ironically, St. John was also the epitome of what was now considered to be the fashionable London gentleman.

Both handsome and confident, Kit was immensely popular with the ladies. The masculine set admired him because he was also a reckless and daring sportsman and a skillful gambler. He frequently wagered stakes whose loss would bankrupt half the businesses in the English capital without the blink of an eye.

Given those accomplishments and his natural physical attributes, St. John had been, since his introduction into society, one of its most popular members. Yet he had become almost too accustomed to winning: at cards, at sporting events, and especially in affairs of the heart. His present boredom with the normal activities of the *ton* had led him to push against the few boundaries that constrained young men of his class.

''Wild'' was the epithet most frequently applied to Kit by his parents' contemporaries. His fellow Corinthians considered him simply ''Top of the Trees,'' their highest compliment. The ladies found him to be frustratingly elusive, although undeniably exciting. And his father...

Again Kit tamped down his resentment. Never before had his father called him a blackguard or accused him of dishonoring the Montgomery name. Despite their differing views regarding proper behavior for a gentleman, both Ryde and his son understood family honor. Its principles had been instilled in the younger Montgomerys since their births. The name Kit bore was old and proud, and he had never sought to blacken it.

"You have sullied our name," his father said, almost echoing that thought. "And this time I intend to assure myself that it will never happen again."

The dreaded words had the desired effect, although Kit's classically handsome face did not change. His blue eyes, surrounded by their sweep of long, soot-black lashes met his father's calmly, reflecting only disdain for the threat.

That was not, however, the emotion which seethed beneath the surface. *Disinherited.* He had certainly been warned. His own brother had attempted to explain his father's growing disgust, but despite Roger's cautions, Kit hadn't listened.

He knew there was nothing in his behavior that differed from that of dozens of other young men about town. Except the possibility that he did it all better than anyone else. That was always his goal, and neither he nor his father had ever stopped to evaluate the origin of that particular characteristic.

"Am I to understand you, sir—" Kit began, his voice as dispassionate as the earl's, only to be sharply cut off.

"Understand me?" Ryde questioned derisively. "If you do, St. John, it will certainly be the first time."

"Do you intend to disinherit me, sir?" Kit continued stubbornly.

The earl laughed, the sound scornful. The small flush that had stained the young man's high cheekbones since the beginning of this interview, the only sign of his discomfort, deepened.

"I swear I would," the earl continued, "if I believed that might make you a better man. I'm afraid instead it would simply make you a poorer one."

"I do not fear poverty," Kit said, his eyes now as hard as those of the man seated behind the massive rosewood desk.

"I wonder what you *do* fear," Ryde said. "If I knew that, perhaps I would have some chance of insuring that your worthless life might eventually bear some snatch of honor."

It was Shakespeare, of course, the phrase easily recognized. After all, St. John had been properly educated—at Eton and then Cambridge, and he had done remarkably well at his studies. There was a fine intellect hidden beneath the outward recklessness, but one which had found nothing after university worthy of challenging it.

Kit excelled at calculating the chances that a certain card would fall, at placing wagers in the betting books, and even at figuring to the minute how fast he must push his horses through a particular stage in order to beat the current record along one of the coach roads. Those were not, however, activities which occupied the intellect long enough to provide the type of stimulation Kit had once found in his studies.

Yet a gentleman was not permitted to undertake anything more mentally challenging after the end of his school days. His family's vast estates were managed by professionals, whose activities were competently overseen by his father. At the earl's death the care of those properties would pass into the hands of Kit's older brother, Roger, who had been trained from birth to accept that role.

But for Kit and other younger sons, aristocrats like him,

there was really nothing important to do. Nothing to occupy their brains or their energies, too much of which were expended on activities that called down the disgust of their elders. Ennui had almost certainly played a role in Kit's misadventures, but even had he recognized that fact, there was still nothing society would allow him to do about it.

"Honor, sir?" Kit repeated softly.

"You have now killed a man through your recklessness. And over a woman, of course. I expect the knock of the magistrates on the door of this house at any moment. And may I remind you that is something which has never happened before in its long history. Until now. Until you," his father added.

"It was a duel, sir," Kit reminded him.

His father was certainly aware of the circumstances. Receiving an explanation of the events which had led to that disastrous dawn meeting was not the point of this exercise. The purpose of the earl's diatribe was chastisement. And humiliation. Kit understood that when he had been summoned.

"I never meant to kill Edmonton," Kit went on. "He shouldn't have died from that scratch. I put the ball exactly where I intended. His surgeon did more, I assure you, to cause his death than I. What he had said, however, could not in all honor be ignored. I do not believe that even you, sir—"

"Forgive me, St. John, but I find that I am uninterested in whatever you believe. *If* you truly believe in anything. I must confess I find myself doubtful of that, also."

"Also?" Kit repeated. Despite his efforts to match his father's control, his quick temper was beginning to rise.

"As I am doubtful that you are capable of change."

"I promise you—"

"I am also uninterested in your promises. I believe I

have heard them all before. Frankly, I am becoming uninterested in *you,* St. John. In your endless escapades and your callous disregard for anything beyond your immediate pleasures.''

Although it was not a fair assessment of the man he was, Kit held both his tongue and his temper. It was better to let his father have his say, to listen in respectful silence, and then to absent himself from the earl's presence, and therefore from his attentions, for a few weeks. It had always worked before.

''So I am going to make you an offer,'' Ryde said. His eyes swept slowly down the tall, handsome figure of his son, standing unconsciously at attention before him.

Kit's clothing was the finest London had to offer, and he wore it to perfection. The coat of navy superfine had been cut by Weston's master hand, its color chosen to emphasize the striking contrast between the blue eyes and the curling, coal-black hair that fell over his forehead. The jacket covered a lawn shirt of dazzling whiteness, an intricately tied cravat, and a striped silk waistcoat.

Fawn pantaloons stretched over his flat belly and down the long, muscular legs of a horseman. The tasseled boots, made of Moroccan leather, were from Toby, and they were polished daily by his valet with a preparation whose primary ingredient was champagne. The whole ensemble had cost more than most families in England lived on for a year.

''And I encourage you to think carefully before you turn it down,'' Ryde added softly.

''An offer, sir?'' St. John said cautiously. This was a deviation from the familiar format of their previous encounters.

''An opportunity,'' the earl amended. ''An opportunity

to add something which has been missing from your worthless existence for the last twenty-eight years. An opportunity to finally undertake something of real value, to give meaning to what has been, up to this point, an empty and meaningless life.''

Again Kit's lips tightened, but he swallowed the angry rejoinder. That life had not been his choice. As the younger son of a peer his options were extremely limited. There was no question, certainly not among the ladies of the demimonde, that St. John was highly unsuited for the clergy, and the only other career available. . .

''You once asked my permission to enter the navy,'' the earl continued.

''I believe I was sixteen at the time,'' Kit said, fighting a smile, despite the seriousness of the situation, ''and enamored of the uniform.''

''Indeed,'' said his father coldly.

That gibe had been a mistake, St. John realized with regret. One did not offer humor in the midst of Ryde's chastisements.

''But still, an honorable profession, don't you think?'' the earl asked. His thin lips lifted, echoing the inquiring rise of one brow, but there was no matching amusement in the cold eyes.

''Yes, my lord,'' Kit agreed, apprehension at the direction of this conversation stirring in his stomach.

''However, I do not believe the navy would accept the offer of your services. They prefer men from something higher than the criminal classes, or so I have heard.''

Ryde's bitter smile had faded. Apparently he took no joy in the vicious blow with which he had just struck his son. Again, St. John fought for restraint.

"The army, on the other hand," the earl continued, "is, as I understand, somewhat more desperate and therefore less discriminating. I assume even you know that Sir Arthur Wellesley is being sent to Iberia to fight the French."

There was a long silence. It was so prolonged that the sounds of carriage wheels moving on the cobblestones of the city street below drifted between the two men.

"You wish me to join him," Kit said finally.

"*If* they'll take you," Ryde said insultingly. "But, being the army, I imagine they will. And I still have some influence. I'm offering to buy your commission. Not a very lofty one, I'm afraid, my generosity being naturally limited by my disgust. But then it will be better than life as a penniless fugitive on the Continent, I suppose."

"And if I refuse?" Kit asked.

"I don't believe it will be a great loss to this family. Your mother shall miss you, of course. And your brother. For a time," the earl added.

The thin lips pursed, and then Ryde's gaze fell to the correspondence spread across the gleaming surface of his desk. His long white fingers, which had toyed with a gold lorgnette throughout this interview, closed around it with purpose now, directing the glass toward the topmost document.

"I accept," Kit said softly.

His father's eyes lifted and rested briefly on the elegant figure before him. "Perhaps Wellesley and Spain can make a man of you," Ryde said. "It's far more than I have been able to manage."

Again his gaze dropped, and although his son stood before the desk for at least a full minute more, the earl never looked up again. There was no way that Ryde could know it would be almost three years before he would see Kit again. And even had he known that, of course, it would have made not a whit's worth of difference in his behavior.

"I'm sorry, Judith, but there it is. He's within his rights to question why this marriage has not already taken place. And, given the circumstances, why it should be any longer delayed."

Judith McDowell contemplated her father's face, reading far more from the furrowed brow and the unsmiling lips than she had from the gruff words he had just uttered.

This had not been her father's choice, she knew. But he had given his word, and to General Aubrey McDowell his word was more than his bond. It was his honor. If honor demanded the sacrifice of his only daughter to repay a debt, then that was how it must be.

"But surely..." Judith said, seeking only to delay that which she had always known to be inevitable. She had been promised to Michael Haviland since childhood, and the fact that they had not already married was only because of her father's reluctance and Haviland's indifference.

"Wellesley leaves for Spain within the month. Michael's regiment will go with him. Sir Roland wishes you to accompany his son. As his wife."

Judith held her tongue, but the breath she took was deep, lifting the lace fichu that lay over her high breasts. Not Michael's wish, she was aware, but his father's. General Roland Haviland had chosen a wife for his son almost ten years ago, and neither Michael nor she had had any say in the arrangement.

She realized that most people would believe this match to be well made, certainly from her standpoint. She had no position, no wealth to bring to any union, and her looks were not those which attracted the attention of gentlemen who were well-fixed enough to overlook those other detriments.

Judith McDowell was tall and slim, with soft brown hair and dark eyes, which were thoughtful enough never to have been described as sparkling. Her complexion was most kindly referred to as olive, and despite the best efforts of her abigail, none of the popular remedies of the day would lighten it. Perhaps even more of a handicap than those were her quick wit and her inability to suffer fools, gladly or otherwise.

Judith had had her Season, of course. Her father and her aunt Jane had dutifully seen to that, although it had not been strictly necessary, given her situation. And it had not been a singular success, if one judged by the number of names on her dance card or by the gentlemen waiting each evening to take her to supper. That didn't make any difference, of course, except as a matter of pride, since she was already unofficially betrothed.

During Judith's time in London, Michael Haviland had called when he was in town, but with his duties his presence in society had been a very rare occasion. The round of parties, routs, and balls her aunt had arranged invitations to was quickly over, and then, gratefully, Judith had been allowed to return to the place she loved best—her father's large, old country house, whose library she had already devoured by the time she was fifteen.

It was almost ironic that it should be in this very room that her father chose to deliver this painfully unwelcome news. Its familiar genteel shabbiness should have been comforting to her distress perhaps—the low, pleasant fire, the tea tray, the dearly beloved books and the worn furniture. These were the things she loved best in the world, and she had truly never missed the whirlwind round of London entertainments that she had so briefly been exposed to.

There were always other things to occupy her time in the country—reading, of course; caring for the animals that belonged to the manor; taking long walks across the moors or along shaded country lanes; and chatting with her elderly neighbors, who welcomed her visits and who had taught her so many things from their vast store of country wisdom.

Judith McDowell's life was, to her at least, full and rich. And the prospect of following the drum in a strange country with a man whom she did not particularly admire was not, she was finding, a pleasant one.

"It's a hard life for a woman," her father said. "You know, Ju, that I would never have wished..." His voice faded, the open expression of that wish forbidden by his conscience.

But, of course, she knew it all. The story had been told to her from childhood, and it had never changed. General McDowell owed his life to Roland Haviland because of an act of heroism on some distant battlefield. This was a long-standing debt of honor which led to the agreement the two had made concerning their children's futures.

"I know," she said. From somewhere within the devastation her father had just made of her ordered and orderly life, she found a smile for him. He was worried about her, of course. He knew better than most, far better than she could, what she would face as an officer's wife on campaign in a hostile country.

Her mother had followed her father to his posting in India shortly after their marriage. Judith had been born there, but her mother's health had been permanently broken by the confinement and the climate, and she had died of an unnamed fever within the year. Judith had been sent back to England and placed in her aunt's care until her father's return several years later.

''Haviland's not the man I would have chosen for you, my dear, but there was no way, of course, for either of us to foresee...'' Again, her father's words drifted into silence.

Not the man I would have chosen. Not the man Judith would have chosen, either, she knew. In her few encounters with him, she had found Michael Haviland to be arrogant, proud, and brusque to the point of rudeness. His looks were not unpleasant, but his manner during his brief visits had been off-putting to both her father and herself.

They had not discussed that, of course, but they knew one another too well to be in any doubt about the impression Haviland had made on each of them. Not only was Judith not in love with her fiancé, she had found little enough to like about him.

However, since she had not yet met a man who caused her heart to behave at all strangely in her very practical breast, Judith McDowell was beginning to believe, as the world already did, that her match with Michael Haviland was the best she might hope for. And of course, it was the wish of her father and his. More than a wish, she acknowledged. It was to them both a matter of their honor. Of a promise made that must be kept, no matter the circumstances.

If the marriage did not create emotions which matched the romantic fantasies written about in the popular novels of the day or correspond to the giggling revelations of those ethereal blond creatures she had encountered in London, whose dance cards were always full and who knew exactly what to say to gentlemen to make them laugh, then it was just as well. There was probably little place for romance in the ranks of an army on the move.

It would be her duty to become the kind of wife a man who has been sent to fight for his country needed. She could accomplish that, she had no doubt. She was far stronger than her mother had ever been, and she was clever about many things, even if she had never learned to flirt.

She would make her father and her husband proud of her strength and resourcefulness, Judith decided. Never by word or deed would she indicate to either that this was not the path she had wished her life to take.

And after all, she acknowledged practically, it really wasn't as if she had any other choice.

Chapter One

Portugal, 1811

The sound of a whip striking the back of a man who has already endured over eighty strokes is a sound like no other. The sharp crack of the leather thongs against intact skin had at first been accompanied by soft grunts of pain, but both those noises had long ago become something else.

The efforts of the small, trembling man to remain silent before his assembled peers had eventually given way to begging and then to shrieks. Now, after a long time, the leather was sodden, and the skin was certainly no longer intact—not one square inch of it. The watching men had fallen silent, and the flogged trooper's head hung loosely between the tripod of lances to which he had been tied.

Major Lord St. John deliberately raised his eyes from the scene before him to find those of his commander. The blue eyes inquired. Colonel Smythe's head moved once, the arc of movement small enough to be undetected by anyone paying less attention to that order than St. John, but it had undoubtedly been a negative.

One hundred strokes of the lash had been ordered, and

they were to be delivered. Lord Wellington's orders on that point had been unmistakably clear, and they were well-known to the men.

Except in this case it was almost certainly the wrong man who was receiving that punishment, St. John thought bitterly. Involuntarily, his mouth flattened as the whip fell again. Mercifully, the limp body of Private Toby Reynolds didn't even jerk in response. At least he would not feel the last twenty, and when it was finally over...

Kit's eyes again moved, this time meeting those of the only woman among the assembled troops. Who was watching *him,* St. John realized, rather than the punishment being administered. Judith Haviland had chosen to attend this public spectacle of military brutality, and when the trooper was cut down, it would be Mrs. Haviland's competent hands that would attend to what remained of the skin of his back.

Her brown eyes were calm and uncondemning as they met Kit's. After almost three years spent with the English army on the Peninsula, Mrs. Haviland had seen every horror known to man, and she had flinched from none of them.

St. John wondered if she understood why Toby Reynolds was being punished. Not the actual charge, of course. That had been read before the first stroke of the whip descended. The man had been caught stealing from the peasants in the nearby village, and theft was something that an army dependent upon the goodwill of the local populace could not afford.

The French army lived off the land and was hated for it. The British would not, not if Wellington could help it. So far the English general's genius for supply had served them well. His forces had seldom gone hungry, not for bread or for beef, which they carried with them on the hoof.

But St. John's regiment had recently been deployed as

an outpost to guard a vital yet remote road against the arrival of French reinforcements. The duty was not unusual for the highly mobile light dragoons, most adept of any of Wellington's units at scouting, intelligence-gathering, and hit-and-run actions.

This time, however, they been sent so far in advance of Wellington's winter encampment that they had apparently been lost or forgotten. At least, the supply wagons had failed to arrive when expected.

Rations had been cut and then cut again. There were still biscuits, but several of the last barrels of salt beef they had received had been spoiled and inedible. There had been no issue of either rum or wine in more than a month. And no pay.

Kit himself had been sent to negotiate with the locals for whatever provisions were available, for the troopers and perhaps more importantly for the irreplaceable horses. The villagers had little to sell, and in truth the regiment had little with which to buy or trade.

Yet up until now discipline had held through the deprivation. Most of the dragoons, seasoned veterans in this campaign, had been on short rations before. They trusted Wellington, knowing from experience that the supplies would eventually reach them and had simply resigned themselves to waiting out the discomfort. Except, apparently, for Captain Michael Haviland, Kit thought.

There was no doubt in his mind that Haviland had sent his batman to loot in the nearby village, and Kit was certain it had not been the first time. There had been items missing from their own supplies in the past, in all likelihood stolen and then traded to the Portuguese by Haviland and Reynolds. When the regiment's stores which were worth bartering ran out, the two had been forced to resort to stealing what they wanted.

This time the batman had been caught and brought back to the colonel to receive his prescribed punishment, a punishment which every man in this army was well aware of and which most recognized as necessary. As, of course, would Judith Haviland.

He might feel differently about the theft, Kit acknowledged, despite the fact that such a thing endangered them all, had he believed the batman had been sent to procure something which Mrs. Haviland needed, either food or clothing.

Not a man here would begrudge her anything, and most of them, himself included, would willingly have taken those hundred stripes to provide whatever she lacked. But the wine which Haviland's batman had been caught stealing was not for Mrs. Haviland. And everyone watching his punishment today was well aware of that fact.

Haviland's drunkenness was no secret to the regiment. How he continued to procure spirits when there was no official issue had once been mysterious and was now no longer. But if he desired further stimulation from drink, St. John supposed, the captain would have to do his own procuring from now on.

Not that it would make much difference whether he did or not. A sober Michael Haviland in the field was not a particular improvement over a drunken one. That had already been demonstrated on several occasions.

The terrible noise the lash made had stopped, Major St. John realized suddenly. The enormous sergeant who had been chosen to administer the hundred strokes was awaiting his orders.

"Cut him down," he commanded.

The peasants from the village had already been generously compensated by the colonel for their trouble and given an apology. They had been invited to witness the trooper's punishment, but had chosen, wisely perhaps, not to.

I damn well wish I had had that option, St. John thought. No matter how many times he had seen this, it was never any easier. Not even knowing that it was necessary. And just.

An army at war maintained discipline. That was only one of the lessons Kit had learned in the years he had spent on the Peninsula. He wasn't sure his service had accomplished what his father had intended, but there were, without any doubt, lessons he had learned that he would never in his life forget.

"May I tend him?" Judith Haviland asked softly.

Kit glanced down to meet those remarkable eyes again. Mrs. Haviland was standing beside his horse, almost at his knee, her left hand soothing over the neck of the bay. Her fingers were slender, and they had not lost the summer's tan. These were not the soft, white hands of a lady, not any longer, but they had proven more valuable than any others in the regiment.

"Of course," Kit agreed. Seeing to Reynolds's injuries was a task he didn't envy her, but one at which she had experience.

"Thank you," she said simply.

She turned to follow the troopers who were dragging the unconscious body of her husband's batman to the large tent which served as the unit's makeshift hospital, and St. John's gaze unconsciously followed.

The bottom of Mrs. Haviland's gray kersey skirt was damp and caked along the hem with mud, as were her half boots. Her soft brown hair had been braided and wound into a loose chignon, but curling strands of it had escaped and drifted around the back of her neck and shoulders as she struggled over the rough, snow-covered ground.

The heavy skirt was not full enough to completely camouflage the contours of the body it covered. Her hips were slim, yet womanly, below a narrow waist that led upward to high, firm breasts.

Conscious suddenly that he was taking an inventory, part of it from memory, of the body of a fellow officer's wife, Kit forced his eyes down to his gloved hands, to the reins threaded loosely between his fingers. And he wondered again at his undeniable attraction to Judith Haviland.

There was nothing in her appearance or her demeanor that would have attracted him three years ago. Nothing that would have warranted a second look from the man he had been then. But, of course, he was no longer that man.

And he *was* attracted to Judith Haviland. It was not a temptation he would ever do anything about, though. In all honor, she was for him the most forbidden of women. However, after fighting against it for three years, the attraction he felt was one he no longer bothered to deny. Not to himself at least.

When Kit reentered his tent, Michael Haviland was waiting for him. The confrontation shouldn't have been unexpected, he supposed, but it was. Somehow he had thought Haviland would have the decency to stay out of sight until the remembrance of this morning's exercise in military discipline had faded. But of course, decency was not something that meant a great deal to Captain Haviland.

"I suppose you took some satisfaction over that," Haviland said angrily. "Beating half to death a man who couldn't defend himself."

He had been drinking. It was obvious by the slight slurring of the word "satisfaction." He was also unshaven and his uniform was stained, but neither of those things was unusual enough to occasion comment. War made men or it broke them. And despite his family's long and distinguished military tradition, it was obvious which effect it had had on this one.

"You're a fool," Kit said coldly. He stripped off his gloves and threw them on the narrow cot, which with his folding campaign desk and his small chest made up the entire furnishings of the tent, and the entirety of his belongings. "You must have known he'd be caught eventually."

"Are you accusing me of *sending* Reynolds to that village?"

"Here?" St. John asked. "Between the two of us? Then yes, of course, I am. And you may thank Smythe's respect for your father that that same accusation was not made in front of the regiment or in the dispatches."

"If it had been, I would have called him out. He knows that. So should you," Michael said. His eyes were bloodshot, and his cheeks were gaunt, almost gray beneath the surface tan.

"You may do so now, you know," Kit offered. He found himself wishing the bastard would.

"So you can kill me, too?" Haviland mocked. "Save your threats and your chivalry for the French, St. John. Everyone knows why you're here, relegated to this bloody backwater unit. Your own father couldn't stand having you in England any longer. You're not fit to sit in judgment on anyone. Certainly not on me."

Kit's fingers trembled over the button he had been pushing through its opening. By a conscious act of will, he controlled them and his automatic response to the contempt he heard in Haviland's voice.

"I may have been responsible for a man's death," he said softly, the blue eyes hard, "but I've never let another man suffer for my crimes. And I have never in my life mistreated a woman.''

Haviland laughed. "That's what this is, isn't it? This isn't about Reynolds or the wine or Wellington's prissing Methodist orders. This is all about Judith.''

"One has nothing to do with the other,'' St. John denied.

"And you're a bloody liar, my lord. One has *everything* to do with the other. But she is *my* wife, you know. I'll damn well do with her what I will. And there is nothing you or Smythe or anyone else can do about it.''

Suddenly Kit was very still, exerting a rigid self-control that would have made his father proud. What he wanted to do with the hand that he forced to move calmly to the next gold button was to drive it into the nose of the drunken coward who stood before him.

Haviland was right. There was nothing he could do. Especially when Mrs. Haviland herself claimed that the bruise which had marred the smooth, fragile line of her jaw this past week was the result of an accident.

There was not a man in the regiment who believed that. And not one who was willing to add to Mrs. Haviland's shame by openly questioning her explanation. Though several of them had come to him privately, however, to express their concerns.

They were not gentlemen, not even by the lowly standards of the army, but they had enough of what Haviland mockingly called chivalry to know that if ever a woman was undeserving of a blow from her husband's fist, it was Judith Haviland.

"An angel is what she is, Major St. John,'' one of the *troopers had said. "You know that, and we know it. And it's not right that that bastard should abuse her.''*

Judith would have been the first to laugh at that complimentary sobriquet, but it was not far from the truth. Not to the men of this regiment, depleted by illness and battle losses to less than half its original strength. Theirs had been one of the units left in Portugal after Sir John Moore's army departed after Corunna, so they had been in continual service since the beginning of this campaign. And had suffered for it.

There were three other married women in camp, wives of enlisted men chosen by lot to accompany their husbands onto the transports. They and the camp followers handled the cooking and laundry, what little there was of either.

But Judith was the only officer's wife, and as such, in a class by herself. And although it was not a fitting task for a lady, with her knowledge of herbs and their effects, it was Mrs. Haviland who saw to their wounds when they were away from the surgeons that accompanied the main force.

She also wrote countless letters for the men, most of whom were illiterate, and in the case of a trooper's death, her letter of condolence always went home to the family, along with the colonel's. She had suffered with them, without a single complaint, all the endless deprivations of war, which no English gentlewoman should have had to endure.

Angel, St. John thought, remembering the earnest, wind-burned face of the Yorkshireman who had called her that. He was right, of course. She should never have to suffer this bastard's abuse again.

"Be warned, Haviland," St. John said in immediate, unthinking response to that realization. "If you ever strike your wife again, I *will* kill you. And you're wise to remind us both that you won't be the first man I've shot. There is not a man in this regiment who would bring charges against me or who would feel compelled to testify at my court-martial even if I did it openly, with the regiment drawn up in square to watch. You might want to remember that."

"Are you threatening me, you noble popinjay?" Haviland asked, his mouth arranged in the smirk Kit had grown to hate.

"If you like," Kit agreed softly. "I prefer to think of it as a promise, maybe simply a word to the wise, but you are certainly free to take it any way you wish."

He shrugged out of his coat and turned away from his visitor. Despite the pervasive winter dampness, his shirt had become soaked with sweat while he supervised the flogging. "Now if you'll excuse me, Captain Haviland," he suggested, "I must remind you that I have other things to do. I'm sure you have duties to attend to as well."

"She won't have you, you know," Haviland said, ignoring the obvious dismissal. "She might like to. You know more about that than I, I suppose. They say you're very…experienced with women. But even if she fancies you, St. John, Judith won't do anything about it. It would go against everything that old prig taught her, against everything she believes."

Kit didn't turn around, afraid that something in his features, no matter how carefully he schooled them, would reveal his disgust. Or more importantly would let Haviland know that his jeering comments had struck home.

"That's a pity for you, of course," Haviland went on, despite the determined lack of response from his victim. "For such a brown mouse, she's really *quite* entertaining. Especially on a cold night like this one is going to be. I'll be sure to think about you while I'm topping her," he promised, his voice full of vindictive amusement. "And who knows? Maybe she will think about you, too."

Only when Kit heard the flap of the tent fall, the movement of the stiff canvas audible even above the rush of blood pounding through his temples, did he allow himself to react. He closed his eyes, thinking about what Haviland had said.

She won't have you, you know. The bastard was right about that. Kit understood Judith Haviland's concept of honor as well as her husband did. As well as he understood his own. He had never believed otherwise.

But it had been the last of Haviland's words which would live in his imagination. And tonight, as he lay on the hard mattress of his cot, alone in this small tent, he would certainly remember them. Along with the dark bruise that was still visible on Judith's clear olive skin.

"How is he?" St. John asked, his voice kept very low out of consideration for the injured man.

Judith Haviland looked up at him, laying the book she had been reading by the light of the brazier down in her lap. It was one he had loaned her from his small collection, a volume of obscure Latin poets she confessed she hadn't seen.

She smiled at him, but shook her head slightly. "I have nothing else to give him," she whispered, her eyes troubled. "I administered the last of the laudanum. When he wakes up..." She shrugged, slender shoulders lifting under the thick woolen shawl. "If I only had something else, *anything* else. I've worried about the effect of spirits on the wounded, but at least with that, as with the drug, there is some blessed oblivion."

She turned to consider the man lying prone on the cot on the far side of the tent. A coarse blanket had been pulled up to his waist, and his ruined back was mercifully covered by a poultice which Mrs. Haviland had almost certainly brewed with her own hands and placed there.

Judith's profile was briefly limned against the low glow of the fire, and St. John wondered suddenly how he could have once thought her to be ordinary. The line of brow, nose and chin the light revealed was classic, pure and incredibly beautiful.

And she is another man's wife. A man who had justly accused Kit of coveting her. A man Kit had threatened to kill if he touched her again. *Touched* reverberated within his head, and the image he had fought since his confrontation with Haviland was all at once there as well, as clear in his mind's eye as the profile outlined against the flames.

Judith Haviland slowly turned back to face him, questioning his silence perhaps. "What's wrong?" she asked, her voice soft.

"Do you have a cup?" St. John asked instead of answering.

Her brow furrowed slightly at the request, but she didn't question it. "Of course," she said.

She brought him the cup, a tin one, battered through its travels, and held it out to him enclosed in the slender fingers he had admired. He produced from behind his back, almost like a conjurer, the canteen he'd brought. He took the cup she offered and, after pouring a small measure of dark liquid into it, held it out to her. When he looked up from that task, her eyes met his, full of wonder.

"Rum." She had identified his offering by its pungent aroma. "Where in the world did you get this?"

"A private store. I've been saving it for an emergency," Kit confessed, unable to resist the urge to smile at her.

"And you're willing to let me have it for Private Reynolds?"

"This is for you—what's in the cup. The rest you may do with as you see fit. I'm only sorry I hadn't thought to give it to you before now."

"It's very generous of you, Major St. John, but I think, if you don't mind, that he needs it more than I."

"But I *do* mind. It's cold, and despite your fortitude, it can't have been easy watching what was done today. Or easy doing that," he said, gesturing toward the figure on the cot.

She shook her head, her eyes falling again to the cup. "I promise you—" she began.

"Drink it, or I shall keep the rest. You can do none of us any good if you fall ill from exhaustion. We've come to depend too much on your strength."

Her eyes lifted again, surprisingly luminous in the dimness of the tent. "My strength?" she repeated, her voice filled with the same quiet humor that so often answered the hardships she had faced for the last three years. "Are you mocking me, Major St. John?" she asked, her lips tilting in amusement.

"I assure you I am not, ma'am. And it won't work, you know," he said, his own teasing grin answering that small smile.

"What won't work?"

"Distracting me. It's been tried before, I promise you. And it's far too late for you to pretend to be missish."

"Missish?" she repeated the word unbelievingly. "How dare you insult me?"

Then she laughed, spoiling the effect of her pretended anger. It was only a breath of sound, almost intimate. Hearing it, Kit realized suddenly that he had no right to be here, no matter the pretense he used.

He had no right to banter with her as if they were at some London party. As he had no right to demand that she take care of herself. No rights at all where Mrs. Haviland was concerned.

Even as he thought it, her hand closed around the tin mug, her fingers brushing against his. An unintentional contact. Kit understood that, but the hot jolt of reaction which flared through his body was no less powerful for that knowledge.

Judith raised the cup and, tilting her head back bravely, drank down the draught as if it were a dose of medicine.

"Good girl," he complimented lightly when she had finished.

She raised her hand, using her knuckle to wipe a trickle of the spirits from the corner of her mouth, and he noticed that the skin on the back of her hand was chapped and reddened from the cold.

"Purely for medicinal purposes, I assure you," she said, a spark of mischief in the dark eyes.

"We are agreed as to that," St. John said, handing her the canteen.

"But I promise you the rest of this shall be devoted to my patients. I assure you, Major, I am not yet a secret tippler."

"I never believed you were, ma'am. Pray send me word if there is anything else you need to care for Reynolds."

He had already turned, preparing to retreat from a situation that was far too dangerous, when her question stopped him.

"You believe Michael sent him there, don't you?"

St. John turned back, his blue eyes carefully guileless. "I beg your pardon?" he said.

For a heartbeat there was silence in the tent. Kit forced his eyes to meet the searching ones of Michael Haviland's wife.

"But you must know that it was Reynolds—" she continued, despite the fact that Kit hadn't answered her question.

"Someone had to be held responsible," Kit said. "Whatever the reason he went to the village, Reynolds knew the penalty."

"I don't understand why you would believe that Michael—"

"Good night, Mrs. Haviland." St. John again deliberately cut off whatever else she intended to say.

"Thank you for the rum," she said softly as he raised the flap of the tent, but St. John did not look back.

When she was alone, Judith turned to look at the man on the cot, but the even rise and fall of Toby Reynolds's mutilated back indicated that he was still asleep. She sat down again in the chair by the brazier, but didn't take up her reading.

Instead she held in her hands the battered tin cup St. John had filled for her. Unconsciously, her thumb moved over the dented metal, as she thought about the man who had just left.

She remembered St. John from London, of course. It would be difficult to forget such a striking figure, especially one who caused a clamor of excitement whenever he attended an event at which the young ladies in town for their Season were present.

Judith knew that St. John was almost certainly unaware they had met before. His eyes had skimmed over her face with patent disinterest then. Sally Jamison's brother had made the introduction, and there had been whispers aplenty after St. John had moved on, without bothering, of course, to lead any of their small party onto the dance floor.

That's simply St. John's way, Bob Jamison had assured them when he disappeared into the crowd. *He don't mean anything by it, you understand, but you're all too young.* An involuntary grin had accompanied that pronouncement.

He means we're far too inexperienced to be interesting, Sally had whispered behind her fan. Judith had joined in the laughter, but she hadn't really understood why they laughed. She did now, of course. Because after all, she was neither young nor inexperienced any more.

Despite the fact that St. John's hair was now cropped close for campaigning, and that the evening dress he had worn that night had been replaced by his now less-than-spotless regimentals, the earl of Ryde's younger son would still have set feminine hearts aflutter in any London ballroom.

The unmistakable aura of danger he had carried with him then had not lessened. If anything it had been intensified through the crucible of war, through his exposure to real hazards. Judith knew his record, his undeniable bravery in battle.

She had never been called upon to treat him, thank heavens. The minor scrapes St. John received in the last three years had all been attended to by the army surgeons. She wondered if her hands would have trembled if forced to touch his body, as they had trembled tonight when she took the mug from his fingers.

They were long and brown, she remembered, the nails short and very clean, despite the primitive conditions in which they all lived. They were the strong hands of a strong man, and yet they had been as gentle as a woman's the day he had touched the bruise on her jaw.

That had been the only time in the three years she had known him that he had touched her, and that had been in shocked reaction to the evidence of the blow Michael had struck her. St. John's eyes had questioned, and she had answered them with a lie.

He hadn't believed her explanation, of course. It was obvious to everyone, she imagined, what had caused that bruise. She usually was more skillful in avoiding Michael when he was drinking, but she had been tired and cold that night, and there really had been nowhere else to go. There was no privacy in the camp, not even inside the tent they shared.

Until that time Michael had been more careful about where he hit her, not wanting his mistreatment of her revealed to his commander or his fellow officers any more than she did. But every day those inhibitions were weakened by drink, by indifference, by anger over his situation.

Her husband had come to the Peninsula to follow his father's grand plan for his career. The general intended for Michael to use this campaign to rise quickly in rank and then return to London and a favored position in the Horse Guards. Instead, this war had slogged drearily along, and Michael's shortcomings as an officer and a man became more evident with its increasing pressures. When he was sober enough to indulge in self-examination, he worried, as she did, that his father's dreams of glory for him were more likely to end in disgrace.

And that was all the more terrifying after the last letter they had received from home. Michael's father had suffered a stroke and was in very ill health. They both understood he must be protected from the knowledge of his son's failings at any cost. At least Michael still understood that, she thought.

She had been so afraid that this last episode would be reported to the colonel. Not by St. John, of course. She knew instinctively that he would protect her from that humiliation. According to his reputation, he was more likely to call Michael out or to thrash him soundly than to be tempted to report his actions to his commanding officer.

The latter would be no protection against the next time her husband hit her in a fit of drunken anger and frustration. There *was* no protection from that. Michael was her husband, and it was his legal right to treat her as he wished.

Judith found that her fingers had whitened over the small

cup, their grip reflecting her growing realization that this was a situation about which she could do nothing. She was Michael Haviland's wife, and however he treated her, she felt she had to protect both his reputation and the life of his aged father.

But sometimes…she thought, her dark eyes again falling to the tin mug she had taken from St. John's long, brown fingers, it must surely be permissible *sometimes* to wish that her life might have taken a different turn.

Chapter Two

"I thought I would find you here," Michael said. Unheard, he had pushed aside the flap of the medical tent and was standing in its opening, watching her.

Judith knew it must be after midnight. Through Mrs. McQueen, her very efficient helper and the wife of one of the enlisted men, she had sent word to her husband that she would be staying in the medical tent throughout the night. She had assumed Michael would, as he did most of the time, fall asleep as soon as his body hit his cot and never give her whereabouts another thought. Instead…

Judith laid down her book, but with a reluctance that made her ashamed. Michael was her husband, and she felt no joy in his presence. There was no leap of pleasure as she had felt seeing St. John standing in this same place. Assaulted by guilt, she forced her lips into a welcoming smile.

"He seems still to be sleeping from the laudanum," she said. She was beginning to worry about Reynolds's prolonged slumber. There had only been a few drops left in the small brown bottle, but perhaps in his weakened condition, she had given him too much. It was so difficult to tell about the proper dosage.

She stood up and laid aside the book, intending to check on her patient. She presumed her husband had come out of concern for his orderly, but his gaze did not even flicker in the direction of Toby Reynolds. Instead it was focused on her face with an intensity which she suddenly recognized.

She fought any revelation of the revulsion that was her automatic response to his look. She knew what it portended. It was not an expression which she had seen in a long time, but she had not forgotten what it meant.

"I understand St. John visited you earlier. Overcome by a paroxysm of guilt and duty, no doubt?" Michael asked mockingly.

"I think he was sorry for Reynolds. Sorry, perhaps, that it fell to him to see to the punishment."

She knew why St. John had been chosen for that role. He was the most popular by far of the officers. That his popularity was deserved by virtue of his courage was a certainty, but it also owed something to the mantle of leadership which had been bestowed on him at birth. The men were willing to follow him unquestioningly where they might have grumbled about the same orders from another officer. The attitude of common British soldiers toward the aristocrats in their ranks was a paradox, perhaps, but it was well-documented.

"Are you pitying St. John, my dear?" Michael asked. He stepped into the tent, allowing the flap to drop behind him, affording them some privacy.

"Not…pity, of course," she said. It would be hard to pity a man who has everything, she thought. "But I do believe he is not as inured to that sort of duty as one would think."

She turned to look again at her patient, the "victim" of St. John's duty. Before she was even aware that he had moved, her husband's hand caught her chin, holding it tightly. He turned her head, at the same time forcing her face up to his in order to put his mouth over her lips. They opened in a gasp of shock at his unexpected tactic, and his tongue invaded quickly, hot and hard, almost suffocating in its demand.

Judith fought not to recoil. She stood motionless, stoically resolved to endure his unwanted embrace. His head lifted suddenly. When her eyes opened at that miraculous respite, she found him looking into her face, his brow furrowed.

"Where the hell did you get drink?" he asked.

"Major St. John brought rum for Reynolds. He made me drink a measure against the cold."

"Made you?" Haviland repeated, his voice full of amusement. "And have you already administered St. John's medicinal draught to your patient?"

"I—" she began, and then she stopped. She had intended to explain that Reynolds was still sleeping off the effects of the laudanum or had simply lapsed again into unconsciousness after she had applied the new poultice. The words faltered, because suddenly she knew exactly where this was leading.

"Transparent as glass, Judith," her husband said, laughing. "I always know whether or not you are telling the truth. Your face reveals your every emotion."

He still held her chin, her face tilted up to his. "And you might do well to remember that, my dear, when St. John is about. *I* may be understanding of your weakness for our gallant major, but I doubt those who believe you to be a candidate for sainthood would welcome the knowledge that their idol has feet of clay. Especially where her marriage vows are concerned," he added.

"How dare you," Judith whispered. She resisted the urge to jerk her head away or to wipe off her lips the moisture his mouth had left on them. Nausea at what he suggested rose into her throat. She had believed that her unspoken and unacknowledged attraction to St. John was unknown to anyone, including Michael.

Her admiration of the major was only an innocent fantasy, a harmless daydream which she never had any intention of acting upon, of course. But Michael's accusation made her realize how those idle thoughts, if they became known, might be misinterpreted by the malicious. "You have *no* right to—"

"I have *every* right," Michael interrupted, his voice still soft and yet menacing somehow. "I have every right in the world where you are concerned. You would do well not to forget that."

He was right, of course, but her dark eyes remained locked on his in a battle of wills which she was determined not to lose.

He laughed suddenly, contemptuous of her small show of courage. "Tell me where you've hidden it, Ju."

"I don't know what you mean," she said almost defiantly.

His hand lifted, away from her chin and threatening. Instinctively she put her arm up, palm outward to ward off the blow. "I swear, Michael, if you strike me, I'll appeal to Colonel Smythe," she said.

"And shame your father and mine before their old comrade in arms? I don't think that would be wise, my dear. And so cruelly unnecessary. My father's health is precarious now, as you know," he reminded her, smiling.

The seconds drifted by in silence, but their positions did not change. Slowly, Judith's arm fell, and she took a breath. This was the choice she faced. Resistance or humiliation for them all, her father and his. And into that familiar equation was now thrown the reality of what Michael had just threatened.

Given the very small world of the English army, any scandal begun here would surely follow them back to England. By protesting Michael's treatment of her, she would hurt two old men who had lived their lives in such a fashion that neither deserved to endure gossip about the actions of their children.

''It's in the medicine chest,'' she said.

Michael's mouth relaxed into a wider smile at her capitulation. With the hand he had raised to threaten her, he suddenly caught the braid at the back of her neck and pulled it downward, forcing her chin to lift again. Tears sprang into her eyes. He lowered his mouth to hers with deliberate slowness, holding her moisture-washed eyes. His breath, hot and almost fetid, stirred sickeningly against her nostrils.

His lips closed over hers as his left hand found the softness of her breast. His fingers gripped hard and then he squeezed, deliberately causing pain. She fought not to give him the satisfaction of struggling against his hold, and she did not try to escape his covering mouth to cry out. After all, there might be someone near enough to hear.

Finally, it was over—as she had known it would be. There was something else in this tent that Michael wanted far more than he wanted her. She had been aware of that for a long time.

''That's my sweetling,'' he said softly, when he had lifted his head. He watched the deep shuddering breath she took, and his lips moved again into a smile, apparently in genuine amusement this time.

He released her and strode quickly to the chest she'd indicated. He rummaged through her meager supply of simples before finding the canteen of rum. He tossed it lightly in his right hand to test its weight and fullness. Again smiling, Michael sketched her a quick salute as he left, allowing the tent flap to drop closed behind him, mercifully leaving her alone.

The attack the following dawn struck the English outpost with lightning swiftness. It came out of the semidarkness almost without warning. Despite the placement of the pickets on the high ground above the road, there had been too little time between the single shot fired by one of the British sentries and the arrival of the first of the French cavalry patrol within the circle of the tents.

They had swept unhampered down the defile and breached the outer ring of security to overrun the camp before the officers could muster any sort of defense. Although seasoned soldiers, most of the English dragoons had been awakened from a sound sleep, stumbling out of their blankets to face cavalry sabers wielded by equally seasoned Frenchmen.

Colonel Smythe and the other officers attempted to impose order. Kit shouted himself hoarse, rallying men to him in the darkness. His efforts had some effect, for although they didn't have time to mount to meet the charge, within a couple of minutes he had gotten them drawn up and firing at the enemy.

The effect of the carbines in the hands of men who knew how to use them was the same on foot or on horseback, and eventually the French began a slow and very professional retreat, melting back into the morning mist along the route they had taken into the valley.

"St. John?" Smythe's voice rang clear in the confusion.

"Here, sir," Kit shouted, moving toward it.

"An advance patrol?" Smythe questioned when they were close enough for conversation, despite the noise of the scattered individual conflicts that surrounded them. Smythe was holding his handkerchief against a bloody cut on his forehead.

"They were as surprised as we were," Kit agreed. "They weren't expecting to find an English outpost this far north of the French lines. I don't think they came to do battle."

"Possibly reinforcements for Massena?" Smythe questioned.

The French commander had given Wellington's army considerable difficulty the previous fall. Rather than risk another encounter after the autumn rains began and yet determined not to abandon Portugal, Massena had dug in, apparently in a desperate attempt to survive the winter and await the promised reinforcements from France.

Intelligence suggested that Napoleon intended to strengthen Massena before the arrival of the English army's own reinforcements, expected some time in March. Colonel Smythe's dragoons had been stationed along this road to notify Wellington of the arrival of any French reinforcements and to delay them until the English commander could move his troops into position.

It seemed too early in the year for any massive troop movements, but the French were hard-pressed for supplies. It was possible Napoleon was sending both soldiers and provisions for his faltering army, which would allow Massena to renew his attack on Wellington instead of retreating back into Spain as the English had hoped. Whatever the situation, Smythe's primary job was to notify Wellington of what was happening in this district, and for that he needed better information about the purpose of the enemy patrol.

"Someone will have to follow them," Smythe said. "I need hard intelligence before I send word to Wellington."

Kit nodded agreement. Although the sky was beginning to lighten, the smoke from the guns was still thick around them, adding to the nightmare quality of the encounter. "And if they *are* the advance guard of a larger force?" he questioned.

"Then get that word back to me as quickly as possible. I need to know the strength of whatever Napoleon has sent."

"Shall we engage them, sir?"

"Not unless you have no other choice. We are ordered to defend this route until Wellington can get us some help, and I need every man we have. We can't afford any more losses simply to give chase to a French patrol. Observe and report, St. John, but avoid a clash. I'll send Haviland's troop with you in case you run into anything unexpected."

"I understand," Kit said.

"St. John and Haviland," Smythe shouted, his voice raised over the confusion, "mount your men."

As soon as Kit had given his own orders, his dragoons rushed to saddle their horses, throwing on their equipment as they ran. Amid the chaos, Kit saw that the men of Haviland's troop were mounting also, according to the colonel's orders, but Haviland wasn't with them. St. John realized that he hadn't seen Haviland since the attack had begun, but given the conditions in the encampment at the time, that was perhaps not too surprising.

"Where's your captain?" he asked Haviland's sergeant.

"I don't know, sir. Haven't seen him. Maybe he's fallen," Sergeant Cochran replied.

There were more than a few dead and wounded men on the ground. In the growing light of day, those who had not been ordered to follow the fleeing French patrol were already beginning to find and give succor to their fallen comrades.

It was possible that Haviland was among the wounded, Kit supposed, but he wondered if it were not more likely that he was hiding in his tent, avoiding the encounter. Then he wondered with self-disgust how much of his suspicion about his fellow officer was colored by Haviland's treatment of his wife. Or by his own admiration for Judith.

"Find him and then follow us," Kit ordered. "Tell him that we are ordered to observe the size of any forces we encounter, but not to engage them. We can't wait on you. We may lose the French if we delay until Captain Haviland has been located."

"Yes, sir, Major St. John," the sergeant said.

His eyes met Kit's in perfect understanding. Haviland's men knew his failings as well as Kit and his colonel did. After all, they were the ones required to follow him into battle. But Kit trusted Haviland's Sergeant Cochran. He was an old India hand. He would do as he was told. And he would make sure Haviland understood his orders. As Kit swung into the saddle, the man was already hurrying to do as he'd been instructed.

St. John knew that as wild and rugged as this country was, if the French got any jump at all on the pursuit, it would be almost impossible to follow them. He really couldn't afford to wait, whatever the cause of Haviland's absence, legitimate or otherwise.

"Taking a break," Lieutenant Scarborough whispered.

He and Kit were stretched out on their bellies, looking down on the beginnings of the valley that stretched north from the opposite end of the pass they'd just traversed. The French patrol had stopped to give their horses a rest and tend to their casualties, apparently unaware that they had been followed.

Kit realized that his squad was heavily outnumbered.

Even with the addition of Haviland's troop, they would not have been a match for the French. They had lost too many men during last summer's campaign and to the winter's illnesses, and then additional casualties had been added in this morning's action.

Smythe hadn't realized how large the French detachment was, of course. Apparently, their attack on the camp had been caused by the undisciplined excitement of the outriders. At finding the English camp asleep, they had rushed into the assault in a headlong pursuit of glory. It was a failing that the English cavalry had often been accused of.

And one I don't intend to be guilty of, Kit thought grimly. His job was to follow this detachment to whatever force they belonged to and then report back on the size of the French reinforcements. Smythe would then be able to provide the hard numbers that Wellington would need to counter any spring push the French made.

It was at that moment that Haviland's squad came riding out of the rocky defile and into the flat, suddenly face-to-face with the French, who reacted quickly. They were re-mounting and offering defensive fire before the English reached them.

"Bloody hell," Kit said under his breath. "What does that fool think he's doing?" It was already a rhetorical question, given what was happening below, but Scarborough answered it.

"He appears to be attacking them, sir," his young lieutenant said calmly enough. "And they're going to cut him to ribbons."

He was right, of course. The English dragoons had almost staggered backwards, faced with the withering French fire. Now Haviland's men and horses were milling purposelessly, with, it seemed, no one to give them direction.

"Rally your troop, damn it," Kit urged under his breath.

He could pick Haviland out. He wasn't giving orders. He seemed almost... The thought was incredible, but watching what was taking place below, Kit was forced to give it credence. The captain appeared to be drunk. He was almost reeling in the saddle. And if that were the case...

"Come on," Kit ordered, scrambling up.

He ran, Scarborough following, over the same rocks they had noiselessly picked their way across only a few minutes before. Despite Smythe's orders, the enemy had been engaged, and Kit didn't feel he had a choice. He couldn't leave Haviland's men to suffer that counterattack, heavily outnumbered and under the command of a drunkard. It would be little less than a slaughter.

He and the lieutenant swung into their saddles at the same time and rode as quickly as the rugged terrain would allow across the ridge, guiding their horses down the steep slope to where their troop waited below.

"Haviland's squad have run into the French," Kit shouted to his men.

He owed them no explanation for the charge he was about to lead, of course. He would offer none that was critical of his fellow officer. However, he was so infuriated by Haviland's actions that he no longer felt a great constraint to protect his reputation. Haviland was not only disobeying the orders of his commander, he was costing the lives of his own men.

As they rode to join the battle, it became obvious that Scarborough had been right in his first appraisal. Haviland's force was being cut to ribbons. Kit assessed the situation as his troop poured down the ridge behind him. Instead of joining the battle surrounding Haviland's scattered command, he led his men direct as an arrow against the French flank.

The shock was enough to drive them back. It wouldn't

take long, however, for them to realize that they still out-numbered the English. Kit and Scarborough began shouting encouragement to Haviland's dragoons, who, given some direction, began to rally and fight with renewed determination.

This was the kind of fighting that the cavalry of both armies was notorious for—close, brutal and incredibly bloody. The dragoons were laying about with their heavy sabers now, and despite the close-packed horses, far too many of those blows struck their targets, slicing through flesh and cleaving bone.

Fighting with single-minded determination, Kit was almost unaware of the passage of time or of the number of men he engaged. His arm was already beginning to tire, however, from the mechanical rise and fall of his saber, when he was hit. He felt the glancing blow on his left arm, but there was no pain.

Just no pain yet, he acknowledged. The impact had been numbing in its force, almost as if he had been struck with a club instead of a blade. Intellectually, he knew that wasn't true. It was a saber wound, and it was probably deep.

He ignored that knowledge and dispatched the man who had struck him. Using his knees, he urged his charger forward to the next target, a captain who seemed to be in command of the patrol.

The Frenchman's eyes were black, and they glittered beneath the visor of his tall helmet, his face grim with determination. Kit raised his sword and slashed hard at the bobbing target of the hat. His blade clashed against the chin strap, just under the Frenchman's ear, and was briefly deflected. Then it slipped off the metal and sliced into the hussar's throat. The Frenchman fell, and the sorrel he'd been riding careened away from the fighting.

As suddenly as it had begun, it was over. There was no

order, perhaps because there was no one left to issue it, but the French turned tail and, deserting the wounded who had been unhorsed, streamed off across the empty plain, pinions flying.

Kit looked for someone else to engage, but there was no one left. There was a slight ringing in his ears, and the pain in his arm had begun, making up in its viciousness now for the small respite the numbness immediately after the blow had given him.

"You're bleeding, sir," Scarborough said. His face was chalk-like beneath the freckles, but his voice was still amazingly calm. Kit's horse suddenly sidestepped the approach of the gray the boy was riding, and Scarborough reached out to catch his major's reins, recognizing how rare that lack of control over his mount was for St. John.

"I have him," Kit said, too sharply.

He felt light-headed, and despite the number of times he'd been in combat, the scene around him had an almost surreal quality. There was a screaming horse he should order someone to kill. A man was lying at his feet, the front of his uniform soaked with blood which still spurted upward like a small fountain with every beat of his dying heart.

Kit's left glove was also crimson, he realized, almost sodden with blood, and it took a long minute of thought to realize that it was his own, which was running down his forearm under his uniform sleeve.

"We need to get that tied up," Scarborough said calmly. "You get down now, sir, and I'll tend to it. It's bleeding bad."

Kit nodded, but the ground appeared a great distance away. Trusting his years of experience and not his strangely distorted vision, he lifted his right leg over the saddle and was pleased to find that it was still able to maintain his weight as he took the left out of its stirrup to join the other on the ground. But he was forced to lean against his horse, his eyes closed against the sudden vertigo.

"Should we go after them?" a voice asked at his shoulder.

Kit lifted his head to find who had asked that reasonable question. The face of Sergeant Cochran swam into focus before him. He nodded, trying to think. At the same time he was aware that Scarborough was touching the left sleeve of his uniform.

Wellington would still need the intelligence about the size of the reinforcements Napoleon had sent. That's what they had been sent to find out. And that reminded him...

"Did you convey my orders to your captain?" Kit asked softly, his language deliberately formal.

The sergeant's mouth twisted. He glanced at Scarborough, who was standing at St. John's other shoulder, working to push the tip of his knife into the seam of the sleeve in order to split it.

Cochran's voice was low when he answered, but there was no doubt about what he said. "I told him right enough, sir. Just what you and the colonel said. But...the truth of the matter is he was drunk, Major. Drunk as a lord."

The sergeant's eyes widened suddenly as he realized what he had said and to whom he had said it. Despite the dead and dying men around them, despite the disaster they had barely escaped, Cochran grinned suddenly, obviously remembering St. John's title. "Begging the major's pardon."

Kit laughed. "That's all right, Sergeant Cochran," he said. "No offense taken. Drunk as a lord," he repeated softly.

It was only what he himself had surmised watching Haviland in action. Or in *inaction,* he thought bitterly.

"I should'a left him in bed, Major," Cochran went on. "I should have known he was going to get somebody killed. But I thought of Mrs. Haviland, and the disgrace, so...I just drug him out. I swear to you I told him just what you told me to, and he understood me. Then when he saw those damn Frenchies... He ordered that charge like he had the whole division behind him. Looking for promotion, no doubt. Stupid drunken bastard," Cochran added under his breath, but not softly enough that it wasn't audible.

Kit nodded. "I didn't hear that last, Sergeant."

He turned to his left to find Scarborough trying to tie his neck cloth around his major's upper arm. Kit gasped a little at the last strong tug on the two ends, and the lieutenant's eyes came up to his.

"I don't suppose you could put your finger over the knot, sir," Scarborough said, smiling at him. "Damned hard to get it tight enough to stop the bleeding using only two hands."

The freckles were pronounced against the drained skin of his boyish face and his fingers were covered with Kit's blood, but Kit would give the boy credit. He had guts and coolness. A little more experience and he would make an excellent officer.

"'ere, sir," Cochran said. "You let me do that."

He stepped around St. John to lay a thick, grubby finger over the knot. Still holding his major's eyes, the young lieutenant pulled again. This time Kit controlled any response as the bandage tightened agonizingly over the wound.

"Where's Haviland now?" he questioned instead of letting himself react to that pain.

"You didn't see?" Sergeant Cochran asked, his voice rich with contempt. "One of His Majesty's bad bargains is that one."

"See what?" Kit wondered if the drunken captain had been cut down in the fighting. And he deliberately destroyed the hope which had leaped into his mind at that possibility.

"He ran, sir," Scarborough said.

"Retreated," Kit corrected.

"That weren't no retreat, begging the major's pardon," Cochran explained. "He didn't order the troop off. When he realized how outnumbered we was, I guess he got scared. Next thing I know, he's heading back through that pass—all alone. I was about to get the men out of there when you hit them on the flank. I knew you'd come to help us, and I wasn't about to leave you to fight the bastards alone."

"Thank you, Sergeant Cochran. I appreciate your courage."

"Not courage, sir. Just..." The sergeant paused and shook his head. "I ain't never run from a battle in my life, and I didn't intend to start now. I've retreated when I've been ordered to, and I'm not ashamed of those times. Live to fight again, I always say. But I ain't never run."

Kit could hear the strong disgust in the veteran's voice, and he had to work to keep it out of his own. Michael Haviland had sealed his own disgrace, and there wasn't much anyone could do about it now. Kit turned his attention to the young lieutenant still standing at his elbow.

"Take what men are fit to travel, Scarborough, and follow the patrol. Not close enough that they know you're there," Kit ordered, trying not to think about the growing pain in his arm or about what her husband's actions today would mean for the rest of Judith Haviland's life. Trying not to think about anything but what he'd been ordered to accomplish. "Bring back an estimate of the size of the force they're attached to as soon as you can. Cochran will go with you.''

Scarborough nodded. ''And you, sir?''

''I don't think I can ride fast enough to keep up,'' Kit said. He knew damn well he couldn't. He was reduced to wondering if he were going to be able to get back to camp. ''I'll go back and report what happened to Colonel Smythe.''

''What about Captain Haviland?'' Cochran asked.

''Haviland can go to the devil,'' Kit said softly. ''I intend to report him as drunk on duty. You'll testify to that, won't you, Sergeant?''

''I'll testify to everything I saw today. You make no doubt about that. But sir, what about…'' The dark eyes were questioning, filled with compassion.

''We do her no good in protecting him. You saw the bruise on her face this week. And you know well enough how it got there,'' Kit said. ''We all knew.''

The man nodded, but he was still concerned, and Kit didn't blame him. These charges meant sure disgrace for Haviland. And that dishonor would touch Judith's life forever, of course.

''You watch your back, sir,'' Cochran said softly. ''He'll know what you intend.''

A good warning, Kit realized. If he didn't make it back to camp, then no one would bring charges against Haviland. Not the enlisted men. They wouldn't be believed if they did. That was simply the way the army worked.

''Thank you, Cochran. You two do the same.''

''You need a hand up?'' the sergeant asked.

Kit wanted to refuse, but he knew he couldn't afford to. His job now was to get the wounded back to camp and to inform Smythe about what had happened out here. Scarborough would see to the French. And Cochran would take care of the young lieutenant.

"Forgive me, Sergeant," St. John said simply. "But I'm afraid that I might."

Chapter Three

"What happened?" Judith Haviland had asked when Kit arrived back in camp with the wounded.

One of the men had died on the way, and St. John could only hope that none of the other injuries would prove fatal. They would need every man they could muster if Wellington ordered them to slow down Massena's reinforcements rather than to fall back before the French advance. If the patrol they'd encountered this morning *was* part of a larger force, then this severely depleted light cavalry regiment would be caught between two much larger French armies.

In view of the situation, Kit simply shook his head in answer to Judith's question. There seemed no point in trying to explain the events of the morning. He wasn't sure he was enough in control of his own emotions to contain his disgust with Haviland's action.

She held his eyes a moment before she turned away to assess the casualties the men were bringing in. Those who had been injured in the dawn attack on the camp had already been attended to, and most of the cots in the tent were occupied.

Toby Reynolds had recovered enough to be displaced by the wounded apparently. Haviland's batman was sitting on top of an overturned box in the corner of the tent. He met Kit's eyes, undisguised hatred in the depths of his, and then he spat into the dirt before he looked away, deliberately turning his gaze from the major who had been ordered to carry out his punishment.

St. John ignored the insult. He couldn't blame the private for his bitterness, but he wondered if it extended to Haviland, the rightful target of his anger.

Kit had stopped in the opening of the tent, leaning against the support pole as he supervised the troopers who were helping the last of the casualties inside. He shook his head when Judith returned to offer him one of the remaining cots. "There are others who need you more," he said. "This has stopped bleeding."

Her eyes studied his features a moment, and she put her fingers lightly against the bandage Scarborough had devised. The neck cloth was stiff with gore, as was the damaged sleeve of Kit's uniform, but there seemed to be no fresh blood on it or on the material of his coat.

It was obvious that he was right about the needs of the other casualties, so she nodded and returned to a corporal who was the victim of a saber cut that had cost him most of his ear. He was still unconscious and had been brought back to camp over the back of his horse.

St. John closed his eyes. He was still leaning against the pole, and he let the sounds of the women who were working on the other side of the tent drift around him. He tried not to think about what had happened, but, against his will, his mind went back again and again to Haviland's charge and its results.

Only when he felt Mrs. Haviland's hand on his arm did he realize that he seemed to have lost track of the passage of time as he had in the heat of the skirmish. He glanced around the tent. Everyone had been treated. The troopers he'd brought in were either resting in the cots or had been released.

"It's your turn," Mrs. Haviland assured him, her fingers working at the knot the young lieutenant had pulled so tightly.

"My men have—"

"Everyone else has been attended to, Major, I promise you," she interrupted. "I've sent Reynolds to Colonel Smythe to report on the injuries. I'm sure he'll want a report on yours as well."

"It's nothing so bad as what you've been dealing with," Kit said, watching her fingers work at the cloth.

"Perhaps I'm better qualified to make that assessment than you," she advised him softly. "A saber cut," she said, when she had loosened and gently pulled the makeshift bandage away from the wound. "And a nasty one, I'm afraid."

Kit glanced down. His was typical of the kind of injury that resulted from a cavalry clash. A flap of flesh and muscle had been sliced away from the bone, the edge of the blade cutting diagonally into his arm just above the elbow. Clotted blood was now holding the raw edges of the wound together, preventing further bleeding. Apparently Scarborough had known what he was doing with his makeshift tourniquet.

"Wiggle your fingers," Judith ordered, her voice sharper than it had been before. She watched intently as he obeyed. "Now move the arm below the elbow."

When Kit had successfully accomplished both, she took a small, but audible breath, and he realized she was relieved.

"I don't believe the bone is broken," she said. "Although, given the location, there may be some permanent damage to the muscle, even after it heals. It may atrophy or shorten. I'm afraid that only time will tell us about that. However," she said, "you would appear to be a very lucky man, Major St. John."

"So I have always been reputed to be, ma'am."

Her eyes lifted from the wound to find his, certainly reading in them the small amusement her comment had caused. His cronies in London had called him the luckiest bastard alive, and apparently his luck still held, even in this godforsaken war.

"You know what the surgeons would do for such a wound?" she asked, destroying his pleasant diversion into the past.

"Amputate the arm," he said evenly.

Kit was relieved that his voice was so steady, but there was a sudden coldness in the pit of his stomach. It was not the horror of the surgery he feared. Other men had endured that and much worse, but he didn't relish the idea of living out his life with only one arm, not if he could help it.

"At a point well above the injury," she agreed.

Near his shoulder, she meant. They both knew that's where the surgeons would make their brutal incision.

"Is that what you advise, ma'am?" Kit asked, working to keep his voice as emotionless as hers had been.

"It would really be the wisest course, you know," she said, truthfully, "given the odds of infection in this climate and with this type of wound. Unfortunately, however, I don't feel that I have the experience to attempt such an operation on my own. So I suppose we must try other, less drastic methods." She paused, but her calm, dark eyes held to his steadfastly.

"I must confess that I much prefer your second option, ma'am. Do your best for it, please."

She nodded, and her gaze returned to examine the injury again. Her fingers touched gently along the edge of the gash. "I only wish that I had—" The sentence she had begun stopped abruptly, the soft words cut off as if she had suddenly realized that thought should not be spoken aloud.

"Had what?" he questioned her sudden silence.

She looked up into his eyes again, hers clearly troubled. "Another, more professional opinion," she finished softly.

Judith Haviland had just lied to him, Kit realized, as she had lied about the bruise on her cheek, and he couldn't imagine why, unless the wound was more serious than she'd indicated.

"First, I'm going to try to clean the blood away," she went on, "and then try to make sure that the wound is free of debris. That won't be very pleasant, I'm afraid, but I've found that an injury heals better if there is nothing closed up within it that doesn't belong to the body. No loose threads from your uniform or dirt from the field."

"I'm completely in your hands, Mrs. Haviland," Kit said.

"Indeed you are, Major St. John," she agreed, smiling at him for the first time. "And I promise I shall do my very best for you. You would be better on the table, I believe."

Kit obediently followed her across the tent, his stride only the slightest bit unsteady. It was a little more difficult maneuvering himself, one-handed, onto the edge of the trestle table she had had the men set up as a makeshift examination area.

Suddenly it seemed very warm in the tent, despite the chill of the morning. He raised his right hand to unfasten the top button of his uniform and was surprised to find his fingers trembling weakly over that simple task.

"I do have some experience, you know," Judith assured him.

Kit realized she had been watching the small vibration

of his hand. "I trust you implicitly, ma'am. Much more than the sawbones, I promise you."

"Well, I shouldn't go that far," she said lightly. She smiled at him again. "Shall I help you with your coat, Major?"

Getting him out of the ruined jacket wasn't easily accomplished, even with her help, and Kit's face was covered with a dew of perspiration by the time they had managed it. The white lawn shirt he wore underneath was also badly stained with blood and damp with sweat. He tried to watch as she cut the sleeve of that garment away, but his head was swimming with blood loss.

"Why don't you lie down?" she suggested when she had finished and glanced up at his blanched features.

"Will that make it easier for your work?" he asked.

"My suggestion was intended to make it easier for *you,* Major St. John," she said. Her soft laughter was again intimate.

"Then I believe I shall continue to sit up, ma'am."

"But you trust me implicitly, remember?" she reminded him, the laughter still caught in her dark eyes.

"As long as I can see exactly what you're doing," he countered, smiling at her.

Despite his determination to play the stoic, Kit found that the rest was an ordeal. With each involuntary flinch of muscle, Judith Haviland's eyes lifted to his face, still assessing.

"I'm not going to faint on you," he assured her finally.

"Actually, I was rather hoping that you might," she said. This time her eyes didn't lift, but the corners of her mouth tilted.

"I wouldn't, however, turn down a swallow of the rum I gave you yesterday," Kit suggested after a few more minutes of her painstaking and extremely painful cleansing of the gash. "Strictly for medicinal purposes, you understand."

It took a moment for her to respond. She handed the basin of bloody water and the sponge she had been using to Mrs. McQueen, before she looked up. "I'm sorry, Major, but I'm afraid that's impossible."

"Blood loss?" he asked. She had said she worried about the effect of spirits on the wounded. Maybe...

"*Rum* loss," she corrected, taking from Mrs. McQueen the needle and thread that the motherly, gray-haired woman was holding out. "Are you ready for this?" she asked softly.

"Of course," Kit said, setting his teeth into his bottom lip. The sewing surely couldn't be much worse than what had gone before. It wasn't, he found, but still it was several heartbeats before he trusted his voice enough to ask for an explanation.

"Rum loss? You've already used it?"

"No," she answered calmly, "but I assure you it's gone."

Suddenly he understood. This was where Haviland had gotten drink last night. Judith had given it to him. Voluntarily or otherwise? he wondered. "Your husband?" he asked.

Her eyes lifted again, holding his for a long moment. In them was regret and embarrassment. As he watched, a small flush spread across her cheekbones. Finally she nodded, and then her gaze returned to the needle which she pushed into the torn muscle of his arm, carefully placing the next stitch.

"There's something I feel I must tell you, ma'am," Kit said softly, wondering if hearing what had occurred this morning wouldn't come better from him than from the colonel or from regimental gossip. No matter who told her, he knew it would not be easy for Judith Haviland to learn the truth.

"Something about Michael?" she asked, her concentration now apparently fully on the neat line of stitches she was setting.

"Yes, ma'am."

"Then I'm afraid that I really don't wish to hear it, Major. Whatever criticism of my husband you intend to make, I hope you will not make it to me. I assure you I am not unaware…"

She hesitated, and then she went on, her eyes still resolutely on her work. "I am aware that Michael is not as…strong as you, but he is my husband, Major St. John. I'm sure you'll forgive me if I say that it would be best that you *not* tell me whatever you feel constrained to say about Michael's actions. Much better for us both."

She looked up, her eyes very calm and very sure. *He is my husband.* No matter what Haviland had done, Kit realized, there was nothing she could do to change that relationship.

Nothing anyone could do, Kit thought with real regret. Judith Haviland was bound to suffer for her husband's disgrace. But he realized thankfully her words had freed him from what he had felt was his duty to tell her.

"Fourteen men are dead, Haviland, through your actions this morning," Smythe said, his voice cold. "Fourteen men who didn't deserve to die, whom this regiment could ill afford to lose."

"Colonel Smythe, I hope that you will—"

"What I will do, I assure you," Smythe went on, overriding the protest, "is report this sorry episode to Lord Wellington. The story of this morning's action will go out in the next dispatches. And those shall be sent as soon as

Lieutenant Scarborough returns from the mission I asked *you* to carry out.''

"Major St. John—'' Haviland began again, only to be once more interrupted.

"I have St. John's report. Which he assures me will be corroborated by Lieutenant Scarborough and Sergeant Cochran upon their return. The charges against you include disobeying an order, being drunk on duty, and the worse by far, desertion in the face of the enemy.''

"None of those are entirely true,'' Haviland said. "There were circumstances, sir, that—''

"This is not a court-martial, Captain Haviland. I'm not asking for an explanation of your actions. I assure you that will be required later. I simply wished to inform you that this is the report I shall send to Lord Wellington.''

"Colonel Smythe, I must protest—''

"Protest and be damned,'' Smythe said, his anger allowed for the first time to break through the carefully detached recitation. "It took Captain Scott more than two hours to sober you up and to get you in a condition to listen to the charges which I intend to lodge. I assure you that after that, whatever you can say will have little bearing on my actions.''

For the first time since he had known him, Kit realized, Haviland looked frightened. His skin was pale and his hands shook, but of course those might be put down to drink as well.

His eyes had met St. John's when he had entered the tent, escorted there by Captain Scott. In them had been the same cold hatred Kit had seen in the eyes of Haviland's batman. It seemed he had acquired two enemies.

"My father's health is precarious,'' Haviland said. His tone had changed. It was softer and less aggressive, and apparently it or his words had the desired effect. For once

Smythe didn't interrupt. "You must know this will kill him, sir."

The older man's eyes reflected his regret, and his mouth pursed slightly before he answered. "That is something you should have considered earlier, Captain Haviland. I'm afraid there is nothing I can do to prevent whatever will happen as a result of your actions this morning."

Haviland's eyes were bleak. It seemed that finally the realization that his "mistakes" were not going to be ignored or forgiven this time was beginning to sink in. The men all knew what lay ahead. Professional condemnation, certainly, but that was the least of it. That would swiftly be followed by personal disgrace, especially given the Haviland family's strong military traditions.

For some reason his father's face was in Kit's head, exactly the way it had looked the last time he had seen the earl. He had never forgotten his words that morning: *You continue to bring dishonor to this family. You may enjoy wallowing in the mud of public censure, but I will no longer allow you to drag the Montgomery name there with you.*

Haviland faced the same kind of public and private humiliation Ryde had described. For the first time Kit felt some fellow feeling for Michael Haviland. Undoubtedly he, too, loved his father and might be forced to live the rest of his life, Kit thought, knowing he was responsible for his death...

"I'm begging you for a chance to redeem myself, sir," Haviland said softly, his eyes focused intently on his colonel, who was, as they all were aware, an old friend and a former comrade-in-arms of General Roland Haviland.

"Surely whatever mistakes I've made, my father doesn't deserve to suffer for them. Please don't send that dispatch, sir. Instead..." Haviland hesitated before he went on. "Give me some mission. I don't care how desperate, how unlikely its chance of success. I'm begging you for an opportunity, Colonel Smythe, to redeem myself. A chance to save my father's life.''

Kit found himself hoping that his commander would relent, and was surprised to feel those stirrings of sympathy.

''The men who died under your command this morning will have no second chance, Captain Haviland,'' Smythe said coldly. ''Why do you believe I should give you one? Your father, I know, would be the first to agree. General Haviland was a fine and courageous officer, and I find that I must live up to his standards. However unpleasant that may be for me personally.''

There was a long silence in the tent. Finally, Colonel Smythe's gaze fell, and his hand idly moved a paper on his desk. It was obvious that the painful interview was at an end.

''If you'll escort Captain Haviland back to his tent and place him under guard, Major,'' he ordered softly, but he didn't look again at the disgraced son of his friend.

St. John had been cradling the elbow of his aching left arm in his right palm as he listened. Mrs. Haviland had devised a sling, which gave some relief, but he knew it would be a long time before he'd be back to full strength and able to help in whatever action Wellington directed this ravaged regiment to take. He supposed that setting a guard over a prisoner would be the extent of the duties given him for the next few days.

As he led the way outside the command tent, holding the flap open for Haviland to follow him, the captain spoke to him.

''You could talk to him, you know,'' Judith Haviland's husband said softly.

Kit turned in surprise, realizing that his prisoner was appealing to him for his help. "Talk to Smythe?" he repeated. "What good do you suppose I might do?"

"He likes you, admires you. Your *nobility*, perhaps." The emphasized word was almost an insult. "And besides, you're the one responsible for bringing those charges."

"Your actions this morning were witnessed by over fifty men. Do you suppose you can convince each of *them* to lie for you?"

"I wouldn't have to. Not if you told Smythe you were mistaken. The men wouldn't go against your word."

"You know I can't do that," Kit said. He had already turned away, heading toward Haviland's tent, when the captain's next words came from directly behind him.

"Not even for Judith's sake?" he asked, his voice still very low, almost a whisper. "Not even to save Judith and her father from disgrace? And to save my father's life?"

The soft words stopped Kit's advance. He turned back, his eyes tracing over the face of the man who made that request. Despite all that had happened, there was in Haviland's features that small hint of arrogance which seemed to indicate that he still, somehow, expected to be able to talk his way out of this.

"I'm sorry for your family," Kit said truthfully, "but you're a danger to everyone here. I won't lie for you, not even to protect your father from learning what you've done. To leave you in your present position would eventually cost other men their lives. I know you, Haviland. I know you too well."

"Not even in exchange for Judith's...undying gratitude?" Haviland asked, his question soft enough that Scott, who had just walked out of the tent behind them, couldn't possibly have heard what he'd just suggested. "I can arrange that, you know," he added. "Judith is very fond of my father. And of her own, of course."

St. John knew exactly what Haviland was offering, knew and was sickened by the idea that he would try to trade his wife's body for his own reputation. Kit held the dark, almost smiling eyes a moment. To his shame, he had felt the smallest breath of temptation. There had been within him a quick, yet undeniable, physical response to that obscene suggestion.

And then he remembered Judith Haviland's hands, work-worn and reddened with cold, moving with kindness over the injuries she had treated today. His and all the others. He remembered her voice, comforting and reassuring to the men she tended, and reacting to his own unspoken fears with amused tenderness.

Slowly, Kit shook his head, rejecting a despicable offer made by a man he despised. Haviland's eyes fell, finally, before St. John turned away and, holding his injured arm protectively against his body, continued across the muddy field of the encampment to the tent where he would make Haviland a prisoner.

"At least five regiments, sir," Scarborough said breathlessly. "All of them looking fresh as daisies."

"You're sure they didn't spot you?" Smythe asked.

"We never got close enough, sir. But they're not more than four hours away, and coming on fast."

"Along this road?" the colonel asked.

"Straight as a die," the lieutenant agreed. "They'll be here well before sundown."

"Two thousand men," Smythe said under his breath. They all knew that he was thinking about his options, which were limited.

There was no time, of course, to send to Wellington for further orders. A messenger would carry the information that Napoleon had finally come through with the promised replacements for his army in Portugal. But as to their own role...

"Thanks to Haviland, we now have wounded who are unable to fight," Kit reminded him.

"And there are the women, of course," Smythe agreed, raising his eyes to meet those of his second-in-command. "We could send them west toward the coast by wagon. I believe that Trant and the militia are still in control there."

Kit nodded agreement. It seemed the best plan. Even if the unit retreated in front of the oncoming forces instead of offering resistance, the wounded would slow them down. And Massena's main army still lay between them and Wellington.

Whatever happened in the next few days, they all knew that this small band of dragoons would be caught between the two larger French forces. Caught and probably crushed.

"In case my own courier doesn't get through, you'll have to see to it that Trant sends word to Wellington of what's happened here as soon as you make contact."

"I, sir?" Kit questioned in surprise.

"You're not in any shape to fight, St. John, even if you're willing to hold your reins in your teeth," Smythe said, humor touching his voice for the first time since the lieutenant's grim assessment of their position. "I need someone I can trust to see to the safety of the wounded."

"We could all move to the west," Kit suggested, reluctant to leave his men, despite the fact that he knew Smythe was right. One-handed, he wouldn't be very effective in a cavalry fight, and the women and the wounded had to be protected. It was not a duty he had anticipated being given. Nor one he wanted.

"The last order I received from headquarters was to guard this route until we were reinforced or removed," Smythe reminded him. "And I have not yet received any instructions from Wellington to the contrary, Major St. John. Given that situation, I can't simply surrender this road to the French.''

"You can't hope to stand against them, sir," Kit warned.

"We can stand," Smythe said softly. "Whether or not we can hold them will be another story."

Scarborough had been chosen to carry the dispatches to Wellington. Kit made it a point to see him off. The boy's pleasant, freckled face was calm and determined, but he was no fool, of course. He knew the difficulties of eluding the French army which stretched across the land before him like a net.

"Take care," St. John advised, handing him the packet he'd brought from Smythe's tent.

"Don't you worry about me, Major," the young lieutenant said. "You see to the lads. And to Mrs. Haviland and the others. You get them safe away, sir. I'll do just fine."

"Of course you will," Kit said. Their eyes held a moment. Both of them knew the enormous odds that they would ever see one another again, and then, fighting emotion, Kit slapped the gray sharply on the rump. He watched until horse and rider had disappeared into the mist of the winter afternoon.

When he turned, Judith Haviland was standing outside the medical tent, her eyes on him rather than in the direction the messenger had gone. "We're almost packed, Major St. John," she said. "In reality, other than the wounded, there wasn't that much to put into the wagons."

"Probably just as well," Kit said. "With the terrain we'll be crossing, the less baggage we're hampered by, the better."

"Baggage or baggages?" she asked, reminding him of the army's slang for the women who followed them, but she was smiling at him. "I know that this particular duty isn't your choice."

"There aren't many choices where duty is concerned, ma'am."

"And all of them are sometimes hard," she said softly.

She had heard then. She knew about his role in the charges that had been brought against her husband, and probably better than anyone else, she would be aware of the impact of those charges on the life of Michael's father. And on her own.

Still, he could read no condemnation in her eyes. They met his with the same steady regard and friendship they had always held. Unlike her husband, Judith Haviland understood duty.

"Colonel Smythe's messenger?" she asked, her gaze shifting in the direction the young lieutenant had taken.

"Carrying the dispatches to Wellington," Kit admitted.

Her eyes came back to his. Despite her knowledge of the import of those messages, they hadn't changed. "We'll be ready to leave in fifteen minutes," she said. Turning, she disappeared into the medical tent.

St. John looked again into the distance where Scarborough had vanished. He could only wish the boy Godspeed, but he knew that if Smythe's packet reached the headquarters of His Majesty's army in Portugal, Haviland's military career was at an end.

As was any semblance of a normal life for the members of his family. Judith Haviland knew that as well as he, and yet, as always, she had made no protest over the blow fate had dealt her. Or any outcry against the unfairness of it all.

That was the same courage with which she had met every hardship of the last three years. And if there was any single virtue Kit had come to admire and to value above all others, since the day his father had sent him into this hell, it was courage. It seemed a shame that only one of the Havilands possessed that precious commodity.

Chapter Four

"**B**loody hell," Kit said, the expletive uttered under his breath, too quietly, he hoped, for anyone else to hear.

"What do we do now, Major?" Cochran asked.

Kit realized that the sergeant was standing at his elbow, his gaze following St. John's over the expanse of churning water they were supposed to cross to reach the coast road.

What St. John had discovered when he arrived at the river's edge were only the remnants of the medieval stone bridge which had once spanned the broad, swift-running current, its destruction almost certainly carried out by engineers acting under orders from Wellington.

It was a highly effective way to direct the enemy's progress and one the English commander had used successfully in the past. Roads that would support the movement of artillery were few in this country, and access to them depended on bridges such as these. Only in this case...

"We go back the way we came," Kit said.

He had already considered his options and had been forced to admit he was left with little choice. There was no way he could take these lumbering carts across the mountains to another bridge, and there were too many wounded who were not yet ambulatory to allow him to abandon that means of transport.

"Whatever happened back there…" Kit paused, further expression of yesterday's merciless reality almost blocked by emotion. "It's certain to be finished by now," he concluded.

In the distance behind them, as they wound their way up the first of the ridges that now lay between them and the road they had guarded throughout the winter, they had heard the noise of their regiment's resistance to the French advance. They had already been some distance away from that fighting, of course, but the sounds of it traveled to them, pushed upward by the land's topography from the valley below.

Kit knew that the men in the wagons, even those most severely wounded, had reacted to that noise just as he had. With guilt, primarily, and with despair that they were not below, struggling beside comrades with whom they had shared every hardship of these last three years.

In the faces of the women had been a resigned sadness. Most of them had lost husbands before in this war. That was the way in the army. By necessity, widows remarried quickly and went on with their lives.

Only one of the women St. John was assigned to protect had not left her husband behind. For Mrs. Haviland it might have been better if she had. It would have been a reprieve for his family if Michael had been killed in yesterday's action. If Kit had been in the captain's situation, death in battle would have been his fervent wish. However, given what he knew about Haviland, it would probably not be his.

St. John had been given three able-bodied men. He had requested Sergeant Cochran and been grateful when Smythe agreed. Two corporals had been sent along to guard the prisoner, who was allowed to ride his own horse at the back of the caravan.

St. John had already decided there was nothing he could have done differently in bringing the charges against Haviland. His first obligation was to the men of this regiment. And it did no good thinking about the consequences of his action. Besides, they now had more immediate problems.

''Turn the wagons, Sergeant,'' Kit ordered.

As Cochran rode off to put that command into effect, Kit looked down again into the current, dreading a return to the encampment they had left yesterday afternoon. It was possible there were survivors of that battle, men who had somehow escaped being killed or taken prisoner, and their addition would strengthen his party. And if there were other wounded, then they, too, would become St. John's responsibility.

Whatever the situation behind them, Kit knew he had no choice but to retrace the journey they had made. Since they were cut off by the river, the road they had followed here led back to the only route over which he could now move these wagons south. There was nowhere else for his small detachment to go.

The bodies they found had been stripped. The peasants in the surrounding countryside were too poor for that not to have happened, especially at the end of a long, hard winter. Kit ordered his men to bury the dead in graves they dug near the site. Colonel Smythe's body had been among them.

It had been little more than forty-eight hours since they'd set out, and yet so much had changed. The regiment to which they belonged had been virtually eliminated, its members either killed or, if they were lucky, taken prisoner by the swift-moving enemy. However, judging by the number of friends they buried, the French had not bothered to take prisoners.

The fact that they had swept through the regiment's resistance so quickly was almost an advantage to their own position Kit realized. At least they were well to the rear of whatever fighting would take place within the next few days.

He had to admit to some relief that the enemy was by now miles ahead of them. Without supplies or resources, he bore the responsibility of taking four wagonloads of wounded men and the women through those same miles of hostile territory.

More frightening than the thought of that was the growing realization that, despite Mrs. Haviland's treatment, his wound was becoming inflamed. He had felt the effects of the fever in his body throughout the afternoon.

He had also been aware that Sergeant Cochran's eyes had focused questioningly on his face from time to time. They had been filled with speculation, although the enlisted man had as yet said nothing. But if Cochran realized he was ill, then Judith Haviland would almost certainly notice.

"Now what?" The sergeant stood again at his elbow, questioning as he had at the bridge yesterday. St. John realized that Cochran had seen to most of the work of the burial, and he blessed his colonel once more for assigning him to this unit.

"South," Kit answered simply. Despite what hostilities they might face, without medicine or supplies, they had no choice but to travel toward Wellington and the main British force still encamped, as far as he knew, at Vedras Torres.

"Shouldn't we spend the night here, Major?" Cochran suggested. His eyes were again considering. "There's water."

"The road parallels the river for the next ten or twelve

miles. We'll do better to find a more secluded spot to set up camp, away from the possibility of encountering more looters.''

Cochran nodded his agreement. They were watching a couple of the women, under the direction of Judith Haviland, bring water to those wounded who were unable to leave their beds in the wagons. Mrs. Haviland had not watched the hurried burials, but had spent the time attending to the needs of the living.

"How are you at poaching, Sergeant Cochran?" Kit asked, thinking of his own responsibilities. "We're going to need something to feed these people tonight."

"Try my hand at hunting, sir?"

"I thought you might range ahead and see if you could scare up some game." In late winter, that would be difficult, but the sergeant didn't question the order.

"I'll do my best, Major. Allowed to use my firearm?"

There was always the possibility that shots might attract the attention of someone, either one of the bandit groups that inhabited these mountains or, perhaps even more dangerous, a band of French deserters. But given the condition of some of the wounded and the journey they faced, there was probably more risk in their going any longer without food.

"If you have to," Kit agreed reluctantly. "Just make sure that we'll have something nourishing to feed them tonight."

Cochran was a good shot, and everyone in the regiment knew it. Kit himself was better, of course, but in this situation he would have to trust in the sergeant's skills.

"I'll bring home the bacon, sir," Cochran said with a grin. "Don't you worry none about that."

"Can you find the ruins of the old mill where we surprised the French outpost last year?"

"Maybe six or seven miles south of here?"

"About that. We'll set up camp near there for the night."

"I'll meet you. You take care of yourself, Major. I'll see to supper, providing the French ain't devoured all the game like they've devoured everything else in this blasted country."

"I'm counting on you, Sergeant," Kit said.

For the first time, he put his right hand on Cochran's arm, the touch of his fingers quick and light as he squeezed the solid muscle, an unspoken expression of his gratitude. Surprisingly, the sergeant's eyes were suddenly full of emotion.

"I won't let you down, sir," he promised softly. "Or them," he added. "You can count on that. There'll be food tonight, Major. I promise you that."

Cochran's vow had been easily made, Kit supposed, but now the sun was setting and the soft sounds of twilight were beginning to infiltrate the glen where Kit had ordered the wagons circled. The location he'd chosen was sheltered from the eyes of anyone passing by on the road they'd been following and near enough to the river to make hauling water convenient.

Kit was beginning to worry less about food and more about the sergeant himself when Cochran finally guided his mount into the circle of the campfires. He was leading a gray gelding, and tied across the saddle of that animal, St. John was infinitely relieved to see, was a brace of rabbits and a few birds.

The women would have to make the game into stew in order to have enough to go around. However, with the hard tack they had been given from the regiment's meager stores, at least no one would go hungry tonight. Kit felt a weight lift from his spirits at the sight of the sergeant's round, honest face.

It wasn't until he had walked over to welcome him, near enough to read Cochran's eyes, that St. John knew something was wrong. The sergeant slid out of the saddle and handed the string of game to one of the women. Then he met his commander's gaze, tilting his head toward the woods that lay between their bivouac and the river. Unquestioning, Kit followed him a short way into the surrounding trees.

"Bad news, Major," Cochran said as soon as they were out of earshot.

Kit couldn't imagine what could be worse than what they had already encountered today, but he braced himself for whatever news was bad enough that the optimistic Cochran had decided no one else should hear it.

"I found a body in the woods."

"A body?" Kit repeated.

"Scavengers had already been at it. Pointed it out to me or I'd never have seen it. About five miles from the old camp."

Cochran's eyes shifted to where the women were working. The birds he'd brought in were being spitted, and they had already skinned the hares in preparation for putting them into the pot. The sergeant watched a moment, apparently reluctant to finish what he'd begun. Finally his gaze returned to Kit's.

"Scarborough," the sergeant said softly. "The boy didn't get very far, Major. Not to Wellington, in any case."

Despite the fact that he thought he had been prepared, Kit felt that blow. He had lost men before, of course, and some of them had been good friends. But even with Cochran's warning and his obvious reluctance to reveal what he'd found, St. John had not been prepared for the boy's death.

He forced himself to ask the more important question, despite his heartsickness. "What about the dispatches?"

"The packet wasn't there. I looked. But the thing is, sir, his horse *was*. That's what don't make sense. French regulars would have taken both. The Portuguese would have taken the horse, to eat if nothing else, and left the pouch. And…" Cochran hesitated before he added the rest. "Not only had he been shot, Major, but the boy's throat had been cut as well."

"Good God," Kit said, feeling a chill of horror. "Why would anyone…" He shook his head in disgust, despite his familiarity with the brutalities of this war.

"Making sure, I guess. Just in case the bullet didn't finish him off. But Wellington won't have had word about what happened to the regiment, Major. Or about us. Whoever took those dispatches, you can be sure they ain't going to frank 'em off to headquarters."

"No, of course not," Kit said, again forced to reevaluate their situation. That was the other thing he'd been ordered to do—the last order Smythe had given him, the last he would ever give anyone. Make sure Wellington got word that Napoleon had finally sent the long-promised reinforcements.

Their number didn't represent enough men to make a difference to any major battle, but still, getting that intelligence through had been Smythe's job. His duty. And now it was Kit's.

"Thank you, Sergeant," he said finally, knowing that no matter how much he had come to depend on Cochran's good sense, this particular problem was his and his alone. "Go on and get your supper. You've more than earned it. And Cochran…"

The sergeant, who had already turned toward the camp, halted at the soft admonition. "Well done," Kit added and again saw the unspoken response to his praise reflected in the man's face.

After Cochran left, St. John stood alone in the darkness under the trees, trying to think. The logical thing would be to send the sergeant south with a message detailing the size of the advance, what had happened to the regiment, and requesting help for the wounded he guarded.

But with his own condition worsening, that was a move Kit was reluctant to make. If anything happened to him, if he became unable to command, then Cochran would be the one he would trust to look after this vulnerable party.

Haviland outranked the sergeant, of course, but officially the captain was a prisoner, which made Cochran Kit's second-in-command. The two corporals, relative Johnny Raws, were not familiar with the country that stretched between their position and the main British force in the south.

"I thought I might check on your arm," Judith Haviland said.

Kit looked up, surprised that she had followed him here. Cochran had sent her, he supposed. Despite the calmness of her voice, he could read concern in Mrs. Haviland's brown eyes. Of course, he warned himself, given the gravity of their situation, that concern didn't have to be personal or even for him.

"My arm's fine. You made a good job of it," he said. "Just as you promised."

Sounds of laughter from the camp came to them on a gust of cold wind. It was the women, probably celebrating the unexpected bounty the sergeant had brought in. Neither of them commented on that, but listening to it, Judith said nothing else for a moment.

"That's not really your reputation, you know," she offered finally.

Her voice was so soft, Kit could not read her tone. And for the first time since he had known her, he was forced to wonder what Mrs. Haviland had heard about him.

The narrow world of London society had seemed so distant that Kit sometimes forgot his notoriety there would almost certainly cause comment here. But the infamous Lord St. John was a very different man from Major St. John, and he found it disturbing that she would refer now to his scandalous past.

"My...reputation?" Kit repeated reluctantly.

"You were never reputed to be a flatterer," she said. "Or a liar," she added. "Will you let me look at your arm, Major?"

"It's inflamed," he admitted.

"And you're fevered, just as Sergeant Cochran suggested."

"I have a score of wounded men and four women to look after. I'm afraid, ma'am, that I really can't afford to be fevered."

He smiled at her, trying to tell her without words that he understood the ridiculousness of the claim he had just made. And the undeniable truth of it as well.

"I see," she said. Her voice was almost amused.

And this time there was something else there, he realized. Some other emotion that had lain, not quite hidden, under that covering amusement. In surprise, Kit realized that in her tone was something which the notorious Lord St. John had certainly heard before.

Had that emotion been in the voice of any other woman he had ever known, any woman other than this, Kit would have been sure what its subtle undercurrent conveyed. But that emotion was alien to their relationship, and so he discarded the incredible idea it had fostered in his heart.

"And you believe that because of the seriousness of your duties, you can deny the functioning of your own body?" she asked reasonably.

"I certainly hope so, Mrs. Haviland," he said, smiling at her again. "At least, until we are well out of this."

"How long do you think it will take for help to reach us?" she asked. "Considering the fact that the French are between Wellington and ourselves."

It was a legitimate question. She had seen Scarborough leave camp more than two days ago and had been aware of the purpose of his mission. Apparently, despite his betrayal of Kit's condition, Cochran had not seen fit to inform her that the young lieutenant would never arrive at English headquarters.

"I suppose," Kit said carefully, "that will depend on the conditions Colonel Smythe's messenger encounters."

"You *do* realize, Major, that if your wound goes septic…"

Her voice faltered suddenly over that horror, but they both knew well enough what she intended to warn him about. If gangrene set in, he would die. His only hope would be the amputation they had discussed before, and that might then be too late.

"I understand," Kit said calmly.

Her eyes were on his face. In the growing darkness he could still read worry in their depths and an undeniable fear.

"Days," she warned. "It will be only a matter of days."

"Perhaps by then we'll be with the surgeons."

"Perhaps?" she repeated.

He fought against the urge to tell her the truth. Not that

it would do any good, but as with Cochran, he trusted her common sense and would value her advice.

"Major St. John, are you afraid that—"

"Of course," he said, breaking in deliberately before she could finish the question. "Of course, I'm afraid," he confessed, forcing amusement into his voice. "I'm not a fool, Mrs. Haviland. Whatever you may have heard in London."

She laughed. "No, I assure you *that* wasn't your reputation either," she said, but her tone had lightened, just as he intended. "Did you even remember that we once met there?" she asked. The smile that was the lingering residue of her laughter still played about her lips.

He didn't, of course. Kit had no idea that he had ever seen Judith Haviland before his arrival in Spain.

"Of course," he lied easily. "How should I ever forget having met someone like you, ma'am?" He was rewarded again with her laughter, as soft and as intimate as it had been within the medical tent that night.

"*That,* sir, is a blatant untruth. A gallant one, perhaps, but certainly a whisker. You have no memory whatsoever of our meeting," she chided, laughing again. "At least be honest, sir."

"I was befuddled with drink?" he suggested, his tone matching the teasing quality of hers.

Her laughter suddenly disappeared, fading more slowly from her eyes.

"I'm sorry, Mrs. Haviland," he said softly. "That wasn't intended—"

"I know," she whispered. "I'm just so afraid of what will happen."

"I assure you, ma'am, Wellington will not abandon us to—"

"Not of this," she broke in quickly. "It's not..." She took a breath, deep and calming apparently, for when she continued there was none of that previous agitation in her words. There was only regret. "It almost seems that here, until we reach the English lines…"

She didn't finish, but Kit understood instinctively what she meant. Here there were other problems, concerns more pressing even than the charges that had been brought against her husband. Here her worries focused on the lives that she guarded. And in the scope of those duties, she could forget for a time that which loomed like a storm above the future of her family.

"I'm grateful, ma'am, for all you're doing." In his own concerns, Kit realized that he had failed to thank her for her care of his men. That was something he had learned early in his brief military career, what a word of thanks or encouragement might mean to someone under his command. Not, of course, that Judith Haviland was. "No one could do more for them than you have done. Not even the surgeons."

"John Penny died today. They buried him with the others."

Penny was the trooper who had received the head injury in Haviland's fatal charge, Kit remembered. He had been one of the most severely wounded, of course. Still, even if he should have been, Kit had not been prepared for that either. Especially not on top of the news about Scarborough.

"I have almost nothing left to treat these men with," Judith went on softly. "No herbs, no drugs. Even the rum you…"

Her voice faltered, remembering her husband's disgrace perhaps. Or his own role in it.

"Do you realize," she said, "if I had had those spirits to cleanse your injury, then…it might all be different?"

"And it might not." Kit found himself comforting her.

"Whatever happened, it was not your fault. Surely you understand that."

She nodded, seeming to agree with his words, but her eyes had fallen, and her hands played restlessly with the fringe of her shawl. He waited, aware of her distress over the incident, but when she went on, lifting her eyes again to his face, it was something different.

"The surgeons feel that in order to heal, a wound must first suppurate. Perhaps that's all that's happening with your arm. Perhaps it doesn't mean—"

"Mrs. Haviland, you must realize that I don't want anyone else to know about this," he said. "I would have preferred that Cochran kept his suspicions about the fever to himself."

"He was worried about you. I understand that you feel it best that news of your illness not become general knowledge. If you'll come to me tonight…"

Her voice faded, but her eyes remained on his face. That soft suggestion had inadvertently been phrased as the age-old lover's invitation. Kit's body reacted, and the reaction was swiftly denied.

That was not something that had ever been within the well-established bounds of their relationship. Friendship, certainly. Mutual respect. But never anything between them that went beyond those two acceptable emotions.

"When everyone else is asleep," she added, apparently trying to induce him to agree. "No one else will know you're there."

Kit's heart responded to the appeal inherent in those words. Their intent was very different from what they seemed to imply, he knew, but still, with her whispered invitation, an unthinkable image had been engendered. And must, in honor, be fought.

St. John nodded, and then he brushed past her in the

darkness, making his way through the shadows cast by the trees toward the safety of the light of the campfires. In his head, unwanted and unsought, echoed again the simple words that Judith Haviland had just said to him.

The bandage was stained, and not with blood. Judith had taken great care in peeling the cloth away from the wound. And when she had, she realized that the fears she had fought since Sergeant Cochran had come to her were not unfounded.

"You were right," she said, fighting to keep her voice even in the face of this setback.

She looked up from the angry, swollen arm to find St. John's gaze. The blue eyes did not reflect the fear that had suddenly tightened her breathing at the sight of what lay under that bandage. His courage was not from ignorance, she knew. St. John had probably seen as many wounds go septic in the last three years as she had. As this one almost certainly had.

The wound and the stitches she had set had almost disappeared, swallowed up by the poisons building under the swelling of proud flesh. Streaks of red had begun to creep upward toward his shoulder. Judith tried to think of anything that was left in her small store of medicines with which she could treat this. Of any plant which grew here that might have some effect on the spreading infection.

That was the problem, of course. She was still too unfamiliar with the flora that were indigenous to the region, despite her determined questioning of the natives she'd encountered during the last three years. Someone's life might depend on her knowledge, she had told herself. And now her worst fears had come true.

"A poultice," she suggested aloud, feeling compelled by the major's trust to offer him some remedy, even if her brain seemed incapable of identifying one. "Something that will draw out the poisons. Or perhaps…a blister," she suggested, hesitating to mention a procedure that seemed to her little more than medieval torture. The surgeons, however, swore by that method as they did by swift amputation. And if she had had the courage to take his arm at first, she thought, then none of this would be happening.

Their voices had been kept so low they were almost whispering, although the camp was asleep. And if not, no one would think it strange that the major had visited Mrs. Haviland's tent for treatment. However, it would be better, they both understood, if the men didn't know about the potentially serious consequences of what she had discovered under that bandage.

"Do you believe those might help?" St. John asked.

"Perhaps," Judith hedged. She preferred the poultice, of course, if only she had access to the right ingredients. "But I must tell you—" she began before St. John interrupted calmly.

"That in all likelihood, nothing will help."

"Yes," she admitted. He deserved to be told the truth. It was his life they were discussing. His life that she held now in her hands, with too few weapons to fight against the unseen, yet terrifying enemy with whom she had become all too familiar.

Would it be better for her, who was not a surgeon and who had never before performed an amputation, to try to take off the arm before the infection could climb higher? She had watched more of those operations than she wished to remember. She knew the procedure, but to actually carry out that ghastly surgery, without the proper instruments and on this particular man… Suddenly her eyes lifted again to his.

St. John's face was dispassionate. She could read nothing

there beyond a genuine need for information. He was in command of this unit and, as he had reminded her, the lives of the people Smythe had placed under his care were his first responsibility.

She had seen men with courage such as St. John's endure a great deal and then go about their duties as if determined to ignore the pain and weakness of their bodies. *I can't afford to be fevered,* he had told her. How could he afford then the other?

"How long?" he asked quietly.

She understood what information he was seeking, because she knew his character. *How long could he continue to command before his body betrayed him, refusing to respond to the demands of his iron will?*

"Five or six days. A week," she guessed. "Perhaps more if we can slow the spread of the poison through the body."

"Can you do that?"

"I still have some dried willow, I believe. But Major, you must understand—"

"I understand perfectly," he interrupted again. "You've been very forthright." There was surprisingly a thread of amusement in his voice. And still no fear.

"Surely Sergeant Cochran can manage whatever needs to be done," she said.

He didn't reply for a moment, and briefly his eyes tried to avoid the question in hers. "Sergeant Cochran will have other responsibilities," he said finally.

"*Other* responsibilities?"

"I'm sending Cochran south in the morning."

"But why?" she whispered. She was aware of how much St. John depended on the bluff sergeant. And when the major became truly ill…

"Because I have no choice," he said simply. "Scarborough was ambushed. Cochran found his body while he was hunting.''

Judith's first thought was for the boy, of course. A quick, burning sorrow that his young life had been so brutally snuffed out before he had a chance to live it. Only gradually did she realize all the implications of that death.

"Then... Wellington won't know what happened," she realized. "Or about us."

"I need a messenger I can trust to get through. None of the others are familiar enough with the country to find a way to circle the French and reach Vedras Torres. We need help for the wounded. I can't take them through the French lines. The best we can hope for—"

"Michael knows the country," she broke into his explanation. She didn't know where that thought had come from, but once it had been voiced, she very quickly realized it was the solution to so many problems. Almost the perfect solution for them all. "He knows it as well as you. As well as Cochran," she argued.

It was only after she had made her suggestion aloud that she thought to question her motives. Had she proposed this to offer her husband a chance to redeem his life? Or had there been some other reason, something less rational? Something dark that grew within her own soul and whose existence she had never before acknowledged.

"Captain Haviland is a prisoner," St. John reminded her.

"But it's a chance," she argued. "Don't you see? It's an opportunity for him to make up for what happened. These men were wounded because of Michael's actions. Who better than he to go for help for them?"

"Do you realize..." St. John began, and then he hesitated.

"How dangerous that will be?" she asked. "Is there less danger in this situation? At least..." She hesitated as he had, examining her motives again even as she tried to convince him. "At least, it's a chance," she whispered finally.

"Forgive me, Mrs. Haviland, but perhaps it's a chance your husband doesn't deserve."

His assessment hurt. She knew Michael's weaknesses, but he was her husband. And when she pictured his father, and her own, she could not be sorry that she had thought to suggest this to St. John, no matter what the major's answer might eventually be.

"Do you love your father, Major St. John?" she asked softly.

The sudden pain in the depths of his blue eyes was unexpected, but she went on, knowing that this man represented her only chance to change the fate of two brave old soldiers. They had played no role in that dawn battle, but they would certainly become casualties of her husband's disgrace.

"Of course," he said. For the first time tonight, despite the terrible truth of the diagnosis that she had given him, there was an echo of emotion in St. John's voice.

"As he loves you. Very much, I'm sure," she went on. "And no matter what..." She paused again, remembering what this man faced. A soldier's fate he had accepted with equanimity, and so she went on, trusting his strength to hear this.

"No matter what happens to you here, even if..." Her voice faltered, but she strengthened it and continued. "Even if your father loses you, he will be able to look back on your life with pride. To glory in your accomplishments, in your unquestioned valor. He will always be so *proud* you were his son. But...for Michael's father, unlike your own—"

"Don't," St. John ordered suddenly.

The shock she felt at the harshness of the single word

must have been reflected in her face, because when he spoke again, the major's tone had softened and was once more controlled.

"Believe me, Mrs. Haviland," he said, "I understand the price of disgrace. And of dishonor. Even of disappointing your father's expectations. You don't have to remind me of that."

"Major," she protested softly, but he had already turned away, picking his jacket up from the table where she had placed it before she'd begun to examine his arm.

She called to him again, softly, from the door of the tent, but St. John didn't stop. Instead, he continued across the center of the encampment and disappeared into the darkness of the woods on the other side.

Chapter Five

"What makes you think St. John will be willing to listen to anything I say?" Michael asked. "I can assure you he never has listened before."

"Because his options are extremely limited," Judith said truthfully.

This was betrayal, and she recognized that, but the more she thought about those options during the long, sleepless night, the more certain she was that only in this way might everyone win. It was so simple a solution. Cochran would be free to assume command if she were forced to carry out the horror of the amputation which was probably St. John's best hope for survival. And with the sergeant in charge, Kit might be willing to agree to that. And for Michael and his father...

"You're not trying to get rid of me, are you?" Michael asked. "Leaving the field open for our gallant major, perhaps?"

And of course, Michael in his shrewdness had hit upon the other question she had considered throughout the night. Why, really, had she suggested this?

"It's up to you," she said. "I'm simply telling you the situation. I'm not urging you to volunteer. I know..." Her voice faded suddenly, but then she forced herself to go on. "I know how dangerous this is. Lieutenant Scarborough had made it only a few miles from the encampment before he was killed. But I thought that you might *want* to do something…" Again her voice faltered before the cynical gleam in her husband's eyes.

"Something so valiantly right and honorable that it would make up for all the wrongs I've ever done before?" he asked.

There was no mockery in his voice, however, and she wondered if he were really considering volunteering to be the courier.

"That's just what St. John's father intended when he sent him to Wellington," he said. "Did you know that, my dear?"

She shook her head. "I don't know anything about Major St. John," she said.

It was not the absolute truth, of course, but she knew nothing about whatever Michael was suggesting. She remembered, however, St. John's reaction last night to her simple comments about his father's pride in his military record. So she wondered exactly what Michael knew about the earl's relationship to his son and how he knew it.

"You think he's such an honorable knight," he said. "But do you know, Judith, we are more alike than you think. He, too, was a constant disappointment to his noble sire. And it's possible, I suppose, that I can use that to my advantage."

"I don't understand," she said, feeling a frisson of unease.

St. John had asked her not to tell anyone about his condition. And of course, the news of Scarborough's death was not something he would want the others to know. Although he had not put her under any restrictions about that, Judith had fully understood that his disclosure was intended to be confidential.

Yet at dawn she had come to her husband in order to betray St. John's trust. For Michael's sake. For the sake of his father and her own. Now her husband was talking about using the knowledge she had given him to his own advantage, and she was sickened again by the way his mind worked.

"Don't worry," he said. "I'll be able to make St. John see it our way. As you said, he really doesn't have many choices left, does he?"

"Michael," she whispered, realizing suddenly that there was no guarantee that if he were given this mission, he would carry it out. If St. John released him, there was nothing to stop him from traveling in the opposite direction, away from the English lines. "You wouldn't..."

For some reason, she hesitated even to suggest such a contemptible action. If he hadn't thought about the possibility, then she shouldn't bring it up.

"I wouldn't what?" he questioned. "Run away and leave you surrounded by the enemy?"

Her fear of his cowardice must have been in her eyes, or her feelings were as transparent to him as he had once claimed. He laughed before he went on. "Leaving you here with our noble major? No, my darling, that I would *never* do."

She wanted to be reassured by that promise, but then he added, "That bastard has had more than enough of life's riches, far more than his share. I promise you I don't intend to give him something which belongs to me. But be warned, Judith, against whatever...temptation you may feel while I'm gone."

His eyes moved slowly down and then back up her figure, obviously taking in the worn, almost shapeless garments that covered her slender curves, even pausing to assess the work-roughened hands and her unbecoming hairstyle. He smiled when he saw the slight blush of reaction creep into her cheeks.

''You really *aren't* up to St. John's standards, you know. If he ever looks your way, my darling, try not to make a fool of yourself. Just remember that it's only the result of his isolation from his own kind. And the lack of more...acceptable women. Only here, Judith, could someone like you possibly be interesting to a man like St. John.''

It was a cruel taunt, especially if he believed what he'd said to her before about her attraction to the major. She was a married woman, and she had been faithful to those vows, in deed and, except for her admiration for the kind of man she believed St. John to be, even in her thoughts.

She had always known that men like the earl of Ryde's son were far above her reach. She had clearly read St. John's disinterest when they met in London. She had never entertained the notion that the handsome aristocrat considered her to be in any way appealing.

St. John had offered her his friendship, and she valued it. They respected each other, she believed, and she would never do anything to destroy that respect. Except, she remembered with regret, in revealing the major's situation to Michael, perhaps she already had.

She swallowed the impulse to reply to her husband's warning, fighting the urge to defend herself from Michael's caustic tongue. She had learned long ago the futility of that. But with his reaction to the information she'd given him, she wondered again if she had done the right thing in coming to him. Had it been the right thing for any of them? Her gaze fell, her guilt over what she had done a burden almost too strong to bear.

She heard Michael's soft laughter, and he put the crook

of his forefinger under her chin, lifting it so that her eyes were forced to meet his. He studied them a long time before he spoke.

"Thank you, my dear, for telling me," he said simply. He lowered his mouth to hers, and for the first time in months, his breath was free of the stench of alcohol. There was no brutality in the kiss he gave her. And no passion.

When he released her, their eyes met again, but they said nothing else. And Judith realized that she now had no control over what she had just put into effect.

"Because you have no choice. And you're certainly smart enough to know it," Michael Haviland said. The same arrogance, the same cold mockery that had always been there, was in his eyes and in his voice, despite his situation.

Kit had not expected to be confronted by this when he'd been asked to speak to the prisoner. St. John had told no one but Judith about Scarborough's death. Cochran had known, of course, but the sergeant could be counted on to keep that secret. He had believed that Mrs. Haviland might be counted on as well, Kit thought bitterly.

"I'll get through to Wellington," Haviland vowed, his normal confidence apparently restored by the possibility this mission offered. "But in exchange, St. John, I want your promise."

"*My* promise?" Kit repeated, although he had known this was the crux of the offer. It was, in reality, the same one Haviland had made to Smythe. Only he had made it to the colonel in terms of respect. And now...

"Your sacred promise. Made on your bloody, precious honor," Michael demanded. "I want your solemn oath that if I go for help, if I carry the news of the French reinforcement and your situation here, that you'll never repeat to anyone the charges you made against me. That you'll never by word or deed divulge what happened that morning.''

"You know I can't agree to that," Kit said.

"Why not? The regiment's destroyed. Smythe's dead. There are only a handful of people left who know anything about what happened that day. And without your pressing them to testify, those few can be trusted to keep their mouths shut. Even if they don't..." One of Michael's brows arched, and he shrugged.

He was right, of course. No one would care what people such as Cochran or the few remaining men of Haviland's troop would say. Too many enlisted men disparaged their officers. They would simply be ignored. They both understood that.

"You can't send Cochran," Haviland argued. "You need him to feed your charges. The other two would be less than worthless for that. They'll end up spitted on some Portuguese bandit's dagger before they stumble across anything fit to fill the cooking pots. I'm your best hope to get these people through this country, and you know it."

"When Cochran leaves, I'll see to the provisions."

Michael laughed and then seeing the quick reaction to his mockery in Kit's eyes, he wiped the amusement from his face. "Perhaps you can. For a while. *But* that will then leave this detachment without a commander. Cochran will be gone, and you propose to be out foraging all day," he said, his derision for the plan still clear, somehow, in his voice. "And when you are no longer able to function?" he added softly. "When you're no longer competent to command? What then, St. John?"

"I'll consider that possibility only if I have to," Kit said stubbornly.

"Possibility?" Haviland repeated in mockery. "If Judith

says you'll not be fit to give orders, then I can assure you it's not simply a *possibility*."

"Did she tell you that?" Kit asked sharply, feeling both anger and fear at her appraisal of his condition.

"You won't even recognize when you have reached that point," Haviland said. "Your mind will begin to play tricks on you. What is irrational will seem supremely rational. Fever does that to a man. You know it as well as I."

Kit couldn't deny that truth. They had both seen the sequence: the rising fever, the trembling physical weakness and the near stupor it produced, followed almost inevitably by wild ravings and the unnatural strength of true delirium. Thinking of that progression, St. John said nothing, until Michael asked the crucial question.

"Who will be responsible for these people then, St. John? Will you trust me to lead them?"

"Perhaps," Kit said.

"But I won't, you know." Deliberately, Haviland belittled that unwilling agreement. "Because then there will be nothing in it for me. I don't care if you *or* they live to reach Wellington's surgeons. It's to my advantage that none of you do. Why should I take any of these men to a place where I'll face disgrace and dishonor? A place where I'll again be made a prisoner. No, my friend. You have one deal left for the game. One hand to play. Or we'll probably *all* die."

Kit expected death. He had already begun to prepare himself for it. And he would willingly die if he could keep the others safe. But that willingness was only in exchange for the lives of the others. Judith's face was suddenly before him. He had seen women caught before between the opposing armies of this war. And the thought of that happening to her was unbearable.

"How do I know you'll keep your word?" Kit asked.

Haviland was right about so much of what he said, despite the immoral premise behind the suggestion.

"Because…" Haviland hesitated. Suddenly, for the first time since Kit had known him, the captain seemed unsure. He looked younger, less cynical, and what Kit read in his eyes was a pain that had never been revealed there before.

"Do you love your father, St. John?" Haviland asked finally, instead of finishing whatever easy explanation of his motives he had begun. "Did you seek his approval? Have you sought his approval your whole bloody life and known that you never quite lived up to his expectations?" Michael's voice was caustic and yet somehow filled with longing. "Do you have any idea what it's like never to measure up? No matter how hard you try?"

Again, as they had in Smythe's tent, his own father's words echoed in Kit's head. *You continue to bring dishonor to this family. You may enjoy wallowing in the mud of public censure, but I will no longer allow you to drag the Montgomery name there with you.*

But, despite that bond which they undoubtedly shared, could he trust Michael Haviland? And did he really have a choice? St. John wondered bitterly.

"Your wife is here," Kit reminded him. However despicable Haviland was, surely he would not desert Judith to face starvation or capture in order to save his own hide.

"Of course," Michael said softly. "The thought of that will travel with me every mile of the way, I promise you."

Again Kit heard an undercurrent, but he couldn't identify it. He wondered suddenly if what Judith had predicted about the ultimate failure of his faculties was already beginning. But that, too, was a chance he would have to take.

"All right," Kit agreed reluctantly. "You have my word."

"I want your oath, St. John. Whether or not I succeed,"

Haviland demanded. "We both know what lies between here and Vedras Torres. I may not make it through. I don't want my father to suffer because of that…failure. I want your word," he said again, "that the story of what happened the morning of the French attack will never pass your lips. Or any other disparagement of my conduct. I want your solemn oath made on your own noble honor." And there was mockery in that, too.

"Then in exchange," Kit demanded, his own temper flaring, "I want *your* oath that you'll do everything in your power to get through. No stratagems, Haviland. No hiding. No cowardice. The lives of these people depend on your faithfulness to this bargain."

"I'm not a coward. No matter what you think."

"On your honor," Kit ordered again, ignoring that claim.

Their eyes held, weighing one another. They were not friends. They had no respect for each other, but they had both been raised according to a code, taught to them by men who had adhered to its rules all their lives.

Slowly, Michael Haviland held out his hand. Kit hesitated, still considering all that was on the table, still trying to assess the man who stood before him and the situation. Finally he allowed his own right hand to close firmly around the other. Only then did the familiar smile appear on Haviland's lips.

"Poor St. John," he said softly. "Forced by fate to make a bargain with the devil."

"And if you don't keep to it, you bastard, I swear I'll hunt you down in hell," Kit promised, his voice as low as the other man's had been, "and I'll bloody well make you wish you had."

But even as he watched, the small, cynical smile widened.

* * *

"Is he gone?" Judith Haviland asked.

Kit wondered if her husband had not bothered to say goodbye, but that was not a question he could ask her. The beautiful oval face was as colorless as poor Scarborough's had been the morning of the battle.

"Almost an hour ago," he admitted.

She released the breath she'd been holding, and the strength of its passage through her slim body was visible. Relief, he thought, identifying the emotion that showed briefly in her eyes, which were then quickly veiled from his assessment by the fall of long, dark lashes.

"Thank you," she said.

"As you pointed out to your husband, Mrs. Haviland, I really had very little choice."

Hearing the bitterness, her eyes flashed up to his. "I'm sorry. Truly I am, Major St. John. I did what I thought was for the best. For *all* of us."

Kit said nothing, still hurt by her betrayal. He deliberately shifted his gaze from her face to watch Cochran supervising the reloading of the wagons.

As soon as they were on their way, the sergeant would ride ahead, not only scouting the territory they must cross for signs of the enemy, but seeking something for the cooking pots tonight. They had made do with only the hard biscuits and water this morning, but their store of those was running dangerously low.

"I'd like to look at your arm again, Major St. John. I think it might help to wrap the rest of the willow I infused under a new bandage. Eventually, you know—"

"You made all the eventualities extremely clear last night," he interrupted. "To me and apparently also to your husband."

She glanced down at his elbow, his left arm bent and held protectively against his body. The crimson uniform sleeve was stretched tightly over the swelling, and that must be excruciating. He hadn't given her a chance last night to replace the bandage she had removed. And she knew the wool would chafe the tender flesh all day as he rode.

"Do you believe I lied to you, Major?"

When she looked up from his arm, the blue eyes were again on her face. She had nothing to hide, and so she let him examine it, meeting his appraisal without fear.

"I believe you used your knowledge of things I should never have told you to your husband's advantage," he said finally.

"And to yours. To the advantage of *all* these people. Surely you can understand that," she argued. "I meant you no harm. I only wanted to help. To…"

Her rationale faded in the face of the coldness in his eyes. Within them was an indifference to her explanation that was as chilling as the aristocratic boredom which had been there the night they met. He hadn't known her then. Surely by now he knew her better than this, she thought. His gaze finally moved away from her face, again checking Cochran's progress.

"You need Sergeant Cochran to hunt," she said, her eyes following his, "and to scout. *You* are needed to lead, so you must stay physically strong as long as possible. No matter what you think of my motives, Major, you know I'm the only one who can help you to do that. Please let me treat your arm."

The cold eyes came back to her, again assessing.

"For their sakes," she added softly.

And for your own, her heart pled, but that was an argument she didn't dare offer because she knew him well enough now to know it would have perhaps the opposite effect of what she sought. Finally, after a long time, he nodded.

She resisted the urge to draw in a breath in relief. Instead she led the way to her small tent and the concoction she had begun brewing some time before dawn, knowing full well that perhaps neither it nor her prayers would make any difference in the progress of the creeping infection.

And if it didn't, she knew also that she would have to try something more radical. *The best hope for survival,* she had told him before. And although she didn't remind him of that this morning, they both knew it was still true.

He had tied a neck cloth around the wound, and when she removed it, she realized that even in these short hours the redness and swelling around the saber gash had grown more pronounced.

"I need you to remove your shirt," she whispered.

He had replaced the shirt she had cut up with a fresh one from his campaign chest. When she had tried to roll up the sleeve to allow her to work, it wouldn't now go far enough above the swelling for her to evaluate how rapidly the corruption was spreading, but she hesitated to destroy another garment of his limited wardrobe.

"I can help you," she offered, seeing the hesitation in his eyes.

Abruptly, St. John shook his head. He reached behind his neck with his right hand and pulled the loose shirt off over his head and then more slowly off the swollen arm.

Judith had cared for innumerable injured men. She had seen them in all stages of undress and had performed services that no gentlewoman, not even a married one, should have to carry out. There was little that was any longer mysterious to her about the masculine body.

But at the sight of St. John's, her breath caught in her throat and even her stomach reacted. And somewhere below. Something roiled within her body, hot and immensely disturbing.

St. John's shoulders were broad, his skin as dark as her own. Despite his coloring, his chest was smoothly bronze, the small brown nubs of his nipples pebbled now with the chill of the morning.

Judith simply stood a moment, almost mesmerized, staring at the expanse of graceful muscle and the perfection of bone structure he'd revealed. The only thing that marred the smooth expanse was a thin line of dark hair that ran down the center of his ridged stomach to disappear into the top of the white knit pantaloons.

"Is it very far advanced?" he asked.

Only with his question did Judith realize that she had forgotten the purpose behind this disrobing.

"No," she said softly, thankful to realize that that was reality. The streaks were there, climbing upward under the dark skin that stretched over the long, firm muscle of his upper arm, but they seemed no farther advanced than they had been last night.

"Perhaps if I blister the wound itself..." she began and realized what an impossibility that would be, given the swelling.

"Try the other first," he suggested softly.

Her eyes lifted, questioning. She had forgotten the infusion she'd prepared. Forgotten almost everything in the sheer physical reaction to his body. She didn't understand what had happened. There had never been anything about Michael's body... *Michael,* she remembered suddenly. *Michael, who was her husband.*

"You said there would be some time..." His eyes met hers unflinchingly, despite what he knew he faced.

"Especially if we're successful in slowing this," she

said, grateful for the reprieve from her tangled emotions that his calm question offered her.

She moved to the other side of the tent for the infusion she'd begun last night, using the last of the dried willow leaves she'd brought with her from England. They wouldn't be as potent as fresh, she knew, but perhaps this would have some effect.

Time, she thought. Only a little time. Enough for Michael to bring help. Enough for them to get the wounded through. To get St. John to the surgeons. *Please, dear God,* she prayed, *just enough time.*

When she had dipped the cloth into the amber liquid, making sure it was thoroughly soaked, she brought it back to where St. John was sitting. She carefully placed the steaming rag over the swelling and heard the inward hiss of the breath he drew.

"I should have warned you," she apologized.

His face was averted, and he didn't turn at her words. He was still angry with her about what she'd done, she supposed. Losing his trust was the price she would pay for trying to find some solution for all that had happened.

There was nothing she could do about that, she thought, as she wound a new bandage over the still steaming cloth. She had done what she thought was best for the people she cared about. For all of them, but she was unwilling to enumerate exactly who *they* were. If her action resulted in the loss of St. John's respect, it was a small enough price to pay for his life.

"Shall I help you with your shirt?" she asked when she had finished tying the ends of the cloth over the poultice.

"I can manage, thank you, Mrs. Haviland."

He stood up again to pull the shirt awkwardly over his head, and she watched him struggle unsuccessfully to get the sleeve down over the swelling in his left arm, but she didn't repeat her offer. He still hadn't looked at her.

"He will do his best," she said softly. At that the black lashes lifted, revealing clear, fever-bright eyes. "He won't betray you," she promised, believing that because she must.

"Or you," he suggested.

But she had no guarantee of that. She was aware that her marriage was not what her father's and mother's had been. It had never been a love match, of course.

There was nothing in her heart of what she should feel for a husband. Nothing of desire. Or of affection, even. She had blamed herself for that lack, and for the shivering revulsion she had come to feel when Michael's hands moved against her body.

That guilt was hers. Innate still. But now she knew that the familiar coldness was not.

"Honor," she said softly.

St. John's blue eyes narrowed slightly, but he didn't question her use of the word in this context. Or the thought which had produced it.

"Thank you, Mrs. Haviland," he said again. And again, he picked up his jacket and walked out, leaving her once more alone.

Chapter Six

They made frustratingly slow progress over the course of the next four days, and two more of the wounded died. The jolting carts were agonizing for broken bones and damaged bodies, of course, and there was little food, a subsistence level only, although Sergeant Cochran did his best to provide fresh meat each night. They had run out of biscuits the day before yesterday and now were wholly dependent on Cochran's skill, or more importantly, St. John thought, on his luck.

Kit shifted his swollen left arm, trying to find a more comfortable position for it, although intellectually he had already acknowledged there wasn't one. His eyes were burning with the growing fever, and more than once this afternoon he had found himself swaying in the saddle. He had also fought the ridiculous urge to discard the wool jacket in hopes that the cold rain would ease the almost unbearable heat of his body.

Mrs. Haviland patiently placed steaming cloths over his wound each night, replacing them with fresh ones as soon as they cooled. She was trying to draw out the poison and reduce the swelling, and she had had some small success with that. But the nightly fomentations had given him little relief from the pain or the building fever.

She had not been able to stop the spreading infection, but still he was grateful, because she had given him four days, and they were now four days closer to the English lines and to help. And if Haviland had reached Wellington...

Kit's wandering attention was suddenly attracted by a horseman, approaching out of the gray curtain of mist and rain. The red coat marked him as English, and seeing it, Kit's sudden anxiety abated. However, the rider was trying to push his tired mount too fast through the sucking mire the roadway had become.

The wagons had fought their way through the mud all day, every slogging step an effort. They had been forced to stop twice this afternoon to free the wheels of the heaviest cart. Unloading and then reloading the wounded had not helped their condition, and the rain had continued all day, slowing this already endless journey, adding hours they couldn't afford.

The approaching rider was Cochran, Kit realized. The sergeant pulled his exhausted mount up beside Kit's.

"The French," he gasped, his beefy face red with exertion.

"How large a patrol?" Kit asked. He had already turned in the saddle, preparing to order the wagons that stretched behind him to move off the road.

"No patrol." Cochran's breathing had eased somewhat, allowing him to get out more words. "Whole bloody French army."

"Massena?"

"Every French bastard in Portugal."

"What the hell..." Kit breathed.

"Starving. Just like we are. Apparently the emperor sent

two thousand more men and no provisions. And Major, there ain't a chicken left alive between us and Wellington. Not after this winter. You can't feed an army on promises. Not even Massena can do that, so he's taking his army home.''

''And they're coming this way.''

''There's not any other. The Beau's blown the bridges on the Targus. Eventually the French will turn east, but not before they reach us.''

''Do you have a suggestion, Sergeant?'' Kit asked.

He was aware that his capacity to think clearly, to make appropriate decisions, had been diminishing, swallowed up by his illness. The warning Michael Haviland had given was still in the back of his head, as it had been throughout the endless hours of these last four days.

You won't even know when you've reached that point, the captain had taunted him. What action the caravan should take was Kit's decision, and his responsibility, but he would value the sergeant's advice. At least he wasn't too far gone in the throes of fever or too big a fool to know he should ask for it.

''Won't do no good to turn around. We can't travel fast enough to outrun them,'' Cochran observed. ''Not in this mud.''

''Then we find a place to hide until they've gone past us.''

The enlisted man's eyes rested on his commander's face a moment before he nodded agreement. ''There are caves in the hills,'' Cochran offered. ''I ran across one not too far from here, but you can't get the wagons up to it.''

''Thompson can't ride,'' Kit reminded him.

''Leave him somewhere off the road in the woods,'' Cochran advised bluntly. ''You got no choice, Major. He'd be the first to tell you that.''

"The French won't take prisoners. Not if this is the full-blown retreat you believe it to be."

The sergeant nodded. "Then leave him a gun."

It was the usual procedure in this sort of circumstance. The welfare of the unit was more important than the life of one man. Every British soldier understood that reality and most accepted it. But, whether influenced by the effects of the growing fever or not, Kit rejected that logical option. It wasn't an order he would ever give about one of these men. Their British stubbornness and will to survive had gotten them this far. He wouldn't abandon them now.

"Put him up in the saddle in front of you," Kit ordered.

"He won't survive the ride, Major," Cochran warned softly. "You know that as well as I."

"Then at least he won't die alone," Kit said.

Except for Thompson, they made it to the shelter of the cave Cochran had found, but it had been another nightmare journey. The women and the remaining wounded had been placed on the backs of the cart horses and Judith was mounted on Scarborough's gray.

In the end, they had to climb the last half mile, walking beside the struggling animals to encourage them. Only those too debilitated by illness or by their wounds were allowed to ride on that final leg. Kit did not choose to be one of them, and he was exhausted when they finally arrived.

The sanctuary the cave represented was only a temporary reprieve, he knew. They could kill one of the horses for food, and they found water in the back of the cave, a cold trickle that slid down the rock wall to collect in the shallow basin it had worn over the years in the stone floor.

But with the countryside overrun with the retreating French and the ever-present threat of Portuguese bandits and cutthroat bands of deserters, Kit knew that the smoke from even a single fire might give away their location. At least for now, however, thanks to Sergeant Cochran, they were relatively safe.

Kit was standing outside the entrance of the cave into which the two corporals had already carried the wounded. One of the soldiers from Haviland's troop had a badly broken leg, and throughout the jolting ride up the rocky slope to the cave, his pain-filled eyes had clearly expressed his suffering, but he had sketched the major a cocky salute as he was being taken inside the shelter.

Kit had already sent Cochran out to scout, hoping that by some miracle the sergeant might stumble across a living, breathing creature in this war-devastated landscape where the French had survived by scavenging for food all winter. And if he did not...

Kit's eyes shifted unwillingly to the thin, rack-ribbed draft horses. One of them would have to be sacrificed, and he supposed then they'd be forced to take their chances with a fire. His stomach roiled with nausea at the alternative.

Again he pushed the unpleasant possibility from his mind, not even questioning why he hadn't already given the order. They had all eaten horse meat at some time during the last three years. That should no longer be as unthinkable to him as it had been when he'd first arrived in this country. But somehow he hadn't been able to make up his mind to order the slaughter.

He would ask Cochran, he thought, closing his eyes against the deep ache behind them and leaning his head against the cool dampness of the rocks. And as soon as the sergeant returned, he would ask him to post sentries for the night.

Kit knew there must be other things he should attend to,

but the ideas seemed to slip out of his brain before he could grasp them. He could almost watch them drifting away from him to disappear into the mist. And he was no longer certain whether that mist was reality or was a growing fog within his own mind.

"I need to see to your arm," someone said softly. "Before nightfall. Before it gets so dark that I can't."

Kit opened his eyes, pushing the heavy lids upward against their determined resistance. He turned his head, which was still resting against the dampness of the rocks, and found Judith Haviland standing beside him in the gathering twilight. He had not even been aware of her approach.

Apparently, as it had during the long horror of the afternoon, his mind had retreated from the worries of the present into more pleasant memories of the past. He had been thinking of England. Of the vast estate where he had grown up. Of summer rains that caressed instead of battered. Of horses grazing in lush meadows instead of being butchered and eaten by those whom they had so faithfully served.

See to his arm? At least he thought that's what she had said, but he couldn't remember why she would want to do that. She had said *something* about his arm.

She lifted her hand to put the back of it against his brow, but he jerked his head away, recoiling from that contact.

He couldn't allow her to touch him. He remembered that, all right. It was too dangerous. That was one of the things he knew he must hold on to. Mrs. Haviland was married. Out of his reach. Forbidden. Any caress of his hand was forbidden. Or hers, he supposed. Even the thought of allowing her to touch him must be fought. And instead...

At his reaction, Judith had hesitated, her hand still raised between them. He wasn't looking any longer at that, however. His eyes found her face instead, tracing over the clear, rain-touched beauty of her skin. Examining the fragile bone structure, too clearly revealed by the deprivations she had suffered. Too exposed. Exposed to his eyes.

He blinked, suddenly reminded that this, too, was not allowed. He was forbidden even to look at her. Forbidden. All of it. All of what he wanted.

"What is it?" she asked softly. "What's wrong?"

He shook his head, unable to find the words he needed to frame an answer to that. The ones that clamored for expression were those he had no right to say. Could not in honor ever say to this woman. And if he died without telling her what he felt, then that was only as it should be. No right, he thought again.

"Major St. John?" Judith whispered, her wide, dark eyes examining his face.

He was frightening her, Kit realized. She wouldn't understand why his lips had flattened into the taut line that was necessary to prevent the escape of those words. Forbidden words. Forbidden thoughts.

But still he *had* thought them. They had drifted through his brain in increasingly vivid images. He was no better than his father had accused him of being, he thought in disgust. Without honor. Even about this.

"Your arm?" she said again.

"Of course," he managed. He tried to straighten his elbow, to move it away from the protected position against his body in which he had held it all day. And he couldn't prevent the involuntary gasp of response to the agony of that movement.

"We'll have to get your jacket off," she said.

Kit tried not to think about that. He couldn't bear to move his arm, and she was suggesting that they pull the woolen sleeve off over that grotesquely swollen flesh. But of course, he knew that was the only way she could treat it. He couldn't understand why he had forgotten that necessity.

"I think tonight we might need to cut the coat away," she suggested. "I can split the seam up the back of the arm."

"They'll hang me," he said with conviction. And if they did, his father would be ashamed of him again, he reasoned.

His argument against cutting up his coat made perfect sense to him. Everything he owned had been left with the wagons they'd deserted. If she destroyed this coat, he would be in enemy-held territory without a uniform. But for some reason, Judith Haviland was smiling at him. She put her hand gently on his arm, thankfully his good one.

"Well, I promise they won't hang you tonight," she assured him softly. "Uniform or not. They'd have to find you first, Major, and we won't allow them to do that. I think you'd better come inside with me. Don't you think that would be better than standing out here in the rain?" she asked gently.

She was speaking to him as if he were a child, but then Kit hadn't realized it was raining. He closed his eyes, lifting his face to the fine mist, and took a deep breath, pulling the cold, damp air deep into his lungs. He liked the feel of the moisture on his skin. It was almost soothing.

There was something he knew he was supposed to be doing. Some duty he was responsible for. So he opened his eyes again, and found that Mrs. Haviland was still smiling at him, her hand still resting on his arm.

He looked down at it. He could almost feel its warmth through the wool of his uniform. Despite the heat of his body, her fingers were burning against his skin. Long slender fingers, always reddened from the cold and the endless hard work she did for everyone. For him and the others.

But they shouldn't be work-worn, he thought. It wasn't right. They should be the soft pampered hands of a lady.

His lady? he wondered. She would be if she married him. And then he remembered, of course, and the sudden, terrible loss created by that remembrance was cold and bitter in his chest. The woman he loved was already married. Married to someone else.

The woman he loved. He examined the phrase which had appeared in his head, knowing that it, too, was forbidden. Still he didn't destroy the words. He found that he couldn't, now that they had finally been allowed expression in his consciousness.

"What are you doing out here?" Judith asked.

"Waiting for Cochran," he said. He had forgotten why he was waiting, but at least with her question, he had remembered that's why he was here. Part of his duty, and he knew that whatever he was waiting to tell the sergeant must therefore be important.

"I'll ask Corporal Timmons to wait for him. Will that be all right?"

She had taken Kit's arm and was guiding him toward the dark entrance of the cave. He followed because it seemed easier to let her do what she wanted than to marshall an argument against it. It was hard to think of the words he wanted to say. There was something else, he knew. Something that…

"Sentries," he said suddenly. The word had popped into his fevered brain like a miracle.

"I'll see to them," she promised him.

And she would. This was Mrs. Haviland. He could trust her. But at the back of his mind was a warning. Something that he should remember. Something his father wanted him to remember, he thought. Maybe when he was inside, in the cool darkness of the cave and out of this terrible heat, it would come back to him.

Maybe.

"How is he?" Cochran whispered. The question echoed slightly because they were at the very back of the cave. Everyone else was asleep, exhausted by the exertions of the day and weakened by the lack of food.

Tonight the sergeant had brought nothing back from his brief scouting trip in the fading light, and perhaps that was just as well. They all understood the risk of building a fire, but it would have been hard to resist the urge to cook if they had had anything to put into the pot.

As it was, sleep was the only escape from hunger and the cold. So they huddled together, still in their drenched garments, drawing what warmth they could from one another.

Judith shook her head in answer to the sergeant's question, and then wondered if Cochran saw the movement in the darkness. There was some shifting moonlight, despite the clouds, and the lighter darkness of the sky outlined the entrance of the cave.

She had watched Cochran come in from the outside, from sentry duty, and make his careful way past the sleepers to the back of the cave. His first concern had been for the major.

"He's burning up," Judith said truthfully. "Everything he said earlier..." She paused, hesitant to reveal Kit's confusion, even to Cochran.

"Delirious," the sergeant suggested.

"Just...wandering. He doesn't seem to have a very clear understanding of what's happening."

"You did all you could, Mrs. Haviland. The sawbones couldn't 'a done no more for him. The major knew it, too.

Don't you go blaming yourself, now. Whatever happens,'' he added.

"You talk as if—'' There had been sharp protest in the sentence she began, and then she wondered what she was protesting. Cochran sounded resigned. But she was not. Not yet, at least. "They would have taken the arm. It's what I should have done,'' she said.

She had known that would be the safest way. That's why there were so many amputations when an extremity was injured. No one could argue about the success of that common practice.

"Could you do that? Can you do it now?'' the sergeant asked.

"Here?'' she whispered, her doubt clear despite the softness of her tone.

"There's not likely to be a better place. We'll probably be holed up here for a while,'' he said.

"Where no one can find us,'' she suggested bitterly. "Not even Wellington.''

"The general can't send men into that French exodus, ma'am. Much as he might want to if...when he finds out about us.''

Judith understood the sergeant's doubt. He had found Scarborough's body. He knew the odds against Michael getting through. Or perhaps he feared, as she had, that her husband might not even try.

"It would be a suicide mission,'' Cochran continued, and he wasn't talking about Michael's, she realized. "One with little chance of success, and the Beau will know that full well.''

"So no one will come. Even if my husband gets through.''

The sergeant said nothing in response. There was, in reality, nothing to say.

"What will we do?" she asked finally.

"Tomorrow we'll kill one of the horses. There's water. We can survive here for a few days."

She looked down in the darkness at the pale oval of St. John's face. *We can survive,* Cochran had said, and if no one stumbled across their hiding place, that might be true. For the rest of them perhaps, but for the major…

"Can you do it, Mrs. Haviland?" Cochran asked again. "Will it help if you do it now?"

She had almost forgotten what he had asked her before. Or had managed to block from her mind once again the thought of the operation she had been thinking about for the last week.

"I don't know," she whispered into the surrounding darkness, and even as she said it, she wasn't sure which of those questions she was answering.

The morning brought a weak, watery sunshine. The two corporals cheerfully helped Judith move the wounded out of the dampness of the cave and into the clearing in front of it. Relishing the small warmth of the winter sun on her back, as she knew the men would be after yesterday's cold rain, Judith cleaned and rebandaged their wounds and, with the help of Mrs. McQueen, saw to their most pressing needs.

All but the major, she thought, who was still on the bed they had made for him at the farthest reaches of the cave. St. John had begun to talk. There were only whispered words and phrases, but some of them were clearly articulated enough to be understandable.

And most of them had been references to his father. Remembering the major's reaction to what she had said about the earl's natural pride in him, Judith had also realized that some of those muttered expressions might be very personal in nature.

Whatever his relationship to his father, it shouldn't be so cruelly exposed to the others. And for some reason, she was still reluctant to reveal the extent of his illness to them as well.

While she had seen to the other wounded, Cochran had killed the weakest of the draft animals, and the women had been set to work preparing the meat for the cooking pot. At least there would be food today, and hot, nourishing broth for the major, Mrs. McQueen had promised her that, and Judith was determined to get some of it down him.

The sergeant had posted sentries on the rocks above the entrance to the cave. Their position here was probably as secure as any they were likely to find, but he had cautioned them all about unnecessary noise. So in contrast to their usual chatter and laughter, the women were subdued as they worked. Under no illusions about what would happen to them if they were captured, they understood the situation as well as the soldiers.

Cochran had agreed to build a small fire, but he had devised a thick screen of interwoven branches that could be placed across the narrow entrance to the cave. The sergeant had laid the wood in preparation for the fire just inside. The opening would draw the smoke outward and the leaves of the screen he'd made would help to break it up. Which should make it less noticeable, he had explained, to anyone who might be looking.

Cochran had followed Judith when she went back inside to check on St. John. The soft, broken monologue the major had carried on throughout much of the night was continuing.

The sergeant watched as Judith knelt to touch Kit's forehead. There was no reaction to the coolness of her fingers against his brow today. No recoil from her touch, as there had been yesterday.

"Maybe the fire will help to keep him warm," Cochran offered.

Judith had been concerned about the coldness of the cave last night. She had known that she shouldn't allow St. John to sleep in his wet clothing, but, against her medical judgment, she had not removed anything but the jacket she'd had to cut away.

At some time in the coldest, darkest hour of the night, she had even thought about lying down beside him to keep him warm, but, of course, she had not done that either. Instead, she had tried to make sure that the blanket stayed tucked about his shoulders. He had thrown it off again and again, fighting against the rising heat of his fever.

She looked up at the sergeant, no longer attempting to hide the worry in her eyes, infinitely glad that she had someone she trusted to share this burden with. "I don't think the cold is bothering him," she said softly.

"You're going to have to try to take that arm off, Mrs. Haviland," he said.

Cochran was trying to help. He understood, as she did, that there was probably only one thing that might make a difference in St. John's condition now.

"I don't know that I can, Sergeant," she said truthfully. "I've never done an amputation before. I have no instruments. And in his condition…"

"He ain't going to get any stronger, ma'am. You know what fever does to a man. Just burns up his strength."

"I know," she said.

He was right. This was a decision that would have to be made today. And it was her decision to make. Perhaps with Cochran's help, she could succeed. At least, she thought, the delirium of the fever would provide its own escape from the pain.

"I'll be outside if you need me," Cochran said. "The women just about have the meat ready to go into the pot. I'm going to start the fire, and then we'll put the branches over the entrance. Will you be needing the light to see to the major, Mrs. Haviland? If you do, we can wait."

"Of course you must not wait. The sooner those men are fed, the better, Sergeant Cochran. The fire will provide what light I need," she said. "I'm going to try to get some water down the major's throat. We'll be fine."

Turning, she stooped to dip her handkerchief in the shallow basin at the foot of the rock wall and then knelt beside St. John. She allowed the water to drip off the cloth onto his parched lips. She had hoped that he would lick it off, an automatic reaction to its coolness. But he didn't.

She rubbed her thumb gently over the fullness of his bottom lip, and it opened slightly. She squeezed the handkerchief, and two or three drops of icy water fell into his mouth. This time there was a reaction. His tongue moved slowly over his bottom lip, touching her finger as well as the moisture.

She smiled at her success or perhaps at that small contact with his tongue, and then she continued the slow process. It wasn't until she stood up to make another trip to the basin that held the water, that she realized Cochran was standing near the entrance watching her.

"That's a good sign, ain't it, ma'am? Taking the water?"

Unwilling to deny the hope she could clearly hear in the sergeant's voice, she nodded agreement. She knew full well, however, that her small success with this would make little difference in the larger battle she fought.

Her eyes were still directed toward the opening, where the sergeant was silhouetted against the morning light, when she heard the first shot. And then another, rapidly following.

Cochran whirled, looking out through the entrance even as he pulled his pistol from its holster. Judith had no idea what he saw, but before he stepped outside, he turned back to face her, laying his finger over his mouth and shaking his head.

Judith nodded to indicate that she understood what he wanted her to do, but since she was hidden in the darkness at the back of the cave, she wasn't sure he had even seen her agreement. Her own fingers closed over St. John's pistol, which she had laid on top of the uniform coat last night.

When she turned back, the gun in her hand was pointed at the entrance to the cave. She saw that Cochran was now on the outside putting the screen of branches over the opening, hiding the entrance to the cave from whoever was out there.

She wouldn't know what was happening outside, not until someone removed those branches and entered the darkness of the cave. But in obedience to Cochran's unspoken command, Judith crouched beside the major, his pistol gripped in her trembling fingers, and almost without daring to breathe, she listened.

There were other shots which seemed nearer than the first two had been. The English soldiers were apparently returning fire. There was an occasional outcry, guttural and sharply cut off. It was the sound a man makes when he's been hit by a ball or by a saber's slash. Judith had heard that noise often enough to know she was not mistaken.

When the firing diminished, a small hope began to grow within her heart. It lasted until the screaming began. The women, she thought. The women. Judith closed her eyes, but it didn't help. Her brain conjured up the images of what was occurring only a few feet from where she hid.

She should help them, Mrs. McQueen and the others. She had a pistol. Perhaps she could…

But if she went to help the women, she realized, then she would reveal St. John to whoever was out there. Even as that thought formed, another sound distracted her. The fever-induced mutterings of the man who lay behind her had begun again.

They were very soft, but if they followed the pattern they had taken last night, they would grow in volume as his agitation increased. And when the screaming outside stopped…

Cochran had told her to be quiet. In this situation that was an order. Here in the back of the cave, hidden from sight, they might escape detection. That had been Cochran's intent, she knew. To provide the best protection he could for the two people he had left hidden in the cave.

The low murmur of St. John's voice was increasing in volume. She turned, leaning over him. She laid her left hand lightly over his mouth, the pistol still gripped in her right, her eyes focused on the screened entrance.

She could hear someone talking out there. Giving orders? The tone was right, but the words were too rapid and still too far away for her to decipher. Not French, she realized, but Portuguese. She had picked up a smattering of the language in the last three years, but not enough to know what was being said.

St. John turned his head restlessly, and her hand slipped off his mouth. She looked down, distracted from whatever was happening outside. The major's eyes were open. She could see them, the whites shining in the darkness of the cave.

Maybe she could make him understand that he must be very quiet. She leaned closer, pressing her own body over his, almost lying on top of him. She put her palm over his mouth again.

"Shhh," she whispered, her lips against his face. She could tell by his sudden stillness that he was listening.

She lifted her head, trying to see his eyes, to read them. He was still motionless, and she couldn't know if he had understood what she was trying to tell him. From outside the cave, she could hear the sound of horses milling around the small clearing where she had tended to the wounded this morning, their morale buoyed by the promise of the sunshine. And where now...

Again, St. John turned his head, escaping the confinement of her palm in order to say something. She couldn't distinguish anything that made sense in the words, and realizing that he was probably too far gone in delirium to heed her warning, her heart began to pound in her throat. Whoever was out there would surely hear him, and then they would come in here and...

Suddenly St. John's right hand reached upward to cup the back of her head. His fingers stirred in the loose chignon, and then his thumb trailed down the side of her neck. Down and back up. Slowly. Caressing the shivering chill of her skin with its fevered heat. Touching her.

Despite what was happening outside, despite the real terror of their situation, a matching heat began to grow inside Judith's body, moving upward, in a warm, honeyed wave of sensation, into her stomach. Her lips parted slightly with the shock of that feeling, breath sighing out in reaction.

What she felt was totally unfamiliar. And it was frightening. Not terrifying in the same way that whoever was outside was terrifying, of course, but still it filled her with fear. Because it was stirring sensations that she had not realized she was capable of feeling, that she should *not* feel.

But she didn't resist when the gentle pressure of St.

John's hand increased, urging her face down to his. His lips opened beneath hers, and his tongue touched her mouth, drifting sensuously across the fullness of her bottom lip. It moved as slowly as his thumb had, when it had glided against the sensitive skin of her neck. This movement too was unhurried. Undemanding.

And then his tongue pushed between her lips, opening them. Seeking admittance. Trying to enter and find hers. His lips were firm, and his mouth had automatically aligned itself into position under hers.

This, then, is what it should be, she thought. This was how a man's mouth should feel against her own. Inside hers. Caressing. And it was nothing like Michael's kiss had ever been.

With that thought came the realization of what she was doing, and she tried to lift her head, attempting to pull her lips away from that heated contact with his. St. John's hand refused to release her.

He said something, the tone of the whispered words seductive somehow, but loud enough that she was afraid whoever was out there must surely be able to hear them. In her terror and confusion, his voice seemed to echo within the cave. Or maybe the whispered words echoed only within her head.

She was frozen, held motionless, because she couldn't decide. And because she was listening. Listening to see if whoever was beyond the screen of branches, all that separated them from certain death, might have heard him.

And then, while she was still listening, she felt the heat of St. John's breath flutter against the corner of her mouth. The warmth of his tongue followed it, touching her lips again with that practiced expertise.

When his head lifted slightly, bringing his mouth to fit again under hers, she didn't resist. He had no idea what was going on outside. And probably, she acknowledged with an uncharacteristic bitterness, no idea even of who she was. But when he was kissing her, he was quiet. That was the reality. The very important reality.

She could hear clearly now footsteps just beyond the opening of the cave. As they came ever nearer, Judith Haviland deliberately lowered her mouth over St. John's. Hers was open, as he had taught her, and it was, against her will perhaps, and certainly against her lifelong values and the precepts of her religion, this time receptive to his tongue.

Her eyes closed and, knowing that this might well be the last voluntary action of her life, Judith Haviland gave in, letting the notoriously experienced Lord St. John demonstrate exactly how a man's mouth should move against a woman's.

Chapter Seven

The kiss went on for an eternity, it seemed, his lips and tongue moving against hers. Demanding now. His mouth ravaged her senses. His long fingers touched her hair, gently tangling themselves in the curling tendrils that had escaped their confinement. Or they caressed the small arch of her neck as she bent above him or moved again over the skin of her throat, trailing a shimmering heat in their aimless path.

It was a long time before the sounds of men and horses faded away outside. And then, for a long time after that, Judith still waited. Her mind occasionally examined the silence in the clearing, but more often it drifted, anchored to reality only by the touch of St. John's lips.

This was sin, and she knew it. On some conscious level she still understood that. It was a betrayal of her marriage vows. She might rationalize that she had given in to this temptation in order to save his life—and her own. But she would always wonder within her own heart if that were the real reason.

Her husband was attempting even now to bring them help, to effect their rescue, while she... *While she lay*

*against St. John's body and covered his hot, seeking mouth
with hers.*

Finally, after it had been quiet a long time in the clearing,
she lifted her head. Her moist lips had clung a moment to
the parched heat of his, as if her very skin was reluctant to
break the contact that had flared between them.

"Don't go," St. John whispered.

Those were the first words she had clearly understood,
and yet she knew that even they were meaningless. To him
she was only a woman, a woman who had pressed the
softness of her body against his. And he had instinctively
responded.

Despite his whispered protest, St. John released her.
Again she listened to the stillness that surrounded them. It
was unnatural. The same terrible brooding quiet that lingered like a pall of smoke over a battlefield when the fighting is done. That terrible, eerie silence of death.

She pushed away from St. John, and his hand fell bone-
lessly, to lie limp and relaxed against his chest. His eyes
were closed, and she knew that he was again asleep, wandering once more through that fevered world of nightmare
dreams and hallucinations from which she had briefly
roused him.

But that meant she might have a few moments before
the soft murmur of his voice began again. A few moments
to tiptoe to the screen of branches that had saved them and
determine the fate of those who had been their friends and
companions. Sergeant Cochran and Mrs. McQueen and all
the others.

She hurried across the stone floor, knees shaking, and
peered through the tangled branches. What she saw in the
small clearing was as eerie as the silence.

Bodies were sprawled in unnatural positions, too awkwardly arranged to be mistaken for anything except death.

Her gaze briefly touched each before it sought the next. She picked out the sergeant's bulk, lying protectively in front of the cave. Then those of the other men. She couldn't see any of the women, and suddenly she realized why.

They had been taken. They would be kept alive and would travel with the bandits as long as it was convenient, as long as they were useful. Or cooperative.

She might have been one of them, had it not been for an accident of fate. And for Sergeant Cochran. She shivered, rejecting the horror of that thought as she remembered their screams. That was almost more obscene to her than the thought of death, especially after the gentle warmth of St. John's mouth.

She closed her eyes against the sting of tears. Crying would serve no purpose. With his final silent admonition, Cochran had given her a job. It was her responsibility now. To take care of his beloved major.

Judith stood a long time behind the screen of branches, watching the shadows stretch across the clearing with the slow movement of the sun and listening to the low murmur behind her. She didn't react to St. John's whispers now, knowing the sound of them no longer mattered. Because now they were truly alone.

It had been shock that held her motionless, she would later decide, looking back on the events of this morning. Perhaps her mind needed that time to deal with what had happened. Eventually, however, she gathered her courage and shifted the framework of branches far enough away from the entrance to allow her to slip out behind it.

She pressed her body against the rocks, again holding her breath, again listening. There was nothing. No movement. There was no living creature in the clearing.

Whoever had been here, bandits she believed, had taken

the horses, except for the one the sergeant had killed. That was still there, its corpse as bizarrely lifeless as all the others.

Moving slowly, like a very old woman, she made herself examine them all. Desperately hoping for a miracle, she checked by putting her cold, trembling fingers against the place in the neck where the reassuring pulse of blood should be.

And was not. Not in any of them. Their bodies, too, had been stripped of everything of value, anything that might be useful in this war-scorched nation.

When she had verified that all the others were dead, she walked back toward the entrance to the cave, to where Sergeant Cochran lay facedown in the mud. His big body had already begun to stiffen, and it took all her strength to roll it over.

She wondered why she wanted to. It was obvious he was dead, just like the others. But for some reason it was important to her that she see his face. His eyes were open, glazed and unseeing now, and again she fought the sharp, demanding sting behind her eyes. She needed Sergeant Cochran to tell her what to do. She needed *someone*.

The sob caught in the back of her throat, and she lifted both hands to push her fingers hard against her mouth, trying to stop the sound. But that noise didn't matter either. There was no one left to hear her cry. No one at all in the terrible, empty silence of the clearing.

The scavengers would come eventually. Both animal and human. That was inevitable, she knew. And they might not be so lucky the next time.

Her almost undeniable need was to go back into the cave and return to the mindless, unthinking escape of St. John's lips moving under hers. Of his fingers tangling in her hair. The warmth of his body lying beneath her own.

She could make endless arguments, some of them even logical, as to why they should stay here. But they could not. They needed to find someone to help them. Even if it were the French, even if they were taken prisoner, it would be better than what had happened here. She would find an officer, demand to be taken to one, demand to be taken to *someone* who would listen to her.

St. John was an English aristocrat, the son of a rich and very powerful nobleman. Someone would understand the importance of seeing that he got medical treatment. She would make them understand. But if she didn't find them some help soon, St. John would die, and then so would she.

She held to that thought as she did the things she had to do. She could not bury the dead. That was a physical impossibility, but she searched the bodies and the impromptu camp for anything that might have been left behind by the bandits.

And she coldly closed her mind to the fact that these were men she had succored, who had talked with her about their families, about the wives and children they had left in England. Now they were dead, she reminded herself, and her responsibility was to the living. They would understand her need.

When she went back inside the cave, she wet her handkerchief again. This time she used the icy water to bathe the major's face. At the first touch, his eyes opened, almost as unfocused and unseeing as the empty, glazed ones of Sergeant Cochran.

"We have to go," she said urgently.

There was no change in the blue depths, and no understanding. His right hand lifted, as it had before, shaping the side of her face. She could feel the calluses, rough against the smoothness of her cheek.

She didn't bother to resist the small comfort his touch gave her. His thumb moved to trail across her mouth, pulling slightly against the dampness of her bottom lip, and she wondered if he remembered what had happened between them.

"We have to go now," she said again, deliberately blocking her own remembrance. "The enemy will find us if we stay here. You have to get up."

She took his right wrist in her hand and began to rise, thinking that if she pulled upward, he might understand what she wanted him to do. Instead, his hand found the fullness of her breast as she rose.

She could not know if his touch were accidental, but it was shattering. Her body recoiled as his had yesterday, jerking away from that contact. Trembling, she released his hand and stood there, looking down on him.

His gaze had followed her, rising as she did. His hand hesitated in midair a moment and then began to fall. It dropped against the heavy wool of her skirt, and his fingers caught a fold, holding on to it as his eyes held hers. Holding her prisoner? Or perhaps...

He was too sick to know what he was doing. In returning his kiss, she had introduced into his fever-disordered brain the idea that she was the kind of woman who would welcome his embrace. And in brutal self-honesty, she wondered what woman would not.

One who is married, her conscience answered. *One whose husband is even now risking his life to save hers.*

She reached down and, using both hands, she pried St. John's long fingers away from her skirt. When she had succeeded, she didn't release his hand, but pulled upward on it again, trying to convince him that he must make the effort to rise.

"We have to go, Major St. John. You have to get up."

The unblinking blue stare did not change. There was no reaction to the growing urgency of her demands. And then, suddenly, she remembered. Something she didn't fully understand, but an idea that had been gleaned from both his actions and from Michael's words. Something that might, just might...

"Your father believes you aren't man enough to do this," she said softly. "He thinks you haven't the courage to stand up and come with me."

Whatever the relationship between the earl of Ryde and his son, it was despicable, she knew, to use his guilt against a man who was too ill to understand this situation. Despicable to taunt him with his father's disappointment.

But watching his eyes, she knew that he had understood something in those words and that they had had an effect. His face began to change, the muscles tightening even as she watched, the handsome lines shifting into hardness. He swallowed, and his tongue reached out to moisten the dryness of his lips.

"My father?" he whispered. "My father thinks..."

When his voice faded, she waited. But as his lids began to drift over the glassy blue eyes again, she cruelly, desperately, added, "He thinks you don't have the courage to get up and come with me. He thinks you are hiding here, Major St. John. Hiding from the enemy. And he is ashamed of you."

His eyes opened again. There had been almost no color before in his face. Only the parchment gray of sickness lying beneath the sun-darkened skin. And that had been stretched too tightly over his high cheekbones, made more prominent by the ravishment of fever. But even so, she could see the effect of what she had said in the quick loss of blood from his cheeks.

He nodded once, and finally he began to move. Slowly. Painfully. Laboriously lifting his injured body in obedience to her demand. In obedience to his father's words.

As soon as she realized what he was trying to do, she bent and put her shoulder beneath his right arm. She could feel his legs trembling as he tried to push up off the stone floor, but with her help, eventually he stood swaying beside her.

"Coat," he said, so low that she didn't hear it clearly.

"What is it?" she whispered.

"My coat," he said again. The request was still soft, but this time she understood. He had told her before, and she had laughed at him, but now... Now that threat, too, was reality. Especially if she were forced to seek assistance from the French.

She helped him lean against the wall. As he had yesterday, he put his head back, turning his cheek against the coolness of the stone. She stooped and gathered up his possessions. The pistol and canteen and the blanket that she quickly folded were pushed into the pack she'd found outside. It had been lying empty in the clearing, but it was still useful for this.

Finally she picked up the uniform coat and helped St. John slip his right arm into its sleeve. When she pulled on his wrist, he leaned toward her cooperatively, and she draped the other side of the mutilated coat over his shoulder.

Then she slipped his good arm around her shoulders and together they made their slow, staggering way out of the cave and across the clearing, leaving behind them the lifeless bodies and the terrible silence.

* * *

"Only a little farther," she pled, as she had begged several times before. Encouragement now, where before she had used the scourge of his past to make him move. She was sorry for that, but it had accomplished the goal of getting him up and out of the cave, which she could not regret.

"No more," he had whispered once, but again she had ignored the exhaustion in his voice to drive him on.

It was not until she estimated they had come almost a mile from the clearing that she felt she could let St. John rest. As she had in the cave, she helped him to lean against the rock wall that rose steeply to the right of the path they were following. She was afraid to let him sit down because she knew if he did, she might never get him up again.

She gave him water from his own canteen and left him while she walked a few feet farther down the path, trying to see beyond the next rise. They had stumbled across this narrow, winding trail only a few yards from the clearing and, knowing that all paths lead somewhere, even in this seemingly empty terrain, she had followed it, thanking St. John's infamous luck. This smooth track alone had made their staggering progress this far possible.

But even with her support and the worn path, it had been a terrible exertion for St. John. She could feel through his clothing the heat from his body, burning against her own.

When she reached the top of the incline, she traced the farther progress of the trail with her eyes. It dipped downward and then rose to disappear over the next ridge. She wasn't sure what she had hoped for. A village, perhaps, some sign of civilization. At least some evidence that she was pursuing a reachable goal. Instead, there was only more of the same rocky, inhospitable terrain they had already crossed.

Judith walked back to where she had left St. John, moving more slowly than before because she was trying to decide what to do. Perhaps they were far enough from last night's camp to take an hour's rest. Then they could—

She looked up and realized that St. John was no longer where she'd left him. Could she have been mistaken about the location? Frantically she looked around. The canteen and pack were lying beside the rock the major had been leaning against. Only, St. John was no longer there.

Her eyes scanned her surroundings. Could he have gone back the way they had come, back toward the clearing? She ran a few steps in that direction before she heard the noise. Something was moving through the bushes to her right, moving away from the trail and down a decline that led to the mountain stream which had been weaving in and then out of sight as they walked.

It was St. John. She could see him now, staggering through the wind-gnarled shrubs and misshapen trees that dotted the side of the mountain. He had already discarded the crimson uniform coat she had draped over his back, dropping it on the ground.

When he reached the edge of the water, he sat down purposefully on a rock, tugging with one hand at the back of his boot. When he had succeeded somehow in getting the right one off, he began to struggle with the left.

He was going into the stream, she realized suddenly. And considering the heat that had radiated from his body, she could even understand his fever-induced madness. She had seen delirious men do things this strange before, their capacity to think burned up by the sickness of their bodies. But the icy water would be an incredible shock to his system, already dangerously weakened by the wound and infection.

She should never have left him alone, she thought, hurrying down the slope he had somehow managed to successfully navigate, even in his condition. She never thought to call out to him. It was too great a risk. A handful of tumbling pebbles, dislodged by her passage, went rocketing down the hill before her. One of them rolled to the water's edge and then splashed into the cold torrent.

St. John stood up and followed it, using the rocks of the streambed as stepping stones, moving across them in his stocking feet with reckless disregard for their slickness. He teetered dangerously once, throwing out his right arm for balance. The left was still held closely against his body. Not even seeming to be aware of its cold, he continued to move out into the current until the icy water was well above his waist.

Then, as she watched, the major sank beneath the cascade of the foaming stream, totally disappearing. Heart thudding, Judith increased her speed, clambering down the shifting rocks as recklessly as he had moved over the stones of the streambed.

She kept her eyes on the spot where he'd vanished, only occasionally allowing them to scan the treacherous ground she was traversing. *Too long,* she thought. *He's been under too long.*

Then he broke the surface, moisture sheeting off his body like silver foil. His head was thrown back, almost in ecstasy. The black hair was plastered to his skull, and the fine lawn of his shirt was transparent, molding to the firm muscles of his chest like a second skin.

His head straightened and the blue eyes opened, somehow finding her face. Judith was standing on the edge of the catapulting stream now, hesitant to plunge into its cold depths after him, again trying desperately to decide what to do.

"Major," she said softly. Unbelievingly, she watched him smile at her. He stretched out his right hand, water dripping from his fingers. He held it out before him in unspoken invitation. In involuntary response to that eloquent and touching gesture, she returned the smile.

But her mind was racing. It was late February, and the man she was supposed to be caring for was already terribly ill. She had let him wander into the middle of an icy mountain stream and now he seemed to be urging her to join him.

"If you'll come out of the water," she said softly, "we'll build a fire. It will warm you."

For some reason that seemed to amuse him. The smile widened slightly, revealing an unexpected flash of even white teeth, their contrast startling in the gaunt, bewhiskered cheeks. And there had been a dimple, Judith realized. She had never noticed that intriguing indentation before. Or perhaps she had never seen him smile. Not this broadly. Not this particular smile.

She took a deep breath and tried again. "Please come out of the water, Major St. John," she said, holding out her hand, as he had done. "It's too cold. It's dangerous in your condition."

Smiling still, he shook his head, moving it slowly from side to side like a mischievous little boy who knew very well he was doing wrong. As if he were almost daring her to do something about his disobedience.

"Your father wants you to—" she began in desperation.

"To hell with my father," he said softly, but each word was distinct and very clear. "To hell with what my father wants. *You* come in."

She took a deep, unsteady breath at the seductive tone of that command. But despite the smile and the outstretched hand, his body was vibrating like a tuning fork. The pervasive shivering was visible even from where she stood.

The skin of his face had been gray; now his lips were

changing to blue with the cold. This would kill him if she didn't get him warm soon. Suddenly there was no doubt in her mind about that.

Not bothering to remove her half boots, she gathered up her skirt in one hand and stepped out into the icy stream. Its cold was so shocking that her breath sucked inward. Without pausing, however, she stepped across to the next rock. And then realized that there was nothing visible on which to put her foot in order to take the next step.

Bravely, she extended her foot into the ankle-deep water and felt around until she found a submerged rock. She shifted her weight forward, and then repeated the process, feeling carefully for the next step. Painstakingly, she made her way into the stream, being careful not to let the swiftness of its current unbalance her.

The water inched upward as she worked her way across. Each step took her deeper into the liquid ice which seemed to pull the air from her lungs in gasping exhalations. Soon she, too, was trembling uncontrollably, and *she* wasn't suffering from a fever. The icy water covered her lower body completely now and was beginning to push around her breasts.

When she looked up again to judge the distance she had to go, St. John's hand was right before her. It looked strong and brown, as competent as always, except for its trembling.

The next step would take her to him, she realized, so she took it. Suddenly, just as she began to transfer her weight to the new stone, her foot slipped off it, and she started to fall.

Her outstretched hand flailed wildly for a second and then was caught. Caught and held firmly by the long fingers of St. John. She fought to regain her balance, body swaying precariously, and finally with the support of his strong, unwavering grasp, she succeeded.

She looked up, breath sawing in and out of her lungs from fear and exertion. And then her heartbeat hesitated. Her breath caught and held, her body seemingly unable to draw in another inhalation. And her sudden paralysis was not in reaction to the cold water swirling about her body.

St. John was no longer smiling. His face was fixed in lines that might have been chiseled from the granite outcroppings that surrounded the stream. Set and still, its darkness framed his eyes, brilliantly luminous with illness and surrounded by the wet, black spikes of his lashes. As Judith watched, the sun touched the moisture that beaded them, which glittered suddenly like a band of diamonds placed around sapphires.

Still holding her hand, he pulled her toward him. His head began to lower to hers, his lips parted in anticipation. Another invitation, one whose intent was as expressive as his outstretched fingers had been. And as compelling. But for totally different reasons.

This time, however, his life did not depend on her kissing him. There was no danger if she didn't put her lips against his, not as there had been in the cave. There was no one to fear. No need to use her mouth to keep him quiet and safe. No legitimate reason at all to respond to this unspoken entreaty.

And yet, somehow, she couldn't make herself move away. She stood, the water rushing around them, as his mouth slowly lowered to hers. It seemed she was suddenly incapable of movement. Incapable of thought. Incapable of protest.

His head tilted, subtly aligning his lips to meld with hers. It was not until the black lashes drifted closed that the spell released, freeing her from her enthrallment. She retreated, stepping away from him. She was still holding his hand, and at the increased pressure on his fingers, his eyes opened again, looking down into hers.

"No," she said. It was all she could think of to say to him. The blue eyes rested questioningly on her face. "Come with me," she urged softly, taking another step backward. And was infinitely relieved when he obeyed.

He didn't look down, but began moving with the same dangerous disregard for the placement of his feet as he had when he had entered the stream. His eyes never left hers as they moved together out of the center of the stream.

She had made it safely to the edge when her foot slid off the slime-covered rock that was barely visible under the shining surface of the water. She had been hurrying, feeling prematurely that they were safe. She had not been thinking about her footing, but about getting the warmth of the wool uniform coat around his shoulders until she had time to start a fire.

When her boot slipped, she struggled to regain her balance. However, her other foot had been no more firmly planted, and St. John had been in the act of stepping across to the same rock. Instead of offering the firm support that had saved her in midstream, he was unbalanced by the pull of her body, so that as she tumbled backwards onto the bank, he fell with her.

Instinctively, he had pulled his hand from hers. His body turned and he used his right arm to break the fall rather than landing solidly on top of her. His long legs had become entangled in the heavy wet wool of her skirt, his lower body stretched out over hers. His chest was propped above her breasts, his weight resting awkwardly on his right forearm.

Judith had landed hard, her head banging against one of the stones that edged the stream. The air thinned and shimmered around her, her vision seeming to darken with the force of the blow, and she fought to stay conscious. In the center of her blurring vision was St. John's face.

As her world shifted slowly back into focus, the blue eyes looked down into hers. His mouth was taut, almost stern. Again, as it had in the cave and in the middle of the rushing stream, Judith's awareness of her surroundings faded into nothingness, everything lost in what was happening between them.

She could feel his growing arousal even through the cold, wet fabric of her skirt. The woolen material was twisted around her legs and his, almost holding them prisoner, locked together by its icy grasp. She was pinned beneath the solid weight of his body. And he seemed to have no inclination to move away. The fever had apparently destroyed his natural inhibitions in this situation, as it usually did in all others.

"Please," she begged softly, beginning to be afraid.

His eyes softened at her tone, the hot blue flame that had been in them smoldering into tenderness. His fingers lowered to the delicate curls at her temple, touching them almost in wonder.

"I won't hurt you," he whispered. "I would never hurt you."

Mutely, she shook her head. She wasn't afraid of pain in this situation. That was the known, the familiar. It was the other that terrified her. The stern, burning need that was etched so clearly in the austere lines of his face, open for her to read. That incredible want—his and, she knew to the endangerment of her immortal soul, hers.

"My lady," he whispered. "My beautiful lady."

With those heartbreaking words, she also knew that she had been right about her original surmise. He had no idea who she was. In his near-delirium, he might have reacted this way to any woman. She might *be* any woman, and it wouldn't matter to him.

Only here, Judith, could someone like you possibly be interesting to a man like St. John. Michael had told her that. And of course he, too, had been right.

"Please," she whispered again. This time she put her hand on St. John's chest, pushing against the hard muscle.

His eyes held hers, trying to interpret whatever was in them. And when he had, his face lowered instead, lips parted, preparing to cover hers.

She did not resist again. Like the poor, mad opium eaters of India that her father had once told her about, her body craved this. Her intellect might deny that need and reject her own desire, reject it for all the right and virtuous reasons, but her body wanted him as desperately as a drug.

And no one would ever know. St. John wouldn't remember. Michael would never find out. Only she would even know what had happened between them. *Never again,* she thought. It was almost offered as a condition in this bargain she was making. A bargain for her soul, which she knew was already lost.

Only this once, her heart begged. *Only now. Only here.* Her lips opened in anticipation as his head continued to lower. And when his mouth finally covered hers, the feel of his kiss was as devastating as it had been in the dark cave.

His tongue demanded, pressing hers to answer. To answer him. To surrender to his surety and control. And she wanted to. There was nothing she wanted in this world now more than this.

As his lips continued to caress, his trembling fingers moved to the neck of her kersey dress. They loosened the small buttons, working slowly, opening them one by one. The resulting rush of cold air against her skin was another almost unbearable sensation. Her body seemed suddenly more sensitive. More responsive to everything around her. To him. Lost in his touch. Drugged with it.

When he slipped his hand inside her bodice, cupping his wet palm over the heat of her breast, she gasped, her mouth opening in shock under his. With that indisputable response, he deepened the plundering kiss. And suddenly she, too, was mindless with need, with desire. Nothing mattered but this. His mouth. His hands moving against her body.

His fingers captured the softness of her nipple between them, rolling it. The sensation of their hardness against the delicate nerves and tissue was so exquisite it was almost pain. Almost joy. As incredible as the feel of his lips, trailing now down the length of her throat, which was fully exposed for their caress. Welcoming, as his mouth moved intractably lower.

She knew what he intended. And her body reacted to that knowledge in anticipation. The liquid response was scalding in its intensity, rushing through her lower body in waves of heat.

What she was feeling was shattering in its newness. She would never have dared to dream of this, because she could not have envisioned it. She had no guides to the place where he had taken her. No experience in its wonders.

Suddenly, St. John's head lifted, his fever-bright eyes narrowed and directed upward. Even passion-drugged, she knew she should have been the one to realize what was happening. After all, this same shower of pebbles had been dislodged by her own descent down the slope that stretched above them. They had bounced noisily down the decline to land at the water's edge. Just as these did. Dislodged, of course, by someone above them.

Judith turned her head, tilting it back, trying desperately

to see who was there. From the angle at which she lay, there was little to see. Little that could be recognized.

Animals. Horses or donkeys. She could see hooves and legs, milling restlessly at the top of the decline. From the horses' position at the edge, she knew that their riders were looking down the slope, as she had looked down on St. John.

And he had been clearly visible here at the water's edge. Just as the two of them would be clearly visible now to whoever was up there watching.

Chapter Eight

Judith. Insuring her safety had been Kit's first thought, of course, when he realized the party of horsemen was above them. From what he could see, they didn't appear to be wearing uniforms, but he knew that might make them even more dangerous. Bandits? French deserters?

His fevered brain was slow in determining exactly who those riders might be. That primitive part of him, however, the part which had been shaped by generations of warrior ancestors, had already ordered his body to react and to do it quickly.

St. John began to struggle to get up, surprised at the unresponsiveness of his legs. It felt as if he were moving through water, his limbs slow and weighted.

Vaguely, he remembered *being* underwater. It had been so cold against his burning skin. He was still cold, he realized. And although he didn't think he was in the water anymore, it still seemed very hard to move. And harder even to think.

Whoever was up there had started down the slope toward them, he realized, as a stone bounced down the decline to land almost beside him. As he lay here, stupidly trying to remember something about being in water, they were coming to take Judith.

Kit rolled off her body, ineffectively kicking at the sodden wool of her skirt, trying to free himself. Somehow his legs had become tangled in her clothing. Maybe that's why it had been so hard for him to move. Maybe that's why it was hard to think, but even as he thought that, he knew it didn't make sense.

The men were saying something. Shouting at him as they came sliding down the slope. They were speaking Portuguese, he knew, but the words wouldn't quite fit together in his head.

But they were not the French, and that was good, because he had just discovered that someone had taken his uniform. He realized its loss only when he had finally stumbled to his feet.

The world swam sickeningly before him, and when he looked down to clear his head, he could see his right arm. There was no familiar crimson sleeve over it. He was wearing only his shirt, and it was very wet. He looked farther down and was reassured to find that he was still wearing his regimental pantaloons, their fine knit plastered against his legs and lower body. And for some reason he had taken off his boots.

Why had he begun to undress? he wondered in bewilderment. *Because he had been making love to Judith,* he suddenly remembered. *Judith. Where the hell was Judith?*

He saw that she was still on the ground at his feet, half reclining, her clothing disarrayed and her upper body propped on her elbow so she could see the top of the slope. Her eyes were moving back and forth between him and the approaching men.

Men, he remembered. He couldn't let them reach her. She would be raped. Repeatedly. Brutally. And then she would be killed, her slender white throat cut with one of their daggers. He could almost see that happening, too vivid in his mind's eye.

He had touched her throat with his fingers. He had watched them tremble over the pale smoothness of her skin, but he couldn't remember when he had done that. Why the hell couldn't he remember?

The men were still shouting, still clambering down the rocks toward them. *Not Judith,* he prayed silently. *Dear sweet God, not Judith. Angel,* flickered in his head. He couldn't recall who had called her that, but he knew it had been a long time ago.

God himself takes care of his angels. That's what they said. But God wasn't here. Not on this bloody, battle-ravaged peninsula. Despite the churches and shrines, St. John had not found the Almighty anywhere here. And he had not found that He was willing to intervene in the natural horrors of this war, despite the repeated prayers Kit had sent up in the last three years on behalf of wounded friends.

So it was up to him to save Judith, he decided. That seemed very logical, and he was relieved that he had finally been able to reason his way to the decision.

Kit fumbled for his pistol, but its familiar weight was not at his side where it should be. Nor was his saber. So he had no weapons. Nothing to fight them with. Nothing except his body.

He glanced down again at the woman at his feet. *My precious love,* he thought. There was something wrong with thinking that, and he knew it. Judith Haviland could never be his love, but he couldn't remember the exact reason for that either.

After all, she had been *making* love to him. He could remember the feel of her lips under his, the softness of her

breast enclosed in his hand. He even remembered how her
mouth tasted, her tongue hot and sweet, moving against his
own. He remembered touching her. So why...

"St. John," she whispered, her eyes wide and her hand
outstretched to him.

She must be so frightened, terrified because she knew as
well as he did what these men would do to her. And he
couldn't let that happen. Not to Judith.

Kit began to run toward the men who had now descended
the slope. He hit the first one with his right fist. The blow
seemed to have no force behind it, and that surprised him
because he had always been considered a fair hand in Jack-
son's practice ring. But this, of course, was very different
from that gentlemanly London pastime. This was life and
death.

Despite Kit's doubts about the effectiveness of his fist's
impact, however, the smaller man went staggering backwards into one of his companions. Kit struck out wildly at
the next man, rushing him, but again the blow wasn't well-
timed or well-aimed.

Kit knew that, but he didn't seem to be able to do anything about it. His arm moved too slowly, as if it were still
fighting against the force of the water that had surrounded
him. Some water. Some time. Why the bloody hell couldn't
he remember?

And suddenly there were too many of them. All of them
were gathered around him. Kit tried to raise his right arm
again, but one of them must have gotten behind him, holding it. He could hear the man there. He tried to turn around
to confront him, but, head spinning, he staggered with that
too-sudden motion.

They were still shouting at him, more loudly now, but
he couldn't make sense of what they were saying. The

words beat at his brain like insects, droning and meaningless. So, jerking his right arm free, he hit another one.

Suddenly someone grabbed his left elbow, wrenching his injured arm backwards and twisting it high behind his back. An incredible agony shrieked through his head. He wondered if that sound were *his* inhuman shriek. Wondered if it had come through his throat or if, as he hoped, it had echoed only in his mind.

Judith, he thought, the blackness roaring into his screaming brain. The pain seemed to be trying to drown the remembrance of the woman he knew he must protect. It was rushing in like the water. So damnably cold and dark.

Judith, he had time to think again, and then Major Lord Christopher St. John fainted from the agony. And he wouldn't think about anything else for a very long time.

It's more than I deserve, Judith thought in voiceless gratitude. *Far more than I deserve after what I have done.*

Still thinking that, she pulled the coarse woolen blanket she had been given more tightly around her shoulders. Despite its warmth and the cheerful fire that blazed on the hearth she was huddled before, she didn't believe that she would ever truly be warm again.

She smiled at the old woman who walked across the hard-packed earthen floor to hand her a steaming mug. Judith took the cup, looking down into the dark, aromatic liquid. It was soup, she realized, thick with meat, its fragrance rich with fat and pungent with some unfamiliar spice.

Judith couldn't remember the last meal she had eaten. She remembered the poor draft animal Cochran had sacrificed. A question about the source of this meat appeared briefly in her mind and was then ignored. She raised the cup to her lips, having to hold it with both hands. But they

were still shaking so much that she was forced to reach out
to capture the cup's elusive rim with her lips.

The first taste whetted the appetite she had suppressed
for days, and she gulped the thick, hot liquid, as unthinkingly greedy as a starving child. For a moment her responsibilities and anxieties were pushed aside in savoring the
incredible pleasure of the soup sliding down her throat,
warming a passage through the center of the endless cold
all the way to her stomach.

"Bom?" the old woman asked, smiling. It was one of
the few Portuguese words Judith knew, and she nodded her
agreement vigorously, returning the smile. The black eyes
filled with amusement at the Englishwoman's approval of
her simple offering.

The old lady said something else, obviously pleased to
find that Judith understood her question. However, her sentences had been too rapidly spoken, the gist of them beyond
Judith's limited vocabulary. Helplessly, she shook her head.

The woman pointed to the cot where the villagers who
had found them had placed St. John. They had had to sub-
due him first in order to bring him here because he had
fought, trying to keep them from reaching her, she knew.

It was not a battle he could have won, of course, no
matter whom he was fighting, but St. John had attacked the
men as soon as they made it down the slope. Once Judith
had been able to see them clearly, it had been obvious to
her that the men who had stumbled upon them as they lay
together by the stream were not the same as those who had
attacked the camp.

For one thing, they had no weapons. For another, they
didn't attempt to harm the English officer, not even when
he charged them. In his weakened condition, however, they
had had little trouble subduing him. All it had taken was
for one of them to grasp and twist St. John's left arm.

With her heart pounding wildly in her throat, Judith had watched him collapse, passing out from the pain or from the cumulative effects of the fever and his recent immersion in the icy stream. She had rushed to him, pushing aside the Portuguese peasants who gathered around him.

Judith didn't understand what they were trying to tell her, but the tone of it had been reassuring. And respectful. When she finally realized from their signs that they were offering to take the two of them with them, she nodded gratefully, tears of relief gathering in her eyes.

They had put the unconscious major up on a horse in front of the bulkiest of their number, handling him now with an almost exaggerated care. She was mounted on another of the animals, whose rider walked beside her until they reached this village, tucked into one of the valleys that separated these rocky ridges. The journey had taken them less than an hour.

Once here, their destination had been the house of the old woman. Acting on her instructions, the men had stripped off St. John's clothing, laying it carefully before the fire to dry.

Then the English officer, totally nude now, had been placed on the room's single narrow cot. Their wizened hostess had issued orders the entire time, watching over their shoulders as the men rushed to follow her instructions.

Those had apparently included directions for removing the bandage from St. John's arm. Her gnarled fingers had reached to gently touch the grotesque swelling around the inflamed wound. The tisking sound she had made with her tongue was universal.

But she had done nothing else about that injury, nothing for St. John beyond seeing to the placement of the blankets they piled over his shivering body. She had instead turned her attentions to her other guest, bringing first the blanket that was draped warmly around Judith's shoulders and then the soup.

Now Judith's gaze followed the old woman as she moved back to where St. John lay, as pale and unmoving as an alabaster statue. Despite the piled blankets, Judith could see the small, steady rise and fall of his chest. His breathing was shallow, but at least, she thought, offering up another prayer of thanksgiving, at least he was still alive. Despite everything, he was still breathing.

Again the old lady spoke, and Judith's eyes came back to her face, trying to make sense of what she was saying. With those twisted, arthritic fingers, the woman touched her own left arm at a spot in the approximate location of St. John's wound. She then made a slicing motion in the air with the flat of her hand, mimicking, Judith believed, the movement of a saber.

Judith nodded agreement. Again the tisking sound came in response. The next question was indecipherable, and mutely, Judith shook her head, raising both hands, palm upward, to indicate her puzzlement.

The woman nodded, and then she moved nearer to the low cot. Without hesitation, she pulled the blankets away, exposing St. John's bare chest. She bent to take the swollen left arm gently into her two hands, probing the area around the wound with her distorted fingers. As she did, she glanced over her shoulder to make an occasional comment to Judith.

Although she was concentrating fiercely, Judith was able to pick out only a few words and even most of those she was not perfectly sure of, or of their context. Once she thought she heard the word for *knife,* but she might have been mistaken.

The commentary which accompanied the old woman's examination ended in an inquiry. That was clear by its inflection and by the black, waiting eyes focused on her face. A question, Judith knew, but which one? And what about the reference to a knife?

It must be obvious to the woman that the arm needed to be taken off or St. John's condition would worsen. Gangrene would set in, if it hadn't already, and he would die.

Was it possible that there was someone locally who could be sent for, someone who might be able to accomplish that amputation? Was that what the old woman had said? Hope flared within Judith's breast. And was then as quickly extinguished.

What would a Portuguese surgeon, living in these primitive conditions, know about such an operation? Judith, who had watched the best surgeons England had to offer while at Wellington's headquarters, might even be more proficient.

Or, she wondered suddenly, was it possible that these kind and cooperative villagers who had found them might carry the two of them through the mountains to the English lines? Was it possible now to get St. John to those very same English surgeons?

Except how would she make any of those questions clear to the old woman? As she thought, trying to remember every Portuguese word she had ever learned, the old woman turned away from the cot and disappeared into the adjoining room, whose doorway was hidden by a colorful cloth hanging.

It was only minutes before she returned, carrying a leather pouch, which she put down on the table near the fire. She smiled at Judith before she removed the black cauldron from the hook which swung over the fireplace and carried it to the table.

As she passed by, the smell of the soup drifted out of the iron pot. Judith's mouth began to water, but the old

woman had already generously shared her limited resources. She certainly couldn't ask for more.

The woman dipped out a portion of the soup and added
cool water from an earthenware jar. She held out the cup
to Judith and then gestured with it toward the bed where
St. John slept.

Judith nodded and, still clutching her blanket around her
damp clothing, rose. She wasn't sure that she could get any
of the diluted soup down the major's throat, but she was
very willing to try. This was exactly the right thing for an
invalid, she thought, as she took the cup from the peasant's
hands and carried it carefully to the cot.

Judith's attempts to feed St. John, however, were not
particularly successful. More of the soup trickled out of the
slack corners of his mouth than went inside. And there had
been no response when she sat down on the bed beside him
and slipped her arm behind his neck. She tried to lift the
major's head, but it lolled lifelessly until she bent her arm
to hold it in place.

Not, of course, that it had done any good. His face was
almost waxen now, his lips still tinged with blue, despite
the covering of blankets and the warmth of the small hut.
Her eyes filled with helpless tears, and she blinked them
away, turning her gaze from his still, sunken features.

The old woman was rummaging around in the leather
bag she had brought from the back room. When she had
found what she was looking for, the crone dumped the contents of the paper twist into a wooden mortar and began to
grind whatever it was into a powder.

Medicine? Judith wondered. Some herbal remedy?
Maybe this old woman knew something about the plants
that grew in this region. Perhaps that's why the men had
brought them here.

When she had finished her grinding, the woman returned

to the fire and swung a smaller cauldron out to dump the contents of the mortar into the liquid that simmered there. And then she removed an object from above the fireplace.

It was not until the crone held the knife out over the bubbling pot that Judith realized what it was. The firelight caught the metal of the long blade, a flare skating along the keen edge like lightning.

An amputation knife? Although it was not curved as the English surgeon's tools were, it was certainly large enough. And more efficient looking than anything Judith might have been able to put her hands on.

When she glanced at the wall above the hearth, she could see other instruments, some hanging on pegs and some, as the knife had been, lying on a board above the fire. One appeared to be a saw such as the English surgeons used to cut through bone.

Judith swallowed her sickness, knowing that instead she should be feeling elation and relief. This woman seemed to be just what Judith had begun to suspect she was—the local healer or witch-woman or whatever the proper term was in Portugal.

Amputation of the diseased arm was what Judith knew in her heart would be necessary now to save St. John's life. She had known that almost from the onset of the inflammation, so she couldn't understand the thick knot of emotion that crowded her throat. She looked down into his face, too still and pale.

That mutilation would not in any way diminish St. John's virility. It couldn't change the man he was. The kind of man who, ill, burning with fever and handicapped with an agonizing injury, had tried to fight off a half-dozen unknown men in order to protect her. Judith would never forget his gallant and heroic defense.

And this operation was necessary to save his life. She

had prayed for the knowledge, the proper tools, and the courage to do it herself. Why then was she suddenly not ready for this to happen? She forced her eyes up from St. John's face, again fighting tears.

She watched as the old woman plunged the blade of the knife she held into the boiling water. At one time surgeons had applied heated irons to a wound to stop its bleeding. Maybe the healer didn't know about tying off arteries, and she intended to use the heated knife to try to seal them.

Judith had heard that hot tar was once used for that purpose, a horrifyingly damaging way to prevent the victim of the amputation from bleeding to death. Maybe the woman didn't know about tourniquets. There were so many things the surgeons had learned, knowledge that wouldn't have reached this isolated and primitive location. Knowledge that the old woman...

Judith took a deep breath, denying her growing fears. Together they could do this, she told herself. The Portuguese healer had the instruments and apparently the courage Judith lacked. Perhaps she had experience, too, but Judith had seen this done so very many times. She understood the most modern way of performing such an operation. Together, she thought again. Together they would succeed.

The men were back. They had come in answer to the old woman's summons. Following her direction, they had pulled the cot away from the wall and carried it to the middle of the small room, handling the bed and St. John easily, despite the weight of his still solid muscle. Now they were all gathered around, waiting for further instructions.

The old woman had looked at her strangely when Judith began to make sewing motions. She shook her head, brow wrinkled in puzzlement, but Judith had persisted. There were few things, however, that might be mistaken for the pantomime she was carrying out, and eventually the woman shrugged and produced exactly what Judith had asked for.

The needle was straight and small, rather than the large curved one the English surgeons used. The coarse thread was not the waxed shoemaker's kind she was accustomed to either, but it appeared to be strong enough to do the job. So Judith nodded her approval, smiling her thanks.

Then she curved her forefinger into a crook and pointed at the wall above the fire where the saw and the other implements hung. The woman's eyes followed the direction of Judith's finger, but then she looked back in bewilderment, shaking her head.

Judith then pulled her crooked finger toward herself, mimicking the motion necessary to pull the arteries out of the newly incised stump so that they could be tied off. The woman glanced toward the wall and back. Judith repeated her gesture.

The crone again shook her head, but finally she went into the other room and returned after a few moments carrying a small hook which appeared to be carved from bone.

It was certainly not the surgical hook Judith had requested. It looked like the sort of thing one might use in making lace. But, she decided, since it was small and sharp, there was no reason it wouldn't work just as well.

Carrying the hook and the threaded needle, Judith walked to the side of the cot. The old woman had begun issuing a stream of instructions to her helpers, who were scurrying obediently to carry them out. One brought the steaming cauldron from the fire and put it down on the left side of the cot. The handle of the long knife still protruded from the simmering liquid.

Others stationed themselves around St. John's unconscious body. Two of the men pulled the blankets off and grasped his legs. Another held his right arm. Two more stretched out the injured left, turning it so that the ugly, swollen wound was accessible.

The old woman's eyes met Judith's. The Englishwoman realized that she had been almost holding her breath, silently praying for success. They had come this far. She would not let St. John die now under the shock of the amputation or from blood loss. He *would* not die, she repeated like a litany.

Suddenly, the healer smiled at her, the movement disturbing the deep wrinkles around her mouth and revealing a set of teeth that looked surprisingly white and intact in her aged face. She reached out, patting Judith's arm reassuringly. The understandable gesture was accompanied by unintelligible words.

Comfort for her fear, Judith supposed. And it was welcome, of course, because the healer didn't seem to be the least bit afraid. Her calmness was infinitely reassuring. So Judith nodded, and the healer nodded again in return.

Then the old woman sat down on the floor beside the bed, crossing her legs under the skirt of her shapeless dress. Surprised, Judith knelt beside her, determined to make sure that whatever happened, St. John would not bleed to death. When the woman reached for the knife, Judith stopped her.

"No," she said sharply, pushing her hand away. There was no tourniquet above the wound. That was the simplest precaution, something that was done routinely in English field hospitals before any incision was made.

The eyes of the men standing around the cot were focused now on Judith's face, shock and puzzlement reflected in each pair. Apparently, judging by the way they had rushed around obeying her instructions, no one ever questioned the old woman's methods. This time, Judith thought with determination, someone would, and it didn't matter to her whether they liked it or not.

"No," Judith said again, shaking her head. If they didn't know the word, they would surely understand the gesture.

The old woman's hand had hesitated, but now she said something, her tone as sharp and demanding as Judith's had been. Her hand again moved toward the knife and was again pushed aside.

The crone turned to one of the men who was watching this exchange, wide-eyed in surprise. In response to the old woman's unspoken command, he moved to where Judith was kneeling and grasped her arm, trying to pull her up and away from the bed.

"No," she said again, jerking her arm away. As she did, she noticed that he was wearing a rope belt tied around the waist of his loose trousers. Excited by her discovery, she pointed to the belt, and startled, the man took an automatic step back.

Judith pointed at the rope again and then turned her palm upward in entreaty. He looked down at the belt, then at Judith, and finally his eyes moved to the old woman. The crone shrugged, apparently signifying permission.

When the man had handed her the rope, Judith slipped one end under St. John's outstretched arm. Then she twisted the two strands together, high on the upper arm, near the shoulder. Looking around, she indicated to one of the unoccupied men that she needed the pestle which was lying on the table where the old woman had ground whatever she had put into the cauldron.

His eyes sought permission from the healer and again received it, along with a verbal acknowledgment this time. The woman appeared to be fascinated by whatever Judith was doing. They all watched as she wound the handle of the pestle into the rope and used it to tighten her makeshift screw tourniquet.

When Judith was finally satisfied that it was tight enough

to stop the flow of blood, she reached up to take the hand of the man whose belt she had borrowed. She placed it over the stick, curving his fingers into position around it and then patting them to let him know that he should keep them in exactly this same place. She glanced up at his face to make sure that he understood. When his eyes indicated that he did, Judith turned back to the old woman and nodded.

The woman said something, pointing to Judith's left hand. The men laughed. Judith glanced at her hand and realized it was empty. She had laid the hook and the needle in her lap while she fixed the tourniquet. She picked them up again, smiling at the old woman.

This time when the crone's hand moved toward the knife, Judith made no protest. There was nothing else she could do. She had done her best, and the rest was in the hands of God. And in the bent, misshapen fingers of this old Portuguese peasant.

Chapter Nine

Something had gone wrong, Judith thought, *dangerously wrong.* Despite her efforts to see this operation done correctly, exactly as the surgeons would have performed it, nothing was happening as she had anticipated.

Before she could think how to voice her protest, the sharp edge of the knife the old woman held sliced into the swollen flesh. Not, however, where the incision should have been made, at least three or four inches above the climbing redness. Instead, the woman had made a cut on top of the original wound.

"No," Judith protested sharply and was ignored. "No," she breathed again, more softly this time because the healer was paying her absolutely no attention. She had not even looked up. She was intently watching instead what was happening under the pressure of the knife. And suddenly so was Judith.

They all were watching, Judith realized after a moment, all with that same horrified intensity. The evidence of the terrible inflammation gushed out of the cut the woman had made, the smell of its corruption strong in the small room.

One of the men hissed, but the old woman said "Ahhh" in the same tone with which one might express admiration for a beautiful woman, a well-prepared meal, or a fine painting. That drawn-out syllable had sounded exactly like an expression of delight.

As if in verification of Judith's thought, the healer looked up to smile and nod at her. Then she turned to grin broadly at the surrounding circle of faces, her strong white teeth again flashing in the dark, wrinkled folds of her skin. Her left hand made a flourish, as if celebrating some accomplishment, and the watching men nodded in admiration.

The old woman handed one of them the knife and voiced a demand. The man hurried across the room to put the knife on the table and returned with several pieces of cloth. These the healer laid on St. John's chest, except for the one she placed on the mattress under his arm, which the men were still holding up.

Then she began to press with both hands on the swelling above and below the cut she had made. The thick discharge increased, flowing out around the outstretched arm and down onto the cloth below.

Judith watched, the hope that had been so strong before fading quickly to despair. The old woman had never had any intention of cutting off the infected arm. That's why she hadn't taken the bone saw from the wall. That's why she hadn't applied a tourniquet.

All of Judith's expectations that this primitive healer might be able to save St. John's life had only been foolishly misplaced hopes, she realized. This old woman couldn't know, of course, the lessons the surgeons had drummed into Judith's head for the last three years. This *healer* didn't know anything.

But the crone was again issuing orders, rapidly and decisively, just as if she knew a great deal. The men had released their holds on St. John's limbs, except for the injured arm. The woman dipped a cloth into the liquid in the cauldron beside her and began to swab at the incision she had made.

She worked for several minutes, seemingly intent on making sure that the fluid penetrated, cleaning out the wound. Then again she pressed all around the area until she was satisfied that no more of the suppuration could be gotten out.

She threw the cloth she had been using on the floor and took a clean one from the pile. This she folded into a thick square and dipped it into the liquid in the cauldron until it was soaked. Then she placed it over the reddened area. Finally she replaced the stained cloth that had rested below St. John's arm with a fresh one from the stack.

When she was finished, she looked up at Judith again and pointed at the tourniquet, questioning its release. Shaking her head, Judith touched St. John's arm at a place an inch or two below the tight clamp of the rope. She made a sawing motion with the edge of her hand there.

The woman's eyes reflected her puzzlement. Judith pointed at the streaks creeping up St. John's arm and again made the sawing motion. Then she pointed to the saw above the fire.

The jet-black eyes followed. When she turned back to Judith, those knotted fingers made a similar sawing motion over her own left arm. Judith nodded. Had she finally made herself clear? Did the old woman now understand what must be done?

The woman laughed and made some comment to the watching men. Her jeering words were accompanied by the same sawing motion over her own arm. They looked shocked, their dark eyes turning in horror to study Judith's face.

Despite her mockery, the crone reached out to touch Judith's hand, the left one, gently patting the back of her fingers, just below the knuckles, and then smoothing her own hand over them. Another gesture of comfort, Judith supposed. Or reassurance.

Was it possible, she wondered suddenly, that the healer's incision and the fomentation, whatever it was, might really work against the poison? Even in England there was a long tradition of less radical treatments than those the surgeons now demanded.

She had brought to Spain numerous recipes for herbal remedies that her elderly friends had sworn were efficacious for a wide variety of maladies. And when she could find the ingredients they called for, she had used them with some success through the long months. Was it possible that this *could* work?

The woman was saying something to her, Judith realized. Then she reached up and grabbed the hand of the largest of the watching men, the one who had carried St. John's unconscious body here by supporting it before him in the saddle. The old woman pushed his hand up until he was holding his arm straight out in front of him. It was corded with muscle that stretched the material of his sleeve tightly.

The healer pointed to that strong arm and nodded. Then she pointed to the bandage she had placed over St. John's arm and nodded again, her head moving vigorously up and down.

Almost against her will, Judith found herself slowly nodding agreement with the woman's confidence in her treatment. *Please, dear God,* she prayed, *please let her know what she's doing.*

Her eyes fell to St. John's face. Deeply unconscious, he had not moved during the entire procedure. He had not flinched under the blade or when the woman applied pressure to the red, swollen arm or placed the steaming cloth over the raw flesh. There had been no response at all in the still, white features.

Unable to resist the impulse, she lifted her hand and placed her cool fingers against the fevered heat of his brow. She did not realize that the firelight, which had earlier illuminated the sharp blade of the knife, played now over the gold wedding band which she wore on her left hand. Or that its gleam had been reflected in the circle of dark eyes surrounding her.

With Judith's help, the old woman replaced the steaming cloths as soon as they cooled. As day faded into night, their vigil over St. John continued, although the men had been banished from the house hours before. The woman lit no lamps, but even after nightfall the light from the fire brightened the room enough for them to carry out this simple task.

Later Judith was given more soup, and too tired and hungry to think of refusing, she smiled her thanks and drank it down. The warmth of the room, the flickering, shadowed light cast by the fire, and the satisfying and unfamiliar fullness of her stomach inevitably took their toll, as the healer had known they would.

When the old woman finally lay down before the fire, pulling the blanket she had earlier given Judith around her own shoulders, she did not disturb the other woman who was already deeply asleep. The Englishwoman's dark head was pillowed on the bent arm she had propped on the edge of her husband's bed as she sat on the floor beside it.

The old woman smiled again in the fire-touched darkness when she thought of the Englishwoman's ignorance. Why should she want to cut off a perfectly good arm because of a little pus?

She shook her head, making again the tisking sound she had voiced before. So foolish. So primitive a method of healing. But then the girl was very young. Who could blame her if she knew no better? One must be taught the proper way to do things.

Tomorrow, the crone thought. *I will show her more tomorrow.* And with the pleasure of having someone to instruct in her arts, the old woman pulled the blanket closer and drifted off to sleep, her mind untroubled and supremely confident.

Far more than I deserve, Judith thought again, looking down at St. John's arm. The wound was still inflamed, still swollen, but she could see it was definitely improved. An incredible improvement over its appearance yesterday.

She studied St. John's face as the old woman pressed around the swelling. He was still asleep. Not asleep, Judith amended, seeing that there was not the slightest response to what the healer was doing. He was unconscious. Deeply unconscious, his breathing as shallow and thready as it had been yesterday.

But he was still alive, she thought, holding on to that. And apparently the old woman knew what she was doing. Judith glanced down again to watch the arthritic fingers moving over the wound. Satisfied by her examination, the woman reached into the pocket of her voluminous dress to remove a small, squat bottle whose stopper had been sealed in place with wax.

She pried out the stopper and dipped one finger into the bottle and began to rub the glutinous ointment it contained over the incision she had made last night. The ointment was faintly blue-green, and a strangely familiar odor drifted upward from it, teasing Judith's memory. So…evocative, she thought, but she couldn't seem to place it.

When the woman had finished applying the salve, she laid a clean, folded square of cloth over the area. As the healer closed the bottle and was about to return it to her pocket, Judith placed her hand on the reed-thin arm and pointed to the container. She raised her brows in question.

The peasant smiled, but not broadly as she had yesterday. This was almost secretive, almost amused. She rose from where she was seated on the side of St. John's bed and gestured for Judith to follow her. With only another quick look down at St. John's face, Judith obeyed.

The room to which she was led was like nothing Judith had ever seen before. It looked like an alchemist's workshop or a medieval apothecary. Her eyes circled it, fascinated by the objects hanging from pegs and strings all around the walls.

Almost everything that could be culled from the bounty of nature was here, both flora and fauna. Some of the plants she recognized, but many more she did not. Even her herbalist neighbors had had nothing like all this.

The woman seemed unaware of Judith's examination of her treasures. She placed the ointment bottle on one of the tables and then opened a small wooden box, from which that same tantalizingly familiar odor escaped.

It reminded Judith somehow of the forest. Dark and dank. Or perhaps more like the cave where they had hidden from the bandits. But still, she couldn't quite grasp the elusive memory.

Suddenly, the healer turned and motioned her closer. For some reason Judith hesitated. It was almost as if, now that she was here, she didn't want to know what the box contained. Hers was an almost superstitious response to the atmosphere of this room, to the secrets it held. Or to the miraculous improvement in St. John's arm, despite the fact that the woman had done nothing that the surgeons believed should be done in such a case.

Medieval, Judith thought again. Even smacking of witchcraft. The dark arts. She took a breath, the very air around her seemingly filled with the scent. Then, berating herself for her irrational fear, she gathered her courage and walked across the room to stand beside the old woman.

At first she didn't recognize what the healer had revealed. And when she did, she realized that it was no wonder she had been reminded of the damp loam of the forest floor or of the cave.

She could not tell what the old woman had originally put into the box. Whatever it had been, it was now covered over by a thick blanket of blue mold. This, then, was where the ointment had gotten its strange color.

The salve that the old woman had just rubbed all over St. John's arm had been made from this decaying mess of organic material. Sickened, Judith lifted her eyes from the contents of the box and back to the healer's face. The woman smiled, nodding her head.

The Portuguese word she said was unfamiliar, of course. But Judith didn't need a name for this. Whatever good had been done by the knife yesterday would surely be undone by the application of this rotting substance to the wound. Despairing, Judith shook her head.

The woman's smile faded, her eyes again puzzled. *"Bom,"* she said, nodding and pointing again at the mold.

At least she understood that, Judith thought, and it was apparently the limit of the verbal communication they would be able to share. But this was *not* good, of course. She looked back at the contents of the box. Nothing that looked like this could possibly be good, not for someone as sick as St. John.

* * *

The days and nights of their endless nursing drifted into a week. Despite Judith's protests, the old woman continued to spread the bluish-green ointment on St. John's arm. And the wound continued to improve. After the third day, Judith had not bothered to object, because the evidence of her own eyes outweighed the natural repugnance she felt at what the healer was growing in that dark, revolting box.

The troubling thing was that St. John's condition did not seem to improve, even as his arm healed. In addition to the salve she smeared on his wound every day, the old woman brewed a decoction which she insisted Judith get down the major's throat.

Although she was more than willing to try, of course, it was a time-consuming process. Judith spent hours every day attempting to get St. John to swallow some of the fluid. And she succeeded, she knew, despite her growing fear and the frustration over his continued unresponsiveness.

However, at the end of six days she could see no improvement. The fever continued to burn through his body unabated, perhaps no longer quite so high as it was when they had been brought here. With each passing day Judith's despair deepened. What did it matter if the old woman could heal the arm, if she could not save the man?

Judith slept beside the bed, curled in the blanket she had been given. She had worried at first about St. John's displacing the healer from her cot, but sleeping on the floor in front of the fire didn't seem to bother the peasant. The old woman awakened each dawn to rush around the cottage with a briskness and energy that made Judith almost envious.

Early one morning, while the woman was fixing their breakfast, Judith again sat down on the edge of the mattress, preparing for the first of the day's many attempts to get some of the witch's brew down St. John's throat. That thought was unkind, she knew, given all that the old woman had done for them, but still there was something almost unnatural about the potions and poultices she used.

Perhaps only unnatural in that, unlike most medicine Judith was familiar with, these seemed to work. Thinking that, her lips curved into a smile, reluctant admiration for the Portuguese woman's knowledge and skill.

For some reason, she seemed to be having more success than usual in getting this particular potion down, Judith realized. She glanced up, and found that the blue eyes which had once, in a faraway London ballroom, skimmed with boredom across her face were now focused intently on it. The shock was so great that her breath caught, and it was several seconds before she remembered to draw another.

"Hello," she whispered.

"Judith?" St. John said. His voice was as low as hers, and it seemed hoarse from disuse. His tone when he said her name had been questioning. Disbelieving, even.

She knew he would remember little of what had happened to bring them here. And probably less of what happened between them. That was, of course, something she devoutly wished for—that St. John would never remember those embarrassing encounters.

But he had never before called her Judith. *Mrs. Haviland.* Or *Ma'am.* Never Judith. And so she found herself wondering exactly what he did remember. She could feel the hot blood climb into her throat and spread over her cheeks.

"Where are we?" St. John asked. He tried to look around, but then he closed his eyes quickly, and let his head fall back to the pillow. He would be fighting the vertigo she knew he would suffer after so many days spent lying flat on his back.

"It's all right," she reassured him.

Without her volition, her hand reached out to touch him, pushing the black silk of his hair away from his forehead and feeling beneath her palm its unaccustomed coolness. The long fever had finally broken.

In response to her touch, the dark lashes lifted again, and the sapphire eyes fastened on her face, moving over it as if he had never seen her before. As if he were trying to recognize her features. Or memorize them.

"It really is going to be all right," she said again, "now that you're awake. Will you drink something for me, Major St. John? It's very important that you try."

His gaze held on her face a long time, searching it, and then he nodded, the movement very small, but obviously signifying agreement. She smiled at him, feeling a resurgence of lost hope balloon within her chest, and it lightened all the black despair of the past few days.

She slipped her arm under his head. She fitted the rim of the cup against his lips and held it there as he drank. He finished most of the liquid before his eyelids drifted downward.

Still she held him, savoring the weight of his head against her breast. Then, once more, briefly, the heavy lids lifted, and his eyes found hers. Found and held. Some silent connection, a message that he was not able to fully communicate to her before they closed again.

Judith gently placed the dark head back against the pillow. He was asleep, that instant slumber into which invalids fall so easily, his now-frail strength suddenly exhausted. He was gone from her again, the bond once more broken, but she was elated.

St. John had just drunk more of the healer's decoction than she had managed to get down him all week. He had

been awake. He had known who she was. All of those were
wonderful signs.

She had not even realized that she was crying until one
of the tears fell onto his sunken, whisker-roughened cheek.
He did not react, but Judith smiled, the movement slightly
tremulous, to see it there. With one finger, she wiped the
teardrop away, and hurriedly blinked back the rest, before
they, too, could fall and wake him.

After that first morning, St. John's recovery was rapid.
More rapid than Judith believed to be wise, but the old
woman encouraged him. And because she had been right
about everything else, Judith acknowledged, perhaps she
was also right about that.

The major had insisted on sitting up a little in bed the
day after he woke. Propped on pillows, he had managed to
swallow almost a cup of broth. St. John's command of Portuguese was far greater than hers, Judith decided, when he
also talked the old woman into shaving him.

She used the keen-edged blade with which she had
opened the abscessed wound, and he looked more like himself without the black whiskers. Much more like the man
she remembered, Judith thought, but she acknowledged privately that perhaps that was not something to be desired.

Those small efforts seemed to exhaust him, and St. John
had fallen almost immediately into a deep sleep and had
thankfully, from her perspective at least, slept away most
of the rest of the day. While he was awake, Judith found
it very difficult to pretend that nothing had happened between them.

She was too aware that this was the man she had kissed,
eagerly covering his warm, seeking lips with her own. In
the cave she had lain over his body, her breasts pressed
like a wanton's against the hard muscles of his chest.

And this was the man who had begun to make love to her beside the mountain stream. The man she had *wanted* to make love to her. To touch her. The notorious London aristocrat, whose conquests with the fairer sex were legendary.

Only here, Judith, could someone like you possibly be interesting to a man like St. John, Michael had told her. That was reality. What had happened between them there was only a fevered dream, and she prayed she could remember that and prayed conversely that he wouldn't remember anything at all of what had occurred.

But when he woke again, late that afternoon, almost at twilight, his eyes followed her as she moved around the small room, helping the old woman with their simple evening meal.

His gaze remained focused on her face as she fed him. Once she looked up to find the sapphire eyes tracing again over her features in what looked like speculation. She was forced to wonder exactly what he did recall because it was obvious, even from the few words they exchanged, that there had been a subtle change in their relationship.

That lingering question was somewhat answered as she began to prepare St. John for the night. When she unthinkingly tried to carry out the more intimate nursing duties that she and the old woman had shared while he was unconscious, the eyes she had been avoiding throughout the day suddenly flared in anger.

"What the hell do you think you're doing?" St. John demanded as she began to pull the blanket down to expose his body.

Her hand hesitated in the completion of that familiar action. "I was only going to..."

The words faded, stopped by the hardening of his features. As it had in the stream, his face suddenly turned to stone. But it happened now for a very different reason. St. John was clearly furious, and that fury was directed at her.

With his right hand, he jerked the blanket out of her fingers. "What the bloody hell *have* you been doing?" he demanded. A flush of color had crept under his pale skin.

She didn't understand why he was so angry. This was only a necessary part of caring for the sick. It was something she had certainly done a thousand times in the field hospitals.

And then suddenly, inexplicably, she was as furious as he. Perhaps her quick rage was a result of exhaustion. Or perhaps she was angry because of the unfairness of his reaction. After all, she had worried about him, cared for him, risked her life for him. *And* her immortal soul, she thought bitterly.

Even in her fury, she could not blame him for that sin, which was hers alone. But, she decided unreasonably, she could certainly blame him for what he had just said. And for the disgust that had been evident in his voice when he said it.

For days she had prayed for his well-being. She had worked like a slave dribbling endless drops of liquid into his mouth in an attempt to keep him alive. She had cleaned his helpless body. She had loved him...

...*had loved him.* The unbidden thought quenched her outrage as suddenly as one might pinch out a candle's flame. Because, of course, it was true.

And it was a truth she could no longer deny, at least not to herself. But the words were sacrilege to the vows she had made before man and God. Even thinking them, allowing them to form, was betrayal. *They* were betrayal, even if they were also true.

Judith Haviland was not a creature of impulse, nor was she given to gestures. Another woman might have poured the basin of water she had brought to the bed over St. John's ungrateful head. Or might have thrown the cloth she was holding at his set face. Judith did neither, of course.

She marched across the room and set both items carefully and deliberately down on the old woman's worktable. Then she opened the door and stepped outside into the coolness of the March night. She leaned against the wall of the small house, partially sheltered from the rain by the overhang of the eaves, and pressed shaking hands against her cheeks.

She had worked side by side with the surgeons for so long that she had apparently forgotten whatever natural modesty she had once possessed. She had tended to Major St. John throughout these long days as if he were an infant.

But he was not, of course. He was a man. A proud, virile man, and she had just treated him like a child. Perhaps it had been acceptable for her to care for him when he was unable to care for himself. Why had she not realized that he would resent and despise her attempt to do so now, especially without consulting him? Without asking his permission.

She could imagine his distaste. No other woman of his acquaintance would ever do what she had done during the last three years. They both knew that. No well-bred, delicate London lady would ever attempt to… Again her mind skittered away from those intimate services she had been accustomed to performing.

But she was *not*, after all, a delicate London lady. She had never been that. And really, what did it matter what St. John felt about her? she asked herself bitterly. Whatever had happened between them would never happen again.

That brief romantic interlude had only been a product of their circumstances. Of her fear. His illness. There were a hundred legitimate reasons for what had happened. Only she would ever know the real one.

So it didn't matter, of course, what he thought about her. It didn't matter if he found her behavior disgusting or crude. Even if he thought her as common as the old peasant woman who grew mold in boxes.

Together they had saved his life. She and that old Portuguese healer. Judith removed her hands from her cheeks and unconsciously lifted her chin. That was really all that mattered. And as for the rest…no one would ever know about the rest, of course. No one.

She took a breath and allowed her mind to linger again on the very few times he had touched her. In the cave, when his fingers had trailed gently and yet so seductively against her throat. In that stream where he had held out his hand as if inviting her to waltz, and where his darkly beautiful face had begun to lower, his mouth open and again seeking hers. And when they had lain together beside the water…

Unnoticed, her anger had dissipated. Her lips had curved into a smile. *And this, too, is sin,* she thought, when she realized what she was doing. The small, remembering smile faded.

Soon they would be back in the English camp, and Michael, who was her husband, would be there. That was her reality. And her future.

A brief, unholy alliance. A fantasy. That's all it had ever been. And now it was over. St. John would again be her friend, and he would never be anything more to her, she knew. Still she fought against the regret, the deep sense of loss.

He was alive, she told herself, and she was at least partially responsible for that. That could not be cause for regret. Never could she regret *anything* she had done to keep St. John alive.

Again her lips tilted upward. This time her smile was resigned. Reflective. Perhaps even slightly satisfied.

Only here, Judith, could someone like you…

Deliberately, Judith Haviland banished the memory of those mocking words. Not even Michael could take this victory away. Major Lord St. John was alive.

Chapter Ten

Judith had no warning and was therefore unprepared when St. John finally asked her the question she had dreaded so long. The question that had been in his eyes after he'd awakened had gradually faded with the passage of time. With its disappearance, she had begun to breathe again, believing that he must have assigned whatever remaining fragments of memory he had about their encounters to the fever. His gaze didn't follow her around the room anymore, and so she had begun to believe that her secret was safe and would remain so.

She smiled at him that afternoon as she brought the bowl of stew to his bed, but she was careful that it was exactly the same smile she had given a hundred other wounded men she had tended. She felt a slight trepidation, however, because they were alone for the first time since they had arrived in this house.

The old woman had gone into the nearby village to deliver a baby. At least that's what Judith believed, judging from the joyful excitement of the man who had come to fetch her and the few words she had been able to pick out of his message.

"Thank you," St. John said as she held out the bowl to

him, but he made no effort to take it. Instead, he looked up into her eyes, holding them with the sheer physical intensity of his.

"I believe I must owe you an apology, Mrs. Haviland," he said.

Her pulse quickened, trying to think how to answer him. Judith knew that whatever she said, she would be treading on very dangerous ground.

"I'm afraid I don't understand, Major St. John. An apology? For what?" She controlled her breathing, thankful to note that the bowl she held did not tremble. Not even now.

"I seem to remember..." His deep voice hesitated over the words, and she held her breath. "If I did anything that was improper, Mrs. Haviland..." Again the sentence faltered. "I hope you know that I would never willingly offer you insult. If, in my illness, I said or did anything that caused you distress—"

"Major," she interrupted. "There was nothing for which you need apologize. Or explain. Nothing...improper," she added.

He held her eyes, trying to read them, she supposed. But she had already dealt with her own guilt, standing one rain-swept night outside this house. She hoped that her eyes reflected only her certainty that nothing of what had happened was his fault.

There is nothing for which you need apologize. That was truth, and she let him see it in her eyes and in what she prayed was the calm serenity of her face. He truly *had* done nothing she hadn't wanted him to do.

In time they would both forget. He because he would believe those fading memories were only dreams. And she... She would forget because she must.

"You need to eat," she admonished almost brusquely. She put the bowl of stew into his hand and turned away, hopefully before he could see those emotions she didn't intend for him ever to find in her eyes.

"English. English."

The Portuguese word had been repeated perhaps three or four times before Kit understood the distant shout. Apparently there was some lingering effect from the fever, which still clouded his thinking.

The feeling that he was operating in a daze would soon be over, he had reassured himself through the long days of his recovery. Soon everything would become clearer, and he would be able to remember all the events of the last few weeks, which seemed to him only a jumble of impressions, their images bleared and distant.

And not all of them made sense. Such as what he seemed to remember about Judith Haviland. Were those images created by his hopeless fantasies, by the strength of his unspoken love? Or was it possible that the encounters between them had really occurred?

The images lingered tantalizingly in his mind, seeming far too vivid to be dreams. Was it possible, despite Judith's denial, that he had touched her? Possible he had kissed her? That they had even lain together—

"English."

The man who had been shouting the phrase outside burst into the hut where they had been living with the old woman for almost a month. St. John had no clear remembrance of their arrival here or of the woman's treatment, but under her care and Judith's he had slowly been regaining his strength.

Mrs. Haviland had told him only that the woman was the local healer. And despite everything that had happened—his wound, the inflammation and high fever that had resulted from it—he seemed finally to be on his way to recovery. Therefore the title Judith had given the old woman apparently had validity.

When the man entered, Judith's eyes had found St. John's face. Kit was aware that the emotion reflected in their dark depths was not one he should now expect to find.

Judith Haviland should be relieved and excited, but somehow he knew that she was not. He could not have explained how he'd arrived at that conclusion or why he was so certain of it, any more than he could explain the uncanny perceptions about her feelings that he had had since he'd awakened.

"English on the road," the man said, still speaking in Portuguese. He was almost gasping in his excitement over having this important news to deliver.

Apparently Haviland had gotten through, Kit thought, and Wellington had finally sent out a party to look for them. And to look also for the wounded that Smythe had placed in his care. St. John felt again a deep sense of regret and even of guilt. None of those men were alive, of course. Only he and Judith were left, the two lone survivors from the entire regiment.

That had been the first question Kit had asked after he'd regained consciousness. He had been grateful when Mrs. Haviland had answered him truthfully. As she answered his other questions which had followed her painful recitation of the events at the cave. Sanctuary, he had thought when Cochran guided them there. But, of course, it had not been. Not for any of the others.

Now Kit listened to the peasant's excited explanation about the English presence in the district with only half his attention. Judith's eyes never left his, holding on his face as he questioned the man. She was waiting, Kit supposed, for some news of her husband.

But there was none. The villager had come away as soon

as he spotted the English column moving along the main road. He thought it would be better if he had something to give them, he explained to St. John. Some sign, proof of their existence. The soldiers would accept some physical evidence of their identity better than they would accept his word.

Given the treachery of the local bandits, the man's suggestion made sense. No British commander would send a detachment into these mountains based solely on the word of a Portuguese peasant.

"My coat," Kit suggested to Judith.

She hesitated only a moment before she obeyed. She brought the mutilated uniform to him and placed it in his hands. Kit tried to think what would be the best thing to send. Not the entire garment, but something that would identify him to whichever English commander Wellington had sent to find them.

Finally he stripped off the regimental insignia and his rank. Those would probably have been enough, after Haviland's message, but there were more than a few stolen British uniforms in Portugal, of course. And more than a few deserters. Reluctantly, Kit also took the gold signet from his finger.

It was the ring his father had given him when he attained his present title. It was the only thing here that he had from the earl, almost the only thing left of what he had brought with him from home. But the signet would identify him more clearly than anything else he could think of.

"Yours, too, I should think," he suggested, looking up from his ring into Judith Haviland's eyes.

"My wedding band?" she questioned.

"I think it's best they have no doubt of who we are."

Judith glanced at the man who had brought the message. Kit knew what she was thinking. There was nothing they could do to prevent the peasant from stealing their possessions, which had more sentimental value, of course, than they had monetary worth. And she was right. There wasn't anything they could do to insure that the man would take these items to the English commander.

"They have shown us nothing but kindness," Kit reminded her softly. Her gaze came back to his face. "We have to trust him, Mrs. Haviland. And we have no reason not to."

Finally she nodded, slipping the slender gold band off her finger and placing it on his outstretched palm along with the things he had chosen. Kit only hoped that his Portuguese would suffice to explain to the peasant what he should do with them.

The English patrol arrived in the village in the late afternoon of the following day, but not before St. John had begun to despair that his message had been conveyed to the column. The lieutenant in command of the detachment was no one he knew, not even by reputation, but it was obvious the opposite was not true.

"I've heard a lot about you, Major St. John," the young officer said in greeting, after Judith and one of the villagers had helped Kit outside.

"Indeed? Lieutenant...?" Kit wondered, as he waited for the man's name, which of his very different reputations had preceded him.

"Standish, sir. Carter Standish, at your service."

"Wellington sent you?" Kit suggested.

There was a flare of surprise in the officer's eyes. He glanced at Judith, and then back at Kit. "No, sir. Advance patrol for the main army. No orders about you, sir."

"Then the army's on the move."

"We left winter quarters two days ago with the intent of

driving the French across the border. Old Hooky's chomping at the bit, pardon the expression. He can't wait to push north.''

''But no one…'' Kit hesitated to ask the vital question, his eyes tracing over Judith Haviland's pale, composed face.

''No one…?'' Puzzled, the lieutenant repeated the broken phrase.

''No one has reported us to Wellington as being in need of help?'' Kit asked, deliberately forcing his gaze away from Judith and back to the young officer.

''Not that I'm aware of, sir. Not that I was told of. Where are the rest of your men, Major? How did you and your wife—''

''My *wife?*'' The tone of Kit's question was too sharp, and he watched Standish's eyes widen. They, too, moved to Judith's face and then came quickly back to his.

''This is Mrs. Michael Haviland, Lieutenant,'' Kit corrected.

''But the villagers told us that the two of you were—''

This time the abrupt interruption was internally triggered. Standish clamped his lips closed over the words he had been about to utter, but he glanced again at Judith, his manner now full of unease. When Mrs. Haviland's dark eyes met his with the same open and steadfast regard which was so much a part of her character, a small flush of embarrassment spread beneath the fine-grained skin of his cheeks.

''Did you say Haviland?'' he asked suddenly, pulling his gaze back to Kit. ''Mrs. Michael Haviland?''

''That's correct.''

Standish's eyes found Judith's again, and his lips tightened briefly before he opened them to speak, his tone softened now with sympathy. "Then I'm afraid, ma'am, that I am the bearer of very bad news."

"Michael's father?" Judith whispered. "My husband's father is General Sir Roland Haviland. Have you had news of him?"

Standish's regretful eyes returned quickly to St. John's, reading in them the realization that Judith had not yet made.

"No, ma'am. No news concerning General Haviland," the officer denied. Then he hesitated, obviously trying to think how to soften the blow he was about to deliver. "It's your husband, Mrs. Haviland. I'm afraid his body was found more than two weeks ago. May I offer you my sincerest condolences on your loss."

Without his volition, Kit's eyes searched Judith's face, which had drained of color. He fought against the urge to hold her, simply to enfold her in his arms and offer what comfort he could. He might have despised Michael Haviland, but as Judith had once reminded him, Haviland was her husband.

There were no tears, however, in the wide dark eyes. She had made no outcry, had expressed no outward sign of grief. And with what he knew about Judith Haviland's abusive marriage, Kit could not in all honesty blame her for that. In fact, it even gave him some small hope that her loyalty to her husband had been only that and not some deeper attachment.

Despite the intensity of his gaze, Judith never looked at him. Her eyes, the pupils starkly distended with shock, remained on the young lieutenant's face. Finally at the continued, painful silence, St. John turned back to Standish.

"Are you sure?" Kit asked softly. "Are you absolutely certain of Captain Haviland's death?"

"There's no doubt, I'm afraid," Standish said. "I understand he was identified by his own batman."

"His batman?" Kit asked in surprise. "A Private Reynolds?"

"I'm afraid I'm not certain, Major. If I heard the man's name, I've forgotten it. Is it important?"

"I suppose not. It's simply... I had thought Reynolds died with the rest of the regiment."

"The *rest* of the regiment, Major?" Standish asked, his voice disbelieving. "How could the two of you... Begging your pardon, ma'am, but how did the two of you...?" Again the question faded, and the color deepened in the boyish cheeks.

"The regiment was massacred by the French advance. By the reinforcements Napoleon sent Massena," St. John explained.

"Reinforcements, sir?" Standish repeated. There was a thread of doubt in the question. "We had no word that Massena had *been* reinforced."

This was the first time St. John would hear the tone. The first time he would notice eyes deliberately shift to avoid meeting his. The first time he would see a gleam of speculation in a man's gaze as it moved across Judith Haviland's beautiful features. All of those would become very familiar to him during the next few months, but Kit would remember this man's reaction to their story as the beginning of the horror that was to follow.

"Because Smythe's messenger and mine were both killed before they could deliver the news. I was ordered to see the wounded and the women safely to the coast road," Kit said, controlling his quick anger at the lieutenant's doubt. "We were sent to make contact with Trant and the militia, but the bridge was blown."

"Then there are other wounded here?"

"No," Kit said softly, reluctantly remembering the

friends he had lost. "There are no other wounded. Just as there is no longer any regiment."

"I see," Standish said. His tone, however, indicated that he certainly did *not* see how something like that could happen.

"Probably not," Kit retorted, the old aristocratic arrogance answering the unspoken but implied suspicion. "But I assure you I'll explain every circumstance," he added coldly. "That explanation shall be made, however, to his lordship. And at the proper time and place, of course."

Surely, St. John thought angrily, his standing with headquarters was such that whatever action he had taken to safeguard the wounded and to carry out his orders should not now be questioned. Not by this green boy, who had probably never seen an action, much less been involved in one.

"Certainly, Major St. John," Standish said, his tone more respectful, a response, no doubt, to Kit's obvious fury. "How long will it take you to pack, sir, and be ready to move out? I'm sure Colonel Prescott will be happy to send an escort to accompany you and Mrs. Haviland to headquarters."

"I should be grateful," Kit said, his words coldly formal. He turned to Judith. "You have my deepest sympathies, Mrs. Haviland, on the death of your husband."

"Thank you, Major St. John," she whispered. She looked at him then, dark eyes luminous now with unshed tears.

She really loved the bastard, Kit thought in despair. *She truly loved him, despite it all.*

Kit turned and walked back into the hut, not bothering to wait for help, from Judith Haviland or from anyone else.

"There is no question, Major St. John, of any misconduct on your part," his lordship said. "I do not wish you to feel that I am in any way censuring the decisions which you and Mrs. Haviland were forced to make during those desperate days. However..."

Wellington's deep voice hesitated. The piercing eyes above the famous hawk-like nose, which had earned him his nickname among his troops, rested on Kit's thin face.

It was the first day St. John had dressed in full regimentals since his return, and the effort of this appearance before the allied commander had taken a toll on his still uncertain strength. He was determined, however, that Wellington would not be aware of that.

Several of the garments Kit wore had been borrowed. None of his fellow officers had begrudged those loans, he knew. Their manner had been as accepting as his rank, position, and military reputation demanded. And thankfully there had been no condemnation in their faces.

They felt, so he had been led to believe by their supportive comments, that if he said Boney had sent reinforcements, then the emperor bloody well had. And if St. John said Smythe had directed him to take the wounded, himself included, out of harm's way, then of course that was exactly what had happened. Not one of them seemed to doubt those statements.

It was only the other that was still whispered about in the officers' mess. And it was the other which had occasioned the kind of titillating gossip that swept like wildfire through the ranks of a bored army, especially one which has gone without anything so interesting to talk about during six long months in winter encampment.

An enlisted man heard to utter such remarks about an officer or an officer's wife might be flogged. But among the members of the officer corps itself, physical punishment could not be used to quash the rampant gossip about the relationship that had existed between Mrs. Haviland and the handsome, aristocratic Major St. John, whose reputation with women was not only well-known, but apparently well-deserved.

Standish and his superior, Colonel Prescott, had clearly heard the peasant's explanation. The translator had repeated his words loudly enough that none of those who had been nearby that day could possibly have any doubt about the situation the peasant described. And of course, the inclusion of the wedding ring seemed to reinforce the story the man had told.

Major St. John and Michael Haviland's widow had been living openly as man and wife for several weeks in the small Portuguese village where they had been found. There was no doubt at all about that part of the oft-repeated tale.

Exactly how that scandalous arrangement had come about was, however, at the core of the gossip. And about that everyone seemed to have an opinion. However, Kit reminded himself, the only opinion that really mattered was the one he had been ordered here today to hear.

"You must know, St. John, there has been a great deal of talk," Wellington went on.

"Talk, sir?" Kit repeated, although he was as well aware of what was being said as was his commanding officer.

"Gossip concerning you and Mrs. Haviland, I am afraid. Somewhat natural under the circumstances, I suppose."

"I was unaware, sir, that you…entertained gossip," Kit suggested softly.

In his voice was an echo of the long generations who had borne the noble name he carried. It was a tone of unconscious arrogance which Kit had acquired from his father. Its coldness might have stopped a lesser man than Wellington from pursuing this line of inquiry.

"Colonel Prescott was told that you and Mrs. Haviland were living together as man and wife. Standish confirmed that was the impression which the villagers had of your relationship,'' the general continued, seemingly untroubled by Kit's disdain.

That was a question, of course. It was not stated as such, but both men understood what information the commander sought.

''I'm afraid, sir, that neither I nor Mrs. Haviland can be held responsible for…impressions,'' St. John said. His tone had not changed. It was still frigid and immensely formal.

But neither had Wellington's eyes changed. The general's lips pursed slightly and were then controlled. ''You know that Haviland is dead, of course. His body was found during our advance. It has been positively identified by his batman.''

''Reynolds,'' Kit said, his tone slightly altered.

In response to that, one of the general's dark brows quirked, questioning perhaps. ''Private Reynolds reached our lines a month ago. He left camp after the battle and made his way south. You are acquainted with the man?'' Wellington asked.

''I had believed Private Reynolds was killed with the rest of the regiment. I was…somewhat surprised to find that was not the case. Were there other survivors then, sir?''

''None that I am aware of,'' Wellington said, not unkindly. ''The two of you seem to be the only ones who escaped the destruction of Colonel Smythe's forces. You two and Mrs. Haviland, of course.''

Kit said nothing, remembering again the men he had led. Men who had fought bravely beside him. Who had protected him, followed him, honored him with their trust. Now they were all gone. Perhaps the emotion of that renewed realization left him unprepared for what came next.

''And the question is, of course,'' Wellington went on, ''what should be done about Mrs. Haviland.''

"Done, sir?" Kit asked, pulling his mind from the past into this equally painful present.

"You must realize that even her status as a widow leaves her unprotected from the unkindness of this scandal, particularly since she was at the time…not yet a widow," Wellington said, obviously choosing his words with care. "That makes the situation even more difficult, I think."

"I'm afraid I don't understand," Kit said, but he was beginning to. The direction of Wellington's comments went a great way toward explaining why the general had sent for him.

"Whatever the truth of what happened in that village, Major St. John, it is the stain of speculation about it which will mark Mrs. Haviland's life. And your own, of course."

Kit said nothing, working to control the growing tumult in his chest, working to remain outwardly calm as the parameters of his world shifted and then realigned themselves.

He had dreamed of Judith Haviland while the idea of loving her had been morally and legally forbidden. And now… Now it seemed that Wellington himself was about to propose that he—

"I had thought to suggest," his lordship continued softly, "that you might wish to do the most honorable thing in this very difficult situation." Wellington's dark eyes had dropped to consider his long-fingered hands, resting together on top of the cluttered desk.

"The honorable thing?" Kit repeated, fighting his sheer physical response to the idea. There was no honor involved in this. There was desire, hot and powerful, coursing through his body. And there was love. He had realized that a long time ago, even when he had thought Judith forever out of his reach.

"No one can force you to do so, of course," Wellington said. "And I do appreciate the differences in your stations.

There is not, I believe, anything in Mrs. Haviland's background that might prevent such an alliance. Her father is General Aubrey McDowell, as you know, a respected retired member of His Majesty's army.''

The commander's eyes lifted again, fastening on Kit's face as if awaiting a response to that commonplace. That was not, of course, what he was seeking.

''You are suggesting that I should offer Mrs. Haviland the protection of my name,'' Kit said. Despite the pounding blood at his temples and the incredible sense of anticipation, his voice was calm. He also knew from long experience at the gaming tables of the more elegant London hells that his features would reveal nothing of his true feelings. Nothing of his growing excitement.

''I believe that might be the honorable thing. Under the circumstances, of course.''

''I see,'' Kit said softly. He wondered if Wellington could hear his heart, which seemed as loud to him as the frantic French drums that beat a prelude to every battle.

''If, however, despite my recommendation, you feel that you should consult your father—'' Wellington began, only to be sharply cut off.

''My father—'' Kit said, his voice like a whiplash. He stopped, sought a breath and control. ''My father has *nothing* to say about this.''

Again the dark eyes of Wellington probed and then lowered from that handsome face. ''Then may I expect you to carry out this…obligation?'' he asked.

''You may,'' Kit agreed.

''May I also suggest you move with all deliberate speed, Major,'' the general said. ''Before this talk becomes more disruptive than it already is. And before the lady herself—''

''I understand,'' St. John said. ''You have made yourself very clear, sir.'' He saluted his commander, forced to do so improperly with his right hand. Then he turned on his heel and quit the room.

Behind him, Wellington pushed himself out of the chair behind the desk and walked across the office in the small municipal building they had commandeered to serve as his headquarters. He looked out the window and watched St. John stride purposefully across the uneven paving stones of the plaza.

Apparently St. John didn't appreciate having his actions questioned, the general decided. Or perhaps he resented suggestions as to the direction his life should take.

Wellington didn't blame the major for his resentment. Being told what he must do was something he himself had never enjoyed. In that, they were very much alike, he thought.

The earl of Ryde's son had, of course, enough natural arrogance, money and position to protect both himself and his wife from the cruelly wagging tongues. Perhaps this marriage would stop the rumors before they could reach London. That would protect McDowell, whom his lordship knew and respected.

The best thing for them all, Wellington thought, believing he had truly achieved that goal. And as far as the British commander was concerned, the minor social affair of Major St. John and Mrs. Haviland had been satisfactorily resolved.

He would not be aware for several days that it was not. And by the time he *was* aware of that fact, it would be far too late to do anything else about the tragedy that was unfolding.

Judith Haviland had spent the last few days simply waiting for whatever came next, her mind numbed by the enormity of what had happened. She had sent her husband to his death, and she could not even be sure within her own heart that that had not been her intent. And if *she* were not sure...

She closed her eyes, trying to think about Michael. She had been attempting to visualize him as he had been the first time she'd met him. Handsome. Charming even. But he had been sober, and that was an occurrence which had happened less and less frequently until, at the last...

Judith took a breath, wondering why she was dwelling on Michael's failings. They had been many, but now he was dead. *And may he rest in peace,* she thought. She really wished that for him. Just to let Michael rest in peace.

Apparently, her husband had been true to his sworn word. He had been killed on his way to Wellington's headquarters. He, then, had kept his part of the bargain. As she would keep hers.

"Mrs. Haviland?"

She knew before she looked up who had spoken her name. Major St. John and the officer's wife with whom she was living were standing in the doorway. She hadn't seen him since the escort Prescott had arranged brought them to Wellington's temporary headquarters.

It had been a much longer time since she had seen him like this. If she had not known of St. John's illness, it would be very difficult to find evidence of it in his appearance today.

His handsome features were still too finely drawn, but it was very hard to criticize them. He was dressed in full regimental regalia, and few men wore the uniform as well as St. John. None, she would venture, had ever worn it better.

She should be delighted to see him so fully recovered, she thought, and yet there was within her heart an emptiness. Never again would their relationship be what it had been through those weeks they had spent together, during those days when she cared for him and had, through sheer determination, kept him alive.

St. John looked more like the man she had so briefly met in London than the man who had once touched her. The man whose fingers had loosened her hair and brushed tantalizingly against her breast. The man whose mouth had ravaged her own.

"Major St. John," she said, fighting those memories.

She nodded dismissal to her hostess. "Thank you, Mrs. Stuart." The woman's brows climbed, but she left them alone, only after she had made her reluctance to do so obvious.

Judith waited until the door of the parlor closed behind her hostess before she turned to St. John. She smiled at him, but he didn't return it. His face was composed, almost set, the blue eyes distant.

"Mrs. Haviland," he said finally.

She was aware that his gaze had scanned quickly over the black gown she wore, a mourning dress she had borrowed from Mrs. Stuart. It was not only too large, but both the color and style were vastly unbecoming, she knew.

At that thought, the guilt she had felt since they had been rescued assaulted her again. She was thinking about how unbecoming her clothing was, about how she appeared in St. John's eyes, when she should instead be lost in grief over her husband.

"I hope you are well," she said.

"Very well, thank you," St. John responded politely.

She had had more comfortable conversations with strangers, Judith thought. And more meaningful. An impossible distance now stretched between them. They seemed to have lost even the friendship and respect they had once shared. She wondered again what St. John remembered and if those memories colored his present treatment of her. The word *wanton* brushed through her mind.

"Mrs. Haviland, you may be aware that..." St. John began before his voice faltered, but his eyes still held hers.

"Aware of what?" she asked finally when he didn't go on.

"I would like to offer you the protection of my name," St. John said simply, abandoning whatever explanation he'd begun.

It took a moment for the words to penetrate. It was the last thing she had expected him to say. The last she might have dared wish for. Hope for. Dream of. And so she waited, repeating the phrase again and again in her head, trying to think of any other possible connotation for those words.

"Protection?" she whispered finally.

Despite her attempts to rationalize what he had said, the physical reaction had already begun. Desire roiled through her body as it had before. Within the dangerous darkness of the cave. And later beside the water, the paralyzing cold of the mountain stream burned away by the heat of his lips.

"There has been some gossip, I'm afraid," he said softly. His eyes were shuttered, hidden. They had always been open, honest in their regard and their appraisal.

Of course, she thought in despair. Why had she not expected this? They had spent several weeks alone. St. John's very honorable offer was the natural result of that time. *Offer,* she repeated. It was a word whose meaning she had not thought about since those far-off days of her brief London Season.

"This isn't necessary," Judith said softly. "Thank you, Major St. John, for your consideration, but I assure you..."

She found that she couldn't continue, couldn't force her mind to compose the formal words of denial. The images were suddenly too clear in her head. All of them crowded into her brain and into her heart, blocking any rational thought.

The memory of the day he had removed his shirt, revealing that darkly bronzed expanse of muscle and bone. The feel of her breasts crushed against his chest. The trembling hand he had held out in invitation. The incredible pleasure of his body on top of hers. The solid weight of it. The breathless anticipation with which she had watched his mouth descend to hers…

To Judith Haviland, marriage had been a prison. A soulless excursion into the empty void of abuse and alcoholism. Now, finally, she had found the man with whom it might be all that it should be. What her father's and mother's union had once been. Joy and companionship. A glory of mind and body joined. One.

But not like this. And not for these reasons.

"I can't marry you, Major St. John," she said softly, denying what she did not deserve. *More than I deserve* echoed again in her head as it had in the old woman's hut.

St. John was alive. And Michael, her husband, was not. Because she had sent him to his death. Perhaps she had even sent him to die because she desired another man. This man.

If this were punishment for her sin, it was apt, and it was even just, she acknowledged. Because she had just been forced to say no to the one thing she would willingly have given up her immortal soul to possess.

Chapter Eleven

"I can't marry you," Judith had whispered.

Whatever Kit anticipated when he had come to her today, it was not this, not an unequivocal denial. He had never before proposed marriage, but Lord St. John had seldom been refused any other request he'd made to a woman. And this was the only one that had ever truly mattered.

"I'm not sure you have a choice," he warned softly.

Her dark eyes widened. He wondered if it were possible she didn't know what was being said about their relationship. But Judith Haviland's innocence was something he had never doubted.

Despite the brutality of these last three years, despite the duties she had undertaken, there was a quality about Mrs. Haviland that proclaimed her lack of cynicism and her belief in the inherent goodness of people. That characteristic had been evident in her dealings with the men of the regiment, and even the roughest had responded with unfaltering respect.

It had also shown, of course, in her dealings with Kit himself. In spite of her denial, he knew that something had happened between them. She had lied to him about that to assuage his guilt for what he had done under the influence of his delirium. Kit was sure that the images which lived in his memory were far too clear to be mere fantasies.

Once he had kissed Judith Haviland. And he had touched her. He knew that, no matter what she said. He was ashamed that he had pressed his unwanted attentions on a defenseless woman, even if his actions had been a result of his illness.

His unwanted attentions, he thought grimly. And apparently they still were. But Mrs. Haviland had been married then, and all of what he felt for her had been forbidden. As had been, of course, whatever happened between them. And now it was not.

"I don't understand," she said.

"Lord Wellington believes it will be better that we marry and put a quick end to this gossip."

It was his strongest argument, and Kit was not opposed to using any card which fate placed in his hand. He had no doubt that once Judith belonged to him, he could win her love. And he was determined to have with Judith the true marriage that Michael Haviland had foolishly thrown away. Even if she had loved her husband, Kit still believed, arrogantly perhaps, that given enough time and the depth of what he felt for her, he could defeat the hold of Haviland's ghost.

"Lord Wellington sent you here," Judith said, interrupting his pleasant fantasy. "Of course," she added, speaking so softly that the comment seemed only to herself.

Her voice was flat, and the words held a trace of bitterness. He wondered if she expected him to deny it. Wellington's suggestion was not the reason he had come, of course, but rather the impetus for acting so soon. The general had given him permission to seek Judith's hand. That was a privilege he had not expected, had not believed appropriate, given her recent bereavement.

"I think he was concerned about the damage to your reputation, Mrs. Haviland. And concerned about your father's reaction to the story when he hears it," Kit added.

He realized that her father's reaction was not something she had considered. Her eyes dilated with shock at his words, the rim of brown almost disappearing in the expansion of her pupils. She had apparently never thought how her father or society would view what had happened. Or what people *thought* had happened, Kit amended. However, his name and position could offer her protection, he knew, if she would only agree to accept them.

"My father?" she repeated disbelievingly.

Despite her question, that argument had obviously had an effect. Kit saw the pain of it reflected in her eyes, and of course, given his own father's undeniable influence in his life, he understood her anxiety.

"We were together for some weeks. The villagers had the impression we were man and wife. That's what they told Prescott. I'm afraid the story has now been too widely circulated to hope to contain the damage it might do to your reputation."

"Damage to *me*?" she asked.

Her eyes seemed to ask another question, but before he could guess what it was, the long lashes fell, hiding whatever had been in their dark depths.

"Not to me, in any case," he said. "I'm afraid my own reputation is such, Mrs. Haviland, that it makes your present situation more difficult."

Her eyes came up at that, and what had been in them before was gone. They were again clear and open to his scrutiny.

"Believe me, I am truly sorry for that," Kit said softly.

He *was* sorry. He had wondered before what she had heard about him, and then that concern had been lost in the friendship she had offered and in her acceptance of the man he had become here on the Peninsula. Now his previously reckless life had stained her. Judith Haviland didn't deserve that blotch on the sterling reputation she had acquired through her service here.

"You have *nothing* for which to apologize, Major St. John," she said emphatically. "And you have certainly done nothing for which you need offer to make this sacrifice."

Her lips had moved into the small, heartbreakingly familiar smile with which she had greeted so many disasters throughout the last three years, and his heart responded. There was no sacrifice in his proposal, of course. Only need. And a desire such as he had never felt before. A desire to cherish and protect this woman. And to love her.

"Mrs. Haviland—" he began, only to be interrupted.

"You have most gallantly defended me, Major St. John, when there were real threats. I promise you that it is not necessary now that you continue to do so. My father knows my character. I assure you he will disregard whatever unpleasant gossip he hears. And perhaps, if we are fortunate, he will hear none."

It was not the answer he had hoped for, of course, but Kit had learned from his years as a soldier. One of those lessons concerned the wisdom of outflanking his opponent. He had come here determined to secure Judith Haviland's agreement to marry him, and he would worry about other considerations only after that particular goal had been accomplished.

"But *your* father is not the only person involved in this situation, I'm afraid," he said. "Or the only one touched by its possible ramifications."

The emphasis was deliberate. The generosity of Judith Haviland's spirit was well-known. If she believed his own reputation was at stake, or his father's regard for him, then she might give in. The silence stretched through several heartbeats, and her eyes again examined his face, seeking answers.

"You believe that—" she said finally.

"I believe," he interrupted, "that this is truly the best solution for everyone involved. I beg you to reconsider. I promise you that this marriage will in no way encroach on your natural grief and regard for your late husband."

Again some emotion touched her eyes and was quickly controlled. Kit had given her his word, and he intended to abide by it. He was not by nature a patient man, but he had once believed Judith Haviland to be forever out of his reach. And now, suddenly, everything he had once only dreamed of was within his grasp. He could wait.

Michael Haviland had mistreated his wife. He had marked her life with violence and dishonor. Kit sought only the privilege of making her forget. And if he did, then the rest of what he wanted would follow eventually.

Again the silence grew, the rush of blood in his ears almost overpowering as he waited. Finally Judith moved. She put out her hand, and surprised by the simple, almost masculine camaraderie of the gesture, Kit took it into his.

It was small and fragile, so vulnerable that again he had to fight the inclination to take her in his arms. To close out the world that whispered scandals about her name and linked it to the notoriety of his. An almost undeniable urge to protect her.

She didn't smile at him as her fingers rested in his. But he saw the breath she drew, almost shuddering in its intensity. And he read her answer in her eyes long before she gave it.

"Then, yes, Major St. John," she said, her voice soft

and very calm. "Given those considerations, I *will* marry you."

Wellington proved as adept at arranging a wedding as he was at supplying his vast army. Kit had no real friends among his lordship's colorful staff, but several of the officers whom he had known socially in London attended the ceremony. As did the woman with whom Mrs. Haviland had been living since their return.

Judith was dressed in another borrowed gown, but Kit was relieved to find that it was not the stark black she had worn on the day he proposed. This was a soft violet-gray, an acceptable color for the latter months of mourning, and its pleasant hue produced an answering blush of color in Judith's cheeks. She looked far less fragile than she had in the too-large, scarecrow black she had worn before.

Jewel tones to bring out the dark perfection of her skin and hair, Kit found himself thinking as he watched Judith walk down the aisle of the chapel on Lord Wellington's arm. At one time Lord St. John had been considered to have a great deal of expertise in feminine fashions.

Kit's mistresses had been reputed to be the best-dressed women in the capital. He would delight in clothing Judith in the finest the London modistes could produce. To be allowed to dress her as she should be would give him infinite pleasure.

Her hand was shaking when she placed it in his. Her fingers were cold, the vibration in them strong. Suddenly Kit remembered touching her like this. Cold and trembling, her lips had once opened under his. Not in fear or disgust, but in an undeniable response to his own passion. Judith Haviland's body had lain acquiescent under his, her lips parted in anticipation of his kiss. His hand cupping the warmth and softness of her breast.

The image was so vivid he knew he hadn't imagined it. He could not have imagined her willing participation in their lovemaking. But it was there, complete and perfect, in his head.

Finally, in spite of the power of that memory over his senses, he remembered to breathe, to think, and even to repeat the vows the clergyman spoke. This was one more thing to be gotten through before Judith Haviland belonged, finally, to him.

The ceremony seemed dream-like. And when it was over, Kit turned to face Judith, aware that others were watching. Aware again that this was little more than a performance. He lowered his head to find her mouth and it, too, trembled under the warm caress of his lips. A contact too brief. Too quickly ended.

He did not release her hand when it was over. She left her fingers trustingly in his, and his was the voice that answered the few well-wishers in attendance. His were the practiced and graceful phrases that carried them out the door and across the plaza to the small suite of rooms that had been provided them.

And finally, after the seemingly endless ordeal involved in satisfying the conventions and expectations of this small, close-knit society, they were once again alone.

"Will you tell me the truth?" he asked.

Judith's eyes came up from the well-cooked slice of the roast he had cut for her. She had prodded it with her fork throughout the meal, between sips of the wine his lordship had thoughtfully sent them, but she had eaten very little.

The woman who owned the house had tried to produce a proper wedding supper, and Kit supposed he should be grateful. Judith, however, had toyed with the rich food. And in the end he had found himself simply watching her pretense at eating. It was another performance, of course, this one for his benefit.

"The truth?" she asked cautiously.

"The truth about what happened between us during those days. The days I was ill. The days you cared for me."

She smiled at him before her eyes fell to her nearly untouched plate. Deliberately, she laid the fork she'd been playing with down and put both hands in her lap. When she looked up at him again, her eyes were amused.

"The days I cared for you?" she repeated, a thread of self-derision coloring her voice. "Do you mean perhaps the day I let you wander into the middle of a mountain stream? I left you alone for a moment, and when I returned, you had taken off most of your clothing to go swimming. Except the water was more suitable for an ice fair than a bathing excursion."

She hesitated, her eyes no longer smiling, before she finished. "I thought you were going to die, in your stocking feet and without your uniform, and it would have been my fault."

Kit laughed. He was pleased to see a spark of answering amusement lighten the seriousness of her eyes at his unexpected shout of laughter.

"I don't see how my stupidity could in any way be considered to be *your* fault," he said.

"You were desperately ill, and I should have taken better care of you. I knew you weren't…entirely rational, and still I left you alone in a vain attempt to see where the trail we were following led."

"That's when the villagers came," he suggested. He allowed his eyes to release hers as he waited for her reply, taking the opportunity to pour wine into the glass she had almost emptied.

This was the crux of the matter. Whatever had happened

by the stream. That was the image he had remembered so clearly during the ceremony today. Kit found that he wanted her to tell him about it, to confess to what he believed he had read in her response.

"Very soon thereafter," she agreed. Her hand closed around the delicate stem of her glass, and her fingers trembled slightly as she raised it to her lips. He met her eyes over the top of the glass and held them.

"And before that?" he probed. "What happened before they arrived?"

Slowly she set the glass down without drinking from it. Her chin lifted, but her eyes didn't evade his. "I'm afraid I don't understand what you're asking, Major St. John."

"I should think," Kit suggested, "that you might try for something a little less formal. Considering the fact…"

"That we are married," she said when he paused.

"There are some who will think it a very strange marriage indeed if you are determined to address me as *Major* St. John," he said. He smiled at her and was relieved at the slight relaxation of the tension that had held her.

"I didn't even know your given name," she said softly. "I don't believe I had ever heard it before today."

"And now you know it."

"Christopher." Her voice was low, the tone ordinary, so he was surprised by the physical response the whispered word evoked.

"Or more frequently Kit," he suggested, fighting that response. It had been a long time since anyone besides his immediate family had employed that childhood nickname. He was most often addressed by his title, of course. Only his mother and his old nurse and occasionally Roger still used the other.

"Kit," she repeated. "It…fits you somehow."

"I'm glad you approve."

"And would it matter if I hadn't?" she asked, smiling.

"It would have mattered a great deal to me," he said softly.

The smile faded, even from her eyes. There was a sudden tinge of color in her cheeks, but her gaze met his unflinchingly.

"Why?" she asked.

Caught by surprise, Kit laughed again. "Do you know, you are the only woman of my acquaintance who would have thought to ask me why," he said. "Most would simply have accepted a compliment they considered their due."

"Is that what it was? A compliment?"

"In your case, Mrs. Haviland, it was simply the truth."

The unthinking use of Haviland's name destroyed the ease that had been growing between them. That was clear from the pain in her eyes. And Kit cursed himself for forgetting and employing the habitual formality he had always used in addressing her. For so long he had forced himself to think of her as Mrs. Haviland. A married woman. Forbidden to him. And now...

"Mrs. St. John," she said.

He looked up to find that her eyes were forgiving, trying to tell him that she understood why he had made that cruel slip.

"Actually," Kit corrected, smiling at her, "it should be Lady St. John."

She returned his relieved smile before she said, "I don't believe I shall ever be able to bring that off, Major."

"Kit."

"And Judith. Safer, I think. At least until we become more accustomed to this...marriage."

"Is it so difficult for you to accept?" he asked.

"I never thought..." she began, and then she hesitated,

obviously considering her words carefully. "I never imagined I should ever be anything but Michael's wife," she
said softly.

Michael's wife. In spite of all Haviland had done to her,
she was still, in her own mind at least, Michael's wife. Kit
fought the thick rush of disappointment. Judith was now
married to him, but not by choice, not as she had chosen
Haviland. She had been forced to wed Kit by circumstances. In order to protect those she loved. And because
he had tricked her.

"Of course," he said. He rose, placing the linen napkin
carefully beside his plate.

Her eyes had followed his movement, and they were
questioning. He had promised patience, had vowed to give
her time, and already he was finding the constraints imposed by that vow to be impossible.

"Where are you going?" she asked.

He turned back and saw that she had also risen. She took
a step away from the table and nearer to him, but he knew
that if he stayed, he would eventually say or do something
he'd regret. Perhaps he was the one who needed time. And
distance.

He needed *something* to fight against the images that had
crowded his brain since the ceremony. The too-vivid memory of Judith willingly lying in his arms beside that mountain stream.

"There's only one bedroom," he said bluntly. "And it
contains one bed." Again her eyes widened, and color
stained her cheeks. "Did you intend for us to share it?"

She said nothing for a long moment. "But where will
you go?" she asked finally, destroying the small, fragile
hope that had begun to grow in Kit's heart.

"There are always places for a soldier to sleep. During

the last three years you and I both have endured conditions far worse than this town offers.''

''There's no need—'' she began, but he didn't listen.

Suddenly he knew that he couldn't stay in this house tonight. He couldn't stay here with her. Not with the ghost of Michael Haviland between them.

''Good night, Judith,'' Kit said simply. He opened the door and stepped out into the waiting darkness.

''So you finally got what you wanted.''

The voice was familiar, but Judith hadn't managed to place it before she looked up, straight into the vindictive eyes of Toby Reynolds. Michael's batman was standing beside her at one of the stalls of the open-air market.

Judith had borrowed a wicker basket from her landlady this morning, deciding that a dose of fresh air and sunshine might lighten her mood. The day had cooperatively provided both, and her small basket was now filled with fresh produce from which she planned to offer her husband a more appetizing meal than the heavy one they had pretended to share last night.

Her normally resilient spirits had responded to being out of doors and to the friendliness, despite her limited command of their language, of the peasants who had come here to sell their goods. She had been feeling better about the situation, despite the fact that Kit had still been absent from their rooms when she had awakened, alone and almost lost in the wide bed.

Now, however, Judith's heart plummeted at what she heard in Reynolds's tone. Perhaps that was because his accusation echoed the guilt her own conscience used to torment her. What he had just said was something she had already acknowledged as the simple truth. She *had* finally gotten what she wanted.

"Private Reynolds," she said, nodding at him. "It's very good to see you again. I'm so glad you escaped."

She was pleased at the normality of her voice. None of her sudden trepidation was revealed in its tone, but Reynolds grinned, apparently seeing through her in an instant.

"You always wanted our pretty major," he said. "Me and the captain knew that. I heard the two of you talking in the tent."

For a moment Judith froze, trying to remember anything improper that Reynolds might have overheard between them. And then she realized that, given his phrasing, he might have meant that he heard her and Michael talking. However, her hesitation caused the batman's leering grin to widen.

"You might'a fooled the others with your act, your *ladyship,* but I knew what you was. And I was right, I see."

"I don't know what you're talking about," Judith said. She could feel the guilty burn of blood in her cheeks.

"It didn't take the two of you long to figure a way to work it. I'll give you that. Clever you are. Sly and clever. A dangerous combination in a woman, I always say. What I don't see is how you got the captain to agree to make that run through the French lines. He weren't no fool. You and I both know that."

She took a breath, trying to think what she could tell him, trying to remember what he might already know. "Captain Haviland volunteered to carry word to Lord Wellington of our predicament and of the arrival of the French reinforcements," Judith said.

"Volunteered?" Reynolds repeated, still mocking. "Is that how it goes, now? I think I'm beginning to get the drift of this. Our noble major wants you, and all the while you're lusting for him. Obvious as a bitch in heat to those of us who really know you. Like your husband did."

"How dare you," Judith whispered. The nausea engendered by his words stirred in her throat.

"One order from the major, and the way is clear," he went on, still smiling at her. "And it worked, of course. He got his Bathsheba. Neat as a charm. St. John took a chance on the captain getting killed, and his bloody luck held, even in that. But then he always was reputed to be a fair lucky bastard."

David and Bathsheba. She remembered the story, of course, with all its Old Testament sin and guilt. King David had sent his captain, Uriah, to be killed in battle because he lusted after the man's beautiful wife. "That's not what happened," Judith denied. "You were there. You *know* what really happened."

Still she hesitated to even speak the truth aloud. But this man knew what had occurred. He knew of Michael's guilt and disgrace, and that her husband had been made a prisoner after that disastrous battle. He also had been in camp when Smythe refused to let Michael undertake the mission that she and her husband had finally forced St. John to allow. Reynolds knew the truth.

"I know that noble bastard tried to have me flayed," Reynolds said. His voice had lost the amused mockery and was filled instead with hate. Its venom chilled Judith to the bone.

"I promise you that Michael volunteered to take that message. He wanted to do something—"

She hesitated again, remembering the purpose behind her husband's gesture. *Something so valiantly right and honorable that it might make up for all the wrongs...*

That had eventually been Michael's wish as well as her own. The aim of that daring journey he had offered to undertake had been to protect his father.

Kit had had nothing to do with that. He had been opposed from the first to letting Haviland go. She and Michael together, however, had given him little option, so he had finally given Michael what he wanted—permission to go— and his own oath never to speak of what had occurred. And if she now revealed what had been done, then the sacrifice of Michael's life would have been made in vain. All of it would be thrown away. Wasted.

"Major St. John had nothing to do with Michael's decision to volunteer," she said.

"It just *conveniently* happened and got him something he'd wanted for a long time? Do you really think anyone will believe that? Especially after they hear that the two of you were already up to no good, and that the captain knew about it. St. John sent a man to his death in order to get you. I wonder if he's found you worth doing murder for."

"No," she said, horrified by the implication. "Nothing you've said is as it happened. Please don't ever suggest—"

Reynolds laughed, revealing stained and uneven teeth. "It's what *I* believe happened, your ladyship. And what others will believe, too. You might'a got what you wanted, you and St. John. But you ain't got off for free, neither of you. Don't you go believing that. Not so long as Toby Reynolds is around."

He insolently took an apple from the basket hanging over Judith's arm and bit into its white flesh with those broken, discolored teeth. His eyes mocked, but he said nothing else to her before he turned away and sauntered across the cobblestones.

Behind him, Judith eventually remembered to breathe, as long and as shuddering an intake of breath as when she had agreed to become St. John's wife. She had married Kit to make the scandal over the weeks the two of them had spent together go away. To protect those they loved. And now, with Toby Reynolds's vicious accusations, she knew without a shadow of a doubt she had failed.

Chapter Twelve

"Considering everything," Wellington said softly, "it might be wise to consider resigning your commission."

"There's no truth in what Reynolds is suggesting. You must know that." Kit's voice was controlled, but the rage that had been building inside him for days threatened to explode.

He had followed his lordship's urgings and the prompting of his own heart when he had proposed to Judith Haviland. Now Reynolds's poison had made their marriage the center of a scandal that was far worse than the previous whispers had been. Something much more dangerous, as Wellington had just acknowledged.

The batman had virtually accused Kit of murdering Haviland by sending him on a suicide mission, one which had already cost Lieutenant Scarborough his life. St. John had supposedly ordered Haviland to make that same impossible journey in hope that he, too, would meet that fate. Then the major could marry Judith, with whom, Reynolds hinted, he was having an adulterous affair.

The batman had woven a sticky web of lies, deceits, and half-truths, which, it seemed, nothing Kit or his superiors said could completely destroy. The story was too grotesquely fascinating, especially after the gossip that had gone before. And especially since it concerned someone like St. John.

Wellington had tried to stop the slander by sending for Reynolds. He intended to warn the man of disciplinary action if he continued his calumny, but apparently Reynolds had carefully walked the line between accusation and implication, walked it too adroitly for the general to take any official action against him.

A lot of what Haviland's orderly said was true, of course. The facts about Scarborough's death, the composition and vulnerability of the small caravan Kit led, the fact that Mrs. Haviland and her husband had both been part of it. But the central claim, that Kit had ordered Haviland to cross enemy lines, could not now be proven one way or the other. And nothing could stop people from making the inference it suggested.

Of course, the batman's story contained no reference to the charges Smythe had brought against Haviland, to his disgrace and subsequent arrest. Kit himself was honor-bound not to reveal any of that information, which might have turned the tide in his favor, although, like the other, there was now no proof that any of that had happened.

His commander's questions had been pointed enough that Kit believed Wellington himself, on occasion at least, wondered exactly what had occurred. Only Judith and St. John knew the entire truth, and Kit had taken an oath not to reveal an important portion of it. And the reasons Judith wanted her husband's dishonor unexposed were, he knew, still as valid as when she'd explained them to him. So they were left with Reynolds's whispers, and no way to disprove what they implied.

Wellington's mouth pursed in thought, but his eyes met St. John's, their gaze considering. ''Those of us who knew

Haviland,'' he said, "did not find him to be self-sacrificing. *Or* heroic. Perhaps that assessment of his character is one reason people are now listening to his batman's story.''

"Those who are listening,'' Kit said, "do so because they *enjoy* hearing filthy gossip. Whatever Haviland was…'' Kit paused, thinking about what Judith's husband had been.

Remembering his oath, however, St. John's lips closed over the true explanation for Captain Haviland's self-sacrifice. He stood silently before his commander, lost in bitterness, again reliving the decisions he had been forced to make.

It was Wellington who finally broke the strained silence. "Reynolds claims that Scarborough had already been lost in the attempt to get word through. Is that information accurate?''

"It is,'' Kit agreed reluctantly. "Scarborough had made it only a few miles before he was ambushed.''

"Private Reynolds avows that you then requested Haviland be attached to your command. Is that also accurate?''

"It is *not*. Colonel Smythe had placed Captain Haviland with my detachment long before Scarborough's body was discovered.''

"A detachment which included Mrs. Haviland?''

"And the other women,'' Kit reminded softly. A muscle tensed involuntarily beside his mouth, and was then controlled.

"Haviland was assigned to your detachment despite the fact that Smythe, shorthanded as he was, knew he would soon be facing a vastly superior French force? Despite the fact that due to your own injury he had already lost one of his best officers?''

Wellington's questions themselves seemed accusations, at least to Kit, although the commander's tone was measured. "I didn't question the reasons for Colonel Smythe's orders," he said. "I obeyed them. As I had always done."

"I see," Wellington said. His eyes remained on St. John's face. "And when you were forced to turn back from the bridge and found that the regiment had been wiped out? There was no one else within your command whom you might have sent to me with word of the French reinforcements and of your predicament?"

"There were only three of us who knew the country well enough to have any chance of reaching the English lines."

"You, Sergeant Cochran, and Haviland?"

"Yes, sir," Kit agreed.

Another silence stretched as Wellington referred to a document before him. St. John could only assume the paper contained Reynolds's sworn statements.

"We've been over this before," Kit said. "I have explained the entire situation as it existed at that time."

His commander's eyes lifted, but he ignored the protest, just exactly, Kit thought, as his father had always ignored him when he tried to defend his actions. "Cochran was too valuable to send, you said, because he was foraging?" Wellington asked.

Kit's mouth tightened, but determinedly he held his temper. "That is correct."

"And could not Captain Haviland have been assigned to see to that? Given that his wife was with your party, it seems that it might have been more appropriate to allow Haviland to remain with the command and send Cochran to me." The sentence had somehow become a question.

Kit took a breath, strong enough that it lifted the muscles under the white facings of his uniform. "I felt Cochran was the better shot," he offered.

"Not better than you, I should think. According to your reputation, at least," Wellington suggested. "But I had forgotten. You were wounded. In high fever by this time and being cared for by Mrs. Haviland.''

''Are you suggesting—''

''I am suggesting,'' Wellington said, loudly enough that his voice overrode the obvious fury in Kit's. ''I am suggesting,'' he repeated, his tone modified now that St. John's angry words had stopped, ''that these are the very questions which will be put to you if you allow this situation to proceed to an inquiry. Don't be a fool, man,'' he advised softly. ''Sell out and go home. You can do no more good here, considering these rumors. And your injury provides the perfect excuse.''

''I'm not looking for excuses,'' Kit said. ''I'm a soldier. I came here to fight the French. I think that perhaps even now we may agree that I have been effective in that endeavor.''

His father would have recognized the glacial glint in the blue eyes. Apparently so did his commander. ''You have proven to be an exemplary officer, St. John. With a record here you may be justifiably proud of. No one can ever take that from you.''

Kit's tight-set features relaxed minutely, until the Beau added softly, ''*Unless* you let them do so with this slander.''

Kit's laugh was bitter. ''I am already stained with 'this slander.' My name *and* my record. Resigning will only appear an admission of guilt. I don't intend to *run* from Reynolds's lies. There isn't one word of truth in what he's suggesting. I swear to you on my honor as an officer that nothing happened as he says it did. Not regarding Captain Haviland. *Or* his wife.''

''*Your* wife,'' Wellington reminded him. ''You married Judith Haviland to protect her. Why the bloody hell don't you do it? Take her home, St. John. Get her away before this becomes something I can't contain. Do it before someone decides to write her father or yours or Haviland's with all the scandalous details. Then there will be nowhere for the two of you to go.''

''I don't believe that will—''

''With you gone, the talk here will die,'' Wellington broke in. ''I guarantee you that. They'll all be too busy chasing the French to have time to gossip like the old women they seem to have become. I'll see to it, damn it. I still have *some* authority over this army.''

''Use it to force Reynolds to tell the truth,'' Kit argued.

''Do you suggest I have the truth *beaten* out of him?'' the general asked, his own temper flaring for the first time.

Suddenly St. John remembered the flogging he'd overseen that snowy morning. It had been Haviland's crime, of course, but it had been the back of his servant and confidant Toby Reynolds which received the stripes. In carrying out Smythe's command Kit had apparently acquired a bitter and vindictive enemy.

''Do it for her sake if not for your own,'' Wellington urged.

This time the silence grew until it filled the small room. Proud, stubborn aristocrats both, they also possessed equally brilliant, tactical minds.

''Retreat and cut your losses,'' the general suggested, as he would have advised any subordinate in a losing position.

''I swear to you, sir, on my honor, that Haviland volunteered for that mission. I never ordered him to go,'' Kit said stubbornly, but the anger had been wiped from his voice. It was tired instead, almost emotionless.

''I never believed you did. But your wife is a beautiful woman. And you're correct about the undeniable lure of a scandal such as this. This gossip will never disappear as long as you are here, living together, your marriage a constant reminder.''

Living together, Kit thought. The bitterest irony of all.

''I can arrange transportation home, if you like,'' Wellington offered. ''The ships carrying reinforcements have already begun to arrive. They'll be returning as soon as possible with the wounded and those whose terms of enlistment are up. I can get you and your wife a cabin on one of them.'' The general's voice was compassionate, but this battle was done, and he was certainly strategist enough to recognize when he had achieved his ends.

''I should be very grateful,'' Kit said.

He saluted, and, as he had before, he turned and crossed the room with the same purposeful stride as the day he had been given permission to propose to Michael Haviland's widow. Nothing in his movements betrayed the enormous difference between what had been his feeling of elation then and the cold desolation in his heart today.

''England?'' Judith repeated softly.

''Wouldn't you like to go home, Judith?'' Kit asked. ''To see your father again?''

Nothing of the agitation he had felt when he left Wellington was in his voice. St. John had walked for hours after that painful interview. He had even ventured outside the walls of the town and into the still dangerous countryside.

None of the English sentries had questioned his destination, either because they had identified him or because they were veterans who had long ago learned the signs of despair and battle fatigue which sometimes drive men to commit acts which are not entirely rational. Kit had walked off his rage and his disappointment. And he had eventually become reconciled to the wisdom of Wellington's suggestion.

He had joined the army because his father had ordered him to, and he had come to Iberia because he had been given little choice. Once here, however, he had found purpose and honor for his life, a sense of pride and accomplishment that had long been missing. Now he must give them up because of one man's lies and innuendoes. About himself and Judith. About their relationship.

But Wellington was right, of course, and Kit had been forced finally to acknowledge that at some point during his aimless wandering. One of the many reasons he had married Judith Haviland was to offer her protection against scandal, and considering the situation, he could no longer do that here.

Kit had discovered that trying to destroy the whispers that haunted their lives was like fighting shadows. They became fleeting and insubstantial when he attempted to confront them. No one said anything openly, or he would have called that man out, of course. What was happening was too subtle for that.

He had clearly witnessed the effects of the batman's libel in the uncomfortable reaction of his fellow officers to his presence. Read it in their eyes when they looked at him. Or at Judith. That had been the most difficult to bear.

"But to resign your commission—" Judith began.

"The surgeons say there are physicians in London I should consult about a course of treatment for my arm. To regain full mobility. To have any chance of success, that must be done before the muscles become completely atrophied."

Her eyes fell to his arm, which in truth was far less impaired than she had warned him it would be. She would probably know that was a lie, he thought. But at least a reasonable one.

"This is what you want?" Judith asked finally, her eyes again on his face, trying to read the truth there.

He smiled at her, his own gaze clear and serene. In those hours after he left Wellington's office, he had made his decision. And he had faced the only guilt he knew he bore for this situation. He had been in love with Judith Haviland—long before her husband had volunteered for that mission.

It was possible that his feelings for her had in some way colored his ultimate decision to let Haviland go. There had been nothing like what Reynolds implied, of course, but still he *had* loved her. Dishonorably, he had desired another man's wife.

Who was now his wife, he thought, and protecting her was what honor now demanded. That was more important than his small role in this war, which Wellington was already winning and would continue to do. Judith was the most important thing now, far more important than his career or even his father's regard.

"I want to take you home," Kit answered her truthfully.

Judith was still watching his eyes, and at what she saw within them, finally she nodded agreement.

The ship did not afford Kit the same opportunities for escape that the town they had left behind them had. There was nowhere for him to go other than the small cabin that had been allotted to the two of them. Space was at a premium, he'd been told, and they were man and wife, of course.

Kit stood in the open doorway of the cabin, still wearing his cloak. The thick red wool was darkened across the shoulders with the cold rain that had pelted them as they hurried from Wellington's private carriage and on board the transport.

He watched Judith press her palm against the mattress of the bed. She had removed her gloves and thrown back the hood of her cloak. A few droplets of rain glinted like diamonds in the dark tendrils that surrounded her features.

"The sheets are damp, I'm afraid," she said, looking over her shoulder at him. The pale oval of her face was alternately illuminated and then shadowed, as the oil lamp someone had thoughtfully lit for them swayed with the motion of the ship.

She was so beautiful Kit's heart lurched painfully in his chest. He could hear the nervousness in her voice, despite her seeming composure and her conversation about something as commonplace as damp bedding. That was an attempt, he knew, to talk about anything except what lay between them.

"But then so are we," St. John reminded her softly.

She smiled at him, but the corners of her lips were slightly tremulous. She would be as apprehensive about this as he. Kit had made her a promise, and he had kept to it scrupulously throughout the brief days of this unconsummated marriage. But occasionally there had been something in her eyes that made him question the conclusions he had drawn about Haviland's death and her grief. Something that reminded him of the image which had leapt into his mind as she put her cold, trembling hand into his the day they wed.

"Come inside," she invited.

She moved away from the bed and over to the low table where the sailor who had guided them to the cabin had placed their borrowed portmanteau.

Kit obeyed, closing the wooden door behind him, shutting out the rain and the low howl of the coastal wind. The resulting silence was almost shocking, as if they had finally managed to shut out the howls of the outside world as well. To be transported back to the few, quiet hours they had once spent alone together.

Judith looked up at the sudden silence, and the same memories he fought were suddenly in her eyes. *Will you tell me the truth?* he had asked, and he knew now that she never had.

''There's a peg for your cloak,'' she said.

Obediently, Kit loosened the fastenings and swung the military cape off his shoulders. He shook it once so that the moisture fell, leaving a pattern like rain over the scarred wooden floor. He was aware that Judith watched him as he moved across the cabin to hang the garment where she'd indicated.

He walked back to face her. He reached out to untie her cloak, and her eyes widened as his fingers came near. He deliberately ignored her surprise and continued to untie the black silk cording. Almost grateful for the opportunity to escape, it seemed, she turned her back when he had finished that task, allowing him to lift the cloak away from her body.

When they'd first entered, the room had been filled with the odor of brine, of tar and hemp; now these were joined by the unmistakable smell of wet wool.

And underlying them all was something that moved in Kit's memory, evoking feelings long denied. That undernote was the pleasant aroma that was uniquely Judith. He was standing so close to her that when he inhaled, the warm scent of her body filled his senses. A delicate combination of rose water and soap. Of clean skin. The fragrance of her hair, spread like a dark, perfumed cloud across his chest and shoulders.

That was fantasy, but the image was no less powerful because it was not real and had not been experienced. Imagination was, of course, the most potent of aphrodisiacs. As was anticipation.

They stirred in his groin, demanding. Needing. He needed Judith. Her comfort and kindness and her concern. Beyond those, he needed to lose himself in the hot, sweet oblivion of desire. To bury the frustrations and bitterness that had tormented him these last days in the welcoming softness of her body.

"The room seems very small," she said, turning back to him.

He was still holding her cloak, so he folded it carefully over his arm, working very hard to regain the control he had imposed on himself for so long. "There's nowhere else for me to go, Judith. I'm sorry for that."

"I'm not," she said, smiling. "I think it would be lonely here without you. And a little frightening."

"You don't like the sea?" he asked, turning to hang her cloak on the peg beside his. Then, as she had done, he put his palm down against the clammy coldness of the sheets. Both actions hid his face for a few moments so, he hoped, she would not be able to read in his eyes what he had been thinking.

"I am *not* a good sailor," she said. "I should have warned you." That appealing touch of self-mockery was in her voice.

"Then I'll play at nursemaid," he said.

"Perhaps if the sea is calm, you won't have to. If," she said, "you are very lucky."

The luckiest bastard alive, Kit thought. And when she smiled at him, there was not even an echo of irony or bitterness in the remembrance of that once-familiar epithet.

The crossing, however, was difficult from the first. The spring storms had apparently arrived early, and waves tossed the heavy transport as if it were a rowboat. Judith spent the first night alternating between bouts of extreme seasickness and exhausted snatches of sleep. Whatever nervousness she had felt at their enforced proximity evaporated.

Finally, she ceased to be ill only because there was nothing else within her stomach to be gotten out. That was when Kit had teasingly plied her with rum, its potency cut with a little water. He poured out a measure of it from an ornately engraved silver flask. A gift from Lord Wellington, he explained, a wedding present and a farewell memento.

Judith certainly didn't want the drink, but Kit had so charmingly cajoled her, she finally gave in. She found that her husband's teasing was very difficult to resist. And besides, she remembered his very practical and competent kindness in tending to her while she was so embarrassingly ill.

She had drunk down the first draught, which, surprisingly, given the state of her stomach, stayed down. She hadn't even protested the second, which produced a most pleasant lethargy.

And at dawn she had awakened to find herself in Kit's arms. Tucked very comfortably beside him, she realized, his body protecting hers from the endlessly rolling motion of the ship.

Her head was cradled on his chest, and her hand had found a very natural resting place on the opposite broad shoulder. He held her, as he had held her in one way or another, through most of the long, intensely uncomfortable hours of this night. And in those hours, she found that their relationship seemed to have moved beyond embarrassment or pretense.

"Are you asleep?" she whispered. She turned her head

slightly, but she couldn't see his face. Given what had gone before, and their positions, that was perhaps just as well.

He must be very sorry of his bargain *this* morning, she thought. One of His Majesty's bad bargains, the soldiers called someone who didn't meet muster. That's what she had been for Kit—a very bad bargain indeed. In so many ways.

"You're supposed to be asleep," he said. The sound of the soft words rumbled beneath her ear, his voice deep and pleasant.

"I have been," she whispered.

"Better now?"

"All better," she agreed. "I'm sorry," she added.

"For being sick?" His question was touched with humor. The tone of his voice was distorted by the position of her ear over his chest, but still, his amusement had been obvious.

"For everything," she confessed softly.

She *was* truly sorry for it all. For the scandal. For the disgrace she had unwittingly brought into his life. He had been forced to marry her, by the constraints imposed on him by his honor and probably by Wellington's command as well.

She knew very well the real reason Kit had sold his commission. A soldier's daughter, Judith knew, probably better than he, how the small world of the British army really worked.

"For everything?" he questioned.

She said nothing for a moment, wondering how she could adequately express her regret for the fact that she had ruined his life. She had never intended that. She had loved him, and because she did, she had allowed herself to reach out and grasp something she knew had never really been intended for someone like her. And now…

"If you mean last night," he said, interrupting that self-castigation, "then I think the scales are still tilted very heavily in your favor."

"The scales?"

"You cared for me far longer than I have cared for you."

"But not like this," she protested, thinking of the events of last night, thankfully clouded by the alcohol-induced haze that affected her this morning.

"No," he suggested softly, "your nursing was in fact far more..." He hesitated, but his deep voice was still relaxed. Still unembarrassed. "Far more intimate," he finished finally.

If she had been able to see his face, she might have been more inhibited. But here, held warmly against the strength of his body, the fingers of his right hand moving slowly, caressing small circles on her back, she felt safe from his possible disgust, and even from her own discomfiture.

"I didn't mind," she whispered, remembering those days in the old woman's hut, removed from the world and from all other considerations except tending to the needs of the man she loved.

"But I must confess that I *did* mind," Kit said. His voice, however, was still laced with amusement.

"Is that why you sent me away that night?"

"I sent you away..." he began, and then the words faded.

She waited a long time, feeling the slow, steady rise and fall of his chest beneath her cheek and listening to his heartbeat. It had quickened when she asked her question, but now it returned to the measured tempo it had held to before.

"I sent you away," he said finally, "because that wasn't the kind of intimacy I wanted."

"Not the *kind* of intimacy?" she questioned. But after

all, she had been Michael Haviland's wife for almost three years. There were so many kinds of intimacy.

"*Not* the kind that involved nursing," he said.

She thought about what he had said, trying not to read more into that simple statement than she should, although her own heart rate had accelerated.

"You cared for me," she reminded him softly.

She pushed up on her elbow so she could see his face. Sometime during the long night, Kit had turned the lamp down very low. The deep shadows it cast drifted again, back and forth, across those handsome, aristocratic features.

"Because you needed me to care for you," he said simply.

It was what he would have done for any comrade, she realized. For any of the men under his command. Whatever St. John had been when he had come to Iberia, he was now the kind of man who would always care for those who needed him. If they belonged to him. If they were his responsibility.

There aren't many choices where duty is involved, he had once told her. And he had been the kind of officer who made the difficult ones. That was all he meant, she had decided, when he added something else, the words very soft.

"And because I wanted to care for you," he said.

Her eyes stung, but she blinked away the moisture, hoping that in the shadows he had not seen it. And that he would never be aware of how much that simple phrase had meant to her.

Only here, Judith, could someone like you... Michael's taunt echoed suddenly in her heart. *Only here...*

Kit had married her because he had been forced to, she reminded herself. Now perhaps he had decided that, since they were wed, he must make the best of his bad bargain

She could not allow herself to read too much into those idle words. Kit was her husband. Caring for her was his duty. And he would fulfill that duty, as he had all the others.

"Thank you for what you did last night," she whispered.

She watched his mobile lips tilt at her politeness. His lean face was relaxed and without tension, as she had not seen it in so many days.

"You're very welcome," he said softly.

His head began to lift. His eyes seemed to be focused on her mouth. As if he intended— Suddenly she was aware again, unromantically, of the more unpleasant aspects of last night. Instinctively, she recoiled, pressing her lips together and putting the tips of her fingers over them. It was a defensive gesture, not prompted by the interpretation he put on it.

"Are you ill?" he asked. He sat up, raising her carefully.

"No," she protested. "No, I'm..." She stopped, and took a breath, reading concern in his eyes now, and certainly not what she had believed might have been in them before. Wishful thinking, she supposed. "A little sick, maybe," she lied.

"Then fresh air," Kit said decisively. "And there's nothing more beautiful than the sea at dawn. Especially after a storm. Would like me to show you?" he invited.

She nodded. At least that would remove them from the confines of this small room. And perhaps she did need fresh air to clear her head, to blow away the remains of the sickness and even the effects of the rum he'd given her, because sometime during their conversation, she had begun to hope...

Kit suddenly swung his long legs off the bed and then stood beside it, stretching with the grace of a big cat. He ran his right hand through the black curls, which were still too short to have become very disarrayed in sleep.

He had removed his uniform coat before he lay down, and she could see the muscles in his back and shoulders, their movement delineated under the thin lawn of his shirt. Her eyes traced down his slim hips and over the muscles of his buttocks and thighs, clearly revealed by the tight-knit pantaloons he wore.

He reached to pull his cloak off the peg and swirled it with the ease of long practice over his wide shoulders. Then he took hers, holding it out with both hands despite his damaged arm, inviting her to step within the welcoming warmth of its folds.

Obediently Judith crawled out of the bed they had shared last night, brushing distractedly at the skirt of her borrowed dress. At least that gave her something to do with her trembling hands. And something to look at besides her husband's body.

The gown was too badly wrinkled, however, for her efforts to do much good, so she wisely gave up the attempt and moved to stand in front of Kit, her back to him. He laid the cloak over her shoulders and reached around her body to fasten the cords.

She looked down, watching the long brown fingers working competently just beneath her chin. They had been just as skillful in their ministrations last night. Holding her, pressing a cold cloth against her face, touching her with compassion. His hands had been as soothing as his calm, low voice had been through the long hours.

They stood a moment when Kit had finished with the cords. She fought the urge to lean into his body, against which she had sheltered last night. Somehow, she had lost the license to touch him, which her illness and the darkness had given her then.

Once more St. John seemed almost a stranger. Someone she didn't know very well at all, despite their enforced intimacy. *Intimacy.* Her mind repeated the word, remembering how it had sounded when he whispered it and what it had seemed to imply. *Intimacy.*

His hands lifted the hood of her cloak and placed the cloth protectively over her head. As she began to tuck in the tangled strands of her hair, she felt his hands fasten gently on her shoulders. He leaned forward and put his chin against the top of her head. He held it there for only a second before he moved, pressing his lips now at the spot where his chin had rested.

Then he stepped back and removed his hands from her shoulders, releasing her. She listened without moving as his footsteps crossed the wooden floor behind her.

Finally she began the prosaic task of pulling on the damp gloves she had stuffed into the pocket of her cloak last night. She could barely see her fingers, her vision blurred by the same unexpected rush of tears she had experienced before.

She had gone through so many things in the last few months, horrors that were truly worthy of tears, but she had not given in to them. Now it seemed she was destined to succumb to that very feminine weakness at the slightest excuse—a kind word or the impersonal touch of her new husband's lips.

The sudden rush of cold air from the door Kit opened was welcome. It broke the pull of emotion, clearing her head and sweeping away the stuffiness of the small cabin. Blinking at the light and trying to banish the moisture from her eyes, Judith turned and found that Kit was watching her from the open doorway.

In his eyes was an expression she had never seen there before. But then, there were so many things she didn't know about him. Still, they had survived the night, and they were leaving behind them in Portugal the painful scandal that threatened disgrace. Together they would build a new life in England.

Home, she thought, finally allowing herself the luxury of acknowledging how glad she would be to leave this country and the memories of the last three years behind. The thought of a new beginning was as welcome as the rush of fresh air into the cabin had been. It banished the shadows and destroyed the pervasive, damp miasma of the long night they had passed through.

From the doorway, Kit held out his hand, an invitation to join him, as clear and compelling as that same gesture had been beside the mountain stream. This time, however, the long brown fingers did not tremble.

This was not a man who needed her care, and not a man who would ever disappoint or abuse her. This was a man who was both strong enough to protect and gentle enough to shelter, as he had done last night.

She smiled at him, and perhaps even at the pink-tinged dawn that gilded the dark panorama of sea and unclouded sky that stretched beyond him. The long storm, it seemed, was finally over.

Chapter Thirteen

It was Roger who met their ship. Kit had written his brother, and Wellington had kindly offered to include the brief message in the diplomatic pouch. He could give no guarantee, of course, that the letter would arrive in England before the transports, but apparently it had.

The missive contained only the barest bones of what had occurred in Portugal. Kit included the news of his marriage, and Judith's parentage by way of an introduction. He also mentioned that his wife was a widow, but deliberately avoided any details about her previous marriage or her husband's death. It was not that Kit distrusted his brother, but the fewer who knew about the controversy they had left behind them, the better.

Despite the contrast between his stolid practicality and Kit's restless wildness, despite the nearly five-year difference in their ages, he and Roger had always been close. And he knew that his brother had protected him from their father's wrath on more occasions than they either would wish to recall.

"This is Judith," Kit said after he and his older brother had exchanged their somewhat restrained greetings.

Roger took Judith's hand, bringing her fingers to his lips. "I'm very glad to have finally acquired a sister," he said.

His blue eyes, very much like Kit's own, seemed to study Judith's face a moment before he said, "My mother asked me to make her apologies. I'm afraid she's been a bit unwell this winter. Nothing serious," he added, seeing Kit's quick concern. "She hopes you'll forgive her. She's waiting for you at home."

"There's nothing to forgive, of course," Judith said. "I'm very sorry she's been ill."

Roger smiled at her. Then his gaze left her face to examine his brother's. "The rest of your luggage?" he asked, rather than voicing the questions which were in his eyes.

Kit glanced down at the battered case which contained both his and Judith's meager possessions. And they were lucky, of course, to have those. "That's all of it, I'm afraid," he admitted. He could see the quick shock in Roger's face, but his brother made no comment before gesturing to the waiting coachman.

The man handled the portmanteau so gingerly that his reluctance to touch it was obvious. His manner bordered on impertinence, something that would surely have set off Kit's uncertain temper three years ago. Now he found the coachman's snobbery merely ridiculous.

Judith's eyes met his, and in them was an amusement that matched his own. *Even the servants are offended by our baggage,* hers seemed to say. *Baggages,* Kit thought, remembering the rag and tag collection of women and children who invariably followed in the tail of the army. That derogatory term might now be used to describe the two of them, he thought. And as he watched, his wife's small smile widened, almost as if she read his mind.

Reluctantly, he pulled his gaze from her face, breaking the connection that had sparked between them. On board the crowded transport, with its enforced proximity, he and Judith had at least reclaimed the friendship they had once shared.

There had still been moments of tension, of course, especially since they had to keep up the pretense that theirs was a normal marriage. They dined with the captain each evening and had discovered to their mutual delight that his love of books was as deep as their own. They matched wits over literary arguments, their discussions far-ranging and very pleasantly ordinary after the horrors they had endured.

Kit and the captain took a long walk around the deck each evening after they had escorted Judith to the cabin. By the time Kit returned, his wife had changed into her nightgown, another outsized garment loaned her by Mrs. Stuart, and was tucked safely between the damp sheets of the bed, pretending to be asleep.

Each night they shared the cabin, but never again the wide bed and so never with the intimacy he had confessed to her he wanted. Given the revelation he had made, Kit felt that the next move must be up to Judith. As yet, she had given him no indication she was ready to make it. Perhaps, he thought, that would change now that they were home.

Kit handed his wife into the carriage and was about to climb up into the seat when Roger stopped him by placing his hand on his arm. "He wants to see you," his brother said softly. "This afternoon. As soon as we arrive at the town house."

His father, Kit realized. "Let me guess," Kit said sarcastically. "Because he's missed me?"

"Because..." Roger began, and then he paused. "Because of what he's heard about Portugal. About what happened there."

For a moment sickness stirred in his throat, and then Kit

realized that this summons didn't necessarily have to be about the scandal. "And exactly what has Ryde heard about Portugal?"

"About her," Roger said, his voice still too low to carry into the interior of the carriage. "About your marriage."

Kit laughed, and shock touched his brother's eyes. He knew Roger could never understand the bitterness of that laughter. Nothing of what he had accomplished in Iberia had reached his father's notice. Or if it had, Ryde had chosen to ignore it.

St. John had led his men well enough to have earned their respect. And even, in some cases, their love as he had been very honored to realize. His actions had been mentioned in the dispatches on at least a half dozen occasions, and Wellington was not known for citing his officers except for extreme bravery.

None of that mattered, of course. Not beside the other. The scandal was all his father had taken notice of, it seemed. All he wished to speak to him about.

"Tell him," Kit said, his voice as low as his brother's, but each word enunciated distinctly, leaving no doubt about the import or the tone of the message Roger was intended to convey. "Tell him I'll see him when I can find time. But not today, Roger. Will you tell him that for me?"

"Don't be a fool," his brother warned. "You really can't afford to alienate him any further."

"I doubt that I could," Kit said truthfully. "Tell him I'll come when I can find time," he said again. Then he shook off his brother's arm and climbed into the waiting coach. It was several long seconds before Roger followed.

They didn't speak of it again. Judith and his brother made polite, idle conversation during the journey home, but Kit took no part in that. He looked instead out the window of the carriage at the countryside they passed, thinking how little anything had changed during the last three years. And how unlikely it was now that it ever would.

"Tell me the truth, damn you," his father said. "About her. The Haviland woman. About her husband's death."

"The truth, sir, is that Judith is my wife. And that Michael Haviland died while on an important and dangerous mission he had volunteered to undertake. He died trying to save the lives of wounded men and the women."

"That isn't what I've been told."

"But you asked *me* to tell you the truth," Kit said softly.

He had known how this would go. It was the same pattern as all their encounters. This one would be no different from any of the others, and he had acknowledged that before it even began. Except, he supposed, this might well be the last of them.

"Do you know that he's been here? In this house," his father said. Ryde was furious. His voice was controlled, as always, but there was a streak of color over his high cheekbones.

"Michael Haviland?" Kit asked with pseudo-politeness, while trying to imagine who his father could be talking about. But then, it didn't really matter who had been here, he decided. Obviously *someone* had rushed to tattle to the earl about the scandal. "If you've been a victim of ghostly visitations, sir," Kit said, "then might I suggest that—"

"Not Haviland, you fool," the earl interrupted, cutting through the mocking suggestion. "His damned batman."

"His batman?" Kit exclaimed, his voice wiped clean of mockery. They had left Reynolds behind them in Portugal, along with his lies. Or so he had believed. But if the batman was here in England, then that explained, of course, how the gossip had arrived before them.

"Only he's not a batman any longer. Or even, apparently, a soldier," his father said.

Wellington hadn't known that Reynolds fell into that group he had so casually mentioned—troopers whose terms of service were up. And with the destruction of his regiment, no one would even try very hard to convince Private Reynolds to reenlist. So, frightened by Wellington's warning perhaps, the batman had beaten them home, securing passage on one of the returning ships. And his first destination, it seemed, had been this house.

"What did he want?" Kit asked. Nothing about this nightmare could surprise him anymore. The gossip Reynolds spread seemed like the mythical Hydra. If one of its heads were cut off, it simply grew another.

"Money, of course," his father said. "A great deal of money, as a matter of fact."

"And did you give it to him?" Kit asked, knowing the answer before his father gave it.

"You know me better than *that,* I should think. I sent him packing."

"But you listened to all his lies before you did."

At the accusation in Kit's tone, the patchy color deepened in the earl's pale face. "Lies?" he asked sarcastically. "Lies about how you sent *another* man to his death to secure something you wanted. Nothing has changed, St. John," Ryde said. "You *still* know nothing of honor."

Kit wondered if there was anything that would ever make a difference in his father's opinion of him. It was his own fault, he supposed. Or the fault of the man he had once been.

That all seemed so long ago. He had stood before this same desk and been told that Spain and Wellington might make a man of him. And in fairness, he thought they had. His father had at least been right about that.

"I know enough about it to realize that honor isn't what the world says about you," Kit said. "And I finally understand that if you have it, there is nothing anyone can do that can take it from you. They may destroy your reputation or even destroy you, but honor is inviolate. And indestructible. I have nothing I need to explain, not to you nor to anyone else, sir, about what happened in Portugal. You are quite free, of course, to believe whatever you wish."

His father's eyes had widened, and his face suffused with blood, but for once it seemed he was speechless. For the first time in Kit's memory, the earl of Ryde had nothing to say to his profligate son.

Kit turned, the movement unconsciously precise, almost military. He walked across the vast salon of the town house, his footsteps echoing, and closed its door behind him. His father had asked him for the truth, and what he had told him, Kit knew, was as near to that as he was ever likely to come.

"We don't have to stay here," Judith said. "We can go to my father's."

"I'm through running," Kit said. "We left Portugal because I let Wellington convince me it would be best. I find now that it wasn't. It has only been construed as an acknowledgment of guilt. I'm not leaving London."

He had been surprised that his father hadn't required that of him. Kit had not seen the earl since their confrontation almost two weeks ago, but he and Judith were still living in his father's London town house.

The first night, his mother had hesitantly suggested that they might wish to dine in their rooms, due to their exhaustion from the journey and their status as newlyweds. Kit had made no comment, and the practice had simply continued. Every day for the last two weeks their meals had been laid in this suite, effectively isolating them from the rest of the household.

Kit saw Roger and his mother on occasion, but never Ryde. And he found that was no longer even a matter for regret. He and Haviland really *had* been more alike than he realized, Kit thought, remembering the captain's bitter questions.

"Do you love your father, St. John? Have you sought his approval your whole bloody life and known that you never quite lived up to his expectations? Do you have any idea what it's like never to measure up? No matter how hard you try?"

Never to measure up, Kit repeated mentally. And he never had.

"Why are you doing this?" Judith asked. "There's no point. We both know now that we can't put an end to what's being said. Not even by staying in town."

He nodded, his eyes tracing over her face. The strain was beginning to take its toll, even on Judith's courage and determined composure. The direct cuts and even the more discreet whispers they had endured in London were far worse than any of the hardships of war they had once faced together.

Then there had been some purpose in the suffering. This was…senseless, meaningless. And it was fueled by one man's lies and innuendoes. When the earl refused to give in to his blackmail, Toby Reynolds had apparently taken the revenge he promised. As he probably would have in any case, Kit acknowledged. He didn't blame his father, because he himself would have given Reynolds the same answer, of course.

"I never meant for this to happen," he said. "I thought I was doing what was best for you."

"If we go to my father's…" she said again.

The suggestion faded when he caught her hand. "I can make arrangements for you to leave tomorrow," he offered.

"For *me* to leave?" she repeated.

"I'm not leaving London, Judith. I'm not running away from their whispers again. I've done nothing wrong."

Nothing except to love you, Kit acknowledged, *long before I had the right.* Although he had searched his conscience, he truly believed that there was no other decision he could have made in Portugal than the fateful one he had come to. The one that had allowed Michael Haviland to undertake the mission that had ended in his death. The mission which had, ironically, saved Haviland's honor and destroyed his own.

"I know," she said. "If you're staying, Kit, then so am I."

"It might be better—" he began.

"No," she said. "If you're staying in London, then so am I."

He still held her hand. He realized that her slender fingers had finally taken on the smoothness they deserved, that he had wanted for them. He released them reluctantly and watched as they fell against the rich fabric of her skirt. Judith Haviland had at last become his lady, and she looked the part.

The gown she was wearing had been cut to Kit's exacting demands. The garnet silk was as becoming to her coloring as he had known it would be. Her darkly shining hair, highlighted with gold by the myriad candles, had been piled high on her head in loose curls. The style emphasized the slender length of her neck and the oval perfection of her face. Under his supervision, Judith had come into her own, as beautiful now in the eyes of others as she had always been in his.

Not always, he acknowledged, mocking his own arrogant

stupidity when he had first seen her, more than five years ago. It was a meeting he had never been able to remember, and it had taken place here in London. So they had come full circle, he supposed. Except now he was the outcast, the one who didn't fit in, and she...

She was the most intriguing woman in the capital. Even Roger had commented on the flattering masculine attention that followed Judith the few times they had gone out to the opera or the theater. Of course, the whispers had followed them as well.

Part of the fascination the *ton* felt was no doubt because Judith was the woman who had lured the infamous St. John astray. A woman worth committing murder for, they whispered. Although he hoped Judith was not, Kit was certainly sophisticated enough to understand that the men who watched her speculated about what she had done to win London's most notorious rake.

They would probably never understand her true attraction, Kit thought. Her honesty and courage had won his heart. They, of course, were looking for quite different attributes from the woman who, they supposed, had ensnared St. John so strongly that he had arranged her husband's death so he could have her.

That belief was in their eyes. Kit saw it clearly, although he believed Judith was unaware of it, at least, he hoped, as yet unaware. But realizing that he couldn't protect her from what was being said, he had finally stopped taking her into society.

Kit himself still visited his clubs and the other haunts he was accustomed to frequent when he was in town. He would be damned if that bastard and his lies would drive him into hiding. But he would no longer allow Judith to be subjected to the snubs and the covertly vicious tongues of the London *ton*.

Nothing was said openly, of course, or within his hearing. Given his reputation with a pistol, few men were brave enough to give him a direct cut. He almost admired those who did.

They were his fellow officers. He had called none of them out, of course, but their actions, and the realization that his own kind had rejected him, hurt far more than the other. He did not even recognize the irony that he now considered himself one with that group of veterans rather than with the far more select circle of aristocrats to which he had belonged since birth.

"St. John?"

Kit raised his eyes from the paper he had been pretending to read straight into those of the speaker. The man who had questioned his identity was no one he recognized.

He was elderly and obviously frail, but the posture was unmistakable. His thin shoulders were erect, and his spine held as straight as a ramrod, despite the ebony walking stick he carried. His black eyes were as piercing, as accustomed to staring down subalterns apparently, as were Lord Wellington's.

It was afternoon, and a pleasant drowsiness had settled over the few inhabitants of White's, the foremost gentleman's club in London. There were none of Kit's onetime cronies here at this hour, of course, which was why he had chosen it.

He made frequent appearances at his club, determined not to let the gossip drive him away, but he seldom came when he might expect his former friends to be in attendance. Kit had found he could no longer bear to be coldly shut out of the circle of which he had once been the acknowledged leader.

"I'm St. John," Kit said. *A friend of his father's?* he wondered. The age was right, but somehow…

The rest of the thought faded as the old man began to pull off his gloves. His hands were as pale as his face, blue veins prominent under the thin skin. Kit's eyes came back to the man's face, and for the first time, apprehension stirred in his gut. There was something in those eyes he should recognize. Something so familiar that it pulled at his mind, urging him to remember.

"Would you stand up, sir," the old man demanded. He held his gloves loosely now in one hand, but his dark eyes had not wavered from Kit's. The words were a command, uttered in a voice that expected nothing less than obedience.

Conditioned during his years on the Peninsula to respond automatically to that exact tone, Kit closed the *Times,* holding its flimsy pages in his right hand, unconsciously using his forefinger to mark his place before he rose. Standing at his full height, Kit almost towered over the visitor.

The old man's eyes were still intent on his. He moved slowly enough that Kit could have avoided the blow, but by that time he understood what was happening, of course. And he knew whose eyes these reminded him of.

The leather gloves were supple from age, but the sound of the blow Roland Haviland struck with them was as shocking in the quiet confines as if it had been a gunshot. Heads turned at the noise, and a few that had been nodding over an afternoon brandy jerked upright. Kit himself, however, didn't react in any way, except for the uncontrollable draining of blood from his face.

The gloves struck again, moving in the direction opposite to that which they had taken before. The shock had faded enough that Kit felt the second blow. And he was humiliatingly aware of the horrified fascination with which the members of this elite establishment were watching this encounter.

"A coward as well as a murderer, I see," Sir Roland Haviland said. His voice had not been raised, and St. John was probably the only one who had clearly heard the accusation.

"I didn't kill your son," Kit said.

"You ordered him on a mission that you hoped would result in his death," the old man accused.

"Not even that, I swear to you. Your son volunteered for a task which he knew was dangerous and necessary. He died a hero's death, Sir Roland. But not, I swear to you, at my instigation."

The dark eyes held to his, wanting to believe him, Kit thought. And he was aware when the decision was made not to.

"Will you not meet me, you bloody coward?" Haviland asked.

"There's no point in this. There's no basis for the story you've been told. It's only one man's vindictive lies."

"You killed my son so you could marry his strumpet wife," the old man said, his voice raised to carry throughout the quiet room. At what he saw in Kit's eyes, Haviland smiled, triumphant, believing that he had succeeded in what he had come here to accomplish. "Send your second to me," he suggested.

Honor isn't what the world says about you, St. John had told his father. It was not, of course, what the world said about Judith either. She would be the last to wish this meeting, or to forgive him for it, no matter what the old man said.

"I won't fight you, Sir Roland," Kit denied. "Our meeting will serve no purpose."

"It will serve *my* purpose."

With those words, Haviland raised the stick he carried in a whistling arc high above his head and brought it down on Kit's shoulder. Again the shock of the old man's action was great enough that Kit didn't try to ward off the blow. St. John didn't move until the stick lifted again.

This time Kit caught it before it struck, and wrenched it out of the frail, trembling fingers. He threw the cane from him, hearing the wood clatter and bounce across the marble floor, the noise it made far too loud in the stunned silence of the room.

"Meet me, damn you," Haviland demanded, "or I'll have my coachman thrash you like the sniveling coward you are. And then I'll have her dragged through the streets like the whore *she* is."

Haviland's voice had risen so that it echoed now against the marble and the fine oak paneling, the words as jarring to the room's normal tranquillity as the obscene clatter the stick had made. Almost against his will, his body flooded with fury and adrenaline, Kit nodded.

Satisfied, the general nodded in return. Then Michael Haviland's aging father turned on his heel, his back still militarily straight, and marched across the marble floor toward the street. He didn't bother to retrieve the walking stick.

Behind him the silence in the club welled like a chorus of condemnation. St. John was not aware of it, of course. He was thinking instead about Judith. And about all that he had lost.

He knew now what he must do. Everything was clear in his mind, the plan of action formed in its entirety as had sometimes happened to him on the battlefield. It was all laid out before him, as plain as if someone had drawn him a map.

There was no doubt and no decision to be made about

what would happen next, because it was exactly as he had already told his father.

They may destroy your reputation or even destroy you, he had said to Ryde, *but honor is inviolate.*

Chapter Fourteen

"**Y**ou can't fight Haviland," Kit's brother said.

"He didn't give me a choice, Roger. Believe me, I did everything in my power to avoid meeting him."

"This is beyond the pale, Kit. Even you must see that. If you kill that old man, you'll be an outcast."

"I'm already an outcast," Kit said truthfully. "But I won't kill Haviland. I promise you that."

"You didn't *intend* to kill Edmonton either. Things happen in a duel that are beyond anyone's control. But even your intent to meet Haviland—"

"He threatened to have his coachman thrash me in White's. Would you and Father have preferred the notoriety engendered by that display?" St. John asked softly.

The reasonable question gave his brother pause, but as the earl would have done, Roger rose to the occasion. "Father and I would have preferred that none of this ever came to pass," he said stiffly. "It's simply another blot on the family name."

"I never meant for it to happen, Roger, I assure you."

"You never do. It's your damned recklessness. If only you would—"

"Please, don't treat me to a lecture," Kit broke in.

"Once you're Ryde, you may control your sons as you wish, but I ask you to remember that you are *not* my father."

His brother's mouth tightened, but he didn't make the rejoinder that almost echoed between them. *Thank God for that,* Kit was sure his brother wanted to say.

"The only thing you must answer for," St. John went on, ignoring Roger's anger, "is whether or not you're willing to serve as my second. And before you refuse," Kit added, modifying the edge that had crept into his own voice, "I should warn you that there is no one else I can ask. At least no one who would agree. I'm depending on you, I'm afraid, and hoping that you may have still have some family feeling for me."

"Kit, surely you must see—"

"No more," Kit said, holding out his hand to stop the flow of unneeded advice. He had known there was no way to avoid the duel when he had looked into Roland Haviland's eyes.

They had been filled with an inflexible determination Kit had seen only once in the eyes of Haviland's son during the entire three years he had known him. And that was on the day Michael Haviland had talked Kit into allowing him to undertake the mission to Wellington.

"Will you second me or not?" Kit asked again.

The brothers' eyes met and held. In Roger's were unanswerable questions and regret. In the other pair was simply resignation. And the carefully concealed knowledge that what had begun in Portugal was, at last, almost over.

Finally Roger nodded. Kit clasped his brother's shoulder quickly and squeezed, exactly as he had once done, he remembered suddenly, with Sergeant Cochran. "Good man," Kit said softly.

This time, however, there was no respect in the eyes that

met his. But, Kit realized gratefully, nor was there within them the slightest awareness of what he intended.

News of the upcoming duel spread throughout the *ton,* as all rumors in London eventually did. The Season was winding down, and aristocratic boredom had set in.

Matches had been made and relentlessly examined to determine which party had gotten the advantage. Fortunes had been won, or more frequently lost, on a horse race or the turn of a card. And there had been at least one affair of honor, but whatever it had been about had apparently been settled to everyone's satisfaction with the first prick of a rapier.

This meeting, it was understood, would be something very different. Haviland was out for blood, of course, seeking revenge for his son's murder. St. John had already killed one man, it was whispered to those who might have forgotten, and his unquestioned skill with the pistol was well documented.

And, it was ventured by those knowledgeable about such things, this duel would be little more than a slaughter. It was true that Haviland had once been a notable shot, but given his age and recent stroke, it was almost certain St. John would be the victor.

The general consensus was that, considering those factors, St. John should never have accepted the old man's challenge. None of those who so vehemently voiced that opinion bothered to explain how he could have avoided it, given Haviland's actions in White's that day. The word murderer was again being bandied in the clubs and gaming hells and even in shocked whispers in spacious, flower-scented ballrooms. And eventually, of course, it reached the ears of the ladies.

The thought that Judith might hear of the challenge never

crossed Kit's mind. With the help of his man of business, St. John had made the necessary provisions for the settlement of his estate. He would instruct Roger to see that they were carried out. Judith would be taken care of. He had seen to that.

What he had not seen to, because he could not have anticipated it, was his wife's reaction to the duel. And ironically, Judith's reaction was the one thing which might have prevented St. John from reaching the fateful decision he had come to that day in White's.

The musicale was no duller than those she had endured during her Season, Judith supposed, but somehow, given her far more exciting, although sometimes terrifying experiences on the Peninsula, the afternoon seemed endless.

She had agreed to attend the entertainment today only because the countess insisted. She wondered if Kit's mother had any idea of what was being said about Judith and her son. She also wondered if this afternoon's public appearance might possibly be some misguided attempt on the part of the Countess of Ryde to try to redeem them both in the eyes of society.

If so, it was destined to fail, of course. No one had been openly rude as the countess had taken her around the room to make her introductions. Most of the women in attendance were old friends of her mother-in-law's. The countess had, therefore, every confidence that this outing could be accomplished without incident. And it almost was.

The newest twist to the scandal was far too exciting *not* to have been a topic of conversation, however, even in these genteel environs. Since the countess and Lady St. John were fellow guests, it had, of course, been a very discreet one. It was not until the harpist had finished her performance and the polite farewells had begun that Judith learned about the proposed duel.

She and her mother-in-law had already reached the entryway, their coachman called and their wraps brought, when the countess discovered she had left her fan in the salon. Judith dutifully volunteered to fetch it.

The comment she overheard when she reentered the room had never been intended for her ears. And she would never have heard it had Lady Marbury been a little less hard-of-hearing or a little less given to making decisive pronouncements on every topic.

"Then there will be the blood of *two* Haviland men on St. John's hands, my dear. You mark my words," the old woman said.

The ringing tones in which she ventured that opinion might well have been heard in the back row of the Haymarket Theatre. They certainly were loud enough to carry to the ears of the slender woman who had hesitated in the doorway of the elegant gold-and-white salon.

"I beg your pardon?" Judith said. At her question, the shocked gaze of every one of the gossiping women focused on her white face. Lady Marbury's mouth opened and then closed, rather like a dying fish, but apparently she thought better of whatever explanation she had been about to make. Her spinster daughter, who was standing beside her, blushed such an unbecoming shade that her complexion almost blended with the puce of her gown. But neither of them attempted to deny the import of the comment.

"Were you speaking of my husband?" Judith asked calmly, her eyes far more demanding than her voice had been.

"Which one, my dear?" Lady Marbury parried adroitly. "I find it so difficult to keep them straight."

"Lord St. John," Judith said evenly. "Who, I assure you, has *no one's* blood on his hands."

"Indeed?" the old woman questioned with feigned politeness. "I admire your loyalty, my dear, but that isn't what we've been told."

"Whatever gossip you've heard about my husband, I assure you that you may discredit both it *and* the talebearer. There's not a word of truth in those malicious rumors now circulating. I was in Portugal. Surely I'm in a better position to know exactly what occurred there than anyone here in London."

"Then why has he agreed to Sir Roland's challenge?"

"Sir Roland's challenge?" Judith repeated. Her breathing was suddenly constricted and the rush of blood through her head so strong she was almost faint with it.

"The duel is to take place at dawn day after tomorrow, I believe. I'm surprised you didn't know, Lady St. John," Lady Marbury suggested archly. "Given your very *close* relationship with both parties involved."

Judith didn't respond to the gibe. She walked across the room, deliberately holding her head high, and retrieved her mother-in-law's fan from the chair in which she'd been sitting. No one said another word as she walked past them and back to the entry. Lady Marbury's smile was triumphant, she noticed, probably because she was sure she had had the best of this encounter and because it would make such an entertaining story.

Judith, however, wasn't concerned with that. She was dealing instead with what she had just been told. Given what she knew of Michael's father, she knew she shouldn't be surprised that he had sought out St. John. The only question was: Why hadn't Kit told her?

When Lady St. John reentered her father-in-law's town house that afternoon, she thanked the countess for the afternoon's outing and then hurried up the stairs. She did not linger in her bedchamber longer than was necessary to remove her gloves and her pelisse before she opened the connecting door to the part of their suite which had hitherto been her husband's private domain.

She found him writing at his desk. If Kit was surprised at her unannounced and unprecedented visit, he hid it well. The blue eyes which lifted to meet hers were filled only with polite inquiry.

"Why?" she asked softly and watched as they changed.

St. John could not know, of course, what she had been told or how much she knew of the situation, but at least he didn't pretend not to understand.

"Because he left me no choice," Kit said simply.

"Could you not—" she began.

"If there had been any other option, Judith," Kit said, "I assure you I should have taken it."

"You won't..." Although her husband had made no interruption this time, her voice faded over the impossibility of voicing what was, to her at least, unthinkable. And she knew Kit wouldn't kill Sir Roland. She knew the kind of man St. John was far too well to believe he would shoot Michael's elderly father.

"No," he agreed finally when the silence between them had lasted a very long time. "Of course, I won't," he said. "We both understand that."

"Kit," she whispered.

At what was in her tone, finally he smiled at her. His blue eyes were very calm, but then he had had several days to come to terms with this. As she had not.

"You have to explain to him what really happened," she said.

"I gave my word, Judith, on my honor, that I would never divulge what occurred. And Michael gave me his."

"And kept it," she said softly, remembering the circumstances surrounding her first husband's death.

Kit nodded. "I have to do the same. Surely you understand that. I can't tell General Haviland or anyone else the truth."

"But you had *nothing* to do with Michael's death."

"No one believes that. Only you and I know what happened. And nothing I've said so far has made any difference in what they've chosen to believe."

"Then I will say it," she said. "*I'll* tell them the truth. And I'll *make* them believe me."

He smiled at her again. Almost for the first time since they had arrived in London, she realized, Kit's smile was as it had been before this had begun, without any trace of bitterness.

They had believed that in leaving Iberia, they could escape. They both knew now that they had been wrong. He had accepted that, but she could not, because if she did...

"They won't believe you," Kit advised. "Even if you tell them the truth, it will make no difference. Except it will defame Haviland's memory."

He was right, of course. She would not be believed. She had already been judged guilty, as had Kit. The truth would only give the gossips more grist for the slow-grinding mill of rumor. Perhaps Toby Reynolds had begun this, but they had all had a hand. All the scandalmongers.

Telling them the truth would not stop the talk because they would simply choose not to believe. The truth was not nearly so interesting as the lies they had devised to explain it away.

"Then I'll go to him. To Michael's father. I'll tell *him* the truth," Judith said. "And I'll make him listen to it."

"You're the one who wanted Michael to have a chance to redeem himself. Remember your reasons? To protect his father and yours—two fine old soldiers—from that very truth. And what we agreed to accomplished that. Would you destroy it all now?"

"If I have to," she said truthfully. "If that's the only way in which I can protect you." Something moved in his eyes at her words, an emotion that appeared briefly, burning within the blue as strongly as a rocket's flare.

"Thank you for that," he said softly. "But I think you, as much as I, are bound by the agreement we made. Haviland gave up his life to protect his father, to prevent him from finding out how far from his image of his son Michael really came. We agreed to those terms. *Neither* of us can now go back on our bargain, no matter how inconvenient it may now seem to be."

"Inconvenient," she repeated, her tone full of disbelief. "This isn't inconvenience. It's foolish, Kit. And it's incredibly dangerous. There is always the possibility…" The thought was too painful to put into words.

"There is nothing you can do to prevent this meeting, Judith. And nothing I can do. Haviland is determined. And you can't in honor reveal Michael's actions which led to his death on that mission, any more than I can."

He was right, she realized. Although she had sworn no oath, she, too, was bound by the sacrifice Michael had made to prevent his father from ever being hurt by his cowardice. And she was, after all, the one who had suggested her husband volunteer. In that, she bore far more guilt for Haviland's death than Kit. She had always understood and sympathized with Michael's reasons for wishing to protect his father. How could she now be the one to destroy the old man's hallowed view of his dead son?

"But I can talk to Sir Roland," she said. "At least I can

try to convince him that you had nothing to do with Michael's decision. I was Michael's wife. Surely he'll listen to me. He'll want to believe that Michael was everything he had hoped he would be. A hero who died a hero's death. I'll *make* him listen," she vowed desperately.

"Judith, he's already made up his mind. He's lost his only son, and he wants someone to blame. Or perhaps he believes that this scandal stains Michael's sacrifice. For whatever reason, he has chosen to hold me responsible for his death."

"But you weren't. Not in any way. Surely I can—"

"He thinks you were part of this," Kit warned softly. "Believe me, nothing you can say to him will change anything."

"But I have to try, Kit. This is my fault. All of it. Surely you see that I have to try."

But Kit had been right, of course. When she left General Haviland's house that evening, she had finally been forced to acknowledge that probably nothing *anyone* could say would change the old man's mind. Michael had been his son, and despite what her first husband had believed, his father had truly loved and admired him. And had convinced himself that Michael was all he wanted him to be.

Sir Roland had chosen to believe instead that she and Kit together had planned his valiant son's murder in order to satisfy their own lusts. Toby Reynolds's poison seeds had found fertile ground to grow in within the old man's stroke-damaged mind.

The realization that she had failed hurt far worse than the ranting denunciations her former father-in-law had made about what he imagined to be her role in Michael's death. Adulteress was the kindest of the appellations he had bestowed. And she knew now how he had managed to force

Kit to agree to meet him. Sir Roland himself had taken great delight in telling her.

She could never explain the impulse that caused her to stop at the door of her father-in-law's study before she climbed the stairs to her rooms. She had lived in his house for weeks, but she had not yet been introduced to Ryde, obviously because he had no wish to meet her. And, considering what she knew about his relationship with his younger son, she hadn't particularly wanted to meet the earl.

However, she acknowledged, the earl of Ryde was a very powerful man and no one, including herself, had more influence on Kit than his father. Her husband would certainly have denied the reality of her assessment, but almost every action he had taken since she had known him had been with some consideration of his father's opinion of him. Before she could change her mind, Judith opened the massive oak doors of Ryde's study.

The man who was seated behind the desk in the center of that vast room was not at all what she had expected. He was smaller and a far less intimidating presence than she had envisioned. His build was slight, narrower than Kit's tall, strongly muscled frame, and his thin face was deeply lined. And his hair, she realized, was almost as white as General Haviland's.

As the doors opened, the earl of Ryde glanced up from the papers scattered over the surface of his desk. His eyes examined her briefly through the lenses of the lorgnette he'd been using. A enormous cabochon ruby, set in the ducal ring he wore on the elegantly pale forefinger of his right hand, had gleamed in the lamplight when he raised his glasses.

She could see nothing of her husband in his features, but she didn't have long to make that evaluation. Apparently uninterested in what he saw, the earl's gaze returned to the material he had been perusing on her arrival. Rudely, he said nothing, treating her almost like one of the servants, who were supposed to be invisible, of course.

Undaunted, and having faced far more terrifying prospects than the earl of Ryde's studied disinterest during the last three years, Judith crossed the expanse of rich Oriental carpet. She stood before his desk in silence for several seconds, but her father-in-law didn't look up again.

Despite the gravity of the situation that had sent her here, Judith fought a smile, amused by his determined attempt to ignore her. She was not, he would find, so easily gotten rid of.

"I have come to ask for your help," she said finally.

Ryde's head lifted, his eyes meeting hers. "Indeed?" he inquired softly, one brow arching in question.

"I am Kit's wife."

"St. John," he corrected her, but at least he was listening.

"St. John," she amended dutifully. "Who plans to meet General Sir Roland Haviland at dawn on the day after tomorrow. I was not sure you had heard."

There was a brief silence, and then Ryde said, boredom injected almost theatrically into his voice, "What St. John does is of little moment to me. My son and I are *not* on terms. I think you, of all people, may imagine the reasons why," he added, before his gaze returned to the papers on his desk.

"Because of me?" Judith said. "Because of what is being said about what happened in Portugal?"

His eyes lifted again, and this time they focused on her face. She supposed Ryde was not often asked to explain himself, especially by a woman.

"I do not approve of my son's actions. I have told him

so. I am taking steps to see that St. John's scandals no longer reflect on this family."

"You're going to disown him," she guessed.

"It's something I should have done long ago. Family feeling, as you may imagine, prevented me. And, I suppose, the misguided hope that my son might change. I have been disappointed in that."

"Disappointed in your son?" Judith questioned softly. "Do you even know him, I wonder?"

The brow quirked again, but the cold eyes did not change. "I have known St. John all his life. Far better than you, I should think."

"Yet you believe what Haviland believes about him. Did you ask Kit to tell you what happened?"

"I did," Ryde said. His eyes said nothing beyond that.

"And what did he say?" Judith demanded softly.

"That your first husband volunteered to give up his life. A very convenient response on Haviland's part. And it certainly accomplished what you and Kit wanted. The story might even have worked, had not someone else survived to recount a very different version than the one you and St. John were putting about."

"Kit told you the truth," Judith said, ignoring the sarcasm, "but not the entire truth. Perhaps when you know it all—"

"I have no wish to 'know it all,' I assure you. The particulars of your sordid affair do not interest me in the slightest. Nor did the story St. John told."

"But it should," Judith said. "Because it *is* the truth."

The earl's features sharpened in distaste, and in his eyes was simply resignation. Judith took a breath, knowing that she would have only one chance. One opportunity to change his father's lifelong perception of St. John.

"Michael *did* volunteer, just as Kit told you, but there

was a very good reason for why he was willing to do so. And a very good reason for why Kit agreed to let him undertake the mission."

"I really am not interested—" Ryde began, but Judith interrupted him.

"This concerns your son. Your own flesh and blood. You *should* be interested."

"I see that you are determined to tell me this sad tale," the earl said sarcastically. "Can I not convince you—"

"No," Judith denied, shaking her head.

There was another silence, and then the earl put the lorgnette he was holding down on the papers and folded his hands. The long, aristocratic fingers appeared to be perfectly relaxed.

"Then I will beg you simply to be brief," he said.

"If you knew your son at all..." she began and realized her mistake. "But obviously you don't. I know, however, the kind of man St. John really is. I know his unquestioned and well-documented bravery in battle. You may verify that with the Horse Guards if you wish. But what won't be in those records is how St. John's men felt about him. They trusted him with their lives, and he never betrayed that trust. He cared for them. And in the end they not only respected him, they loved him."

The dark eyes considered her, but she could see no emotional response in them. To those who had never been in battle, perhaps it was difficult to understand how important those attributes were in an officer.

Judith took another breath, trying for calmness, trying to think what she might possibly say that could make a difference in a relationship that had become set and static long before she met Kit. And when she spoke again, it was not really about St. John at all.

"I have just come from Michael Haviland's father," she

said. There was a brief reaction to that in the dark eyes watching her, and she knew she had surprised him. "Whose son was a coward and a drunkard whose men despised him," she added softly.

Judith had not told General Haviland about his son because of what Kit had said to her, but she did not feel that telling Ryde broke the unspoken agreement she had made with Michael. And as she had told Kit, she would do anything to protect him. Perhaps now only his father could do that.

"Despised him? As did his wife, of course?" the earl suggested. One corner of his mouth moved, twitching in amusement.

"I won't make excuses for the failure of our marriage. I will tell you, however, that Michael's drunkenness caused him to make an error in judgment that cost the lives of men under his command. It was not the first time that had happened. This time, however, Michael also disobeyed a direct order not to engage the enemy, and then, when he had, he ran away from the battle, leaving his men. He was disgraced, and we both believed news of it would kill his father."

Her voice was very soft, but there was no other sound in the vast room. In the earl's eyes for the first time was something other than boredom.

"And your son," Judith went on, "who had been wounded when he led his men into that same battle to rescue Michael's troop, was given the job of guarding my husband. Along with the task of seeing that the women and the wounded were taken to safety."

"A task at which he failed," Ryde said.

"Perhaps," Judith acknowledged. "Ultimately. But not because he was a coward or because he didn't do his duty. And not even because he made bad decisions. Kit failed because of circumstances beyond his control, by acts of war. He was forced by those same circumstances to let Michael go for help. And because…'' She hesitated, remembering her role in this. "Because we both begged him to give Michael a chance to redeem himself. In exchange, Kit gave his sworn oath that no word of Michael's disgrace would reach his father.

"And the ironic thing is," she said, her voice almost a whisper now, "Haviland would probably not have believed it, even if it had. We tried, all of us, to protect him from the knowledge of Michael's guilt, but I think he would have found it impossible to believe his son could do such a despicable thing."

"Misguided faith," Ryde suggested sarcastically.

"But faith, in any case," Judith reminded him softly. "Faith in a son who didn't deserve it. And you, on the other hand…"

"I know my son," Ryde said stubbornly.

"No," she said. "Not if you can believe what Toby Reynolds says about him. If you can believe St. John would send a man to his death in order to win a woman, any woman, then you don't know your son at all." Again a silence fell between them, but there was a subtle difference to the quietness this time.

"Why would Reynolds lie?" the earl asked.

"I don't know. The simplest explanation is that Kit had a hand in punishing him for something he didn't do—or rather for something Michael had ordered him to do—and he wanted revenge. I think it's far more complicated. I think that, as Michael did, Reynolds saw in Kit what he himself lacked. Courage and honor."

"Honor," the earl repeated quietly, but there was no mockery in his voice. "Is that what you believe this duel represents? Honor? Neither of St. John's choices will be honorable," Ryde said, "I assure you of that."

"Neither of his choices?"

"There are only two, of course. He may kill Sir Roland—"

"He won't shoot General Haviland," Judith interrupted. "Kit isn't the kind of man who would ever do that."

The earl's mouth moved again and then was still. "A fascinating observation. Especially given St. John's past. May I ask your basis for that...insight on my son's behavior."

"He won't shoot General Haviland because it would be wrong," she said simply.

The earl laughed. "Because it would be wrong," he repeated.

"Wrong to kill a sick old man. A man who believes he himself is doing the right thing. The honorable thing. Kit won't do that."

"Then he must delope and admit that what Haviland accuses him of is true."

"No," Judith said again, thinking about that possibility. "For *your* sake, he won't do that. And because it isn't true."

"For my sake?" the earl said sharply.

"Because he loves you," she said softly.

The earl said nothing for a long time. His fingers had found the lorgnette and turned it idly, over and over, but he didn't look again at the work on his desk.

"There's nothing I can do, you know," Ryde said, and she believed she heard regret in his voice. And, for the first time in the course of this painful interview, emotion there as well.

"If you are right in what you say," Ryde continued, "and mind you, I do not concede that point...but if you are right, then there is only one thing St. John can, in all honor, do.''

"In all honor," Judith repeated, thinking about all the implications of that simple phrase.

"If he refuses to delope and admit he is in the wrong, and if, as you assert, he will not shoot Sir Roland, then..." The earl's voice faded.

Judith knew very little about dueling, but the earl, who knew far more than she about how such things were done, understood, of course, the decision St. John had already made.

"Then the best shot in London will deliberately miss his target," Ryde finished softly. "And after he has, he will simply stand and wait for his opponent's bullet to kill him."

Chapter Fifteen

It was a long time after she left Ryde's study before Judith again opened the door which connected her rooms to her husband's. She almost expected to find Kit still seated at the desk where he had been working this afternoon.

He was not, of course. The room was empty, the low, banked fire in the grate its only light. She walked across to his desk. It seemed that she could still smell the candles which had burned there. The scent of their expensive wax filled the room, along with the completely masculine odors of fine leather and starch and sandalwood.

There was a gilt-edged volume on the desk, its thin pages opened to a passage in the Psalms. It was too dim in the firelight to read the text, but the words were familiar, of course. They had both listened to them read aloud beside isolated graves on the Peninsula too often to ever forget their import. And their undeniable comfort. *Yea, though I walk through the valley of the shadow…*

Lying beside the Bible were several envelopes, all of them addressed in her husband's bold scrawl. Each had been sealed in wax and stamped with the signet he wore, the same one he had sent as a means of identification in Portugal. She touched the top letter, tracing with one finger the imprinted design the ring had left, and she realized in surprise that the wax was still soft.

Her eyes lifted, circling the room again, but she had not been mistaken. Apparently Kit had finished his correspondence and gone out. Judging by the scent of the candles and the softness of the wax, she had missed him by only a few moments.

If only she had gathered her courage more quickly, she thought. But that phrase encompassed almost the whole of their relationship. *If only...*

She looked at the letter she had touched and, without thinking about the propriety of her action, turned it over. It was addressed to his brother Roger. She pushed that one aside to read the next, which said simply "Ryde." There was another for Kit's mother. And the last...

The last was addressed to her. *To my beloved wife Judith.* The words blurred suddenly as she looked down on them. She drew the tips of her fingers slowly across the inscription, as if she could feel with them the phrase she could no longer see. *To my beloved wife...*

She had been Michael Haviland's wife, but she had never been Kit's. She had been wed to him, but nothing of what the other implied had ever occurred between them. A fevered kiss. An unspoken, delirium-induced invitation, accepted and then interrupted by the cruel circumstances of war. That was all they had ever had.

And now the word he had written would never have meaning. There were too many barriers, and far too little time left to attempt to overcome them. If only they had had enough time, she thought. *If only...*

Unconsciously, she picked up the letter. She was not sure what she intended to do with it. Perhaps carry it with her back into her chamber. Or maybe the urge to hold it, to touch the phrase he had written, had grown so strong that it was irresistible. She could not have read it. Not here in the shadowed, fire-tinged darkness. Not through the blur of tears.

"That's not for now," Kit said.

She looked up to find him standing in the doorway that led to the balcony. With the breath of the night breeze behind them, the sheer draperies swirled and billowed into the bedroom as if they were alive.

Obediently, she laid the thick letter back with the others. She knew what they were. Farewells, dutifully written to his family. And, of course, that word *did* include her. Not his wife, perhaps, but now at least part of St. John's family.

He had given her that. He had freely offered her his name in Portugal. To protect her, and instead...

"Part of the dueling ritual, of course." His voice was dispassionate, perhaps even a little amused.

"Did you write these before? Before the other duel you fought?"

"Every duelist pens his farewells," he said, his voice still mocking. "And when the duel is over, he throws them with a great deal of relief into the fire. Exactly like the rubbish most of them are."

She looked down on the letters. Her eyes had adjusted to the dimness enough that she could now distinguish the individual elements of the seal. The rampant lion, the crest, and the Montgomery motto. Automatically, she translated the archaic Latin phrase. *Without honor, there is nothing.*

"And your opponent's letters?" she asked. "What do you suppose happened to those?"

But instead of answering her, he asked, "What are you doing here, Judith?" He stepped into the room and turned to close the doors behind him. The silk that had seemed so alive suddenly went limp, falling still and dead against the black glass.

"I know what you intend to do," she said.

When he turned, his voice was still calm, his eyes unreadable in the darkness. "What do you think you know?" he asked. He didn't move any nearer to her. He stood before the shrouded windows, little more than a silhouette.

"Your father told me."

His laughter was a breath of sound. "My *father* told you?" he repeated unbelievingly.

"He said there are only two options in a duel. And you, of course, won't take either of those. Because in this situation, both of them would be wrong."

"Then…it follows there must be a third option," he said softly.

She knew suddenly that he was smiling. She could hear it in his voice, and her heart ached with the need to see him smile at her again.

"Ryde says you'll deliberately miss your shot and let Haviland shoot you."

Still he had not moved, but she knew that the smile was gone. He really had not intended her to know, of course.

"When did you speak to Ryde?" he asked calmly. But she was aware that he hadn't denied what his father suggested.

"Tonight. After I returned from General Haviland's. And you were right, of course. Sir Roland didn't believe me."

"I know," he said, his voice now almost comforting. "It doesn't matter, Judith. None of it matters anymore."

"Will you do what your father said?"

"I always do what my father says," Kit said. Again his voice held amusement. Whatever decision he had come to, he was at peace.

He was a man who had faced death a hundred times. In battle and sport. His peace with dying had been made long ago, she supposed. Long before she had known him. Certainly before she had become his wife. *My beloved wife Judith.*

"But there's nothing for you to be afraid of," he said. "Whatever happens, you'll be taken care of. And after a while, even the talk about this will die. Some new scandal will distract them. All this will simply be...a memory."

She nodded, her eyes on the letter because she could not see his face and because his voice was too much now as his father's had been. Without emotion.

Whatever she had hoped for when she came here, there was nothing, apparently, that he needed to say to her. He had given her his name. For honor's sake. That was all he owed her. More than he *owed* her, she amended. Telling him what she felt for him now would only be another burden, she knew, added to this heavy one he already bore.

Please don't die, because I love you. And because I need you. I need to know you. I need long days to learn about the man you are. And I need time to make you love me.

Those were not words she had any right to say to him. And even if she had that right, would saying them make anything about this better? He had been ordered to marry her, and he had obeyed, out of his sense of honor.

Now her own honor forbade that she voice the demand she had no right to make. *Please don't die, because I love you...*

"Go to bed," he suggested, his deep voice touched with the same kindness it had held when he cared for her on board the ship the night of the storm. "There's nothing to be afraid of," he said again.

"I know," she whispered.

But before she turned away, her fingers closed over something, and furtively she took what they had grasped from the desk. Like a common thief, without honor, she crushed the letter he had not intended her to see between the folds of her rail. And she carried it with her when she left his room.

In the quiet darkness she left behind, Kit finally remembered to breathe. He thought of what she had said about meeting his father. Ryde and Judith, he thought, savoring the image. His mouth curved again, almost a smile.

In Judith, his father had probably met his match. In many ways, they were alike. People who never took the easy way out, who never bent or faltered, no matter what was demanded of them.

Not like him, he thought, remembering what he had written. It had taken him a long time to compose those two letters. They both contained things that would perhaps have been better left unsaid, but he had been unable to control the impulse that made him put it all down. That made him write the words he had never had the courage to say to either of them.

To his father. For whom his life had been a constant disappointment.

And to Judith. For whom he had been... *For whom he had been nothing,* he acknowledged with painful honesty. Whatever he had imagined happened between them beside the stream that day must have been only that—the product of his fevered imagination.

He was her friend, and she had never indicated by word or deed that she desired any other relationship with him. And now that was just as well, he supposed. She had lost the husband she loved. And in all probability...

He drew another breath, inhaling deeply enough that the sound was audible in the stillness of the room. There was no point in revealing to her what he felt. There was nothing to be gained, of course, by telling Judith that he loved her. That he *had* loved her, long before he had the right.

The confession he had written would do nothing but make her unhappy. He knew her well enough to know that she would regret that she hadn't understood what he felt. And regret, perhaps, that there had been nothing of what he wanted between them. Without that letter, at least her memories of him would contain no loss beyond the loss of his friendship. And they both had endured the loss of friends. She would endure again.

He was a fool, Kit decided suddenly. There was no point in hurting Judith. If writing down his feelings had been cathartic, so would be the destruction of what he had written.... *Thrown into the fire like the rubbish most of them are.*

He walked across the room and looked down at the letters he had left on the desk. He pushed them apart, trying to find the one with her name. And then, not finding it, he went through them again. But for some reason there were only three of them. And the one with Judith's name...

When he flung open the door to her room, she didn't even look up from what she was reading. She had not taken time to light the lamp. She had knelt instead by the fire, holding the letter out to the soft, golden light of the flames.

He could smell the wax from the seal she had broken in her haste. It had fallen in scattered pieces on the hearth, and they smoked and sizzled there in bloodred droplets.

It was too late. If there had been any doubt before, that hope was destroyed when she finally raised her face to his. Her eyes reflected the firelight, golden and luminous with her tears.

"Why didn't you tell me? Oh, Kit, why didn't I know?"

Her low words were anguished. Tortured. He knew that he had been right before. This was a burden that he had no right to ask her to bear. Because tomorrow...

That thought was like a blow, stunning in its intensity,

sickening. He believed he had been prepared to face with honor whatever vengeance Haviland wanted to take. His father was right, of course, as he usually was. Because there had always been only one other option. One outcome.

"How could you not know?" she asked softly. "How could you not know how I feel? How I've felt about you for so long."

He felt the pain of that. The initial, protective numbness of shock had worn off, to be replaced now by a sense of loss that was deeper and more agonizing than any he had ever known.

She laid the letter down on her lap, its whiteness disappearing against the pale cotton of her gown. He could still see her hands, slender fingers holding his letter, their skin a darker cream than the gown, touched with the gold of the fire.

"I never intended for you to know," he whispered. "It's too late. It's all come too late."

"No," she said simply.

She put the letter aside and rose. There was no awkwardness in the motion. He watched as she crossed the room toward him. She moved silently, on bare feet, coming to him out of the darkness, as if she moved in a dream. And it was his dream, of course. Long held. Long denied.

When she was very close, she hesitated, her eyes tracing over his face, and then she smiled at him. "First," she said, "I admired you for what I knew you were. I watched you silently, from a distance. Then you became my friend, and I was so honored by your friendship. I thought it was far more than I deserved. And then somehow…"

She paused, her dark eyes glowing. What was in them was unexpected. Unasked for. But, as the gift of his name had been, he knew it was freely given.

"I loved you long before I should have," she whispered.

"Long before I admitted it, even to myself. Long, long before I ever dreamed of this."

She held out her hands to him, both of them, and unthinking, he caught them tightly in his. "But I could not know…" she whispered. "That you, too… And I would never have known."

"Judith," he said softly. His throat closed with the force of how much he loved her. Courage and honor and strength. She was all that he had learned to value in the last three years.

And she was his. Finally, in every way that God intended, she was his. That, too, was in her eyes. It would have taken a far stronger man than St. John knew himself to be to have refused.

He had once imagined the scent and softness of her hair tangled over his chest and shoulders. Now the fragrance of it surrounded him. They lay together like spent swimmers, at peace, safe at last on this new and alien shore. The ocean might pound behind them, but here the threat of its waves was nothing. Less than nothing.

He watched as his fingers found one dark, curling tendril of her hair and held it up to the light. It blazed suddenly, a thread of gold running along the long darkness of the strand.

The memories ran through his mind as quickly. Droplets of rain caught in her hair, flashing like diamonds, as the ship's lantern swung slowly back and forth. Her lips parted in anticipation as he lay on top of her, their legs entwined, caught in the cold, wet fabric of her skirt. Her eyes when she had placed her trembling hand into his on their wedding day. *Why didn't I know?* she had asked, and his heart repeated it.

It had been revealed tonight in every movement of he

body. Every response. Every sighing breath he had evoked as he made love to her. Every vow and promise. Like lovers' promises, whispered into the darkness, those would melt away in the sun.

St. John's eyes moved to the windows, but there was as yet no hint of dawn behind their blankness. Time. Even hours, perhaps, to know her. To claim her. To brand her with the heat and power and force of his love so that no matter, in the long years ahead, whoever else touched her...

For them, of course, there was no future. As there was no past. No echoes of guilt or regret. Here there were only the two of them. These hours. These minutes which were moving out of his grasp as the tide slips inexorably away from the shore.

She turned her head, and her eyes opened. What was in them had changed. The wonder of discovery had been joined by the knowledge of desire and need. Fulfilled and yet still wanting. Exactly as it should be.

"I thought I was to blame for what I couldn't feel," she said softly. "For what I couldn't be to him."

He didn't answer her with words. He turned, pushing his mouth into the now familiar softness beneath her jaw. Her head moved, tilting upward, welcoming his caress.

His lips trailed down the ringed column of her throat, tasting the salt-slick dampness of her skin. The scent of her body, heat released, drifted around him, perfumed subtly like her hair. Clean and faintly rose-sweet.

His tongue laved the shadowed hollow at the base of her neck and then traced over the delicate collarbone. Examined its fragility. Caressed. It touched finally against the small, hard nub of her nipple. Circled slowly before his mouth closed over it and suckled. Pulling strongly. Demanding.

She gasped, the sound an indrawn breath, almost lost

against the silk of his hair. At that, his head lifted, and his eyes examined her breast, its rose areola surrounded by the dark cream of her skin and the hard masculinity of his fingers.

Fire-touched, heat-scented, her body at last lay open to him. He had explored its mysteries and had shown them to her. And he would again. He lowered his head, nuzzling against the dampness his mouth had left on the nipple. He turned his face so that the beard-roughened skin of his cheek moved over and then around her breast. She moaned, and his knee pushed between hers. Demanding still.

Her legs opened and then drifted apart. Boneless. Welcoming. Her slender body arched upward, searching for his. He lifted over her, aligning their bodies into a position as old and unchanging as time. His palms cupped the outside of her breasts, and he lowered his head between them. Breathing in. Inhaling the fragrance of her skin. The essence of her body.

He pushed into it. Despite the times he had made love to her, he was so hard, so tight, engorged with a need that was as sharp and painful as starvation. Never to be fully sated. Never satisfied.

Her hips responded as they had before, moving upward to meet his thrust. He raised his head, and his palms found now her face, shaping themselves to its contours, feeling the fragility of bone. He held her, watching her eyes as his body lowered again and again to hers. An invasion that was slow and measured and controlled.

The first time had been little more than an explosion of need. His and hers. He had not left her behind, despite the pain of what he felt. The boiling force of his desire had seemed to take over his body, overpowering, but he had, even then, protected her from it. This was Judith, and he would always protect her. Without thought. An instinct only, perhaps, but one that could never be overridden, not even by his want.

This was something different. Deliberately different. A subtlety measured in millimeters of motion perhaps, but precise as a fencing lesson.

As he had written what his heart contained, never intending that she should read it while he lived, he wrote now what was in his soul, inscribing it on her body. Indelibly. One chance to make it last forever. The unchanging expression of his love. One unfading memory to shine in the darkness of loss.

"I love you," he said. *My beloved wife Judith.* There had been nothing of what he had written on those pages that was not true. As was this. Truth and honor. And courage, finally, to confess it all. No matter what happened tomorrow.

Her fingers lifted to touch his mouth. To trace its shape. To press against the words he had finally uttered. Then she brought them to her own lips and held them there. Her eyes were still locked on his.

His body swelled with love. Need. Want. Desire. Heat. The force of it drove him against her. Out of the coldness and into her warmth. After a long time, her eyes closed and the tears seeped slowly from beneath the dark sweep of her lashes and, touched by the firelight, shimmered over her temple to be lost in the cloud of hair that spread across the pillow.

He lowered his head, even as his body arched and thrust above hers. Slender hips answered, responded, as he had never dreamed they could. Her eyes opened only as need exploded and then dissolved, the hot moisture of his seed spilling into the receptacle of her body as her tears had slipped over her skin.

And, as the response he felt moved in shivering force

throughout her frame, he watched it also happen in her face. The wonder of it was reflected clearly in the darkness of her eyes, as had been the golden firelight when she knelt before the hearth and read what he had written.

My beloved wife Judith… Finally, and always, she was.

He dressed without waking her. He moved through the dark room, pulling on familiar garments that now seemed terribly strange. And when he was dressed, except for the cloak he had thrown over the chair near the door, he came back to stand beside the high bed. Her body lay fully exposed, the forgotten sheets at the foot, twisted and disordered by their lovemaking.

Judith was lying on her side, her hair spread across the pillow behind her head as if blown by an unseen wind. One hand was before her face, and he imagined the feel of her breath feathering against it, just as it had whispered over the skin of his body while he lay, unsleeping, beside her. Holding her.

He wanted her again. Even now. Even given what had passed between them during the long hours. He had taken her again and again, beyond satisfaction into exhaustion. She had refused him nothing. Her generosity of spirit extended even to this.

And he had made love to her in every way he could devise, imprinting the memories of each on his brain and his heart, just as he had pressed the signet into the warm, soft wax of the seals. Indelibly fixed there. These memories would be the last he would think of as he waited today for Haviland's shot.

His spirit would not be there, not under the shadow of the tall trees that sheltered the secluded site from the growing light of day. It would be here. Still. Sheltered by something very different.

St. John did not believe in ghosts. Not in the coldly rational part of his mind. But he had seen things on battlefields that he could not explain away. And now no longer tried.

If it's possible, my Judith, he thought. *Here. Always.*

He wanted to touch her. To run his fingers one last time over the warm, alabaster velvet of her skin. To feel her shuddering response to his touch. To see in her eyes...

But he could not bear what would be in her eyes. It was better then that this goodbye never be made. Last night had been enough. *Far more than he deserved.*

Involuntarily, without his conscious direction, his strong brown fingers, tanned and hard from years of war, reached out and found a solitary tendril in the dark curling mass of her hair. He wrapped it slowly around one finger, being very careful to put no pressure on the strand. He held it there a moment, its warmth and softness almost alive. Almost enough.

And then he slowly unwound the curl and let it fall. It did not lose the shape of his finger. It lay instead beside her cheek, moving slightly, up and down, with the deep, even breaths she took as she slept.

When he turned away in the near-darkness of pre-dawn and walked to the door across the silent room, still she did not awaken. Not even when it closed, very softly, behind him.

Chapter Sixteen

The morning that broke over the tall trees represented England at her finest, the pale light of dawn as golden as the firelight had been the night before. A light fog hovered, floating over their boots, softening, with its white peacefulness, what would happen in this place.

Ritual, he had told Judith. And now, most of that had been completed. The recitation of the rules they all knew. The examination of the grounds. The loading of the two beautiful and very deadly pistols. All of that was done. Finished.

His brother asked finally if he had any messages. Kit was forced by the question to pull his mind from where it had found refuge, a fire-touched distance, infinitely far away.

"Nothing, thank you, Roger."

His brother nodded, regretfully, St. John thought, but still he resisted the urge to touch Roger's shoulder comfortingly as he had done before. His brothers were all dead, their bones and ashes scattered across battlefields almost as far away in time and distance as the bed he and Judith had shared last night.

Kit did not bother to examine the pistol he had been

given. The pair had belonged to his grandfather, and he knew them well enough to know that there was no need. They always fired straight and true. There would be no mistake.

The clatter of the arriving carriage was loud enough to drag him again from his self-absorption, especially when he recognized the crest on the door. Large, black, and well-sprung, the coach, pulled by four magnificent grays, flew across the grassy expanse toward them. The small assembly watched in silence as the earl of Ryde's carriage was pulled to a halt, just before it seemed that the racing horses would careen into the participants.

Kit couldn't imagine what his father was doing here, and for a moment he wondered if the occupant of the coach might be Judith. It was the kind of courage she possessed, of course.

Could she have come in another attempt to change Haviland's mind? he wondered. It was obvious to him that would be fruitless. And Judith could not know that her presence here was the one thing that would make this unbearable.

The slight figure who descended from the carriage was not his wife, however. Ryde's eyes briefly met his before they found his brother's and held a moment. Kit wondered if his father were surprised to see Roger here, his attendance such a departure from his conventional lifestyle. It was not to either of his sons, however, that the earl spoke.

That he spoke at all, interrupting the formality of these proceedings, was as stunning as his unexpected arrival. The rules about that were very clear as well. Those not parties in these contests had no role. Ryde knew the ritual, of course, although to Kit's certain knowledge his father had never engaged in anything so scandalous as a duel.

"I'm afraid I have very bad news for you," Ryde said

to Roland Haviland. He had not looked again at either of his sons.

"I am not interested in your 'news,' Ryde," the old man replied. His eyes shifted purposefully to his opponent, evidently intending to ignore the earl's interruption.

"I have proof that what has been said about my son's action in Portugal is false. You should be interested in that."

The general's eyes came back to him. "What kind of proof?"

"A sworn statement to that effect from the same man who told you those lies. Who has told us all that same lie."

"A statement you coerced from him? Or more likely bribed him to make?" Haviland suggested contemptuously. "It makes no difference what Reynolds says now. We have all heard the truth."

"What he says *now* is the truth," Ryde asserted, his voice still calm. "And truth should always make a difference."

"My son is dead. Murdered under the cover of battle so his wife could become your son's whore. That is the only truth of this. I need hear no other."

"Perhaps this might change your mind," the earl said, his voice still controlled and yet somehow ringing through the clearing. He held out a small, flat packet.

Kit knew immediately what it was. So would Haviland, because they had both seen such packets a hundred times. Military dispatches, still folded as tightly as they always were.

"These were found among Toby Reynolds's belongings when I had them searched. He had given me the address of his lodgings, of course, in hopes that I might change my mind about paying him to keep quiet. And he had been foolish enough to hold on to these. I suppose it's possible he did that because he intended to use them later to blackmail you.''

"Me?'' Haviland questioned, his eyes widened a little in surprise. "How could he possibly have thought to blackmail me?''

"These dispatches were written by Colonel William Smythe shortly before he was killed in battle. They are addressed to his commander, Lord Wellington, and they concern *your* son, Sir Roland. They detail *his* actions in Portugal. His very disgraceful and cowardly actions. You will find, I'm afraid, that they have great bearing on this matter.''

Of them all, only Kit could know the full significance of what his father had found. Smythe's dispatches had never reached Wellington, of course, because his chosen courier had not gotten through. He had been found by Sergeant Cochran, his throat cut and the dispatch case he had carried missing.

For an instant the image of that smiling, boyishly freckled face invaded Kit's mind. Scarborough, who had tended his wound on the battlefield and had probably saved his life. Scarborough, who had died alone, and apparently at the hands of a comrade. Someone he would have trusted.

"Have you come here in an attempt to blacken my son's name? In a fruitless effort to save St. John's worthless life? It won't work, Ryde, no matter what lies you've paid Reynolds to tell. Or to write.''

"The writing is Smythe's. That can easily be verified at the Horse Guards if you wish.''

"I *don't* wish,'' Haviland said bitterly. "I don't need to have anything verified. I knew my son. Nothing you can say makes any difference to this. I have issued a challenge to St. John, and he has already accepted it.''

The old man's eyes shifted from the earl to St. John.

"Do you wish to admit your guilt in my son's death and withdraw from this meeting like the coward you have proven yourself to be?"

Only one option, he had told Judith. There should still be only one, but before he could frame an answer, Kit found himself caught within the golden, seductive net of memory, reliving the short night they had shared. Remembering those brief dark hours.

What did it matter what anyone said about him? He knew he had done nothing wrong, as Judith did. Did it really matter then what anyone else believed? Did anything matter beside what he had found, finally, with her?

His eyes met his father's. The earl was still holding out the papers that would damn Michael Haviland as the drunken coward he had been. That would brand and disgrace his family forever.

It was even possible, Kit realized suddenly, that Haviland was the one who had sent Reynolds to stop Scarborough. With orders to see to it that these papers never reached headquarters and perhaps even with permission to do so by any means.

He didn't know that, of course. Reynolds had certainly proven capable of devising his own villainy. And Kit had given Michael Haviland his word that nothing of what was in those dispatches would ever be revealed. His word in exchange for Haviland's. An oath sworn on his honor.

He was bound by it still. If Kit asked, he knew his father would not reveal the contents of those papers. He would understand the importance of the vow Kit had made.

"I had nothing to do with your son's death, Sir Roland," Kit said. "He volunteered for a dangerous mission and was killed as a result. I have done no wrong that I *can* admit to."

There was a small relaxation in the watching men, a hint

of movement. Kit realized the others had been waiting a long time for whatever he would say. Frozen, motionless, they had simply awaited his response. It could have been nothing else, of course, but the memories of last night had almost defeated him.

"Put them away," he said to his father. "I gave him my word." The earl's eyes held his, searching as they had not in a very long time. Looking into his soul, it seemed. But Ryde was the one who had taught him the lessons of honor. He had demanded those of Kit all his life. So St. John did not doubt his father's obedience to them now.

Kit turned to Roger and nodded. The rest was only ritual, but it must be played out, of course. They had all come here to insure that this was done as it should be. With honor.

Ten paces. Such a small distance when they had stepped them off and turned to face one another. It seemed to Kit that he could see, in the split second before he fired, every line in the old man's face, put there by grief and by love. Both of those Kit understood, better now than he ever had before.

His ball went where he directed it, as straight and as true as any he had ever fired from his grandfather's pistol. It whispered over the top of the shoulder of the old man's coat.

When they examined it later, Kit believed they might be able to see where it had brushed the fabric. He controlled his urge to smile. Well done, he thought. Exactly as he had intended. No one could ever claim that he had tried to miss.

Now there was nothing to do but wait. Despite the fact that time had seemed to hesitate, he knew it would be a matter of only a heartbeat. Maybe two, even if the old man were very slow.

He watched the muzzle of the long dueling pistol line

up and steady, carefully aimed at his heart. There was no reason for the general to hurry now that Kit had fired. And the distance was so slight that there was also no possibility, given the time to do it right, that Haviland might miss.

Judith, Kit had time to think. One heartbeat, sending the rich heart's blood to his brain to form that word. It was his last thought before the second shot shattered the breathless, waiting silence under the elms.

Judith woke, her mouth dry, parted in a voiceless scream. Her heart was racing, threatening to tear its way out of her chest. But the noise, whatever she thought she heard, had not been in this room. She sat up in the disordered bed, jerked upright by a sound that was not a sound. By a scene that she could not have seen.

She looked around the still, silent bedroom. The fire that had burned on the hearth last night was out. Even the ashes were cold and gray, like the thin light that crept into the room between the folds of the draperies. She fought to control her breathing, holding on to the thought that it had only been a nightmare. Only a dream. And Kit...

Her eyes searched the bed where he had lain beside her. And then the room again. He wasn't here. There was no one here. She was alone, and the sudden desolation that depressed her spirit was as black as the glass had been behind the limp, lifeless curtains last night. She couldn't understand why Kit would leave her.

She looked again at the windows, gauging time by the growing light as she had done so often in Portugal. It was only a little past dawn, she realized. Only a few minutes past sunrise.

The rest of the room was still shadowed. And empty. She shivered and, sitting alone in the bed they had shared she pulled the sheet around her trembling, naked body to fight its emptiness.

"Kit," she called softly, and then she waited.

Her voice echoed hollowly in the vast room, but he didn't answer her. She lay back in the tangled bed, remembering the dream. That was exactly what would happen tomorrow unless someone stopped it. But the earl had told her there was nothing he could do. And Kit could not, in honor, follow any path other than the one he had been forced to take.

But Michael had already died to protect his father, and now Kit would die also. For that same reason. And it wasn't right. Two deaths to prevent a proud old man from learning the truth about his son. No matter what Kit had told her about her own honor, she knew a second blood sacrifice on the altar of the Haviland family tradition was no more right than it would be for Kit to shoot Sir Roland. And not honorable, no matter what Kit thought.

She would have to tell General Haviland the truth, even if it meant breaking her word, destroying her honor. There were higher laws than the rules men devise to guide their lives. Kit might choose to abide by man's law, but she would not. Not any longer.

It took her only minutes to dress, moving quickly through the cold half-light of dawn. She wondered if any of the servants were awake. The earl's coachman would be surprised at her request, of course, but he would obey it. And she would make Michael's father hear the truth. And make him believe it.

"My lord!"

The shocked exclamation of Haviland's second rang even more loudly than Roger's anguished cry. The surgeon ignored both, rushing past them to the field where the combatants had, only seconds before, solemnly paced off the distance.

"He's not hurt," the earl of Ryde said calmly. "I didn't hit *him*."

The pistol he held out at arm's length did not waver even now. It was not until the surgeon had reached the general that the earl began to lower his gun. His eyes moved to Kit's and then briefly met the shocked gaze of his elder son. Amusement lurked in their depths as they studied Roger's stunned face.

"This is an outrage, Ryde," the general's second said furiously. "I have *never* seen anything like it. It is against every convention of the code we have come here today to honor."

"Outrage?" Ryde repeated, watching the surgeon pick up the shattered pistol he had shot out of the old man's hand. "It would be outrage if I allowed that obstinate old martinet to put a ball into an innocent man. That, sir, would be outrage."

"But the rules, my lord—"

"The rules be damned," Ryde said, "and you and Haviland be damned with them. My son has done *nothing* wrong. I don't intend to stand by and watch him shot for that fool's mistaken pride."

"How dare you, sir," Haviland said. His voice and face were rigid with anger.

"I *dare* because I'm right. Your son was a coward and a drunkard. These papers prove it, but you wouldn't look at them. You don't *want* to know the truth. But be warned, Haviland, I'll never let you kill my son to protect the reputation of yours."

"There's not a word of truth—"

"Truth is *not* what people believe, sir. Truth is what happened. You can't change this, no matter how much you might wish to make it something else. And I suspect you knew the truth about your son all along. A man seldom reaches manhood without some evidence of his true character revealed. Especially to those…who love him."

"Whatever is written in those dispatches are lies," Haviland said.

"Smythe lied? St. John lied? Your son's wife lied? And now even Reynolds?" Ryde enumerated mockingly. "All of them lied. Even you aren't that big a fool. And neither, I believe, is the world, despite however foolishly they have thus far behaved in this."

The silence grew again, almost as heavy as that before the second shot. "Your choice," Ryde said finally to break it. "*You* will be the one to admit you were wrong, General Haviland. And you will do it publicly. Or I shall see that these papers are introduced into evidence in the military inquiry of the incident which I will demand. And I assure you I have influence enough with this government to see that investigation carried out."

Sir Roland's features had changed, the lines deepening somehow, his face aging before their eyes. But still he made no answer to the earl's demands.

"I warn you," Ryde said softly. "I've had enough of this. Enough of you and of this scandal. You *know* the truth because in your heart you knew your son. Put an end to this insanity before you also put an end to whatever good name he once had."

"What do you want?" the old man asked.

"A public admission that you and Reynolds were wrong about St. John. You may arrange that however you wish. You may claim to have received a letter from your son, written before his death, verifying exactly what Kit has said from the beginning. That Haviland volunteered for the mission that cost him his life. That his wife was faithful. That *nothing* of what my son did was dishonorable or in any way led to Captain Haviland's death.''

The old man said nothing for a long time. ''How do you know that I shall be believed? And that what occurred here today won't simply spawn more gossip.''

''I can vouch for my sons.'' The earl looked at the others in turn, assessing before he spoke. ''The rest are bound by their own honor to abide by whatever settlement the two of you reach. And I will personally challenge the man who reveals anything of what happened here. It seems I've not lost my touch,'' Ryde said.

There was an undeniable note of pride in his father's voice, Kit thought. The earl himself had taught Kit to shoot, endlessly exacting and demanding in those lessons, as he had been in every other. Everything had to be done over and over again until it was right. Until it was perfect. Always perfect.

''You have my word,'' the general agreed.

''A wise decision,'' Ryde said. ''And your promise that you'll never slander my son's name again? Or his wife's. I want your oath, sir.''

''On my honor,'' Haviland said.

Ryde nodded. His eyes found Kit's finally. ''Without honor,'' the earl quoted softly, ''there is nothing. Perhaps that's a lesson I taught *too* well.''

''No,'' Kit denied. There were so many things he should say to his father, he supposed, but he could not think how to word any of them in the face of what Ryde had done for him.

That his father had shot the gun from Haviland's hand went against every precept of honor Kit had ever been taught, and yet it also transcended them. *I won't let you kill my son to protect yours.* And it had been a very long time since he had heard that particular certainty in his father's voice.

"Take the coach," his father suggested. "They're still fresh enough for a run." The dark eyes gleamed again with amusement, but given the earl's next sentence, Kit wasn't sure exactly what had prompted it. "I'll ride back with your brother. I'm sure there are some *things* he wishes to discuss with me."

"Thank you, sir," Kit said. The fact that he was alive and would be allowed to remain alive was beginning to become a reality. How do you thank someone for again giving you life?

"I imagine she's waiting for you," his father said, his eyes strangely soft.

Kit nodded, his throat too thickened with emotion to answer, and then he began to walk toward his father's waiting carriage.

"And Kit," the earl said.

St. John turned back.

"Tell her I did it for *my* sake."

"Sir?" Kit asked.

"She'll understand. It seems she understands a great deal. More than I ever did," the earl said. He cleared the unfamiliar emotion from his voice. "Go on, boy. She was told this duel would take place tomorrow. But by now, of course…"

Again Kit nodded. And, giving in to an impulse he didn't pause to examine, he put his hand on his father's shoulder and squeezed it gently, exactly as he had Sergeant Cochran's.

The earl's eyes met his, and then his arms reached out, enclosing his younger son and holding him tightly against his chest for a moment before he stepped back.

"Go on," he ordered gruffly. "And Kit... Godspeed, my dear son."

It was General Haviland's housekeeper who explained to Judith why she couldn't see him. And when she had been turned away from his door, Judith sat a long time in the countess's phaeton, letting the scope of her error sink in. She had never even asked. Had never bothered to verify what she had been told. She had simply assumed the information Lady Marbury gave her was correct.

Now she knew that it was not. The duel she had come here to prevent had already taken place. This dawn and not tomorrow's. That was, of course, why Kit had left her. Why he had stolen away from the bed they shared last night without waking her.

"Home, my lady?" the coachman turned finally to ask.

Because she could think of nothing else she could do and nowhere she could go besides home, she nodded. Kit had been right last night, and she had been wrong. It had been too late, she thought, as the horses began to move. It had all come far too late.

Judith was not waiting for him as his father had suggested she would be. Kit had bounded up the stairs, taking them two at a time, finally beginning to realize that, thanks to his father, it really was all over. The long nightmare was at an end, and finally he and Judith...

He flung open the door, almost exactly as he had done last night, but she wasn't there. The bed was as he had left it. Shadowed. Disordered. And the letters he had written to his family were still on his desk.

Only one thing was missing. The small, infinitely precious body of his wife. He could not imagine where Judith had gone. It was still early enough that she couldn't have had an engagement. And his father had told him she believed the duel to be tomorrow, so it made no sense that she wasn't here where he had left her sleeping. Where else could she be?

When Judith pushed open the door, she saw him. He was standing by the long windows, and their light enriched the darkness of his hair and made the strong, handsome planes of his face almost luminescent when he turned.

Her eyes widened, but she didn't come into the room. Instead, she hesitated on the threshold trying to decide if the shadowed figure limned against the light was real. Or if he were only a figment of her desire. Her need.

All the way home she had remembered. How his body felt beneath her hands. How it tasted against her tongue. How it moved above hers in the darkness, teaching her things she had never dreamed existed between a man and a woman. Instructing her heart as well as her body.

Remembering it all. And then the image from the dream would intrude, thrusting into her mind with all its horror. She had not begun dealing with that. Her mind was numb, and that was how she wanted it. She had managed to maintain a distance from the agony all the way home, waiting to think again until she reached these rooms. And then...

He had said nothing. Surely if this were really Kit, and not something she had conjured up with her grief, then he would speak to her. One word. Her name. Something, surely, to let her know.

"Judith?" he said softly.

She took a breath. And then another. That had been his voice. There had been nothing extraordinary about it. A little puzzled perhaps. Questioning.

She blinked, because her eyes were burning, and was infinitely relieved to find that he was still there. She took a step into the room and then another. His cloak had been thrown over the chair, and it hadn't been there this morning when she had left. There had been no sign of Kit's presence in this room.

She put her fingers on top of it, moving them against the familiar coarseness of the wool. It was damp. An English morning's dampness. And then she remembered to take another breath. Almost acquiring again the familiar pattern and rhythm of breathing. Her eyes examined his body, tracing over it carefully, and then they returned to his face.

"I dreamed you were dead," she whispered. "And when I woke, you weren't here. I was so afraid, Kit. So I went to tell Michael's father the truth. And they said…" She took a shuddering breath, remembering the shock.

He smiled at her. "I told you there was nothing to be afraid of," he said softly, his voice comforting.

"And Michael's father? The duel, Kit? What about—"

"He's fine, my darling. And it's over, Judith. All of it's finally over."

It took a moment for the assurance to penetrate the sense of dread that had held her since she had awakened, alone, in this cold, dark room. "How can it be over?" she asked, wondering.

"Ryde said to tell you…" Kit hesitated, because he wasn't sure what his father's message was intended to convey, just as he couldn't be sure of what had passed between the earl and his wife.

They were the two people who had never deviated from the path of honor. At least never before. Until this morning. And they had both done what they had done for love of him.

"Ryde stopped the duel by shooting the pistol out of Haviland's hand," Kit explained. "He said to tell you that he did it for *his* sake, and that you would understand what he meant.''

''I had told him that what you intended today was done to protect him. Because you loved him so much that you couldn't bear to dishonor him. You were willing to die— for his sake.''

''Then...'' Again Kit hesitated, trying to understand.

''And today, Ryde also did what he did for *his* sake, Kit. Because he loved you more than his honor. He was willing to do anything, even destroy that cherished honor, to protect you.''

The impact of that realization was evident on the hand some features, and she hesitated to ask about the rest. What Kit had told her, however, didn't begin to explain why he believed the situation had been completely changed by his father's actions.

''What will General Haviland do now?'' she asked. ''Surely he will—''

''It's over, Judith,'' he said again. Simply. That was really all she needed to understand.

''Are you sure?''

''On my honor,'' he said, smiling at her. ''You have my word, my darling. And my father's.''

She shook her head slowly, but her eyes held his and in them began to grow what had not been there since she had left the general's door. Hope. Hope for the future neither of them had believed last night they would be allowed to share.

And now, it seemed, they would. Because a man who had lived his entire life by the rules and narrow conventions that he truly believed in had broken them. *For my sake,* Kit thought, unconsciously repeating his father's words which he hadn't understood.

''Then...'' she said softly.

"It's over," he said again, perhaps because he, too, was finding that hard to believe and to accept what it meant.

She came to him then and gave him her hands, just as she had last night. He took them and brought them both to his lips, pressing a kiss on the tips of her fingers.

My beloved wife Judith. Always. And now, truly, forever.

* * * * *

The Rebel

by
Georgina Devon

Georgina Devon has a Bachelor of Arts degree in Social Sciences with a concentration in history. Her interest in England began when the United States Air Force stationed her at RAF Woodbridge, near Ipswich in East Anglia. This is also where she met her husband who flew fighter aircraft for the United States. She began writing when she left the Air Force. Her husband's military career moved the family every two to three years and she wanted a career she could take with her anywhere in the world. Today, she and her husband live in Tucson, Arizona, with their teenage daughter, two dogs and a cockatiel.

Chapter One

Andrew Dominic Wentworth, Earl of Ravensford, paused in the act of bringing a glass of Irish whiskey to his mouth. The door to the library where he lounged had opened with a vengeance and then slammed shut. The delicate scent of lavender filled the room.

'I am tired of dancing to your tune,' a husky female voice stated.

A smile tugged at Ravensford's lips. A wife or mistress. In his experience, they were the only women who occasionally danced to a man's tune, and then only for something in return. Mothers and sisters did whatever they wanted regardless of what they were told or what was involved.

'You will do exactly as I tell you,' a man's light tenor replied.

A low, feminine growl followed the arrogantly

superior words. 'What if I don't? What if I tell you no?'

The man chuckled low in his throat. 'Then I will be forced to do something you won't like, and we both know what that is.'

The woman groaned, her husky voice ending in a sob. 'What do you want?'

She sounded completely defeated. The man must have a powerful hold over her. For some strange reason, Ravensford felt disappointment. He had wanted her to win their contest.

'That is more like the dutiful miss I know you to be.' Sarcasm and gloating filled each word.

'Only because you have something I value highly.' The woman's rich, nerve-tingling voice caught on the last word.

Her voice was incredible. The deep, almost growling tone demanded attention at the same time as it created an image of a sleek feline. Ravensford found himself entranced. Never had a sound aroused him so, not even his former mistress's voice when she was in the throes of passion.

He was a connoisseur of women, often finding himself embroiled with a second before he was free of the first. Why hadn't he seen this woman—or heard her? For if he had, he would have remembered her voice. He had never heard one so sensual and arousing. Just sitting here listening to her made him want to experience her in other ways.

With very little enticement he could be enthralled. He imagined the woman to be small and supple like the cat her low, raspy tone brought to his mind. For a brief instant he wondered if she would purr like a contented feline when a man stroked her. It was an errant thought and one he had no business thinking where a respectable woman was concerned. And respectable she must be or she would not be in his mother's establishment.

The Countess was fanatical about other people's morals, an unusual trait in someone of her generation. More often than not, he had found others of his mother's age to be more risqué than most people closer to his age.

However, it was time he made his presence known. He took another sip of the liquor and started to rise.

'I want you to stay close to the old Countess. I have need of some of her possessions.' The last word was said with a repulsive snicker.

Ravensford decided not to stand. Something was afoot. Something unsavory from the man's words, and something that involved his mother.

'Haven't I been doing exactly that?' Exasperation and perhaps remorse tinged every word the woman spoke.

Ravensford's curiosity increased. The urge to reveal his presence was strong, but he resisted. It was his experience that when one avenue was cut off a person would find another. Words were not enough for him to have the couple arrested. Nor did he want to. The woman was reluctant and he found himself unwilling to harm her when he did not even know her. His best course was to tell his mother that someone in her household intended to rob her, even though he doubted it would do any good.

As for him confronting the two now, that would not do either. He had no evidence but their words and, even with his rank, he could do nothing without more substantial evidence. Nor would he want to. He had spent his life championing those not as fortunate as himself. The game laws, Corn Laws, all of those were biased for the wealthy. As were the criminal laws. No, he would not do anything until he actually caught the pair in the act of stealing.

He had arrived at his mother's Irish estate early this morning. Derry House and the surrounding farms had been part of her dower, and she returned to them on a regular basis. This time, she had summoned him to attend her. Never a good omen.

'You have been a good little girl so far,' the man said, focussing Ravensford's thoughts back on the couple. 'See that you remain such.' His light tenor was at odds with his implied threat. 'Best you go before someone notices us.'

There was a sharp inhalation. 'Until you command my presence again,' the woman finished bitterly.

She definitely did not like dancing to the man's tune. Ravensford wondered if she disliked the job or the man or both. And what was his hold over her?

The sound of footsteps followed by the opening and closing of the door told Ravensford he was alone once more. The large centre log in the fireplace cracked and split, sending sparks scattering through the room. The servant who had started the fire had forgotten to put the screen in front. He rose and stomped out any little flames before they could do damage to the Aubusson rug.

While the thought of someone stealing from his mother was unpleasant, he found himself intrigued by the turn of events. Perhaps a dull, but comfortable and mandatory visit to his parent would become an entertaining proposition.

If nothing else, he had a mystery to occupy his mind. He did not recognise the man's voice and was not sure he would notice if he were to hear it

again in ordinary circumstances, for it was not remarkable. The woman was another story. He
would remember her deep-throated purr in his
dreams. Whatever she did in his mother's household, he would soon find out. Then the game
would begin.

A wry grin twisted his well-shaped lips. With
the luck he had been having lately, she would be
a drab tabby and married.

He finished the whiskey and strode from the
room. Action was always preferable to inactivity.
It was a maxim he had put to frequent good use in
the House of Lords. He was sure it would be so
here.

Ravensford propped one Hessian-shod foot on
his knee, careful not to rub dirt on his beige pantaloons. He was as casual in his dress as his mother
was meticulous, but casual did not mean dirty.
Then there was his valet, who would make him
miserable for several long minutes if he returned
messed up after so short an absence.

Across a small space, his mother reclined on a
gold-lined chaise-lounge, looking frail to the point
of ethereal. Her silver hair was cut fashionably
short, an ideal foil for the oval perfection of her
creamy complexion. She was a handsome woman
and had been the toast of the *ton* in her first Sea-

son. A pale lavender afternoon dress, trimmed lavishly with Brussels lace, accentuated the slim curves of a young girl. All in all, she was very well preserved.

Ravensford wished her mind were as tidy as her person. She was, to put it generously, scatterbrained. He did not relish the task of telling her about the proposed robbery. Still, he had to do his duty.

There was no sense waiting. 'Mother, I overheard a conversation today between a man and woman. They plan to rob you.'

'Nonsense, Andrew.' She dismissed his warning with a wave of her elegant hand. 'You always were an imaginative child. I had thought you beyond that.'

His jaw clenched before he forcibly relaxed it. This was nothing he had not expected. 'I am, Mother.'

'Well, I cannot believe that anyone in my employ would be so ungrateful as to do what you suggest.'

'Is there someone new who might be in need of money?'

She scowled at him. 'There is Mary Margaret, but her brother-in-law is the curate. She grew up here. Her father was one of my tenants. No, it is not her.'

'Someone else?' he asked, even though his suspicions now lay with the mysterious Mary Margaret. He did not know his mother's tenants, having spent very little time here.

'No, Andrew, there is not.' Exasperation tinged every word. 'But if you insist on this, I shall line up all the servants and demand the guilty party to step forward.'

This was no more than he had expected. He should have known better than to tell his mother. Still, an irritation he rarely allowed himself to feel toward his parent made his next words harsh.

'That would be the worst thing you could do. The thief would be on his guard after that and we would never catch him.'

'Then be done with this nonsense. No one in my employ would do so despicable a thing.' She waved a languid hand, the wrist drooping like a wilted flower. 'I did not summon you here to be told such foolishness.'

Ravensford knew when a subject was ended. To continue pushing her would only make her do up as she threatened. He had not expected her to give credence to his words; she rarely did. He would have to bide his time and catch the pair in the actual act of stealing. Then he would not need his mother's belief or cooperation.

'Now, Andrew,' she continued, her voice light

and musical, 'I asked you to visit for a very specific reason.'

He put the other matter aside for the moment and made himself smile indulgently at her. 'I surmised as much, Mother, and I am at your service. What exactly is it that you wish me to do?'

'My goddaughter, Annabell Winston, needs to have a Season.' She reached for the teapot. 'Do you still take your tea plain?'

'Yes, please.'

In spite of the foreboding edging up his spine, he waited patiently while she poured him a steaming cup of tea. There was no sense prodding her. That route only caused discord without accomplishing any increase in speed or comprehension.

'Now, we shall be arriving in London in early May to give the child plenty of time to assemble an appropriate wardrobe. I expect you to make sure everything is in order.'

He took a swallow of scalding tea and realised that somewhere along his parent's thought processes he had missed something important. 'What exactly do you expect me to do?'

'Really, Andrew, don't be so dense. It isn't like you.' She sipped daintily at her cream-and-sugar-laden drink. 'You are to have the town house properly opened and prepared for us. The ballroom floor very likely needs to be refinished if we are to have a successful coming-out ball for Annabell.'

It was an effort not to groan. The idea of protesting passed through his mind, only to be discarded. His mother had that light in her blue eyes that preceded intense activity—by him.

'And what else am I to do?' he asked, knowing he would not like any part of the answer. His comfortable bachelor life was about to be turned topsy-turvy.

'Oh, very good, Andrew. I knew you would get into the spirit of things once I explained them.' She beamed at him, the charm of her smile identical to his own. 'Vouchers for Almack's are a must. As are invitations to all the private events. The child will likely want to attend Astley's Amphitheatre and all those disgustingly plebian entertainments. Of course, we mustn't forget Covent Garden and Vauxhall.'

Ravensford finished a pastry in one gulp, dreading the answer to his next question. 'And who will be escorting Annabell about since you are not capable of getting out much?'

Her smile widened. 'Why, you, of course. I know how much you enjoy her company and she adores you. Why, the two of you make a perfect couple. It would be delightful if this visit brought about a closer union between you. Your father often said so.'

A twinge of sadness tightened his chest at the mention of his sire, but no matter what his parents had wished, he was not going to marry a miss barely out of the schoolroom. Others might do so, but not he. He preferred women with experience.

'I am not in the market for a wife,' he stated baldly, knowing that nothing short of bluntness got through to his parent and too often not even that.

'So you say.' She leaned gracefully back into the pale yellow silk cushions of her seat, only to bounce forward again. 'I nearly forgot. My companion will help chaperon since it would not be proper for you to escort Annabell alone.'

'Your companion? I thought Miss Mabel left to care for her father.'

'She did, she did. I already told you that I have hired a new companion, Mary Margaret O'Brien.'

Ravensford resisted the urge to shake his head. His mother had mentioned hiring the chit, but not making her a companion. It was the perfect position for a thief. He put the suspicion aside as his mother continued blithely on.

'Quite proper and all, but not of the Quality. Still, a very obliging young woman. She shan't bother you. She is quiet as a mouse.' A complacent smile curved the Countess's lips as she once more leaned back into the plump cushions. 'And her looks are too unusual to be considered attractive. She won't cause you any problems.'

Ravensford narrowed his eyes. In his experience, whenever his mother considered something to be unimportant it ended up being a nightmare. He vividly remembered the litter of puppies she had foisted on him just six months ago. They were supposed to be a *bagatelle*, nothing more. They had ruined his stable and very nearly cost him his head groom. After much cajoling, he had managed to place every pup but one with a good owner. Wizzard ruled Ravensford's country estate with a benign paw. But that was neither here nor there. Right now he had to keep his mother from creating another disaster.

'You do plan on accompanying Annabell whenever possible, don't you?' he asked drily.

'Don't be a goose, Andrew. Of course I do. What kind of godmother would I be otherwise?'

There was no polite answer, so Ravensford made none. Thankfully a tap on the door saved him from his mother's habit of pursuing an answer to her questions.

'Come in,' the Countess said.

Ravensford heard the door open seconds before the faint scent of lavender wafted through the room. Could this be the woman from the library?

His pulse quickened. Still, he did not turn his head to look. Better that he appear completely uninterested.

'My lady,' the newcomer said.

It was she. Her voice purred like that of a contented cat. His gut tightened pleasurably.

Ravensford caught movement from the corner of his eye. Seconds later she was in his line of sight. His entire body responded.

She wore a plain olive-coloured wool gown that hugged the ample curves of her bosom before slipping gracefully past a tiny waist and narrow hips. In profile, her nose was slightly turned up at the tip and her lips were plump and very pink. The watery sun coming through the many-paned window shot blue highlights through her ebony hair which was long, parted in the middle and caught in a severe chignon at the nape of an elegant white neck.

'Mary Margaret,' the Dowager said, 'I asked you here to meet my son, Lord Ravensford. You and he will be spending a great deal of time together in London while you chaperon my goddaughter. My son shall provide the cachet for you to be accepted into the homes of the *ton*.'

Ravensford kept himself from wincing. His mother was not known for her tact. That discomfort faded as the young woman turned to face him.

His mother was right. The chit was not a traditional beauty. She was an exotic temptress.

Her hair lay like a smooth satin cap against her head. He would have likened her to a Madonna because of the demure style and calm scrutiny in her eyes, but there was too much of the unusual in her looks. Her face was heart shaped with winged brows and high cheekbones. Her chin was pointed and with a dainty cleft. But it was her eyes that held him captive. They were green as the finest emeralds and tilted at the corners like a cat's. Her features intensified his impression of her voice, as did her movements when she took a step closer. She was lithe and graceful, flowing like a feline that glides along the ground intent on its own world.

She was amazing. Too bad she was also untrustworthy.

'My lord,' Mary Margaret murmured, making a shallow curtsy.

He rose. 'Please be seated, Miss O'Brien.'

'Thank you.' She took the chair closest to her and sat ramrod straight, yet gracefully as a cat positioning itself to watch the world.

He eased back down and waited to see what more his mother intended and how the woman would react. Much could be told about a person by watching them. It was a trait he had cultivated and which made him very successful in getting some of his less than popular bills through the House of Lords.

'Mary Margaret, we will be staying with my son in London. You will be in charge of completing anything my son has not finished so that the house is ready for us to entertain.'

The woman nodded her head, keeping her huge eyes turned to the Countess. Ravensford found himself wanting to provoke her to speak. He wanted to hear her voice now that he could watch her body and face at the same time. She fascinated him.

'Will you be sending Miss O'Brien ahead, Mother? That would be best if you intend her to make sure that everything is in order.'

It was a provocative idea, and his mother's answer would tell him much about where the Countess placed the woman socially. That she did not think the chit a person of Quality did not mean she thought the girl should be alone with a man. Propriety was propriety.

'Why, that is an excellent suggestion,' his mother said. 'I should have thought of it sooner.' She turned her attention to the other woman. 'I believe you should go ahead. Andrew, arrange for Mary Margaret to depart immediately. With luck and good weather, she should be in London within two weeks. That will give her plenty of time.'

Ravensford thought that some colour mounted Miss O'Brien's high cheeks, but she was so composed he could not be sure. She might be his mother's new companion, but his parent did not consider her of consequence. Inexplicably, Ravensford found himself irritated with his mother. She was often oblivious to the feelings of others, and he had thought himself inured to it. It seemed he was not.

'It would be better if I escorted Miss O'Brien. A woman travelling alone is fair game for anyone.'

No respectable woman travelled with a man unchaperoned, but Mary Margaret O'Brien was considered a servant and therefore had no reputation to lose. Even though part of him rose in anger at this lack of regard for the woman, another part of him looked coldly on. She intended to steal from his mother. The trip would allow him to watch her.

The fact that his gut tightened in anticipation was nothing. He must put aside the very physical reminder that she was an enticing woman and remember only that she was a woman out to steal from his mother. That was where his focus should be.

Mary Margaret O'Brien glanced at him, her expression unreadable. She would be a good card player.

Or a good thief.

His mother frowned. 'I really don't see that your presence is necessary. Several outriders will do just as well.'

Ravensford looked blandly at his mother. 'I disagree. It's obvious that Miss O'Brien is gently reared or you would not have her for a companion. The trip to London is long and not always safe. I must insist on accompanying her.'

His mother's frown turned to a glare. It was not often that he refused to do her bidding.

'If you insist,' she said ungraciously. She stood up and moved to the fireplace where the bell pull was, casting Ravensford a you-will-pay look. 'The two of you should not linger here. There is much too much to be done. I will order the travelling carriage to be readied for departure tomorrow morning.'

Ravensford groaned. He should have known that, once he insisted on thwarting her, she would make the result as unpleasant as possible. That was her way of seeing that he did not refuse her in the future. She had used that method on him all his life and it usually worked.

He remembered the time shortly after his father died when he had suggested they have Raven Ab-

bey modernised. She had not wanted anything
changed. To her Raven Abbey was a symbol of
her life with her husband. But Ravensford had insisted. Before he had even had time enough to determine whom the architect should be and what
should be done, the Countess had hired Nash and
determined the entire structure should be redone in
the Egyptian mode so popular at the time. He still
had difficulty visiting his country seat.

During the entire exchange, Miss O'Brien had
looked straight ahead. Never once had she so much
as glanced at the two people who were deciding
her immediate future. He would have felt like chat-
tel. Part of him rebelled at what they were doing
to her.

'You are dismissed, Mary Margaret,' the Countess said haughtily. 'I am sure you have much to
do before you leave.'

Miss O'Brien rose quickly and curtsied to the
Countess. 'My lady. I shall be ready whenever you
wish.' Then as though reluctant, she turned to him
and dipped down. 'My lord.'

He rose quickly. 'I will send a maid to help you
pack.'

Her incredible eyes widened momentarily. 'That
won't be necessary, my lord. I have little to take
and nothing I cannot pack myself.'

He met her calm gaze. 'Someone will help you.'

'Really, Andrew, don't be importunate,' his mother said, only barely covering her disapproval with disdain.

Ravensford ignored his parent.

Miss O'Brien bowed her head in acceptance even though Ravensford sensed that the chit was far from compliant. 'Thank you, my lord.'

'You may go, Mary Margaret,' the Countess said coldly.

A flash of what might have been anger entered the younger woman's eyes, but was gone so quickly that Ravensford decided he had been mistaken. He would not have blamed her had she taken offense at his mother's words and tone.

He watched her leave the room, intrigued by her walk. Tall and regal, she held herself as though a book balanced on the top of her head. She was magnificent. Too bad she was employed by his parent. Otherwise he would offer a *carte blanche* and the devil take the results.

No woman had ever made him react this strongly. Try as he might, the idea of her in his arms and in his bed created an unquenchable fire in his loins.

'Andrew!'

He turned his attention back to his mother. 'Yes?' he asked, pretending that he saw nothing unusual in her command.

'The girl is nobody. She does not need your attentions or your help. Leave her alone.'

Irritation tightened the corners of his mouth. His mother was used to having her way. 'I do not intend to do her harm.'

'See that it remains that way.' The Countess chopped her normally languid hand. 'Now be gone. I must rest.'

Ravensford made an ironic bow and left. He would arrange for a maid to help Miss O'Brien, a loyal servant who had been in his mother's employ for years, despite what his mother and the girl wanted. Perhaps his mother's personal maid, Jane. She would know if anything in Miss O'Brien's possessions really belonged to his mother, and she would come to him immediately if that were the case.

Chapter Two

Mary Margaret left the drawing room as sedately as her thumping heart would let her. Behind her the Countess and Earl talked as though they were alone. To them, she was a servant, and the aristocracy talked in front of their servants as though they did not exist.

She carefully closed the heavy door. The butler stood nearby, waiting for orders. She smiled at him before turning and hurrying down the hall toward the servants' stairs and the back entrance.

She had to tell Thomas immediately. He would be furious. Nor did she want to go to London. This was home and she had never been farther than the nearby village of Cashel.

And there were Emily and Annie to take care of.

She rushed out the door, not bothering with a

cape, and sped down the path that led to the trail through the pastures. As curate, Thomas had a small cottage near the church. She hoped he would be there and if not, then at the church.

She was out of breath when she got there. She pounded impatiently on the door. After what seemed an eternity, Annie answered.

Her niece was small for her age, with large green eyes, a pointed chin and a wealth of black hair. She had been crying.

Mary Margaret fell to her knees and gathered the child in her arms. She stroked back the long hair, dread filling her. 'What is the matter, sweetheart?'

'Hiccup.' Annie squirmed away and rubbed at her eyes. 'Daddy…was angry.'

Mary Margaret closed her own eyes, wishing she could blot out the misery in her niece's and knowing she could not. 'Where is your mama?'

Annie jerked her head toward the bedroom.

'Stay here, sweetheart,' Mary Margaret said calmly, even though she was far from calm. The last thing she wanted was to upset Annie further.

As curate, Thomas had a modest cottage. The large rectory was occupied by the parish minister. Thomas had spent many afternoons and Sundays trying to ingratiate himself into the Countess's good graces in the hope that she would provide him with his own living. So far, he was unsuccessful. That was just one of the reasons Thomas wanted her to steal for him.

She knocked before entering the room. Her only sister sat hunched on the bed, one hand cradling her cheek. Mary Margaret rushed to her.

'Oh, Emily. Let me see.' She pulled Emily's hand away and frowned. 'You will have a bruise.'

'I walked into the door.'

Mary Margaret moved away to the water basin where she wet a cloth. Taking it back to her sister, she said, 'No, you did not. Thomas hit you. But why?'

Emily refused to meet Mary Margaret's eyes. Compassion and anger warred in Mary Margaret. Emily had been a beauty, her hair dark as a raven's wing and her eyes blue as the sky. Now she was worn beyond her twenty-six years. Mary Margaret hated Thomas Fox, hated him with a passion that, in her calmer moments, shamed her.

Emily shrugged. 'Who knows?'

Mary Margaret was afraid she did. He had not liked her defiance. What would he do now?

'Emily, leave him. Come away with me. We will take Annie.'

'And go where? Neither of us has money to even feed ourselves for one day, let alone care for a child.' Bitterness tinged every word. 'No, I must

stay. At least Annie is fed and clothed and has a
roof over her head.'

'Come to the big house with me.'

'Ha! The Countess cares less than nothing for
the likes of us.'

'But the Earl is here. They say he is compassionate, and so he seemed.'

A slight gleam of interest entered Emily's dull
eyes. 'The Earl is here? Perhaps that is why
Thomas was angry. He might fear that the Earl will
take his mother away and just when Thomas is
getting close enough to ask her for a better living.'

She had not thought of that and her fear
mounted. He would be furious when he found out
that they were all leaving for London shortly. Unconsciously she started wringing her hands.

'Oh, dear, Emily.' She fell to her knees in front
of her sister and grasped Emily's hands. 'Please,
please come away with me now. Please.'

'Why?'

'We are all leaving. The Earl, the Countess,
and…me. Going to London.' She rushed on. 'I
have a little put aside. I will send you more when
I get my first quarterly salary.'

Emily sagged. 'I have nowhere to go.'

Desperate as she was, Mary Margaret knew Emily was right. There was nowhere to go. No one
would believe that the saintly, wonderful Mr Fox

beat his wife. Not even the vicar. Nor could she go to the Countess. As Emily had said, the woman would not care.

Wearily she stood. 'Where is Thomas? I must tell him.'

Emily sighed. 'At the church.'

Feeling more defeated than when her parents had both suddenly died of influenza and she had had to shoulder the burden of caring for her younger sister, Mary Margaret trudged from the room. The church was only a five-minute walk away.

She entered the darkened sanctuary and had to give her eyes several moments to adjust. Thomas was at the front talking to Mrs Smith, one of the farmers' wives. Mary Margaret sat on the nearest wooden bench to wait.

When Thomas finally headed her way, she could tell by his walk that he was furious. She gulped back her fear and resisted the urge to flee. Unpleasant as her news was, she had to tell him.

He stopped short of her, arms akimbo. He looked like a golden god towering above her. With his blue eyes, sun-bright hair, perfect physique and immaculate grooming, he looked to be everything a woman could want and everything a parish could desire in their spiritual leader. How false.

Unbidden, the image of the Earl formed. He was

not breathtakingly handsome as Thomas was.
Ravensford was rugged, more earthlike in his masculine appeal, with auburn hair and piercing green
eyes. He was also more powerfully built, giving a
sense of protection to those around him—or so she
had felt. He was oddly disturbing to her.

'Why are you here?'

Thomas's demand effectively ended Mary Margaret's thoughts. She stood, not willing to have
him lord it over her.

Taking a deep breath, she rushed the words.
'The Countess, the Earl and I are leaving for London immediately.'

'What?' His voice filled the tiny church, echoing
off the centuries-old stone walls.

It was all Mary Margaret could do not to cringe.
She had learned to fear Thomas's anger.

'The Countess is taking her goddaughter to London for a Season. I am to go ahead with the Earl
to prepare the town house.'

Thomas's hand moved as though he meant to
slap her. Mary Margaret stepped back. How could
they have ever thought him the answer to Emily's
prayers? How his charm and seeming devotion to
her sister had fooled them.

'When?'

'Tomorrow. The Countess is to follow.'

He paced away, his boots ringing on the stone

floor. Coming back, he ordered, 'Do as the Countess wishes. There are bound to be more opportunities in London for you to steal from her.'

Mary Margaret blanched. She had secretly hoped he would tell her to quit, that London was too far away and did him no good.

When she spoke she was glad her voice did not quaver. 'But how shall I get home? Even if I do manage to get her jewels, I don't know how to get back from London.'

His fine mouth sneered. 'That is your problem, one you will solve since Emily and Annie will be here.'

His implied threat was only what she had expected. He knew she would manage somehow to keep him from hurting them more. He was ordering her to do an immoral and illegal act. Even though she hoped to thwart him and still save her sister and niece, the anger toward him that she usually held in check burst out.

'If you harm them, if you so much as lay a finger on Annie or hit Emily again, I shall turn myself into the authorities and I shall tell them all about you.'

He laughed. 'Very noble. But no one will believe your story about me. I am the younger son of Viscount Fox. It would be your word against mine—and you are nobody.'

The sense of defeat gnawed at her. She fought it off. 'They might not believe me, but it would do your reputation no good to have the accusation made public.'

His narrowed eyes told her she had finally succeeded in getting past his armour. 'Do so and I will make you rue the instant you opened your mouth.'

She never doubted him. Her hands clenched in the folds of her gown.

'Now, get out of here. I will be waiting for your first report and your final return.'

His cold words washed over her nerves like a scratch on a blackboard. She was defeated. Again.

She retraced her steps to Derry House. She came even with the Gothic folly the Countess had built last summer. Honeysuckle mingled with climbing roses, acting like curtains for the structure's windows. Soon they would bloom and their scents would fill the air. A brook raced along behind. Birds cavorted overhead and roosted in the eaves. It was a haven she had frequently gone to during her short time with the Countess.

Her feet took her toward it now.

She reached the door just as a rustle caught her attention, followed by a shadow disengaging from an interior wall. Her heart thumped and her left hand rose to her throat.

'Miss O'Brien,' a male baritone said.

She recognised the Earl's voice instantly. The deep tone slid like velvet along her senses. Even in the dim, filtered light she could see the glint of his copper hair. His teeth were a bared white slash.

She forced herself to relax. Her hand fell to her side and her breathing evened out. 'My lord.'

He advanced on her until he was close enough that she imagined she could feel the heat from his body. Awareness of him rose within her like a tidal wave reaching for the full moon. She shivered.

'Do you come here often?' His tone was conversational, yet she thought she detected an underlying current of interest. But why?

'When I feel the need for privacy.' She answered him bluntly and boldly, knowing she should be more respectful, yet needing that privacy very much. He was too disturbing, increasing her discomfort.

Instead of finding solace in her hidey-hole, she was finding a very disquieting part of her nature. Since watching her sister fall in love with a man like Thomas Fox, Mary Margaret had made herself impervious to men. The Earl was slipping past her barrier. Even his voice aroused her senses. What would it be like if he touched her?

Shocked at her own forwardness in even thinking such a thing, she drew herself straight. Proper ladies did not have such thoughts, not even ladies born of yeoman farmers.

'And you wish me at the devil instead of invading your solitude,' he murmured, a hint of amusement making his voice rich and creamy.

'I had hoped to be alone,' she said, keeping her tone even in spite of the tremors shifting through her body.

She was never this bold, but desperation drove her. He disturbed her too much, and she needed time to think through what she was going to do. Relief flooded her when he moved forward, as though to pass her and go out the door that was behind her. The relief was short lived.

He stopped beside her, close enough that she could feel his warm breath. She had never been this close to a man who was not family. She licked suddenly dry lips.

'You look upset, Miss O'Brien. Is there anything I can do?'

Her eyes widened. He sounded genuinely concerned. For a moment, but not longer, she found herself tempted to pour out her problem. He was a powerful man. He could help her, help her sister and niece, if he chose. Then the moment was gone.

She had heard many things about this man standing too close to her. The young female servants said he was known for his mistresses and his charm. The men admired his abilities in sports. He was what the fashionable called a Corinthian. She had even heard that he was a champion of the downtrodden.

All she could think of was that he was the Countess's son, and the Countess cared nothing for those beneath her.

No, no matter how tempting the Earl made his question sound, she would not answer. She had too much to lose and, as far as she knew, nothing to gain by confiding in him.

'Thank you for your concern, my lord, but I am fine. I am a solitary person, that is all.'

His eyes met and held hers for a long time. She realised with a thrill of apprehension that she could not make herself look away. For her, he was more dangerous than Thomas.

'Then I shall leave you.' He nodded before sauntering from the building.

Mary Margaret barely made it to one of several chairs positioned around the folly before her legs gave out. She gripped the arms until her knuckles turned white and she lost feeling in her fingers. If she reacted this strongly to him after such a brief exposure, how was she going to survive the trip to London in his company? This was madness.

And yet…was this how Emily had felt the first time she saw Thomas? She had never understood

Emily's immediate attraction to Thomas, and when they had wed after only knowing each other a month she had been shocked. Perhaps now she could understand.

But none of this solved her problem. Even with the threat to Emily and Annie, she was not sure she could bring herself to steal from the Countess. In the back of her mind, she had hoped to devise a plan that would outsmart Thomas. So far, she had not.

She chewed her bottom lip.

This trip to London might be better than she had thought. It would give her time to formulate something without having Thomas constantly coming upon her and demanding that she act immediately or he would hurt her sister. Not even Thomas could be so impatient as not to realise how much more time it would take to gain access to the Countess's jewels now that she was going to London. It was her only hope.

She rose with a sigh. Tired as she was, she still had to pack her meagre belongings. The day was nearly over and tomorrow would be here all too soon.

She made her way to the manor's back entrance. From there, she climbed the servants' stairs to the third floor. Wearily, she pushed open the door to her room and froze.

'What are you doing here?'

Jane, the Countess's personal maid, looked over her plump shoulder. She was a round woman, her apple-red face as full as the rest. Iron-grey hair worn pulled tightly back made her look like a dumpling. She was not the merry character her person resembled.

'What are you gaping at, girl?' Jane demanded.

Mary Margaret tamped down on the anger brought about by this invasion of privacy. 'Who let you in?'

'Don't be daft. I let myself in.' Jane straightened out and turned to face Mary Margaret.

'I told the Earl that I don't require help to pack.'

Jane snorted, her full mouth and button nose prominent. 'His lordship does as he pleases. He ordered me here even though waiting on you is beneath me.' She cast an unfriendly look at Mary Margaret. 'Don't be thinking you're better than you are. The Earl is in a hurry to do his mother's bidding, missy.'

She turned her back on Mary Margaret and marched to the plain oak dresser. She pulled out the few neatly folded clothes and eyed them with a jaundiced look. 'Least they are clean.'

Mary Margaret had done her best to tolerate this invasion, but this last was too much. 'They are more than clean. They are decent and come by honestly. More than some can say.' She stalked to the other woman and took the maligned clothing from Jane's plump fingers. 'I do not need your disparaging comments or your help. Please leave.'

Jane's brown eyes narrowed and her lips thinned. 'Don't be getting above yourself, missy.'

Seeing that she was only making matters worse, Mary Margaret tried another track. 'I know my place very well, and I am far beneath your notice. You are a busy woman and have other things to do. My meagre packing should not detain you.'

'True,' Jane said with a haughty sniff. 'But if I don't help, his lordship won't be happy.'

Mary Margaret considered the Earl for a minute. He was the source of quite a bit of her uneasiness, and she liked him less by the instant. 'He will live. Surely I am not the first person during his lifetime to refuse his bidding.'

'That's as may be. *I* have never gone against his lordship's orders unless my lady has bid me differently.'

'I have no doubt of it,' Mary Margaret murmured, weary of the confrontation and the conversation. They went in circles. 'Perhaps it would be enough for you to see my few belongings.'

Jane looked down her tiny nose as Mary Margaret took out the remainder of her belongings and spread them on the narrow bed. A travelling dress, two day dresses, boots, pattens, one pair of slippers, a nightdress with a plain robe, and underclothes completed her wardrobe.

'What about jewellery?'

Mary Margaret pulled a simple gold locket from beneath the collar of her dress. Inside were tiny pictures of her parents. 'Only this.'

Jane looked disdainfully at the unadorned piece. 'Anything else?'

Mary Margaret curled her fingers protectively around the locket. It was all she had left of her parents. The farm her father had worked had passed to someone upon his death, the furniture and personal items going to pay debts and hers and Emily's education with the vicar where Emily had met Thomas. She pushed away the painful memories of loss and regret.

'No, I have nothing else,' Mary Margaret said. 'Except my portmanteau. Would you care to examine it? Or watch while I pack?'

Jane took the only chair, her ample dimensions flowing over the sides. 'I will watch.'

Mary Margaret bit back a sharp retort and started folding clothes. The sooner she was done the sooner she would be alone. Minutes later, she stuffed the last item into the now full portmanteau.

'Harumph! You will never get the wrinkles out,' Jane stated, standing.

'I will manage. I am, after all, merely a servant, and not even an important one.'

'True.'

Without another word, Jane left, her ample form squeezing through the sides of the door. Mary Margaret released a sigh.

Why did the Earl care about her packing? It seemed such a small and silly thing for him to be concerned about.

He was very disconcerting, as was her reaction to him. If he told her to do something, she would be hard pressed to refuse him simply because she found him so mesmerising. Hopefully she would see very little of him. Most gentlemen did not like travelling in a carriage, so he would probably ride most of the trip. In London he would be too busy to pay attention to her.

She rose and went to the single window. Using her handkerchief, she rubbed a spot clean and gazed out at the immaculately groomed garden. Green speckled with other colours met her eye. Above, clouds scudded across a pale blue sky. This evening would bring rain. Nothing unusual in Ireland. Spring was her favourite time of the year, a time of new beginnings and birth.

How she wished Emily would run away with her and start anew. But so far she refused. And because of that, Mary Margaret had to do as Thomas ordered. When she had initially refused his orders, he had threatened to do more than blacken Emily's eye or Annie's jaw. So she had agreed. But somehow she would thwart him and get Emily and Annie from him. No matter that the law said a wife was her husband's property and a daughter the same until given to another man in marriage.

A robin flew by the window, its little chest covered by a red vest, and alighted on the nearby tree. His colourful feathers reminded her once more of the Earl of Ravensford.

He was a ruggedly handsome man, not at all classical in looks. His eyes sparkled with something deeper than humour that was more compelling than mere charm, although she was sure that he had more than his fair share of that attribute. Then there was his mouth that hinted at passions she could only guess about. When he had spoken to her, she had been hard pressed not to lose herself in the fantasy of his lips on hers. A silly thought and totally impossible.

She sighed at her own weakness, her finger tracing a pattern in the glass. Before she quite realised what she had done, there was a man's profile etched in the window.

With the strong, patrician nose, the picture could only be of Ravensford. He was a forceful man, used to having his own way. She also knew he could be dangerous for her.

She put her palm to the glass and smeared out the image. If only she could as easily banish him from her mind. Everything seemed to lead back to him.

With a sigh, she turned away. These melancholy thoughts helped no one, and tomorrow she began her long journey to London with the Earl as her protector.

A shiver chased down her spine. From fear or anticipation, she knew not, only that she felt alive as never before.

Chapter Three

Stone-grey clouds scuttled across the early morning sky. Damp, cold wind rippled through the trees and whipped Mary Margaret's cape into a frenzy about her legs.

She started down the first marble step, wondering when the Countess would appear and order her to return inside the house and go out the servants' entrance. The Countess had done that Mary Margaret's first day. The butler and footmen had watched impassively, but one of the young female servants had snickered. Mary Margaret had not made that mistake again—until today. It was nerves.

The travelling carriage, with whatever the Earl and his mother had thought necessary, waited on the gravel outside the front entry, scant yards from her. The horses champed at the bit and pawed the

ground, their breath mist on the rising wind. It
would storm soon, spring forgotten in winter's dying hand. Travel would be hard.

In her hurry, she tripped in her skirts. Her feet
skidded on the slick stone, and she pitched forward. The hard marble raced toward her face. She
flung a hand up to break her fall, dropping her
portmanteau.

An arm like a band of iron wrapped around her
waist. A firm hand caught her elbow and helped
steady her. In seconds she was pressed against an
unyielding chest.

She took a breath to still her beating heart,
knowing she had been saved from a nasty accident.
Thinking herself once more in charge of her emotions, she tried to move away from the man who
held her. The grip tightened so that she twisted in
the no longer needed embrace, intending to set the
importunate person in his place. She might not be
a lady of Quality, but she was a lady and no lady
was held so intimately by a man who was not her
father, brother or husband.

Eyes the colour of newly scythed grass met hers.
A mouth she had thought sensual yesterday curved
into a wicked smile, showing a dimple in the left
cheek that threatened to weaken her knees. Still,
the Earl's grip on her waist did not loosen. If anything, it tightened.

The look he bent on her took another turn, becoming slumberous and intense. Awareness of his body pressed so tightly to hers shivered along her every nerve.

After an eternity, his arm slid away, gliding along the curve of her waist and skirting the swell of her hips. It was nearly a caress and she felt it through all the layers of her dress, pelisse and cape. Heat threatened to engulf her entire being.

She forced her eyes to look away from his and her knees to bend in a curtsy. 'Thank you, my lord,' she murmured, not sure what she thanked him for. Part of her mind knew he had saved her from a disastrous fall, yet another part of her mind understood that he had awakened something in her that had been dormant. 'Thank you for stopping my fall,' she said at last.

'You are welcome,' he said, his voice low and husky as though he had an inflammation of the lungs. He had not sounded this way yesterday.

'Are you unwell, my lord?' she blurted.

His smile became rueful. 'Nothing so mundane. Let me help you down the rest of these steps. They are treacherous in weather such as this, and it would not suit my mother to have you injured and forced to remain here.'

He spoke the truth, yet she sensed more beneath his words. Instantly she scolded herself. His hand

still held her elbow and it made reasonable thinking hard. Her reaction to him scared her. Scared
her as nothing else ever had.

'Thank you, my lord,' she murmured once
again. 'But I am on my guard now and able to care
for myself.'

She bent to retrieve her portmanteau. His hand
was before hers.

'I can carry it.'

'I am sure you can, but I shall do so.'

He gave her a mocking half-bow that brought
the blush of embarrassment to her cheeks. What
would the other servants say about this? What
would his mother say when she heard the gossip?
The Countess would not be pleased. Perhaps it was
just as well that she was leaving.

From beneath her lashes, she watched Ravensford hand her portmanteau to a footman. His shoulders appeared broader than yesterday, the many
capes of his coat accentuating them. His hair sparkled like copper even in the dull light coming
through the clouds. She shook herself in an effort
to dispel his draw.

He turned at that moment. 'You are cold. Get
inside the coach. There are blankets and heated
stones. A bottle full of hot water as well. Another
full of hot chocolate.'

'Are you travelling in the carriage, my lord?' All those comforts could not be for her.

'Later. Perhaps.'

He helped her into the carriage, his hand lingering. Her gaze went to his touch before rising to his face. The look he gave her was one she did not understand, but knew instinctively meant danger to her.

He released her. 'Drink all the hot chocolate. It will help keep you warm until we stop for lunch.'

She looked at him. 'Surely it is for you.'

'I think not.' He chuckled. 'Too sweet for my tastes. I like a drink that burns its way down and keeps me warm.'

Almost she thought he meant something besides what his words said. In her fancy, she could think he spoke a special language just for her. This would not do.

She fell back on the security of protocol. 'Thank you, my lord.'

He gave her a quizzical look before turning away. She breathed a sigh of relief. His regard was too disturbing.

Ravensford made his way to his mount. Could a woman with a voice and looks such as hers truly be the innocent she portrayed? Or was this all part of her plan to steal from his mother? Both were questions he could not answer yet, but he would eventually, no matter what he had to do.

Ravensford mounted, and with a wave of his hand to the groom holding the horse's reins, he set out. It would be a long journey.

He glanced back once, wondering if his mother was up and watching. No pale face looked out from a window. The Countess was still abed, as he had expected.

The weather rapidly worsened, and Ravensford considered riding in the carriage—a big lumbering vehicle designed to carry luggage, not people who were in a hurry. And they were in a hurry. There was much to be done to his town house in order to bring it up to his mother's standards and very little time to do it in.

Riding his horse and getting drenched to the bone would accomplish nothing, while if he rode inside he would be able to question Miss O'Brien about herself and her future. Not to mention take in his fill of her exotic features. The last was a consideration he pushed from his mind. His duty was to learn enough to outfox her, not to become entangled with her.

He signalled the coachman and outriders to stop. His mount was tied to the back of the vehicle and the ancient steps let down. Ravensford entered in time to see the woman hurriedly stuff something under the neck of her gown, as though she did not wish him to see whatever it was. He wondered if it was something to do with her mission.

Mary Margaret saw the Earl's gaze on her neck. Homesick already, she had been gazing at the pictures of her parents in her locket. The moment was too personal to share with someone she did not know, so when she had heard the coach door open, she had put the locket back.

Warily, she watched the Earl take the seat opposite her, back to the horses, and make himself comfortable. She had not thought he would join her, no matter how awful the weather became.

'I thought gentlemen preferred to ride,' she said. 'Nor should you be the one to sit facing away from the horses.'

His right eyebrow rose, a burnt slash across his broad brow. 'Gentlemen do as they please, and it pleases me to get inside away from the wind and rain and to sit where I am. 'Tis too bad the others cannot do the same. I would call a halt if I thought this storm would let up soon. Unfortunately, it looks to follow us to the coast.'

Mary Margaret felt her mouth drop in surprise. 'You care about their discomfort?'

Ravensford frowned. 'They are human beings, are they not?'

She nodded, clamping her teeth shut. She had

already more than overstepped the gap between an earl and a tenant farmer's daughter. She did not need to compound her error with more inane comments.

Silence fell, but she was intensely, painfully aware of his nearness. She could hear him breathing and cast him fleeting glances from beneath her lashes. He lounged at his leisure, or as much as was possible with the carriage swaying from side to side and jolting with every numerous hole in the road. His right hand gripped the leather strap for stability. He had long fingers, covered by riding gloves.

She saw his muscles bunch beneath the folds of his coat. Confusion spread through her as she remembered the strength in his circling arm when he had caught her up. No man had ever held her so close, yet it had felt right—and exciting.

She turned her head sharply, hoping to forget the sensation of his touch by looking anywhere but at him. He was a disturbing man. More so because of what she had to do—unless she could outwit her brother-in-law.

'What do you see in the rain that is so interesting?'

His voice was deep with the refined tones of the British aristocracy. Yet there was more to it than that. There was a warmth that seemed to stroke her nerves, heightening her senses.

She shook her head at her fancifulness. This had to stop. He was so far above her as to be as unattainable as the sun. Not that she wanted him. She was not so susceptible nor so stupid as to let her imagination run that wild.

He probably treated his women poorly. He certainly would never marry such as herself, and she would never be a man's mistress—not that he had asked or even intended to do so. So, there it was. She was being overly silly and all because he was handsome and had a voice that made her insides feel like warm pudding.

She said the first safe thing that popped into her head. 'We shall have to stop soon if this rain continues. The road is becoming a morass.'

'True.'

He leaned forward to look out the window, moving so close to her that she felt stifled. She wondered if he did so on purpose, if he knew how his proximity affected her. She drew back, putting as much distance between them as the confines would allow. He shot her a glance that in her mind seemed to say he knew how disturbing his nearness was.

'I am hoping to reach a small inn on the outskirts of the next town. At least there we can stable the horses and all get warm food and a place to sleep.'

Instead of shifting back to his place, he stayed watching out the window. The dim carriage lamp showed his profile, his arrogant nose a-jut and his jaw a firm statement of strength. Golden stubble dotted his face, surprising her. She had thought he would grow a red beard because of his hair. She was wrong.

After her heart had raced itself to a near stop in sheer exhaustion, he finally sat back. He slanted her a speculative glance. She met his study with as much aplomb as she could dredge up. She had never been uncomfortable around men, but she was with him. Her skin prickled and her imagination ran amok, neither one being a condition she enjoyed, or so she told herself.

'I hope you won't find the lack of comforts at this place too much of a hardship, Miss O'Brien.'

That was the last thing she had expected him to be concerned about. 'Me? I should think your lordship will have a greater problem than me.'

A bitter smile twisted his fine mouth. 'I bivouacked in the Peninsula. I am used to Spartan accommodations. It is you I am concerned for.'

Was he baiting her? And if so, why should he think this would do so? 'I am sure you are, my lord. However, I too am used to not being coddled.'

'Really? Where did you live before coming to stay with my mother?'

His voice showed only mild interest, yet Mary Margaret was instantly on her guard. There was no reason a man of his standing should be interested in her past. But once the question was asked, there was no reason to lie. She would tell him her life's story, except for Thomas's treatment of Emily, and the Earl would quickly find himself bored.

'I am the oldest daughter of one of your mother's tenant farmers. My parents are gone and my sister is married.'

He picked up the earthenware container of hot chocolate. 'Would you care for some, Miss O'Brien?'

The abrupt change in conversation nonplussed her. 'Please.'

Somehow he managed to pour her a cup without spilling the liquid. She took it, startled by the shock when her fingers accidentally brushed his. The jolt felt like the spark caused when her feet brushed along a carpet and then she touched something.

'You are very well-spoken for a tenant farmer's daughter,' he said while she took a sip of the hot chocolate.

She wondered if he always jumped from topic to topic. It was very disconcerting.

'My mother's father was a vicar. She…married beneath her. She taught us diction and everything she knew. When her knowledge ran out, she did chores for Reverend Hopkins in exchange for lessons in Greek and Latin for us.'

'Who is us?'

'My sister Emily and myself.'

'You are very well educated. Most women of my acquaintance are only barely conversant in those languages. Many can't even speak French fluently.'

His praise embarrassed her. She was not used to compliments in any form, let alone from someone of his position. His mother certainly had not thought her accomplishments worth much.

By the time her first quarter with the Countess was over, she would have barely enough to keep herself and Emily for a year and that was if they lived as frugally as their upbringing had taught them and did small chores in exchange for food. Still, they would manage. They had to.

Thankfully, the carriage lurched because she had no answer to his praise. The liquid in her cup sloshed over the rim and on to her lap. She bounced forward as the vehicle stopped.

For the second time in one day, she found herself in the Earl's arms. If it were not so disturbing to her peace of mind and calmness of body, she would find it amusing. As it was, she could barely breathe. His face was too close, his arms too tight, and his lips too enticing.

'Catching you seems to be my job today,' he murmured, continuing to hold her.

She stared up at him, a distant part of her awareness wondering why he did not release her. The majority of her awareness thrilled to his touch.

She watched as his gaze travelled from her eyes to her mouth. Hunger, or some other strong emotion she could not name, drew harsh lines in his cheeks. If she didn't know better, she would think he intended to kiss her. She was being silly.

His face lowered until his warm breath caressed her skin. The scent of lemons and musk filled her senses. She knew she should struggle. She was not the type of woman men kissed unless their intentions were less than honourable. She had nothing to offer and no family to defend her.

His mouth skimmed hers and she melted against him, knowing even as she did so that she was making a terrible mistake.

'My lord,' a male voice said from outside the coach.

Ravensford thrust her away so quickly Mary Margaret's head swam. She blinked several times in a vain attempt to clear her senses.

'My lord, we are stuck solid in the mud.'

'Damnation, I was afraid of that,' the Earl said, opening the carriage door and jumping out without a backward glance at Mary Margaret.

Unconsciously, the trembling fingers of one hand went to her mouth. He had nearly kissed her. His lips had brushed hers. She still felt weak as a kitten. He had such power over her without even trying.

Taking a deep breath, she composed herself as best she could. She pulled a handkerchief from her reticule and dabbed half-heartedly at the spill of chocolate that had started the whole episode.

From the open door came the sounds of men cursing. She edged to the door and looked out. The back wheel on her side was sunk up to the axle in mud. The two outriders, the groom and coachman were all trying to lever the wheel out of the hole. She knew her weight was not making their effort any easier.

Gathering her cape close around her neck, Mary Margaret leapt from the carriage to what had once been the dirt road. She landed with a splat and sank several inches. Rain pelted her. Thank goodness the wind had stopped or the weather would be truly beastly. As it was, she was a country girl and could stand in this rain for hours if need be.

'What do you think you are doing?' the Earl demanded, stalking toward her. He stopped barely a foot from her, his face a mask of irritation.

His angry voice surprised her. 'I am getting out of the carriage to lighten the load,' she said in a voice that implied that her action was self-evident. Still, she backed away.

'Get back in.'

'When they are done,' she said calmly, hoping the quiver she felt didn't sound in her voice.

'Get back in or I shall be forced to throw you in.'

She edged back, the mud sucking at her feet and making movement difficult. 'I am used to weather like this. Besides, without my weight the work will go quicker. This is better for everyone. I should feel badly if my staying dry in the carriage meant everyone else had to work harder and longer than necessary.'

'Very noble,' he said sarcastically. 'But I meant what I said. There is no reason for you to suffer like this.'

While he spoke, he stripped off his great coat and then his inner coat until he stood in his shirt. The rain instantly plastered the fine linen to his body.

Try as she would, Mary Margaret could not keep from looking at his chest. Muscles rippled beneath the soaked material, and his shoulders looked broad enough to bear the weight of the coach without help from anyone else.

'Miss O'Brien,' Ravensford said dangerously. He took several steps toward her.

The sound of her name grabbed her attention and she looked up at his face. His eyes seemed to spark in the grey light. Had he seen where her attention had been focussed? She hoped not. She would be too humiliated if he had.

He loomed over her. Dimly she perceived that the other men were watching them, waiting to see what would happen. Her hair had loosened in sodden ropes and she pushed them off her face. The Earl's hair dripped water down his face. They were both being ridiculously stubborn and doing no one any good.

She knew defeat when he stood scowling down at her. She turned and scampered back into the carriage as best she could with mud clinging to her boots like a lover clings to his fleeing mistress. A fanciful thought if she had ever had one, she decided, once she was safely inside the vehicle and away from the Earl's menacing presence.

The rain beat on the roof in rhythm to the men rocking the carriage. Mary Margaret clenched her teeth and hands, hoping they would succeed soon. Everyone was going to be cold, wet and dirty.

A sudden jolt and lurch accompanied by a loud sucking sound told her they were free. She relaxed against the squabs, only belatedly realising her soaked clothing would ruin the velvet cloth. She pealed off her cape and spread it on the seat beside her. The Earl would be joining her soon and they would continue on their way.

The coach moved slowly forward.

Seconds dragged into long minutes and Ravensford did not appear. She looked out the window and saw him mounted on his horse, his coats on once more. His beaver hat provided his face a modicum of protection from the steady downpour.

She relaxed back on to the seat with a sigh, torn between irritation that he was riding in the awful weather and relief that he was not sitting in the carriage with her. She sat engrossed in her confused thoughts until the carriage finally rumbled to a halt.

She quickly realised they must be at the inn that was the Earl's destination. Ravensford himself opened the door and extended his hand to help her out. Reluctantly, she put her fingers into his and met his eyes. His anger sparked at her, and she realised that a confrontation with the Earl lay ahead. And all because she had tried to help.

Chapter Four

The rain pelted her face as she looked defiantly up at Ravensford. His hair dripped water beneath the brim of his beaver hat. Lines radiated from his eyes. On most men of his station the creases would be the results of too many long nights spent gaming, wenching and drinking. She doubted he was any different. The knowledge was small comfort.

When she hesitated, he nearly yanked her from the coach. She gasped and put her free arm on his chest to keep herself from tumbling.

'When I tell you to do something, Miss O'Brien, I mean exactly that.'

'Yes, my lord,' she muttered, twisting her arm in a vain attempt to free it.

'Here,' he said, releasing her while using his one hand to unclasp his great coat. He shrugged out of it and swung it around her.

'I cannot.'

She reached to pluck it from her shoulders, but his hands gripped hers. His eyes blazed down at her.

'What did I just say?'

'I have forgotten,' she said in a spurt of unusual rebellion.

'No, you have not.'

He fastened the top button before grabbing her again and urging her toward the inn's door. The dried dirt on her hem and shoes quickly became mud again. She noticed that his Hessians were coated.

The door opened before the Earl could grasp the handle and a round, squat man stood before them and tisked.

'My lord, I was not expecting you,' the proprietor said, his hands wiping futilely at his pristine white apron.

'I am sorry to discommode you, Littleton. I had hoped to make the coast this evening and therefore not need your services. This storm put paid to that.'

The innkeeper nodded before turning and leading them down a narrow hall. 'My parlour is unoccupied, my lord.'

At the Earl's prodding, Mary Margaret followed the owner to a small room where a fire blazed.

Heat engulfed her. Warm, welcome heat that made her garments steam and smell of wet wool.

'Please, my lord, I will send a girl to fetch your coat for cleaning. And soon—'

'Whiskey for me and tea for the lady,' Ravensford said, interrupting. 'And whatever you are cooking. See that my servants are cared for as well.'

'Yes, my lord. Mutton and potatoes. Ale as well for the others.'

'Plenty of it, Littleton.'

'Yes, my lord.'

The landlord was barely out of the door when Ravensford turned on her. 'Take the coat off, Miss O'Brien. The last thing I need is for you to get an inflammation of the lungs.'

'I am much hardier than that…my lord,' she added.

'And stop "my lording" me. Call me Ravensford.' He slanted her a cool smile. 'All my acquaintants do.'

Instead of responding, she gingerly slid his coat off. It dripped water and mud on the floor.

A knock preceded the door opening and a serving woman entering. 'The landlord sent me to fetch your coat, my lord.'

'Thank you,' he said. 'And please send someone

to get Miss O'Brien's cape from the coach. It will never dry there and will need cleaning.'

'Yes, my lord,' the woman said, taking the coat from Mary Margaret's hands and bundling it up. 'I will be right back to mop up this mess.'

'If you will bring the mop I will do it,' Mary Margaret volunteered, feeling badly about the puddle.

The woman gaped at her. Ravensford scowled.

'That is…I am used to cleaning up.' She knew she was making matters worse, but the words continued to tumble from her mouth.

'Why don't you show Miss O'Brien to her room? Her portmanteau should be there by now and she can change.'

The servant cast him a grateful glance. Mary Margaret realised her offer to mop the floor had made the woman feel awkward. Chagrined, she clamped down on any other words and followed the maid up a narrow flight of stairs to a small corner room. It was neat and clean with a single bed and wash stand. Her portmanteau was on the bed.

The woman left before Mary Margaret could thank her. Just as well. She would not have known what to say.

Half an hour later, she had struggled out of her wet clothing and donned dry ones. The lukewarm water in the wash bowl was brown from dirt, but she felt much better. Hunger rumbled in her stomach. Indecision kept her stationary.

Surely she was not supposed to join the Earl for supper. Which left the public room. The idea of going down among a group of men she did not know was daunting. But not so much as the thought of spending her small hoard of coins. The money was only for an emergency. She did not have enough to spend on anything else if she was going to take Emily away at the end of the quarter.

She sighed. Hungry as she was, she had been hungrier before and lived. She crossed to the bed and sat down. Exhaustion moved through her.

A knock on the door startled her.

The servant stuck her head in and said, 'His lordship be waitin' for you.'

Hunger warred with caution. Hunger won.

Minutes later, Mary Margaret entered the private room and was assailed by the smell of mutton and gravy. Her stomach growled.

'Not a second too soon,' Ravensford said with a grin. 'Have a seat, Miss O'Brien. We will eat and then we will discuss your habit of disobeying me.'

Her pleasure died. She turned to leave, knowing

that eating would only make her uncomfortable now.

'I believe I told you to sit down,' Ravensford said in a dangerously calm voice.

Mary Margaret looked back at him. His mouth was a thin line. His hands paused in the act of carving the leg of mutton. Things were going from bad to worse.

'Thank you, my lord, but I am not as hungry as I thought.' Her stomach chose that moment to put the lie to her words.

'And I am not accustomed to people disregarding my instructions, Miss O'Brien. That is the crux of this situation.'

She straightened her shoulders.

He placed a large slice of mutton on a plate that would have been hers and followed it with vegetables and gravy. Her mouth watered.

'When I tell you to do something,' he said, fixing his own plate, 'I mean for you to do exactly that. This afternoon when I told you to get back in the coach, I did so for a reason.' He took his seat, pointing toward hers with his fork. 'You got out with good intentions. I am sure you meant to lighten the load. What you really did was make the other men feel embarrassed. It is their job to take care of such situations and having a female expose herself to weather such as that made them feel even worse than they already did that the coach had hit a hole. Particularly John Coachman, and he already felt bad enough. It was much kinder for you to remain in the carriage.'

Her attention left the food and focussed on him. 'I had not thought of it that way. I had only meant to help.'

'So, when I tell you to do something, Miss O'Brien, believe that I know best.'

His autocratic manner was irritating, but she recognised the validity of his words.

'Now, please be seated. The food is getting cold.'

She did as he bade. She had thought herself no longer hungry, but the instant the food touched her tongue she was ravenous. She was nearly through when he offered her tea.

'Thank you, my lord,' she murmured, realising too late that he intended to pour for her. 'I should be doing that.'

'So you should.' He shifted the teapot, cream and sugar to her side. 'And I believe I told you to call me Ravensford.'

She stopped putting cream into her tea. 'I know, but your mother would be scandalised.'

He grinned, looking like a small boy who has pulled a prank. She could see the charm he was famous for glinting in his green eyes.

'Yes, she would be, but she isn't here.'

A picture of an irate Countess formed in Mary Margaret's mind. She smiled. 'I will try, my— Ravensford.'

'That's the way.'

He poured himself a drink and lounged back in his chair. He watched her over the rim of the glass. Mary Margaret felt like a bug pinned to a mat for someone's pleasure.

'I am very tired, m— Ravensford. And I am sure that tomorrow will be an early day. Do you mind if I go to bed?'

His scrutiny intensified. The angle of his cheek and jaw sharpened. 'Yes, I would mind, Miss O'Brien, but I will allow it. The last thing I want is for you to become exhausted before we even reach London.'

Feeling like the fox fleeing the hounds, Mary Margaret jumped up, nearly spilling her half-drunk tea. 'Thank you.'

She scurried to the door, only to find the Earl there. His large frame blocked her exit. She gazed up at him, trying to ignore the blood pounding in her ears.

He caught her chin in his well-shaped hand and rubbed his thumb back and forth over the tiny cleft below her bottom lip. She was unable to look away. He could do anything to her and she doubted that she would be able or even willing to say him nay. She gulped hard, her eyes wide.

'You are tired,' he murmured. 'I hope your bed is soft and to your satisfaction. If not, I will have you given another room.'

She did not know what to say. His solicitousness was unexpected and inappropriate. Yet a glow of warmth started in her stomach and spread. No one since her parents had cared for her like this.

'I will be fine, my lord,' she managed to mumble.

He stroked her chin one last time and let her go. Stepping away, he said, 'Ravensford. And remember, if the bed keeps you awake, I will see that something is done.'

She nodded and backed out of the door, never once taking her attention off him. Any second she half expected him to take her in his arms. They would both regret that later. So she watched him until the door closed behind her.

Only once she was safe in her room did she berate herself for over-dramatising the situation. The Earl was only interested in her comfort. If she arrived in London too tired to do what must be done to the house, then the burden would fall to him. Naturally he did not want that to happen.

But there was the caress.

She shivered beneath the thick covers. Why had

he touched her and looked at her as though he wanted to devour her? He could not be attracted to her. Surely not.

Her fingers plucked at the bedcover, finding a feather and pulling it out. What if he were interested in her? She could never be a man's mistress and he would never offer marriage. A hollowness settled in her chest.

She fell asleep, telling herself the Earl was only being considerate. She could not, would not let herself think his behaviour was for any other reason. To do so would be insane.

Downstairs Ravensford finished his drink. He wondered what hold the man in the library had over Miss O'Brien. She was a very attractive woman and well educated. While he had been angry at her leaving the carriage earlier, he had also admired her desire to be helpful. Most—no, *all* the women of his acquaintance would have stayed huddled warm and dry in the vehicle, never thinking about the servants outside in the cold and wet. She had qualities that he valued.

He templed his fingers and gazed unseeing at the fire as he brought his focus back to the problem. It did not matter that he was beginning to like her. His goal was to find out who her accomplice was and to keep them from being successful.

If seeing to her comfort did not win her trust, he could seduce her. Women always talked to their lovers. A drastic measure, but so was her plan to steal from his parent.

The idea was instantly gratifying, something he would not have thought possible. Never in his entire life had he set out to cold-bloodedly seduce a woman. He hoped he would not have to do so now—or so he told himself. It did not sit well with his idea of honour, even as the idea made his blood pool in areas best ignored.

They started early. The sun shone brightly, already drying some of the smaller puddles on the road. Mary Margaret had not slept well. She refused to breakfast with the Earl. She was not hungry and it was not proper. She had done so last night, but that did not mean she intended to continue doing so.

A brisk breeze swept across the coaching yard as she made her way to the carriage, carefully stepping around mud puddles. She was glad to have her cape back, clean and dry.

Reaching the carriage, her gaze still on the ground, she saw a pair of shining Hessians. She licked suddenly dry lips and looked up to meet Ravensford's gaze.

'Are you thirsty, Miss O'Brien? There is lem-

onade and hot chocolate in the carriage.' A smile
tugged at one corner of his mouth.

'No, thank you. Whatever gave you that idea?'

His smile widened to a wolfish grin. 'The way
you licked your lips. And you did not join me for
breakfast.'

Did she detect a trace of irritation in his voice?
He still smiled at her, but the showing of teeth
resembled that of a large predator.

'No, I am not hungry, either.'

She looked away and started up the carriage
steps. His hand caught her elbow and she halted,
one foot still on the ground.

'I took the liberty of having the proprietor pack
biscuits and ham for you to have later.'

She looked over her shoulder at him. Why was
he doing this? She was nobody to him. He should
be ignoring her.

'Thank you,' she muttered.

Hastily, before he could say or do anything else,
she scampered into the coach. His hand fell away
from her elbow and she breathed a sigh of relief,
or so she told herself. As yesterday, she found
blankets and hot stones. He was doing everything
to make this journey as comfortable for her as possible. She did not understand any of this. Nor did
she want it. She might have to steal from his

mother if she could find no other way to save Emily and Annie.

Nervous melancholy gripped her. Somehow she had to outsmart Thomas. To escape her thoughts, she settled herself in the blankets and tried to sleep. She was exhausted and soon drifted off.

She woke with a start when the carriage jolted to a stop. Strands of hair had come loose from her chignon and she pushed them behind her ears, curious to find out what had made them stop. Peering out the window, she saw the outriders digging dirt and placing it in a large hole directly in front of the carriage.

Ravensford came over. 'They are filling any areas that might cause us to break an axle or become stuck. The last thing we need is a repeat of yesterday.'

'How clever.'

Ravensford gave her a scrutinising look. 'Have you never travelled?'

She shook her head. 'People of my station do not go far from home, my lord.'

He had the grace to look nonplussed. 'Forgive me. I didn't think.' He glanced at the men who still worked. 'Are you finding everything to your satisfaction?'

She was grateful he had changed the subject although this new one was not much more comfortable for her. 'You do too much, my lord. I don't need all of these luxuries.'

She could feel his gaze on her, giving her the sensation that the sun burned down on her exposed skin. Never had a man made her this aware of her senses.

'I already explained why you must arrive in London ready to work.'

'Yes, you did. I don't need all of this to do so. I come of hardy farmer stock.'

'You don't look it,' he murmured, his voice low and caressing and creamy. 'You look as fragile as an orchid and just as exotic.'

She gaped at him, not able to look away any longer. The intensity of his perusal seared to her toes. Confusion held her still. What was he doing?

She jumped to the first conclusion that came to mind and blurted, 'I won't become your mistress.' Instantly embarrassment overwhelmed her. 'That is—oh, dear. I didn't...I don't...'

He watched her, a gleam in his eye. 'Don't worry, Miss O'Brien, I have not asked you.'

The blush that had mounted her cheeks turned to flames. Not even a cool breeze could ease the heat that consumed her. Without considering how rude it would seem, she fell back into the coach and pulled the curtain over the window. She heard Ravensford chuckle softly.

Mortification made her stomach churn. She was such a fool.

Thankfully he did not join her for the rest of the journey. If he had, she would have had to jump out the other side of the carriage. His presence would have been too much to bear. What was she going to do for the rest of the journey? She would not be able to avoid him unless he wanted her to.

Agitation still held her when the carriage finally stopped and the scent of salt water greeted her. Impatient and not wanting Ravensford to open the door for her as he had got into the habit of doing, she opened the door herself and jumped out. She narrowly missed a puddle.

They were at a quay. At the end of the pier floated a sleek ship, probably Ravensford's. He probably called it a yacht.

'We'll be boarding immediately,' Ravensford said, coming up behind her and putting his hand to her elbow.

She had not heard him and it was all she could do not to jump. Her embarrassment rushed back so that she barely felt his fingers on her sleeve.

'I've never sailed before,' she said, not wanting to come anywhere near their last exchange of words.

He smiled down at her. 'You'll enjoy it.'

She let go a sigh of relief. He seemed focussed on sailing. She looked up at him, noting the sparkle in his eyes. 'You must like it.'

'I do.'

His valet came up. 'My lord, be careful. The mud will dirty your Hessians.'

'I shall endeavor to be careful,' Ravensford replied with a look on his face that Mary Margaret was sure hid amused resignation.

With that reassurance, the valet continued on his way, ordering the servant carrying the Earl's trunk to tread cautiously. 'Don't, whatever you do, Tom, drop that in water. That trunk is made of the finest leather.'

Mary Margaret watched the procession, amazed that someone could spend his entire life focussing on another person's clothes.

'Why so glum?' Ravensford asked.

She answered without thinking. 'That poor man is obsessed with your clothing. How boring his life must be.'

'Why do you think that?'

She glanced at him to see if he was having fun with her, but he seemed to be seriously waiting for her reply. 'Because there is so much more to life, and so much of it more important than what one wears.'

'Have you heard of Beau Brummel?'

'Who has not? I find his fixation with fashion to be very shallow.'

As they talked, the Earl continued to steer her toward the end of the pier. Up close the yacht was impressive. A gangplank connected it to land, bobbing with each wave. Mary Margaret gulped. She was not sure this was a safe means of travel. Still, at Ravensford's urging, she stepped forward.

It was worse than she had imagined. Her feet seemed to move without her volition and she was sure that if Ravensford released her elbow she would pitch over the side and into the water.

'Captain, please show Miss O'Brien to the guest cabin and see that she had everything she needs.'

'Yes, my lord.'

Mary Margaret turned to Ravensford. 'Thank you.'

He smiled at her, his eyes dancing in his unfashionably tanned face. The sun buffed his hair into strands of copper.

'I will expect to see you for lunch. It will be served on the deck under that canopy.' He pointed to a bright red and white covering that shaded a small table and several cushions.

Joining him for anything was the last thing she wanted when her knees threatened to melt under her every time he looked at her. But she had no polite refusal.

'As you wish,' she murmured.

Two hours later, she lay prostrate in the double-sized bed of her cabin. Sweat beaded her forehead and upper lip and her stomach buckled with each rise of the boat. Mary Margaret thought she had never felt worse.

'Miss.' The cabin boy's voice penetrated the closed door. 'His lordship requests your presence.'

She mumbled something.

'Pardon?'

'I…I cannot,' Mary Margaret managed to get out. 'I…am not…feeling…well.'

What seemed like an eternity later, the door opened. It was all she could do to force her eyes open. Ravensford entered without permission. He took one look at her and went to the wash basin where he dipped a cloth into the tepid water.

'Why did you not tell someone?' he demanded, squatting down by the bunk and wiping her forehead.

'I…did.' He raised one bronzed brow. She took a deep breath and stated defiantly, 'I told the…boy who…knocked. Ask him.'

Indignation at his refusal to believe gave her the

strength to grab the cloth from his hand. She wadded it up and pressed it to her mouth.

He frowned. 'Why didn't you tell me you get seasick?'

She squeezed the cloth until her knuckles turned white. 'If I had known I would have said something. Besides—' she fought the nausea down '—how else would I get to England?'

'True.' He rose on legs long accustomed to ships. 'I will be back in a moment.'

Mary Margaret stifled a moan. The last thing she wanted was to have him near her. She knew she was not a pretty woman and being sick did nothing to enhance what looks she had. Nor did she want him being around if she lost control of her stomach. She could think of nothing more humiliating.

With a groan she rolled to her side, facing the wall, and curled into a tight knot. Surely she could survive until they reached land.

The ship lurched, or so it seemed to her heightened nerves, and she wrapped her arms around her middle. At the same time, the door opened.

'Here, I've brought something for your nausea.'

The Earl's deep voice would have been arresting any other time. She turned her head just enough to look balefully up at him.

'Unless it is poison,' she muttered, closing her

eyes so as not to see the rocking cabin, 'there is nothing you can do to help.'

'Keep your eyes open and focus on something.'

Instead of answering, she curled up tighter, wishing he would go away. His hand on her shoulder shocked and angered her.

'For pity's sake, go away and let me suffer in private.' She heard him chuckle, and her wrath grew. 'How would you like to have someone bothering you when you wanted to die?'

'I tried to shoot my benefactor,' he said, all the humour gone.

'What?' She rolled on to her back to see his face.

His smile was twisted. 'It was after Salamanca.' His eyes took on a faraway look, but only for a moment. 'Now, drink this. Stevens prepared it. He claims it has ginger root and will do wonders.'

'Ginger root.' She reached with trembling hands for the mug. 'My mother would give us ginger root in warm water when we had stomach aches. It always worked.'

'Good.'

He kept hold of the mug, his fingers warm against her own. Part of her was glad. She shook so badly that without his help she would likely spill the contents. Still, some of the contents dribbled down her chin.

'You should be sitting up more.'

He took the cup from her, set it down on a table with rails to keep the cup from sliding off, and turned back to her. While he did that, she manoeuvred herself into a semi-sitting position.

'I would have helped,' he said.

Which was the last thing she wanted. Even as sick as she felt, his touch still disturbed her in ways she did not want to experience.

'Thank you, but I can manage on my own. It should not be long before the ginger settles my stomach.'

He studied her dispassionately.

Mary Margaret felt even more dishevelled and grimy than before. Unconsciously she raised one hand to smooth her tangled hair back from her face. Large strands had worked loose from her chignon. She had to look a fright.

His gaze intensified. 'Drink your ginger root tea and after I will brush your hair.'

Heat mounted her cheeks, receded and came back. The idea of him stroking her hair was exciting and tempting. She told herself that having her chignon in place would make her feel almost well. That was the reason she was so tempted to let him care for her. Nothing else. She resisted.

'After I finish the drink I will be more than able to care for myself.'

'You are as weak as a kitten.'

He put the mug to her lips and tipped it so that she had to swallow. He had moved so quickly and she had been thinking about his fingers in her hair that she was caught unawares and more of the liquid dribbled down her chin. He kept the mug to her mouth until she finished. After he laid the empty container down he took the cloth from her unresisting hand and gently wiped the tea from her chin.

'Since you don't want me to brush your hair, I will take you on deck. Some fresh air will make all the difference.'

'I do not think I am up to being moved,' she mumbled.

'You look better already, and you will be glad you did,' he said, reaching down.

Before she knew what he was about, he had lifted her to his chest. She gasped. 'What are you doing?'

He shook his head as though she were a dense child and smiled down at her. 'What does it feel like, Miss O'Brien? I am taking you up on deck. The sea is calm and the fresh air will make the ginger work much faster.'

'But…but…'

Her mouth worked but nothing more came out.

His arms were comforting and strong. His heart beat steadily against her cheek. This was awful.

Ravensford strode to the door of her cabin and out.

Chapter Five

The cabin boy stood outside the door. When he saw the couple his mouth dropped open. Mary Margaret gave him a hesitant smile and wished herself anywhere but here.

'Put me down,' she hissed, her nausea abated by shock. 'This is not appropriate.'

Ravensford shrugged. 'This is my yacht and I shall do as I please. Right now it pleases me to take you on deck.'

'What if I lose control and…and…?'

'Vomit on me? You shan't be the first.'

He was insufferable.

The Captain was coming down the stairs when he saw them. He stopped in his tracks. 'My lord? May I be of assistance?'

Ravensford grinned at him. 'Make sure no one is coming down as I am going up.'

'Yes, sir.' The Captain retraced his steps. 'All clear, my lord.'

'Thank you.' Ravensford started up.

Mary Margaret was appalled. She should have never come on this journey, no matter what Thomas threatened. Never. She would not be able to look at anyone on this boat knowing they had seen this débâcle. They would think there was more between herself and Ravensford than that of servant and master.

She groaned and buried her face against Ravensford's chest. His heartbeat was oddly reassuring. He was a large man and held her easily, his arms surrounding her comfortably. She felt protected. She belonged in Bedlam.

'Here you are,' he murmured, setting her down.

Her feet hit the deck and she swayed. Immediately his arm was back around her waist, holding her tightly to his side. What had seemed protective just seconds before was now something entirely different. The breath caught in Mary Margaret's throat as the heat of his body penetrated their clothing. She did not know which was worse, being held in his arms or being held to the length of his body.

'I am perfectly able to stand on my own,' she finally managed to say, pushing against his chest.

He looked down at her. 'Are you sure?'

His concern took her aback. 'Yes. Quite.'

He released her. She stumbled backward and tripped over a chair that had been placed beside a table that was laden with food. She twisted around, reaching for something to hold on to. Her left ankle twisted.

'Oh,' she moaned as her left leg went out from under her.

Ravensford grabbed for her.

The last thing she wanted was for him to hold her. She had had more than she could tolerate already. She scooted away. Her hand caught something cold and hard. She realised it was the ship's railing just instants before she tumbled over it.

She hit the water with an icy splash. She sank down, her skirts pulling her deeper. Fear galvanised her. She struggled to the surface and gasped for air. She did not know how to swim. Her legs tangled in her skirts. Her arms flailed.

Ravensford watched in horror as Mary Margaret disappeared over the side of the yacht. Without even thinking, he shed his coat and boots and dived into the water. He surfaced several feet from her just in time to see her sink beneath the surface for a second time.

He dived again, kicking with all his strength. The salt water burned his eyes, but he had to keep her in sight. Mercifully he caught her. He circled her waist with one arm and thrust upward with his legs and free arm.

He thought his lungs would burst, but he had to get them to the surface. Her skirts twisted around his legs, making it next to impossible to get any power, and added to her weight. Without a second thought, he ripped the woollen fabric from her body. The loss of weight made her seem nearly buoyant. He kicked hard, sending them upward.

They popped into the air and both breathed deeply. Ravensford trod water, one hand under Mary Margaret's shoulders and the other moving in circles to help keep them afloat.

'Stay calm, sweetings,' he murmured. 'Everything is fine. They will get us.'

Her large, scared eyes clung to his. She nodded, her lips trembling.

'Breathe,' he commanded. 'Breathe.'

It was only minutes before the yacht lowered a boat. To Ravensford, watching Mary Margaret's pale face, it seemed like an eternity.

He felt the heat seep from his own body and knew Mary Margaret was in worse shape. She had been in the water longer and was slimmer. He had to get her out of here.

'Hold on to my neck,' he ordered, rolling to his side. Her teeth chattered and her lips were blue, but she nodded and did as he said. 'That's my girl.'

Her wide, frightened eyes stared into his. He forced a smile and started kicking. They moved slowly toward the oncoming boat. Hands reached for them not a minute too soon.

Ravensford thrust Mary Margaret into the arms of the first seaman and pushed her into the small vessel. When she was safely on board, he followed.

She huddled on the wooden seat, a tiny, bedraggled ball. Her shoulders shook. He slid next to her and gathered her close. Using his hands, he chafed her arms.

'Are there no blankets?' he demanded, his voice harsh with worry.

'No, milord,' one of the two seamen answered, never stopping in his rowing.

Disgusted, Ravensford pulled her on to his lap. Anything to warm her chill skin. She did not protest. She did not say a thing. That, more than anything else, scared him.

'Come on, sweetings, rail at me,' he ordered, rubbing her back and arms.

Instead of speaking, she burrowed deeper into the warmth of his body. He groaned.

Finally they reached the yacht and a rope stair was lowered. There was no way he could climb it and carry Mary Margaret.

'You have to let go of me,' he murmured, stroking the hair from her face. 'You have to climb that rope.'

She looked from him to the ladder. Her jaw clenched, and he felt her tremble. But she rose from his lap and gripped the rope. Slowly, she climbed.

He followed closely behind, ready to catch her if she slipped. Only now that she was nearly safe did Ravensford notice her clothing. He had ripped her skirts away so that only her pantaloons remained. They were translucent.

He swallowed hard.

Her derrière swelled enticingly against the white fabric. Her hips flared out into shapely thighs.

He climbed up behind her, noticing that the Captain was trying to keep his gaze averted from Mary Margaret's near nakedness. Ravensford smiled wryly. The Captain was a better man than he. He had completely given up on looking away. But that did not mean he would leave her exposed like this for everyone to see.

He grabbed his coat from the deck and wrapped it around her before lifting her and striding to the stairs. Her head fell back on his shoulder. Her face was white and her breath came in little sobs. All he wanted was to comfort her.

Minutes later, he shouldered open her cabin door

and entered, closing it behind them. He laid her gently on the bed.

Her eyes opened. 'I have never been more scared in my life,' she whispered, her lips still blue.

'And all my fault,' he said, smoothing her loose hair back from her forehead.

She smiled wanly. 'No. I am the one whose clumsiness sent me pitching over the side.'

He took his coat from her and quickly wrapped a blanket around her, careful to keep his gaze averted. 'If I had not insisted on taking you on deck, it would have never happened.'

Her eyes closed and she sank back into the pillow.

He gazed at her, unable to resist the memory of her nearly naked in his arms. Her full, rounded breasts pressed against his chest, their tips rosy and taut from cold as they strained against the thin fabric of her chemise. Her rounded hips and slender thighs snuggled into his loins. His body tightened painfully. He closed his eyes, knowing that he could not stop himself from picturing her naked and in his bed.

Her hand on his arm drew his awareness. He took a deep breath and looked at her.

Her black brows were drawn in worry. 'Are you getting sick, my lord? You look in pain.'

He groaned. Seducing her and getting her to tell

him everything about the plan to steal from his mother was supposed to be a last resort if he could not win her trust. Picturing her naked in his bed was not going to accomplish his goal.

He forced himself to speak clearly instead of rasping like someone pushed to his physical limit. 'I am fine, Miss O'Brien. You are the one who is not feeling well.'

He straightened and moved away. Still, the outline of her body under the blanket did things to him that made his skin-hugging wet pantaloons even tighter.

'I am not seasick any more,' she said, a hint of amusement in her voice.

The deep purr of her voice slid along his nerves, adding to his discomfort. He had to get out of here or he would ravish her—immediately, without any regard for what she wanted.

'I will get Stevens, Miss O'Brien. He will have just the thing to keep you from getting a fever.'

He strode from the room, shutting the cabin door firmly behind himself. For long moments he stood with his back to the wall, taking deep breaths and trying to tame his body. It was no use. Every time he saw her he was going to see the way she looked lying in that bed, her luscious figure as good as bare.

'My lord,' Stevens said, coming up the tiny hall-way, 'are you ill?'

He released a bark of laughter. Ill with desire and there was only one cure for that. 'No, Stevens, but I fear Miss O'Brien might become so if she is not given one of your possets.'

The valet became brisk. 'Tut, tut. We cannot have that, my lord. The Countess's maid told me the responsibility Miss O'Brien will have in London. There is no time for the young woman to be sick.'

'Right you are,' Ravensford managed. 'No time at all.'

'You go change, my lord.' Stevens gave his master an appalled look. 'That is—'

'I can take my own clothes off and put others on,' Ravensford said. 'The results won't be as polished as when you assist me, but I will be decent.'

His thoughts flicked again to Mary Margaret. What would it be like to have her undress him? He could not think of that right now.

'Of course, my lord. Then I shall take care of Miss O'Brien. Do not worry about a thing.'

Only my sanity, Ravensford thought, as he watched Stevens enter Miss O'Brien's cabin. No woman had ever aroused him this quickly and completely. His reaction was as disconcerting as it was pleasurable.

Nor had any woman aroused his protective instincts as she had. He could tell himself all he wanted that he was concerned because her brush with death had been his fault, but he knew that was only part of it. Mary Margaret O'Brien was beginning to matter to him.

Mary Margaret tugged at her hair with a brush. They were docking any moment now and her hair was still damp. If she put it in a chignon, it would never dry. If she wore it loose, she would look like a doxy.

And her dress. She wore her second-best dress. Her travelling outfit was at the bottom of the sea. Her chemise and pantaloons were stiff from salt and would have to wait until they stopped for the night before she could properly wash them. Everything was a mess.

But she was not seasick. That was a great comfort.

A knock on her door preceded the Earl's voice. 'Miss O'Brien, we are docked and will be unloading immediately. We have a ways to go before we reach tonight's inn.'

She jumped up, twisting her hair into a knot. Heat suffused her entire body. Only when she had changed clothes had she realised that her pantaloons and chemise might as well not have existed

for all the cover they had given her. Ravensford
had seen every inch of her as though she had been
naked. And so had the crew. The last thing she
wanted was the Earl in this cabin.

'I am ready, my lord,' she said hurriedly, breathlessly. 'I will be out.'

'Good. I will meet you on deck in five minutes.'

'Yes, my lord.'

'Ravensford.'

She heard him move away. What had he thought
about her dishabille? Had it disgusted him that she
had not even realised her exposure and so had not
shown any modesty? She moaned. Nor had she
thanked him for saving her life.

With a groan she realised that one hand still held
her hair twisted into a knot on her neck. She
quickly jabbed several pins into the thick tresses
until they were secure. She would worry about drying her hair later. As it was, the strands smelled of
sea water and salt. She would have to wash it when
they got to the inn. Until then, there was nothing
else she could do.

This trip was horrible. Her only consolation was
that it could not possibly get worse.

She was wrong. Having the gaze of every crew
member watching her walk the gangplank was excruciating. The only thing that got her through the
gauntlet was pride. Ravensford waited for her.

His eyes smouldered as she approached him. His gaze swept over her. She remembered all too clearly how she had looked when she rose from the bunk to change and caught sight of herself in the mirror. He had seen her all but naked.

Embarrassment flooded her cheeks.

'You look none the worse for your ducking,' he said, extending his arm.

She sighed and considered walking past him, but that would only add to the speculation so rampant in the faces of the men watching them. She stopped and laid her fingers lightly on his arm, nearly wincing from the heat he radiated.

'I owe you a great debt, my lord.'

He frowned. 'You are a stubborn woman. How many times must I order you to call me Ravensford?'

She quirked one brow at him, and instantly regretted it. His smile could charm the chemise off a lady of Quality, let alone someone as susceptible to him as she was.

'I would berate you over not using my name,' he murmured so no one else could hear, 'but it would do no good.'

She did not answer, thinking herself lucky they were in public and the heat in his gaze could not be directed at her in a more physical manner. She was weak enough to succumb.

'Let me help you up,' he said, stopping and putting his large, strong hands around her waist.

Totally immersed in what she imaged his kiss would be like, Mary Margaret was taken by surprise. 'Wha...what are you doing?' she babbled.

He smiled down at her. 'Lifting you into my phaeton.'

She looked up and gulped. He was too close and the contraption he wanted to put her into was too high. She gripped one of his forearms with each hand and pushed him until he released her. She stepped back.

Raised in the country, Mary Margaret had never seen a carriage like the one before her. It was high off the ground, with room for two only. The finish was a glossy hunter green with thin black lines outlining the curves. Two prancing chestnuts stood impatiently in the traces, a young boy in the Earl's livery holding them in place. Altogether a dangerous means of transportation.

'What kind of vehicle is this?'

He laughed. 'This is a high-perch phaeton. The fastest carriage on the roads.'

'And the most deadly,' she said flatly.

He sobered instantly. 'Not with the right driver.'

She stepped away, not wanting to be any closer to the thing than she had to be. 'Isn't there another

carriage I can ride in? The baggage must be somewhere. I will go with it. 'Tis only proper.'

He caught her as she turned away. 'I am considered a fair hand with the ribbons, Miss O'Brien.
I won't tip you into a ditch.'

''Is lordship be a prime member o' the Four-in-
'and Club, miss,' the young boy said proudly.

Ravensford smiled at the lad. 'Thank you, Peter.'

'Whatever the Four-in-Hand Club is,' Mary
Margaret muttered.

Scandalised, the youth spoke up again. 'It be a
group of swells what knows how to 'andle the ribbons like no others. 'Is lordship is the best.'

'Thank you again, Peter,' Ravensford said. 'I
think I can deal with this on my own now.'

The lad flushed.

'I can get you to the inn much quicker this way,
Miss O'Brien. You can eat and be in bed by the
time the baggage carriage reaches the inn. Think
about how nice it will be to have a full stomach
and a nice soft bed that does not move.'

She eyed him. He had a point. Exhaustion ate
at her and her stomach fussed at her. She looked
back at the phaeton.

'I promise not to spill you,' Ravensford said as
though reading her mind.

'Well…'

'Up with you, then,' he said.

Before she realised what he intended, his hands were around her waist and lifting her up. It was either step into the carriage or continue to be held aloft by him. Entering the phaeton was more dignified and less intimate than his hands wrapped around her waist.

She sat down gingerly, feeling the carriage sway slightly. When Ravensford climbed in, the vehicle bounced on well-sprung wheels. The breath caught in her throat. Then he sat beside her, and she scooted to the very edge of the seat, only to look down. The ground seemed a long way away.

She sighed.

'I won't bite,' he said, a wicked grin belying his words.

Before she could think of a suitable reply, Stevens hurried up with a blanket. 'This is for Miss O'Brien,' he said, handing it to her. 'It would not do for you to catch an inflammation, miss, after your ducking.'

She took the warm wool covering. 'Thank you, Stevens. This will be very nice.'

Ravensford took the blanket from her without asking and spread it over her lap and legs. His gloved fingers moved over her thighs with a sureness that made the breath catch in her throat. Seconds before she had worried about falling out and breaking her neck. Now she knew the greater danger was sitting so closely to the Earl.

They could travel as fast as the wind and it would still be too slow for her peace of mind and body.

Chapter Six

The carriage came to a sudden halt and Mary Margaret jolted awake, her cheek bumping against something hard and unyielding. Dazed, she pummelled whatever her head had been resting on.

'That is my shoulder, if you don't mind,' a deep voice drawled.

Memory came back in a mortifying rush. She was in the Earl's high-perch phaeton which he had stored here in England while he had been in Ireland. The baggage carriage he had hired was somewhere behind them.

'Pardon me, my lord.' She sat up and straightened her bonnet, which had fallen to one side of her head.

'Let me do that.' He angled around after handing the reins to his tiger.

'Thank you, but I can manage.' The last thing

she wanted was for him to touch her. He had already had his hands on her more than enough these last twenty-four hours.

He ignored her—as usual.

He carefully set the bonnet to rights, leaning back to get a better look. He shifted it slightly to one side. She glared at him. He smiled lazily. His eyes held hers captive as his fingers dropped to the ribbons tied under her chin. He undid the knotted bow and retied the silk into a rakish bow just under her right ear.

'There. A lady's maid could not have done better.'

The urge to say something scathing nearly overwhelmed her good sense. But she managed not to make a difficult moment more so.

'Thank you again,' she muttered, trying hard to keep her resentment from coming out.

He jumped abruptly from the carriage and held an imperious hand up to her. Another touch. She sighed. The only way to stop this was to grit her teeth and do what was necessary so that she could get to her room.

He smiled up at her, the emotion reaching his eyes and making the corners crinkle. Somehow he knew his touch bothered her. She never had been good at hiding her feelings.

'Come along. You need some food and rest.'

Her gaze skittered away from his. His voice had been deep and dark, hinting at things she only barely understood and definitely did not want to delve into. Still, her heart pounded and her skin tingled when she put her fingers in his. He helped her down, continuing to hold her hand longer than was necessary.

'Thank you,' she murmured. Then added with some asperity, 'I can walk on my own, just not on a boat.'

Even to her own ears her words had been breathy and disturbed. No wonder he continued to gaze at her, his fingers wrapped firmly around her skin. Was it her imagination, or was his face closer? Her heart skipped a beat.

He laughed. 'I hope never to have such an experience again. You scared ten years off my life.'

A strange fluttering started in her stomach. 'Well, I can assure you that the ducking did not prolong mine any.'

Belatedly, she realised that he still held her hand. She pulled but, instead of releasing her, he tucked her fingers into the crook of his elbow. His attentions were too marked. She caught one of the outriders watching with a smirk on his face. She looked away.

'I have bespoken dinner and rooms. There should be no delays before you seek your bed.'

She started shivering. He took off his many-caped great coat and wrapped it around her.

'Come,' he said, leading her to the front door.

She followed without protest, too shocked by his behaviour to do anything else. He treated her as though she was a lady of Quality and someone whose comfort he cared about. He made her feel safe.

She stumbled inside, Ravensford's arm supporting her. The landlord stood eyeing them. His gaze went from her to the Earl.

'My lord,' the owner said, rushing forward. 'Your rooms are ready and supper will be served immediately. I kept the parlour for you.'

Ravensford nodded his head. 'Thank you, John. Please show Miss O'Brien to her room so she can change into dry clothes.'

The landlord nodded, casting a scandalised look at Mary Margaret. 'Will your man be bringing in the luggage, my lord?'

Ravensford nodded. 'I will wait for you, Miss O'Brien, before starting supper.'

Mary Margaret felt dazed. Too much too fast. With fingers numb from nerves, she pulled the Earl's coat off and handed it to him.

'I would be happy with toast and butter and a pot of hot tea in my room.'

'I have bespoken dinner, Miss O'Brien, and I would like your company.'

Aware of the landlord watching them, she nodded. 'As you wish, my lord.'

'I will expect you as soon as you have freshened up.'

He turned and strode back to the coach yard. He had not been this high-handed with his mother. When she had requested something, he had agreed. Did he treat all other women this way, or only her?

'This way, miss,' the landlord said, breaking into her thoughts.

She followed him up a flight of stairs. He paused and opened a door.

'His lordship's room is across the hall.'

She glanced sharply at the man, wondering if there was more to his words. His countenance was bland.

'Thank you.'

'Dinner will be served downstairs, in the room next to the commons.'

'Thank you,' she said again as she slipped inside.

She shut the door slowly, giving the landlord time to back away. Immediately there was a knock. This time it was one of the Earl's servants, delivering her portmanteau.

'Thank you,' she said once again, smiling at the man.

When she was finally alone, she turned to view her room—and froze. This had to be one of the best, if not the best, available. A large four-poster bed took pride of place with a massive wardrobe and elaborate nightstand grouped around it. The fire was ablaze with two chairs pulled cosily close. Flowers in muted colours rioted beneath her feet.

She shook her head in amazement.

Another knock brought a sigh of exasperation. Who was it this time? She opened the door to a bobbing maid.

'His lordship ordered a bath.'

Another maid appeared, lugging a hip tub. Before Mary Margaret could protest, everything was arranged and the maids were gone. She was cold and grimy and the steaming water was an invitation she could not resist. It felt so good to get the salt out of her hair.

She was clean, warm in her second-best dress and half-asleep when the summons came. The maid who had brought the tub said, 'His lordship sent me to escort you to his private dining room, miss.'

Mary Margaret's first inclination was to plead exhaustion. She could not be so rude. Ravensford had taken every care for her comfort, the least she could do was go down and thank him. She did not have to stay. With that self-deluding thought, she followed the maid.

The maid left her at the door.

Mary Margaret took a deep breath and told herself that the tightness in her chest was due to the soaking she had taken earlier. The same for her shaking fingers. Resolutely, she knocked. His deep baritone bid her enter and the air went out of her lungs.

She chided herself for overreacting. He was her employer. If he ever found out that the sound of his voice made her stomach feel like lightning was striking it, he would laugh.

In one fluid motion she turned the handle and entered. He stood near the fire, one forearm resting on the mantel, one booted foot propped on the andiron. His brown jacket fit his lean form loosely. The collar of his white shirt was open. His casualness accentuated the rugged lines of his face.

Her pulse jumped.

To hide the delight she felt, Mary Margaret bobbed a curtsy and averted her face so that she talked to the fire. 'Thank you for everything, my lord. You have been more than kind. I must return to my room now.'

His low chuckle was like velvet stroking her

skin, but his voice was firm. 'It's Ravensford and you will eat something first.'

'I'm not hungry.' She backed up. The room was suddenly overly hot.

He smiled and a dimple peeked out of his left cheek, softening the harsh lines of his jaw. She wondered if he knew how devastating his smile was. Probably.

'Truly, I am more tired than hungry. But I thank you for offering.'

He lifted one brow. 'Another argument over dinner, Miss O'Brien? This becomes boring.'

She lifted her chin. 'Then you will not wish my company, my lord.'

He laughed. 'Very good, but not good enough. Sit down and be done with this.'

He moved to the table placed just in front of the fire and lifted the cover off one of the dishes. The aroma of roast beef filled the room, making her stomach growl. Lunch had been a long time ago. She blushed at the indelicacy.

He eyed her knowingly. 'Come, eat some of this and then I promise to let you go.'

He was right, she needed to eat. She sank into the chair he had indicated.

He carved a large piece of beef and set it on a plate, added some potatoes and peas, and set it all in front of her. Next he handed her the tea and let her lace it with cream and sugar. He poured himself an amber-coloured liquid with a smoky scent.

He sat after loading his plate with twice what he had put on hers. Neither spoke much for a while.

Ravensford watched her eat with dainty dispatch. He could almost image delicate whiskers twitching. When her pointed pink tongue darted out to lick a drop of tea from her lip his gut clenched. Pictures of her lying practically naked in the bunk raged through his mind. Blood pounded in his ears. He took a deep breath. He wondered if she knew how arousing she was. Perhaps not.

She looked up and caught him looking at her. He smiled.

'You eat like a cat, delicately and focussed,' he said.

She laid her fork and knife down. He watched her magnificent bosom swell as she watched him. He knew she wanted to say something, probably not complimentary, but was restraining herself.

After a long pause, she said, 'My lord, why are you treating me like this? I am not Quality, nor am I your responsibility.'

He leaned back in his chair, finished with his food even though half of it still remained on his plate. He sipped his whiskey and eyed her over the glass rim. Why was he treating her this way?

He had set out to gain her trust, but that did not

mean he had to treat her like a prized companion
or force his presence on her when she did not want
it. Nor did he have to be the one to dive in to save
her. Any one of his sailors could have done so.
Just as Stevens could have nursed her through her
seasickness from the beginning.

Why was he doing this?

The answer was startling, although he instantly
realised it should not be. His reaction to her was
stronger than he'd had to any other woman. His
body was like an adolescent around her, aroused
and aching all the time.

'Be my mistress. I will pay you well and you
will no longer have to endure my mother's slights.'

She dropped the cup of tea she had just lifted to
her lips. It hit the table with a thump, sending
scalding tea all over the cloth. Neither one paid it
any mind.

'You jest, and very cruelly,' she said.

Amazed at his bluntness, Ravensford shook his
head slowly. 'No, I don't believe I do, Miss
O'Brien—Mary Margaret. In fact, I have never
been so serious about asking a woman to become
my mistress as I am now.'

Her bosom heaved in agitation and her eyes
flashed anger. Even knowing she was about to refuse him, he enjoyed the show. She was not a tra-

ditional beauty, but she appealed very much to him.

She licked her lips and his loins tightened. He downed the whiskey, wondering if it would numb his nether parts. He could only try, for it was obvious she was not going to help him in that area.

She stormed to her feet. 'I am not...not a loose woman. I might not be your equal, my lord, but that does not make me someone you can take advantage of so cavalierly.'

He stood, admiring the way fury put colour into her high cheeks and brought a flutter to her breasts. How he wanted her.

'My apologies, Miss O'Brien. It was my baser self speaking.' He gave her a roguish grin. 'But should you change your mind, don't hesitate to tell me.'

She stalked to the door. Turning, she asked, 'May I be excused?'

Sarcasm was something he had not heard in her throaty voice before. He did not like hearing it now, but he deserved it. He had overstepped the bounds of propriety.

He bowed her from the room, wondering how he was going to survive the rest of the journey in such close proximity to her.

It was just as well that she had refused him. She

was a potential thief, not a potential mistress—no matter what his body said.

Mary Margaret woke before the sun was up. She sat up, only to fall back on to the pillows. Her head felt like a herd of sheep pounded through it. Her throat hurt. Her heart ached.

She moaned.

She did not know which felt worse, her body or her spirit. Just moving was an effort, but remembering last night was a nightmare. Ravensford had asked her to be his mistress and she had turned him down. Shame warred with anger and regret with relief.

She rolled to her side, ignoring the tightness in her chest, and buried her face in the pillow. The linens were still damp from her tears of last night. Exhaustion was the only reason she had been able to sleep, and even then her dreams had been full of loss and longing.

How could she face him today? With luck, she would die of consumption and not have to. She was being a coward. Ravensford was the one who should be ashamed, not she. He was the one who had acted improperly, not she.

She flipped on to her back, fists clenched, jaw clamped. Her head protested with a sharp pain at the temples. No matter how she felt, she needed to get up. They were leaving at dawn.

She managed to dress herself. Determination held her upright when she swayed on her feet. She had survived worse. She would live through this. However, a cup of tea laced with honey and cream would be very nice.

When the maid knocked, she was ready. Carrying her portmanteau, she followed the woman downstairs. Ravensford sat in the common room and chose that moment to look up from his ham and ale.

He rose and walked to Mary Margaret, his stride loose-hipped and easy. To her jaundiced eye, he looked like nothing had occurred between them.

'Please join me,' he said, stopping just short of her, his fresh citrus scent filling her senses.

She studied him through narrowed eyes. 'No, thank you,' she said, her voice a painful rasp in her throat.

He frowned. 'You are sick. Come and have some tea and toast. I will send for Stevens to fix you another one of his possets.'

She shook her head and winced. 'I don't want anything to eat and would prefer to have my tea in the carriage.'

He took her by the arm and propelled her toward his table. She resisted the urge to dig her heels in.

When they reached the seats, she forced a false smile to her lips.

'You must not have heard me, my lord, but I prefer to take tea in the carriage.'

Ravensford gave her a tight stretch of lips. 'I know what you would prefer, but you and I have some things to discuss.'

She blanched.

'My lord,' the proprietor said, coming in through the door from the kitchen with a laden tray. 'The lady's tea is ready.'

Ravensford resumed his seat and the landlord set out the teapot, cream, sugar, cup and saucer, and a plate of scones with butter and marmalade. In spite of her sore throat, the smell of warm bread and steaming tea drew her. When the proprietor looked expectantly at her, she gave in.

'Please bring some honey,' Ravensford said, 'and see if someone can find my valet.'

The landlord hurried out on his errands.

Mary Margaret felt Ravensford's gaze as she fixed a cup of tea and a scone. When she glanced up at him, his attention was on her fingers as she broke off a piece of the pastry. His gaze followed her fingers and the scone to her mouth. A dark hunger entered his eyes, making them appear hunter green in the dim light of the room. She shivered.

His eyes met hers. 'I want you.'

His voice was deep and husky. His mouth was a grim curve of sensualness. Her stomach churned as her body went from cold to hot. The scone dropped from nerveless fingers.

'I...I told you last night, my lord,' she said, her voice a harsh whisper.

'That was last night. Tell me again,' he demanded, his gaze never leaving her face.

Her chest constricted and she felt as though she was suffocating. The room was unbearably warm. One hand fluttered to the high neckline of her dress.

'I am not that kind of woman.' She took a deep breath. 'Please stop asking me.'

His lips thinned, but he leaned back in his chair. 'My apologies,' he finally said, his voice nearly normal. 'I have never wanted a woman as I want you. I find it harder than I would have thought to take no for an answer.'

She gulped, more uncomfortable than she could remember being in a long time. Turning her face away from the intensity of his, she started to rise. One of his large, strong hands caught her wrist, keeping her sitting.

'Please don't go,' he said. 'You need the food and tea. I will leave.'

She nodded, unable to reply.

But instead of standing, he said, 'We will put this behind us—for now. You are under my protection and it was ungentlemanly of me. However...' he gave her a rueful grin '...I think it would be best if you make the rest of the journey in the baggage carriage with Stevens. You are sick and the exposure of the phaeton would not be good for you, and I am not at my best around you.'

He stood abruptly, bowed and left her.

She stared after him, nonplussed. Everything had happened so quickly and her head felt like it was packed with cotton. At least she did not have to continue travelling in the Earl's company. He was as much a temptation to her as he claimed she was to him.

Stevens said from behind her, 'Miss O'Brien, do you know where his lordship has gone? He sent for me.'

Still dazed, she turned to look at the valet. 'I don't know.'

'You have a cold,' the valet said. 'I will fix you another posset.'

Even as she murmured her thanks, he left, moving swiftly and purposefully. She knew that in a short time the posset would arrive. She wished her heart could be cured as easily as Stevens's posset intended to cure her inflammation. Right now she felt as though her world would never be the same again.

With a sigh, she drank the now-lukewarm tea.

Ravensford watched Mary Margaret climb into the baggage carriage. Even though she was bundled up as though she expected a snow storm, he could still make out the line of her hips. He shook his head in exasperation. He was like a boy still wet behind the ears where she was concerned.

Besides, he had not arranged this trip so he could seduce her—not originally. His plan was to gain her trust and get her to tell him about the plan to rob his mother. Now he would be lucky if she even spoke to him again.

He sighed and turned away from the inn window. Stevens stood patiently by the door, waiting for instructions.

'See that Miss O'Brien has every comfort,' Ravensford said, taking a full purse from his bed and giving it to the valet. 'I shall be travelling on ahead. With good weather and no problems, I can be in London within the week. You will be much slower.'

'Yes, my lord,' Stevens said, taking the money.

'I know I can count on you.'

A smile of genuine pleasure lit the valet's face before he left. Ravensford turned back to the window. He had not planned on travelling ahead, but even as he had said the words he had known they were for the best.

Mary Margaret had refused his offer of protection; the last thing she or he needed was for him to continue importuning her. Much as he desired her, his actions disgusted him. He did not believe in taking advantage of others, particularly those less fortunate than him.

So why was he so determined to have her? He did not know, but he was going to stop this stupidity once and for all. A separation was the best thing for him.

Unfortunately, she very likely agreed.

Chapter Seven

❦

Excitement held Mary Margaret spellbound as they reached the London outskirts. Not even Steven's severe countenance could dampen her spirits. He was frowning at her because she insisted on opening the window so she could see everything better. He did not want her to have a relapse from the cool spring air.

She had not seen the Earl since he passed them on the road their first day out from the inn. She told herself it was better this way, but no amount of reasoning eased the ache in her heart. She would have never thought it possible to care for someone she barely knew, but against all logic she did.

So what if there was no excitement to her day and each hour dragged by? She was used to life's easy flow. If she was bored, then it was her own fault as her mother had so often said. When they reached the Earl's town house she would use some of her precious money to send Emily a letter. Her sister would love to hear all about London.

In order to have plenty to write about, Mary Margaret concentrated on the outside. There were people everywhere, dressed in all manner of styles. Vendors crowded the streets.

The coach slowed and she noticed that while there were still plenty of pedestrians, they were more stylish. The men resembled the Earl, the women the Countess. More phaetons and curricles passed them, all drawn by prime horseflesh. The houses were larger and more ornately decorated.

Shortly, the carriage stopped. Stevens got out without giving her a glance. She told herself that was as it should be. Still, a rebellious part of her missed the Earl's attentions.

She chided herself. Not only was she silly, she was wicked. The Earl had made his intentions clear and they were not honourable.

Gathering the skirts of her only presentable dress into one hand, she jumped out. Before her stood a house more grand than the Countess's estate in Ireland. She craned her neck to see up to the roof. Four stories, all with elegantly carved windows and cornices. The house fit her impression of Ravensford—powerful and magnificent.

Belatedly, she realised they were at the servants'

entrance. She could not image what the front looked like. An open door emitted delicious smells so she entered and found herself in the kitchen. A man speaking French and waving around a butcher's knife could only be the chef. Young boys scrambled to do his bidding, whether they understood him or not. Several girls scrubbed big copper pots.

She stood in the middle of the jumble, not knowing what to do or where to go. She had just decided to go back outside and fetch her portmanteau when a short woman stopped in front of her.

'You must be Miss O'Brien. I am Mrs Brewster, the housekeeper. Come along, now. No sense dawdling in the Frenchie's domain. Gaston fixes the best meals in London, but his temperament is volatile.' She shook her head and started off without glancing back to see if Mary Margaret followed.

Mary Margaret trailed the housekeeper's tiny, black-clad figure from the kitchen. Just past the green baize door were a narrow set of stairs. Mrs Brewster started up them. Two flights up, the housekeeper took a turn and came out on a wide landing. Delicate carpeting muffled their steps. Silver sconces with wax candles flooded the area with light. They were in the family portion of the house.

Three doors down, the housekeeper turned to face Mary Margaret. The older woman's face was narrow and lined at the mouth and eyes. Her brown hair was thick and braided tightly to her head. A delicate white cap perched properly on her crown. Her hazel eyes looked Mary Margaret over. She must have liked what she saw because she smiled.

'His lordship told me to put you here. If there is anything you'll be needing, let me know. A boy will bring your luggage up shortly. I will have a tray sent up. I am sure you are hungry and thirsty.'

Mary Margaret smiled in relief. She had been afraid that Mrs Brewster would somehow know the Earl had asked her to become his mistress. If the housekeeper did know, she was still treating Mary Margaret like a respectable lady.

'Thank you, Mrs Brewster. Thank you so much.'

The older woman smiled gently. 'I know how strange it can be your first time in London. And I know what a large task you have ahead of you. I'll do my best to help you.'

Mary Margaret blinked back tears. She was exhausted. Mrs Brewster opened the door and Mary Margaret entered, hearing it close behind her. She stood transfixed by the grandeur of the room. Surely there was some mistake.

She yanked open the door and, seeing Mrs Brewster's figure just disappearing around the corner, ran after her. 'Madam, Mrs Brewster,' she gasped when she caught up with the other woman, 'there must be some mistake. I am the Countess's companion, not a guest.'

Mrs Brewster shook her head. 'No, miss, there is not. His lordship picked the room himself.'

Mary Margaret took a step back. Oh, dear. Even after her refusal, Ravensford had continued to get her the best rooms available in the inns they stopped at, but she had thought that was just consideration and that things would return to a more normal aspect once they reached London.

'Thank you, Mrs Brewster.' She continued backing away, watching the other woman for any hint of what she felt. There was none. 'I am sorry I bothered you.'

'Quite all right, miss. I thought you might be surprised.'

There was nothing to say to that. Mary Margaret nodded and turned around. She needed privacy to come to grips with this most recent incident.

But first she had to become accustomed to her room.

It was nearly the size of her sister Emily's entire house. No wonder Thomas was so bitter if he grew up like this. He had fallen far.

Shamrock-green silk curtains were pulled back to admit the late afternoon sun. The ceiling-to-floor windows looked out on the back of the house and an Elizabethan garden and maze. A wrought-iron gazebo snuggled in one corner. She would have to explore it as soon as possible.

Under her feet was the thickest and most luxurious carpet she had ever seen. Vines and ivy dotted with delicate pink roses spread like a verdant jungle. Two Chippendale chairs, upholstered in pink-striped silk and green trim were grouped cosily around a mahogany pie table with inlaid sandalwood designs.

And then there was the huge four-poster bed with its green and pink curtains and mountainous pillows. She would be lost in it. But the Earl would not.

She flushed and buried her face in her hands. How could she think such a thing? The memory of his smouldering gaze while he waited for her reply gave her the answer. She might not want to be his mistress, but she wanted to be more to him than his mother's companion.

She took a deep breath and regained her composure. He was far above her, and she was supposed to steal from his mother.

She shook her head to clear it of the troubling thoughts and strode across the room to another door. It was a dressing room. She laughed, not a happy sound. She had three dresses to her name and a ruined cape, one pair of boots that the constant rain and mud had taken a toll on and a pair of leather slippers. She did not need this room in the least.

She shut the door with a firm hand. Still, Ravensford had been more than generous with her. She would have so much to tell Emily, and even a desk to write on, she noted. The light, fully stocked lady's desk nestled between the two windows. She sat at it and took a sheet of the Earl's embossed stationery. She dipped the quill in the ink and began.

It was dusk when she finished. A knock on the door caught her attention. Her dinner waited, as did a bath when she was finished eating. Life with the Countess had not been anything near like this.

Three weeks later, Mary Margaret wiped her brow before finishing the arrangement of a large bouquet of lilacs from the Earl's garden. The vase, overflowing with the lavender blooms, sat in the salon between two floor-to-ceiling windows that faced the front street. The town house was as ready as she could make it with the help of the entire staff. When she had been in doubt about something, the Earl's secretary had provided the needed information. Even Ravensford's valet, Stevens, approved.

The Countess and Annabell Winston were to arrive today. She waited in apprehension, hoping the

Countess would be pleased but knowing that she would find fault with something. That was how it had been in Ireland; she did not expect it to be any different here. But that was all right. She had done her best, and she had a sense of satisfaction.

'Well done, Miss O'Brien.'

She jumped. The Earl's butterscotch baritone sent shivers down her spine.

'I didn't mean to startle you.'

'I did not hear you, my lord. And thank you.' She made her hands relax at her side. 'I could not have done it without the staff and your secretary. Mr Kartchner has been invaluable.'

'I find him so. And my staff is the best in London. I am glad they could be of assistance.'

Silence fell between them. A long, awkward silence that made Mary Margaret search her brain for something, anything to say. Nothing came to mind.

'How do you find your room, Miss O'Brien?'

For some reason that was the last thing she had expected. 'Lovely. I have never seen anything so beautiful, let alone lived in something so magnificent.' She laughed nervously. 'I pinch myself every morning to make sure I am not dreaming it. I am sure that I should be on the fourth floor with the other servants.'

He frowned. 'I don't care how my mother treats you, I will treat you as you deserve.'

'Thank you, my lord.' Her voice was tight. He always made her feel awkward.

'And stop thanking me and calling me "my lord". I told you to call me Ravensford.' His eyes darkened. 'Or have you forgotten?'

She had forgotten nothing—not his order to call him Ravensford or his offer of *carte blanche*. 'Yes, m…' She caught herself. It was better to humour him. 'Ravensford.'

'Better.'

He pivoted on his heel and strode from the room, taking her by surprise. It was as though he had suddenly lost interest in their conversation. What a ninny she was to have been so totally caught up in their interaction. It was obvious that he did not regret her turning down his offer to become his mistress. That knowledge, as much as she hated to admit even to herself, was a disappointment. Against her better judgement, she had secretly hoped that he was avoiding her because he did not want to lose control and ask her again.

Not that she wanted to be his mistress—because she did not. But it would be nice to know that he still found her desirable. She shook her head in bewilderment at her conflicting emotions. She had to stop this.

Sounds of commotion penetrated the salon door. Her heart jolted. The Countess must have arrived. Hastily wiping her hands on her skirts and wishing she had had time to clean up and change to a clean dress, she rushed into the hall and on to the foyer.

Boxes and trunks were strewn around with more coming in. The Countess stood in the middle of everything and presented her cheek for Ravensford to kiss, which he dutifully did.

Beside the Countess stood a young girl who looked barely out of the schoolroom. Her bright blonde hair was cut short and fashionably frizzed around her elfin face. Her blue eyes sparkled with curiosity, and her feet danced. She was as excited as a person could be and not explode.

Mary Margaret smiled. The child would be a delight.

The Countess caught sight of her. 'Miss O'Brien, I want you to meet my goddaughter, Miss Annabell Winston.'

Annabell turned her dazzling smile on Mary Margaret. 'I am so pleased to meet you, Miss O'Brien. Godmother has told me about everything you have been doing.'

'Don't gush so,' the Countess said.

The girl quieted, but nothing could dim her exuberance.

'Miss O'Brien has worked diligently and accomplished a great deal,' Ravensford said.

'I shall be inspecting everything once I have rested,' the Countess said, sweeping up the stairs. 'Is my room prepared?'

'Yes, my lady,' Jones, the butler said, following in the Countess's wake.

Mary Margaret followed more slowly, trailing the Earl and Annabell. She had overseen the final preparations, arranging the flowers and ensuring that the fire was properly laid.

The Countess entered her rooms in a swathe of servants and family and stopped. Her gaze swept the immaculate blue drapes and bedspread. She took in the rich carpet underfoot

'Whoever brought those flowers in here should be let go, Andrew. You know I loathe lilacs.'

Mary Margaret paled and wanted to sink into the floor, but she could not let the Countess think someone else was responsible. If anyone suffered, it should be she.

'My lady, I am truly sorry. I did not know you disliked the flowers when I brought them in.'

The Countess turned on her. 'I should have known. Next time check before you do anything.'

'Yes, my lady.' Mary Margaret bowed her head in submission even though she railed at the Countess's high-handed treatment. This was nothing different from when she had been in Ireland.

'You are dismissed,' the Countess said, unfastening her cape and letting it fall to the rug where it was quickly picked up by her maid, Jane.

Mary Margaret breathed a sigh of relief and made her escape. Things did not look good for her stay in London. Thank goodness her quarterly salary was due soon. Somehow she would return to Ireland then and convince Emily to leave Thomas and come live with her. She would not let herself think anything else.

Ravensford waited for the door to close behind Mary Margaret before turning to his mother. 'That was unnecessary, Mother. She has worked harder than anyone to ensure the house is ready.'

The Countess eyed him narrowly. 'I will not be spoken to like that by you, Andrew.' She turned away from him. 'Annabell, you will be in the Green Room. Jones will see that your luggage is taken there.'

Always the perfect butler, Jones managed to keep his face blank, but his gaze darted to the Earl.

Ravensford spoke smoothly. 'That won't be possible, Mother. The Green Room is already occupied. The Rose Room has been prepared for Annabell.' He turned to the chit. 'The colour will compliment you more than the Green Room ever could.'

Annabell giggled. 'You always were a gallant, Ravensford. I see that you have not changed.'

He made her a playful bow. 'I aim to please.'

'Well, you don't please me, Andrew.' The Countess cut across their banter. 'Have whoever is in the Green Room removed.'

Ravensford gave his parent a noncommittal look. 'No, Mother. Everything is fine the way it is.'

'Out,' the Countess said, waving her hand at everyone. When she and Ravensford were alone, she said, 'You have put that woman in there, haven't you? Well, I won't have it. She is not a proper companion to start, and even if she were, the Green Room is for important guests.'

Ravensford sauntered to the window and watched the carriage traffic on the street below. 'I believe this conversation is taking us nowhere, Mother. Miss O'Brien is staying where she is, and Annabell will be perfectly happy in the Rose Room.' He turned back to his mother before moving to the door. 'I hope you will be well enough to come down for dinner. Gaston has prepared your favourite foods, and you know how temperamental he can be.'

'Andrew—'

He walked out. Leaving his mother in a snit was not the best of things to do, but he had no intention of obeying her orders. His only worry was that she would make Mary Margaret's life miserable. He knew his mother well.

Thank goodness his parent did not know he had asked Mary Margaret to be his mistress. Any hint of that and the Countess would throw Mary Margaret into the street without a second thought.

At least he had kept away from her. He had learned early in life that there was no sense in tempting himself with something he could not have. Time cured everything—or made everything available.

A week after the Countess and Annabell's arrival, Mary Margaret donned her best gown, which had been her second best before the accident with the sea. It was dove grey wool, much like her other two dresses. Instead of dancing slippers, she wore her everyday shoes, the worn black leather doing nothing to enhance her toilet.

She turned away from the full-length mirror. She had never had more than a hand-held mirror her entire life. This one, where she could see her entire self, was an unheard-of luxury. Although right now she could do without it.

Determined to make the best of an awful situation, she carefully braided her waist-length hair and piled it atop her head. The style was a departure for her, but she knew it showed her long neck to advantage. She carefully loosened a few strands near her temples so that they curled around her eyes. Next she pulled her gold locket from underneath her bodice so that it showed like a bright spark.

Her reflection in the mirror looked like what she was—a poor companion.

Pride straightened her shoulders. She would not fare well at this ball, but there was nothing she could do. The Countess was not going so she must chaperon Annabell. Things could be worse. Annabell could be like her godmother. Instead, the girl was young, lovely and sweet.

On that uplifting thought, Mary Margaret marched from the room resolved to get through the evening ahead. At least she was not Emily, at home in Ireland wondering when Thomas would drink too much again and lose his temper.

Yes, things could be much worse.

Ravensford put Annabell's white satin-lined velvet cape around the chit's shoulders. She had been early, eager to experience her first visit to Almack's.

Ravensford heard footsteps on the landing and

looked up to see Mary Margaret. She filled his senses.

''Tis a good thing my cape is securely fastened, Ravensford,' Annabell said with a touch of humour. 'Otherwise it would be on the floor from your lack of attention.'

Ravensford gave her a quick grin, but his focus returned to Mary Margaret. He watched her finish descending the stairs. She moved with the flowing grace of the cat she so reminded him of. His loins tightened.

The weeks of avoidance had done nothing to cool his ardour. Too bad she had refused his offer of *carte blanche*. Too bad she was a potential thief, he told himself, determined to stop reacting to her. It was bad enough that he desired her. Worse that he had so little control over his response to her. No other woman in his life had ever made him react as completely and physically as she did. It was an unsettling situation.

'Oh, Mary Margaret,' Annabell said, her youthful voice full of disappointment. 'Why did you not tell me you don't have a ball gown? I would have loaned you one of mine.'

'Silly child. Nothing of yours would fit me. I am just fine the way I am. A chaperon is not supposed to be fashionable, merely present.'

'But I don't want you to be a drab mouse.' Annabell's lips formed a pretty little pout.

'You are a good-hearted child,' Mary Margaret said. 'Now we must go. It might be fashionable to be late, but this is your first time. We must make sure that you have plenty of opportunity to savour the event.'

'You always think of me,' Annabell said.

Mary Margaret smiled.

Ravensford watched the byplay, free to study Mary Margaret without having her aware. Annabell was right. She looked like a drab little tabby. Anger at his mother tightened his jaw. His parent had thrown Mary Margaret into the clutches of the *ton* without a thought for the woman's wardrobe or feelings.

The thoughtlessness was typical.

To cover his unreasonable reaction, he said, 'Jones, fetch Miss O'Brien's cape. The weather will turn colder.'

Always the perfect butler, Jones turned to Mary Margaret for directions. She said calmly, too calmly, 'That will not be necessary.'

'Yes, it will.' Ravensford had had enough. He was taking charge and they were leaving. When she did not answer, he said, 'Well?'

She turned coldly to him. 'I do not have a cape.'

'Of course you do. You wore it on the trip here.'

She eyed him as though he was an exotic specimen. 'Yes, and the continual rain and mud ruined it. Now may we leave?'

He turned to Jones. 'Fetch one of the Countess's evening capes.'

The butler blanched. 'Yes, my lord.'

'Tell Jane that I order it.'

'Yes, my lord.' Looking like a man about to face his worst nightmare, Jones headed up the stairs.

'Oh, Godmother won't be happy,' Annabell said softly.

Irritation made Ravensford sharp. 'I don't care what she likes or doesn't like. Miss O'Brien requires a cape. Mother will provide.'

Annabell eyed him askance but kept any further opinions to herself. Mary Margaret turned away from him so that he could not tell how she felt. However, her shoulders were tensed and her hands clenched.

A fresh spurt of ire made him stalk away. 'I will be in the library. Notify me when the cape arrives and we can finally be on our way.'

He was being unreasonable and he knew it. His mother was always inconsiderate of others and particularly of servants and those she felt beneath her. She was the reason he had decided to champion those less fortunate than himself. He had watched his father, caught by love, flinch every time his wife slighted someone. Father had been a mild man, concerned about others. Ravensford had always thought it his father's misfortune to love a woman so completely different from him. But their marriage had been happy. They had been devoted to each other.

Now he had to contend with Mother. But he had learned young that loving someone did not necessarily mean you liked that person.

As he had expected, Jones sought him out. 'My lord, the Countess requests your presence.'

Ravensford tossed off the remainder of the whiskey he had just poured. 'Thank you, Jones.'

The butler bowed and withdrew.

Ravensford barely glanced at the two women as he passed them in the foyer. Standing up to his mother was something he rarely did. Normally he let her actions pass him by. Her being in Ireland most of the year made things much easier between them. He mounted the stairs, determination hardening his resolve to make his mother do yet another thing she would not like—and all for Mary Margaret O'Brien.

The Countess bade him enter after making him wait for several minutes outside her door. His mood was not improved.

She sat beside a dainty Chippendale table, her chair a match. A book lay open on her lap.

She turned a baleful eye on him. 'What is the meaning of this, Andrew? The chit is a servant. She has no need for one of my cloaks. Nor will I loan her one.'

Ravensford felt his teeth grinding, but he managed to keep his voice cool. 'Then give her one.'

'Andrew, you overstep yourself. Your father would never have treated me like this.'

'Nor would I if you would be generous enough to help Miss O'Brien out.'

'I pay her. Let her purchase her own clothing. And you have ensconced her in one of the best suites. That is more than sufficient.' She waved a delicate white hand as though to push the entire situation away.

Many times in his life he had been tempted to throttle his mother, but never so much as now. This anger was out of character. Another thing to lay at Mary Margaret O'Brien's feet.

Tired of arguing, he strode past her and into her dressing room. Riffling among her clothes, he grabbed the first cape he came to. Holding it in a clenched fist, he re-entered his mother's boudoir.

The Countess stood, her white hair a halo around her furious face. 'How dare you, Andrew. Put that back. Now.'

Ignoring her, he stalked to the door, opened it

and left. She was too conscious of appearances to follow him. Downstairs, he flung the black velvet cape around Mary Margaret's shoulders.

'We are leaving.'

Chapter Eight

Ravensford reached the front door before Jones, who rushed up and held it open. Outside, the carriage waited. A footman hurried to open the door and let down the steps, then handed Annabell and Mary Margaret inside. Ravensford followed, flinging himself down on the seat beside Annabell. He noted that Miss O'Brien had her back to the horses.

A sardonic smile curved his lips. 'I see that you know your place, Miss O'Brien.'

'As do you, my lord.'

Her sharp words were a slap in the face. He nodded ironically. 'I am out of line. Pardon me.'

'Whatever possessed you, Ravensford,' Annabell said. 'I could have loaned Mary Margaret a cape.'

'One I have no need of.'

Ravensford scowled from one to the other. 'Typical.'

He put a stop to discussion by rapping his cane against the ceiling, telling the coachman to go. The carriage lurched forward.

No one spoke for some time. As they turned down King Street where Almack's was situated, the excitement was too much for Annabell who began to chatter. Soon both women were caught up in anticipation. Ravensford, who had cut his eyeteeth on Almack's, expected an evening of boredom.

They entered to the general hubbub of dowagers sitting in chairs along the wall, couples performing a country dance, and clusters of men flirting with chits. Normal.

Ravensford scanned the room, looking for any familiar faces. He caught Mrs Drummond Burrell frowning at them. Her attention was on Mary Margaret. The Duke of Wellington had been denied admission because he was not in evening dress; Ravensford wondered if the patroness was about to come over and tell Mary Margaret she could not attend. It would be a fitting end to an awful beginning.

Just as Mrs Drummond Burrell took a step toward them, Sally Jersey caught her arm and whispered something. Both women glanced their way, Sally with a mischievous smile and Mrs Drummond Burrell with dislike. Ravensford took that to mean Sally had intervened.

He ushered his charges farther into the room and deposited them near a group of young bucks. He raised an eyebrow and one of the youths separated and came to them.

'Ravensford,' the young man said. 'Didn't expect you here. And with such lovely companions.'

Ravensford bit back a sharp retort. Potsford was always effusive where women were concerned. But the youth did not deserve the sharp edge of his tongue. It was not Potsford's fault this evening had started so abysmally and promised to continue on that way.

'Annabell, Miss O'Brien, may I present Mr Potsford. This is my mother's goddaughter, Annabell Winston, and her chaperon, Miss O'Brien.'

'Pleased to meet you.' Always on the lookout for an heiress, Potsford lost no time. Bowing to Annabell, he said, 'May I have the pleasure of the next country dance?'

She blushed delicately. 'Please.'

'Until then, may I escort you to the refreshment table?' he asked, offering his arm.

Blushing prettily again, Annabell laid her fingers on his arm. The two headed off.

'He will be disappointed,' Ravensford said drily.

'Why ever for?' Mary Margaret asked, defence of her charge making her raspy voice catch.

'Because she is not an heiress.'

'She is a delightful young woman and will make some lucky man a wonderful wife.'

'But not Potsford.'

'You members of the aristocracy are all alike.'

'Too often,' he drawled. 'Come dance with me.'

She scowled. 'You mock me, my lord. This is a waltz. Even I know a woman cannot dance the waltz unless a patroness has approved.'

'No,' he murmured, wondering why he did such outrageous things around her. 'I don't mock you. Or are you afraid?'

She angled her chin up. 'Afraid? Of what?'

He gave her a lazy smile. 'Of what I might do— or say.'

More than that, she was scared of what she might say or do. Much as she deplored her reaction to him, he made her blood pound and her stomach churn.

'No.' Even to her own ears, her voice sounded breathy and unsure.

He laughed outright. 'Stay here.'

Mary Margaret watched him angle through the crowd. His broad shoulders, clad in a bottle-green evening coat, were an arresting sight, as were his muscular thighs in black satin casing. To her mind, he was the most attractive man here. Seeing other women follow him with their gaze, she knew her opinion of him was widely held. He was probably going to find a woman of his own station to dance with.

She turned away, her chest tight. The last thing she wanted was to see him with another woman.

She found a single chair in a corner and sat down. She did not have to be in Annabell's pocket, only make sure the girl did not dance more than twice with any one man and stayed out of dark areas. At least she could enjoy the music. She had always loved to dance and sing. Music brought her solace.

She felt a tingling awareness seconds before she heard Ravensford's voice.

'I have someone I want you to meet,' he said.

Surprised that he had come back, Mary Margaret jumped up. The woman with him was the same one she had seen earlier talking to another woman and smiling at Ravensford. She must be his latest interest, although she appeared a little old for him.

'Lady Jersey,' he said, 'I would like you to meet Miss O'Brien. She is the chaperon of my mother's goddaughter. Miss O'Brien, this is Lady Jersey, one of the patronesses.'

The woman arched one immaculate brow. 'How do you do, Miss O'Brien? Now, I would like to present the Earl of Ravensford for your consideration as a waltz partner.'

This was the last thing she had expected. There was a spark of mischief in Lady Jersey's eyes and an intense emotion in Ravensford's that she could not identify. Both waited for her answer.

She took a deep breath and gave the Earl her hand. There was nothing else she could do without drawing attention to them.

'Thank you, Sally,' Ravensford murmured.

'My pleasure,' Lady Jersey said before bubbling laughter escaped her red lips. 'I shall dine out on this for many a day. The much sought-after Earl of Ravensford needing help to get a chit to dance with him. Oh, yes, I shall enjoy telling this one.'

Ravensford winced but said nothing more.

Mary Margaret heard what Lady Jersey said, but dismissed it as a woman teasing an attractive man. She wanted to run. The last thing she wanted was for this man to hold her as intimately as the waltz required. When he slipped his arm around her waist, the dance floor tilted. She needed all her willpower not to melt against him.

Instead, she demanded, 'What do you think you are doing? I am here as a chaperon, barely one level up from a servant. I cannot dance with you. What will people say? What will your mother say?'

He drew her close. 'No more than they already are.'

She gasped and looked around. People watched them, some annoyed, others amused and more scandalised. She stiffened.

'I don't belong here.'

'You have as much right as anyone.'

'I have never waltzed.' Desperation made her voice husky.

He grinned raffishly. 'Follow me. I won't lead you astray.'

He dipped her and twirled her, making her momentarily lose her train of thought. It was hard to concentrate when a man you were inexorably drawn to held you tightly and made the world around you spin.

'I am not of your world,' she managed breathlessly. 'They know it. Lady Jersey knew it when she introduced us.'

His grip intensified until less than the proper twelve inches separated them. His face was close enough that she could see the golden striations in his green eyes. His nostrils flared.

'"My world", as you put it, is hide-bound. Too many of us are only concerned with our own entertainment.'

She stared up at him, seeing a determination that

she had not realised he possessed. 'Are you a reformer?'

His mouth, those wonderful lips that she always fantasised on hers, twisted. 'I try.'

She had wondered. Too many times she had watched him reach out to those beneath him not to have pondered why he did so.

'Is that why you are so active in Parliament?'

'For the most part.'

The knowledge that he cared enough for those less fortunate than himself to stand up in Parliament and fight for their rights hit her with a jolt. Not only was he a handsome man with great wealth, but he was a caring man. The attraction she had felt for him from the beginning increased beyond anything she had thought possible.

The music swirled around them. She moved with him, their feet gliding over the floor. She felt removed from reality, caught in a dream with only him and her. He was her perfect lover.

Heaven help her. Heaven help her heart.

She swayed to a stop in his arms. The notes faded away. The other couples drifted from the floor.

He held her attention.

'Doing it too brown,' a male voice drawled.

Mary Margaret started. Behind Ravensford stood a man as dark of visage as her imagination often painted the devil. Silver wings flew from his temples and a scar ran the length of his right cheek. Dark eyes, nearly black, watched them dispassionately. His entire person was slightly dishevelled, almost disreputable, but she knew that could not be or he would not have been allowed inside. Almack's was much too proper to allow in a rogue.

'Ah, Perth,' Ravensford said without turning. 'Always in the nick of time.'

Perth shrugged. 'I do my best. But there are times when no one can help you.'

Ravensford gave a mirthless chuckle. 'Spoken like a true friend.'

He still had not released her, and Mary Margaret, realising they were creating a spectacle, tried to step away. Several young girls tittered behind their hands.

'But already too late,' Perth said, holding out his hand to Mary Margaret. 'May I introduce myself since Ravensford is remiss. I am Perth.'

'The Earl of Perth,' Ravensford added.

'Another earl,' Mary Margaret said, giving Perth her hand. He brushed her fingers with his lips.

'My pleasure. Would you care for some rataffia? Yes? Ravensford will be happy to get it.' There was a wicked gleam in his eye.

'Always in command.' Ravensford touched his brow in salute before moving away.

Mary Margaret was nonplussed. With Ravensford went her sense of warmth and security, although she would never tell him that and could barely admit it to herself. She did not have the experience to deal with a man of Perth's calibre. She slanted him a glance through lowered lashes. She had a feeling he could be as cruel as he could be kind, if he was ever kind. Yet he had put himself forward to interrupt the scene she and Ravensford had created.

He guided her to a seat. 'The old Countess hired you to play nursemaid to her goddaughter?'

She nodded, still not sure what to say to him.

'Don't pay Ravensford's mother any mind. She has been the trial of his life.'

She nodded again, knowing now that she should say nothing. The last thing a servant or employee should do was talk about her employer.

His mouth split into a grin showing white teeth. Much like a predator.

Mary Margaret cudgelled her brain for an excuse to get away. Jumping up, she said, 'I see Annabell over there with Mr Potsford. I should go to her.'

He made her an ironic bow. 'As you wish.'

She did not wait.

'You certainly scared her off,' Ravensford said. Having just arrived with the drink, he now sat on the vacated chair.

'Your inamorata is a scared tabby. I thought you more adventurous than this.' He gave Ravensford a lascivious grin. 'Especially after taking up with the "Delightful Delilah". Lord, but she led you a merry chase.'

'She did.' Ravensford smiled at remembered antics. 'I am getting too advanced in age to deal with another such as she. Too exhausting.'

'Hence the tabby?'

His friend's disparagement of Mary Margaret was oddly irritating. 'She is no tabby. And I have not taken up with her. She is my mother's companion and Annabell's chaperon.' He cast Perth a wicked glance. 'And she has already turned down my offer.'

'Aha. That explains everything. I've never seen you dance like that with one of your mother's companions,' Perth said drily.

Determined to shake Perth from his high perch, Ravensford stated, 'She plans to steal something from my parent. I am keeping a close eye on her to see that she is unsuccessful. I thought that having her for a mistress would keep her nearby.'

'Ah…everything is clear.'

He angled to face Perth, intending to set him straight when his attention was caught by Annabell. 'Blast that chit. She can't go off with Potsford.'

'Definitely not. The puppy is as broke as shattered crockery.'

Perth's sarcasm was lost on Ravensford as he headed off. The last thing he needed was for Annabell to add another indiscretion to this evening— and hers would be much worse. Mary Margaret was not on the Marriage Mart and neither was he. Annabell was.

He caught up with the pair just as Mary Margaret gripped Annabell's arm. 'I believe Mr Potsford has taken ill and must leave, Annabell. Let us not keep him.'

Potsford looked ready to protest until he saw Ravensford over Mary Margaret's shoulder.

The Earl took Annabell's elbow in a firm hold. 'Miss O'Brien is right. It is time we left as well.'

'Quite right. Getting late,' Potsford said, edging away.

'But…but I don't want to,' Annabell said.

Ravensford stared her down. 'But you are.'

'His lordship is right, Annabell,' Mary Margaret said. 'The Countess will be wondering where we are and curious about the night.'

'I doubt that,' Annabell said rebelliously. But after an admonishing look from Mary Margaret, she acquiesced. 'I shall stop at her room if she is still awake and tell her everything. She always talks about how exciting her first Season was, she will enjoy this.'

Mary Margaret gave the girl a warm smile. 'I thought you would.'

Ravensford doubted that his mother cared about anything except her own comfort, but perhaps he judged her too harshly. She had always listened to his tales of wonder and woe. It was just when people she considered beneath her were involved that his parent could be unlikable and uncaring.

While they waited for the carriage to come around, he watched the two women. With all their differences in station and character, they seemed to genuinely like each other.

Mary Margaret O'Brien was a conundrum. She was educated, gentle and caring, yet she intended to steal from his mother. While part of him couldn't blame her, he knew the plan had been concocted in cold blood, something he would have thought the woman laughing softly with Annabell was incapable of. But he knew differently. He could still hear her wonderful voice agreeing to the deed.

The carriage arrived and they returned home with the two women discussing the evening and him watching the companion. The candles from the coach lanterns cast first shadows, then light, on the sharp angles of Mary Margaret's face. One minute she was a tigress, all temptation and dark. The next she was a kitten playing gently with Annabell.

At all times she was a mystery.

Chapter Nine

Mary Margaret breathed deeply of the roses that surrounded the tiny white iron gazebo. Like the Gothic folly the Countess had in Ireland, this gazebo had become her sanctuary. No one ever found her here.

She had peace and quiet to think about last evening. She had had a wonderful time. Ravensford had made the waltz seem like a part of them. For a large man he was very graceful. Even though he had held her closer than proper, she had not minded. Being close to him was too thrilling for anything else to matter.

She sighed and closed her eyes, wanting to relive the experience again.

'Miss, his lordship requires your presence in the library.'

Mary Margaret sat bolt upright. She had not

heard anyone. Now a young girl stood in front of her twisting her hands.

'Susan, you startled me. I did not hear you.'

'Pardon, miss.'

Still the girl did not stop wringing her hands. 'Whatever is the matter, Susan?' Mary Margaret stood and went to the girl. She put a gentle hand on the servant's shoulder. 'Never say you are afraid of me?'

'Oh, no, niver.' The young girl sighed. 'Not you, miss. But, his lordship is in an awful hurry…'

Mary Margaret gave the maid a quizzical look. 'Then I will go upstairs and freshen up. Then I will report to him.'

'Yes, miss.'

Mary Margaret smiled at the girl who was barely more than a child. 'What are you afraid of? Surely not the Earl.'

Susan chewed her bottom lip. 'I shouldn't be talkin' to ye, miss. But…his lordship is changed since he returned from Ireland. All of us says so.'

Curiosity filled Mary Margaret. Susan was right in that Mary Margaret should not be gossiping with the servants, but then she was very nearly one herself.

'How?' she asked, hoping she only sounded mildly interested.

The girl sidled closer and her voice lowered.

'Temper, miss. He has a temper. Niver had one befores. Like he's bothered awful by somethin'.'

Mary Margaret's heart skipped a beat. It could not be because she had refused his offer to be his mistress. Nor could it be because of Thomas's plan to have her steal some of the Countess's jewellery. Ravensford knew nothing about that. Still...

'Oh.' Her voice scraped. In spite of her conviction that the Earl did not know, her nerves had still got the better of her. She started again. 'Oh? I thought he was always volatile.'

Although when she thought about it, he had not shown any impatience or anger during the discussion she had sat in on between him and his mother before they left Ireland. She would have lost patience with the Countess. The woman was as scatterbrained as she was high in the instep. Yet he was constantly losing his temper with her.

'No, niver, miss. He's ever so easy goin' and friendly. But no more.' Her shoulders drooped as though she had lost something personal.

Mary Margaret wondered at the girl's reaction. Ravensford had always seemed concerned about his people, but she had not realised how involved with him they were. He must be a good employer and landlord.

'And just now you were afraid that if I refused his summons he would be angry with you.'

'Yes, miss.'

'Don't worry, Susan. I will go. But first I must tidy up a bit.'

Mary Margaret left the girl in the kitchen and went up to her room. Alone, she went to the full-length mirror. Her hair needed straightening; pieces had come loose from the chignon and curled around her eyes like errant tendrils of thread.

Unbidden came the memory of Ravensford brushing her hair back from her face after she had nearly drowned. His warmth and concern had eased much of her panic. At the time, she had not recognised how his strength had sustained her. Realising now was like being struck by lightning— searing and surprising.

When had she come to depend on him so much? She did not know. It had just happened. She had only been in his company a month.

This was awful.

Right now, this instant, she could imagine his touch on her, his fingers warm and sure against her skin—as they had been last night. Never in her wildest flights of imagining had she envisioned the ecstasy of being caught up in his arms, dancing the waltz. Never.

Delight suffused her. Using the hairbrush as Ravensford's hand, she began to dance. She hummed the waltz tune from last night as she twirled around the room, smiling up at her imaginary partner. Faster and faster she went, her emotions soaring.

'Umph!'

It was a rude awakening to trip against a pile of books she had stacked in the middle of the room preparatory to returning them to the Earl's library. She sat down on the floor with a thump, the brush falling from her fingers. Her foot hurt like the dickens where she had smacked it.

She sighed. This loss of control was getting her nowhere. She had to rein in her imagination and her emotions.

A knock on the door reminded her that she had to attend Ravensford. Susan was very likely worried sick that she had changed her mind and was not going downstairs.

'I am coming,' she said loudly enough for the maid to hear.

She rose and dropped the brush that had started it all on to the dresser. A quick glance in the mirror showed her hair still looking unkempt and a sheen on her face that flushed her cheeks and reddened her lips. She was a sight.

But she was already late. She wet her hands in the ewer and quickly slicked them over her hair, hoping the strands would stay in place long enough for this meeting.

Mary Margaret straightened her shoulders and headed toward the library where she knocked and waited for Ravensford's permission to enter. Silly pictures of her waltzing around her room brought a smile to her lips, lips suddenly dry. And her palms were wet. No matter how she tried to prepare herself for his presence, her reaction to him always overwhelmed her better sense. It scared her.

His baritone 'Come in' jolted her into action. She stumbled through the door as soon as the footman opened it. He shut it behind her before she even realised she was in the library.

A slight smile curved Ravensford's lips. 'Do you always make an entrance like that? If so, you should be on the stage.'

She flushed, but quickly regained her composure. 'I was woolgathering, expecting to be kept waiting longer than you did, my lord.'

'Procrastination is not one of my failings,' he said, moving from behind the large mahogany desk where he had been sitting when she entered. He bore down on her. 'How many times have I told you to call me Ravensford? After all we have been through it is more appropriate.'

She felt like he was suffocating her with his nearness. She took a step back.

'I cannot do that.'

He moved closer, frowning. 'Don't give me any

of that nonsense about being a servant. You are no more a servant than I am a duke.'

She raised an eyebrow. 'Exactly, my lord. It would never have occurred to me to make the comparison you just did. That more than anything says I am a servant.'

A strange light entered his eyes. 'Did you feel like a servant last night? You didn't act like one. Not in my arms.'

His words caught her off guard. They were the last things she expected him to say. In her mind she was the one who still thought of last night. The dance should be gone from his memory by now.

Unconsciously she raised one hand in a symbolic attempt to fend him off. His stance dared her to lie. She took a deep breath, prepared to tell him anything but the truth.

'No,' she whispered, appalled at her answer even as the word slipped out.

He was beside her in a second, his hands gripping her shoulders. 'I knew it.'

Shivers chased down her spine, followed by heat that curled in her stomach. His mouth was inches from hers and coming closer. The breath caught in her throat. Her gaze clung to his. She did not want to miss anything.

'You are supposed to close your eyes,' he said, chuckling deep in his chest.

Lethargy crept through her limbs as she did his bidding. She could feel the warmth of his breath against her skin. This was how she remembered him.

His mouth closed over hers and her heart jumped. His lips teased at hers, his tongue trailing along her flesh. His hands roamed over her back until one settled at her waist and pulled her close, so close she could feel his chest rising and falling. She swayed into him, opening her mouth to allow him to deepen the kiss.

The hand at her waist slid lower until it cupped the swell of her hip. The other hand rose to the base of her neck and angled her head to one side so he penetrated better.

Her heart pounded. The blood rushed in her ears. Her stomach rioted. Never, in her entire life, had she felt like this. Alive and tingling, ready for anything.

He broke away from her, panting. She whimpered, her hands circling his neck as she tried to pull him back.

He laughed, but it was shaky. 'Easy, sweetheart. This is not the place, much as I want to finish what we have started.'

She blinked and came to her senses. Slowly. Slowly enough that his lips brushed hers before he finally released her.

She swayed and grabbed on to the nearest object, the back of a chair. He was close enough that she could see the black of his pupils. They seemed to fill his entire eye. He looked as though he had just woken, sensual and…and something she could not explain. Excited? Hungry?

She felt bereft, his warmth no longer enfolding her.

'I will come to your room tonight,' he murmured, bending just enough for his lips to brush hers.

His mouth on hers struck sparks that she feared would start an inferno inside her. She closed her eyes and tried to control her reaction to him. He was catnip and she was a cat. Her fingers shook from the effort not to reach out to him.

'After everyone has gone to bed,' he promised, his voice like a liquid caress along the curves of her body.

'After everyone has gone to bed,' she parroted. *After everyone has gone to bed.* Her eyes snapped open. She glared at him. 'No, you will not.'

A sardonic light entered his eyes, making them sharp as facetted emeralds. 'Coming to your senses?'

'How dare you? How dare you treat me like a…a lightskirt? I won't be your mistress, and every time you ask me you insult me. You treat me like

I am lower than the servant you continually say I am not.' She thrust her balled fists on her hips. 'Well, let me tell you. I would rather be the lowest of servants than your mistress.'

He stepped away, his eyes brooding, and made her a mocking bow. 'I hear you very well, Miss O'Brien. If you are not careful, the entire household will hear you.'

She sputtered to a stop as his words penetrated her indignation. She gulped air and turned away, unable to face him. She had behaved as wantonly as a loose woman. But she was not one.

When she had finally achieved a modicum of calm, she turned back to him. 'If you will excuse me, I have much to do.'

'I don't excuse you, Miss O'Brien.'

She froze in the act of moving to the door.

He stroked the signet ring on his left hand, drawing her attention to the fine sapphire. 'I want you to go to Annabell's modiste and get yourself a wardrobe suitable for a London Season.'

She gasped. 'You jest. First you try to seduce me, then ask me to be your mistress, and now you propose to send me to a modiste I cannot afford to patronise.'

'I am deadly serious, Miss O'Brien. And I intend to pay for everything.'

'You summoned me for this? Well, my answer is no. You will not pay for anything of mine.'

'Oh, but I will,' he drawled.

'No, you will not,' she reiterated. They were at it again. He was ordering her about and she was defying him.

'This continual contest of wills is boring, Miss O'Brien,' he said, turning away and going to sit behind his desk. 'Your appointment is at three. I shall expect you down here at half past two.'

Affronted to the core, she glared at him. 'I don't need anything. While I don't have much, and none of it is up to the standards of the *ton*, it is sufficient for me.'

'But not for me,' he stated.

She bristled. 'What have you to do with my wardrobe, pray tell?'

'It offends me.'

'Offends you!' Hurt, followed rapidly by anger, suffused her. 'How shallow.'

'I can be.' He shuffled a stack of papers and lined them up perfectly. 'I have sent word to Madame Bertrice that she is to provide you with a complete wardrobe.'

'You are mistaken, my lord.' She tipped her nose in the air.

'I think not.'

She ground her teeth together. They were very

close to a shouting match. Children would behave as they were. A smile tugged at her lips.

His eyes held a hint of humour. 'We are behaving as children.'

Some of the tension eased from her. Her shoulders relaxed. 'My exact thought.'

'Good. Then you will stop arguing with me and be at Madame's by three o'clock.'

Her face turned to stone. He was stubborn and used to having his own way. 'I did not say that.'

'I will have the carriage brought around by half past two.'

Mary Margaret knew a dismissal when she heard it. Just as well. She was done arguing with his lordship. She simply would not go. With barely a curtsy, she left, her ire up and her determination firmly in place.

Ravensford watched her go and knew she would disobey him—it was written in every line of her magnificent body. For the life of him, he did not understand why she brought out the stubborn streak he had worked so hard at eradicating. His father had told him once that the trait would cause him problems.

Shaking his head, he returned to his desk and re-read for the third time the Bill he intended to introduce to the Lords. His mind refused to concentrate.

Pictures of Mary Margaret O'Brien insisted on penetrating his thoughts. Her voice intruded on his dreams. She was an enigma he longed to unravel.

And that kiss. He had not intended for that to happen. After she had refused his offer of *carte blanche*, he had decided not to ask again. But kissing her had ignited a fire in him that nothing short of full possession could quench. He wanted her, and having sampled the excitement of her, he meant to have her. To hell with her plan to rob his mother.

As his mistress she would have enough jewels that she could give hers to the man who wanted her to steal his mother's. She would even have some left over. He would shower her with everything.

Now he had only to convince her that accepting his offer would be better than stealing.

That decided, he once again tried to read his Bill—and could not. As satisfying as the thought of having her for his mistress was, there was something wrong about it. He felt as though something was tarnished.

His secretary chose that moment to enter and Ravensford forced his attention to matters having nothing to do with his mother's companion.

Mary Margaret paced the confines of her room. The carriage waited for her. It would wait forever.

Part of her, the weak part, longed to have beautiful clothing. She had never had anything that was not serviceable. Some had been attractive in a practical manner, but never designed solely to make her look good.

But she was not allowing the Earl to buy her clothes. Men of his station bought clothes and other things for their mistresses. She was not his mistress. Nor was she going to be.

The hurt that had exploded in the library was now a dull ache. With time, she would make that go away too. So what if he desired her and nothing else? She had not even dreamed that he would desire her. She was a farmer's daughter with nothing to recommend her, not even stunning looks.

She stopped and her reflection in the mirror confronted her. The grey frock made her look drab, as though she was sick. In a fit of pique, she stalked to the mirror and, using all her strength, turned it to the wall.

'There,' she muttered, dusting her hands off. 'I shan't have to look at myself any more.'

The initial satisfaction was quickly replaced by the subdued knowledge that she knew by heart what the mirror showed. She did not need to see her reflection to know her clothing did nothing for her. And how she wished it might.

That weak part of her wanted to look pretty for

Ravensford. She did not want to be his mother's lowly companion who was good enough to steal a kiss from in the library when no one was around. She wanted to be the woman on his arm whom he proudly squired about town.

She wanted the moon. She was a fool. She dashed her fist across her eyes. She was not a watering pot.

A timid knock on the door, followed by Susan's hesitant, 'Miss, his lordship wants to know why you are late,' pulled Mary Margaret from her melancholy admission.

Surprise tightened her shoulders. She had not really expected Ravensford to keep track of the time and the appointment. She had thought he would be out about his business at the House of Lords, fully expecting her to do as he ordered. In her limited experience, men did not interest themselves in women's dress. Her father had never cared and nor did Thomas, whose money went on his own back.

Ravensford's persistence must come of the stubbornness she had glimpsed in him this morning. Nothing else that she could think of would explain this determination.

She crossed to the door, opened it and looked down at the maid's large brown eyes. She regretted putting the girl in the middle, but she was not going.

'Susan, please tell his lordship that I am indisposed and sorry for any inconvenience I might cause.'

The girl gulped. 'Yes, miss.'

'Oh, and would you please return this to the Countess?' Mary Margaret picked up the neatly folded black velvet cape and handed it to Susan.

After Susan took the garment, Mary Margaret closed the door behind the maid's retreating figure and crossed to the window. She looked out on the gardens, which were in full, riotous bloom. If she opened the glass, the scent of roses would fill the air. She did so and drew in a deep breath of the glorious smell. Perhaps she would be allowed to pick some of the blossoms and put them in a vase in her room. Then, perhaps not. It did not matter. She was mentally chattering, trying to keep herself from thinking of Ravensford's reaction when she did not appear as he commanded.

A second knock on the door froze her rambling mind.

'Who is it?' she rasped through stiff lips.

'Who do you think?' Ravensford asked, irritation evident in his inflection. 'I am not used to having my orders ignored.'

She closed her eyes and took a deep breath. 'I

told you before. I don't need those clothes. Nor will I go to the modiste.'

Her voice was raised enough to penetrate the thick wood of the door. She belatedly wondered how many servants were listening to this clash of wills. Why was he doing this?

The door opened. He stood, elbows akimbo, and glared at her. 'You are not missing the appointment.'

She crossed her arms over her chest. 'Yes, I am.'

His eyes narrowed. 'Do you want to embarrass Annabell again?'

'Embarrassment will not adversely affect her.'

He relaxed against the door jamb. 'But your clothing might. How you are dressed impacts on how the *ton* perceives Annabell. If you look poor and provincial, then she looks the same.'

Doubt sneaked through Mary Margaret's determination. 'That is silly.'

He shrugged. 'Of course, but that does not change it.'

The last thing she wanted was to hurt Annabell's chances of a successful Season. The girl was so excited and had such high expectations.

'What about Potsford last night? He did not seem the least bit put off that Annabell was with me.'

'I introduced them. He thought she was an heiress and he is on the lookout for one. He would not have cared if she had the face of a horse and the body of a hippopotamus.'

Mary Margaret flinched at the blunt, uncomplimentary description. 'What an awful picture that creates.'

'It was meant to,' he drawled. 'Appearances are everything to society. Annabell has a moderate dowry. She needs to marry well or at least respectably.'

She sighed. She had come to care for the girl, and the last thing she wanted to do was adversely impact on Annabell's Season.

'I will go, but only if the dresses I purchase are paid for from my salary.'

He straightened. For an instant, she thought mirth flashed across his face. She must have been mistaken because, when she squinted to see better, he was solemn. There was a twitch at his mouth but nothing more.

'Hurry. The horses have been kept waiting for far too long.'

He turned and left without a backward glance, as though he expected her compliance. His arrogance raised her hackles, but she had said she would go. Very likely he was returning to whatever business her failure to show had taken him from.

As dignified as a rushing woman could be, she

sped down the stairs and past the butler who held open the front door. She barrelled through the coach door the footman held and nearly into Ravensford. He grinned sardonically.

'Haste can make for some interesting seat mates.'

For what seemed like the hundredth time since she'd met him, she blushed. He constantly disconcerted her, although this last had been her own doing.

She plopped down. 'I did not think you were going. I am capable of doing this on my own.'

'But, I'm sure, not to my satisfaction.'

She drew herself straight, a set-down on the tip of her tongue, one she could not deliver. 'I am sure that nothing I can afford to buy will be to your satisfaction, my lord.'

She turned away as they set off. When he said nothing further, she tried to lose herself in the changing scenery. London was fascinating. She had never been outside of Cashel, and that country town was not even the size of one of London's hamlets.

But it was impossible to ignore him. She was too conscious of everything that had happened to them.

It was with relief that she felt the carriage slow down and stop. A small, very discreet door sat back from the street. There was no name on the outside. Nothing that she could see to tell the customer this was a dressmaker's shop, if it was. She gave Ravensford a questioning look.

'Madame Bertrice's. She does not advertise. She does not have to.'

He got out as soon as the footman opened the door and let down the steps. Turning back, Ravensford offered his hand.

Mary Margaret eyed his fingers warily. Even covered by fashionable gloves, they looked strong and demanding. She had no doubt that his touch would sear her flesh even though she also wore gloves. After their bout of lovemaking in the library, she did not trust herself near him. He did things to her.

But she could not ignore him. It was not done.

Taking a deep breath, she put her hand into his. She was right. Heat surged up her arm and tightened her chest. She cast one disconcerted glance at him before studiously watching where she put her feet.

'I won't let you fall, Miss O'Brien,' his honey-smooth baritone mocked.

'I never thought you would,' she answered primly, refusing to look him in the face and meet his unspoken challenge.

She had spent her life trying her best to meet

difficult situations without flinching, but now more than ever she felt cowardly. She had stood up to him as much as she thought herself capable of doing for one day.

The rest of the day, she was going to concentrate on not letting her desire for beautiful clothing overcome her determination to save for Emily. Soon she would be able to collect her quarterly wage. She would send it to Emily and tell her to leave Thomas. She could not get carried away here.

Chapter Ten

Once she was safely on the ground, his hand slid to her elbow and guided her toward the door. He opened it without knocking, and they entered one of the most elegant rooms Mary Margaret had ever been in.

Discreet beiges and creams, with just a hint of gold, covered the chairs, settees, floor and single window. Several delicate tables held vases with a few select flowers. A light floral scent filled the air.

Mary Margaret was entranced.

A petite woman glided toward them. She wore an elegant black gown with a single row of white lace at the bodice and wrists. Her blonde, almost white, hair feathered around a face smooth as a newborn's, yet her eyes spoke of years of experience.

'My lord Count,' she murmured, calling him by his continental title and offering her hand.

Ravensford took her fingers with grace and charm. Lifting them to his lips for the briefest of touches, he murmured, 'Madame Bertrice, allow me to introduce Miss O'Brien. She is the woman I spoke to you about.'

The modiste smiled at him before turning her attention to Mary Margaret. Bright blue eyes took in everything about Mary Margaret in what seemed seconds.

'Ah, just as you said, my lord,' the woman murmured, her accent settling into a brisk mode. 'I have just the thing. It was returned by one of my clients because the colour is too strong. It will be perfection on Miss O'Brien.' She crooked a finger at Mary Margaret. 'Come this way, please. We must see what alterations the gown needs. The original owner was not as shapely as you.'

Mary Margaret missed her step. She was not used to people speaking so openly of one's proportions.

Madame winked. 'You will find, Miss O'Brien, that the aristocracy is not so delicate as others in their mode of speech.'

Mary Margaret could only nod.

She was further discommoded to have to undress in front of Madame and an assistant. Both women behaved as though nothing was out of the ordinary, which gradually eased Mary Margaret's discomfort. She knew women who had their dresses made by others always disrobed thus, but she had never had that luxury.

The gown they brought out was stunning. The colour was the deep pink of wild roses, so rich it was nearly mauve. There was no adornment. They slipped the silken folds over her head and smoothed the material down her sides. The bosom had been let out and they quickly set about sizing it. Minutes later, they finished and turned her toward the single mirror.

Surely that was someone else, she thought, even though she knew intellectually that the reflection was hers. The deep pink put colour into her normally pale cheeks, even her lips. And the cut of the dress was masterful. She understood why Madame Bertrice did not advertise her location. Any woman seeing another in a dress like this would do anything to find out who had made it.

She looked like a long-stemmed rose, ready to sway in a passing breeze. She looked regal and beautiful. She knew, with a sinking heart, that she could never afford this dress on her salary, not even if she worked all her life.

She squeezed her eyes shut on her reflection.

Temptation was something she so rarely felt—until recently. First Ravensford and now this vanity.

'It is beautiful beyond words, madame,' she said regretfully. 'But I cannot afford this dress. I am truly sorry.'

The assistant tittered, only to be swatted sharply by Madame. Mary Margaret ignored the young girl the best she could, but it was not easy. Pride was a commodity she could not afford.

'Nonsense, mademoiselle. This gown is nothing. A *bagatelle*. To me, it is worthless.' She shrugged eloquently. 'I would be much better served by having someone of your uniqueness to wear it before the *ton*.'

Hope lit Mary Margaret's face. If only…

'Come, Miss O'Brien,' the modiste pursued, 'why would I tell you something that was not true, for I can see that you doubt me?'

'I don't disbelieve you, I simply cannot see how that can be. Any woman would be delighted to have this gown.'

'Then it is settled,' Madame stated.

'But I did not say I wanted to purchase—'

'Oh, but you did. Not in so many words, but I can see the longing you feel. Do not worry. The Count has provided me with much business in the past. The matter of this single garment is nothing.

Now come along and show his lordship what miracles a fine garment can create.'

Before Mary Margaret could protest further, Madame swept from the dressing room. The maid tittered again, watching her from lowered lashes. Mary Margaret felt trapped with nowhere to go but out to Ravensford. So be it.

Head high, shoulders back, she retraced her steps to Madame's receiving room. Ravensford was in conversation with the modiste and did not look up immediately. Mary Margaret took several deep breaths, wondering if she should return to the dressing room before either of them realised she was here. Just as she decided to do so, Ravensford glanced up. An arrested look came over him. Mary Margaret flushed to the top of the gown's bodice.

Ravensford had always found her to be an exotic beauty, but now she was devastating. The thin silk accentuated her full bosom and small waist. The colour made her eyes sparkle. His loins tightened painfully.

'Superb, madame,' he said softly, never taking his gaze from Mary Margaret. 'We will definitely take that one.'

'But of course,' Madame said complacently.

'I am glad you approve,' Mary Margaret said with a tinge of sarcasm, her deep husky voice rasping. 'Now, if you are both done studying me, I will go change.'

'By all means,' Ravensford said. As soon as she was out of the room he turned to Madame. 'I want a complete wardrobe for Miss O'Brien. Expense is not a consideration.'

'But of course.'

He eyed her sharply. 'Miss O'Brien is a lady of Quality.'

'I never thought otherwise, my lord.'

'Send this gown immediately along with a cape.'

'Tomorrow, my lord.'

Mary Margaret joined them and Ravensford contented himself with the knowledge that Madame would be discreet and her clothing impeccable. He escorted Mary Margaret to the waiting coach and could not resist the temptation to rest his hand on the small of her back as she entered the vehicle. He felt her skin jump under his fingers. She was not indifferent to him. Satisfaction curved his lips.

He followed her into the closed carriage. He had chosen this vehicle in the hope that fewer people would see them. Much as he wanted her to be dressed as befitted her beauty, he did not want everyone to know that he clothed her. He had no real excuse for doing so and others would realise that. The rumour mill would soon have them an *on-dit*, and while he intended to bed her, he did not intend for the whole world to know it. He had to trust to Madame's desire for more business from him and the loyalty of his servants that no one would talk.

He settled across from her, breathing deeply of her light lavender scent. He had always thought of the flower as a way to preserve and freshen clothing and linens. But from the moment he had first heard her speaking in his mother's library, the scent had taken on a sensual connotation that he knew would stay with him for life.

'You will wear the gown at the ball in Annabell's honour.'

She looked at him from the corner of her eye. 'I will wear it when and where I choose.'

He crossed one Hessian-covered leg over the other. 'You are the most argumentative woman it has ever been my misfortune to encounter. Can't you ever do as you are told without first fighting?'

She turned away and in a tight voice said, 'I have done as others have bid me all my life. But only you have tried to make me do things that I find to be inappropriate.'

Even as she finished speaking, a furtive look crossed her face. He grinned sardonically. She must be remembering the man who had ordered her to steal his mother's jewels.

'Are you sure?' he pursued.

Her chest rose and fell and she seemed to be struggling with a strong emotion. For a moment he was contrite, but he pushed the weakness away. Now was the time for her to tell him everything. Or at least hint at it.

'Yes,' she said shortly, refusing to meet his eyes.

His jaw hardened. There was more than one way to make a cat howl.

The remainder of the journey home passed in a strained silence that Ravensford did nothing to break. Let her stew in her own lies.

Ravensford fingered the grey pearl necklace. Matching ear drops, bracelets and a ring nestled in the nearby satin-lined box. The set would go perfectly with the mauve gown Madame Bertrice was altering. Unfortunately it had not arrived for tonight's visit to the Drury Lane Theatre. It did not matter. He could no more give Miss O'Brien the set to wear than he could fly to the moon. No matter that a large part of him wanted to defy convention and his mother in order to see how the Irish woman would look dressed as befitted her exotic beauty.

He returned the jewels to their case and handed them over to Stevens, who looked scandalised. Ravensford quirked one eyebrow.

The valet sniffed. 'Please allow me to get a fresh cravat, my lord. The one you are wearing has developed a crease where there should be none.'

Ravensford barely managed not to laugh out loud, which would have offended the valet. He should have known that Stevens cared nothing for the jewellery and everything for his master's toilet.

'Thank you, Stevens, but that won't be necessary. I realise that I am a trial to you but, as you know, I am not a dandy. I would not be happy to have you leave me for another, but I would understand.'

The valet gave his gentleman an aggrieved look. 'I could not leave. I waited years for you to hire me. You have the best shoulders and legs in all of London. You are a credit to my skills.' He sighed dramatically. 'If only I could impress upon you the importance of dress.'

Surprise stopped Ravensford from speaking for a moment. He had had no idea his valet felt so strongly about dressing him. For his part, he considered himself to be a well set-up man, but he had several friends he would describe as better physical specimens than himself. Perth was one.

Humbly, he said, 'Thank you, Stevens, for your devotion.'

The gentleman's gentleman gave his master a tight smile before handing over Ravensford's gloves and cane. Ravensford took the accessories and left. The ladies would be in the foyer shortly.

Half an hour later, Ravensford tapped his cane impatiently against his right leg and wondered why he had ever thought he should be on time. Women certainly did not consider promptness to be important.

He handed his *chapeau* to the butler. 'If the ladies come down, I will be in the library.'

He turned to leave and caught a glimpse of grey. Mary Margaret, dressed in her drab gown, and Annabell, dressed in white muslin trimmed with blue ribbons, were descending the stairs. His attention stayed on Mary Margaret. Even dressed dowdily, she aroused him.

She stood proudly, watching him. Her movements were delicate and flowing, her eyes brilliant as diamanté and her hair silky as a raven's wing. Dressed by Madame Bertrice, she would take the *ton* by storm.

She had stunned him in that pink dress. The neck had been lower than anything she ever wore, drawing his imagination to the hollow between her breasts. In many ways, it had been more erotic than her soaked chemise and pantaloons. The dress had been provocative.

He swallowed hard.

'Ravensford,' Annabell said in her high, light voice, 'you are being rude. You are putting Mary Margaret to the blush.' Her laugh filled the air.

He had to physically shake himself. His perusal had been too intense and too long. To hell with convention.

'I knew the gown would become you,' he said.

She looked nonplussed. 'This gown?'

Annabell's laughter trilled out.

Ravensford coughed to hide his own discomfiture. His mental picture of her in the pink dress had made him forget that she wore the grey. Never in all his thirty-two years had he behaved this gauche. In the end it was worth it. Her nervous laugh, low and throaty like a warm purr, filled the foyer and sent liquid desire coursing through his limbs.

'Thank you, my lord.'

'Andrew, what are we waiting for?' his mother said shrilly from where she stood on the landing, twenty feet above them. 'We will be late.'

He pulled his focus from Mary Margaret and made his parent an ironic bow. 'So we will, Mother. The coach is waiting.'

The butler showed the younger women out while Ravensford waited to assist his mother. The urge to throw convention to the wind and take Mary Margaret's arm was great, but he knew that doing so would only make matters worse for her. His parent would never condone his interest in the companion. He wondered why it mattered.

Mary Margaret kept her gaze focussed out the window of the carriage. The Countess and Annabell sat across from her, facing the driver. Ravensford sat beside her, his thigh brushing hers every time the coach lurched. She felt like a cat treading across Cook's oven, scorched and wary.

The scent of him filled her senses. He was so close that, if she turned her head, her mouth would brush his shoulder.

Memory of his kiss held her motionless. Her stomach rolled over slowly and her hands trembled. The urge to touch him, to invite his touch in return, filled her. Shivers chased sparks down her spine.

She closed her eyes and forced herself to remember why she was here, and it was not to be seduced by the Earl of Ravensford. In days her first quarter would be complete. Once her wages were in her hand, she could leave the Countess, somehow return to Ireland, and take Emily and Annie away from Thomas. That was why she was here.

She sighed with relief when the carriage finally stopped. The Countess and Annabell descended first. Ravensford followed, turned back to her and offered his hand. She stared at his gloved fingers, telling herself that allowing him to help her down would not make her breath go short and her stomach clench. She lied to herself and knew it.

Fighting to keep from trembling, she put her hand in his. His fingers closed over hers. Her eyes met his, their gazes locked. Her world narrowed to him and his touch. Nothing mattered, not her sister Emily, not her niece Annie, not the people around them.

No matter how many times he helped her from a carriage—and it seemed he did so constantly—she did not think she would ever become inured to his touch. For her, he was magical.

'Andrew,' the Countess demanded, rapping their clasped fingers with her closed fan.

He glanced at his mother and the spell broke. Mary Margaret jerked her arm back and hid her hand in the folds of her skirt.

'Mary Margaret,' the Countess said imperiously, 'see to Annabell, as you should have been doing all the time.'

Mary Margaret nodded, resisting the urge to dip a curtsy. Afraid to look at Ravensford and see his disgust at her weakness in succumbing to him yet again, she skirted away, holding her head proudly as her mother had taught her. The Countess might treat her as a nonentity, but she did not have to act downtrodden.

Annabell frowned at the situation. 'Godmother can be the most autocratic person in the world. Pay no mind to her, Mary Margaret.'

The younger girl linked her arm through Mary Margaret's and steered them to the doors where they waited for the other two. Mary Margaret could just hear the Countess's hissed words.

'Andrew, have you no pride? The chit is a servant, and barely that. Bed her if you must, but don't ogle her in public.'

Mary Margaret blanched and glanced at Annabell to see if the girl had heard. Annabell was smiling at a young man who stood nearby, her attention fully occupied. Thank goodness.

Mary Margaret could not hear Ravensford's reply but imagined it was one of indignant denial.

The Countess swept past them, Ravensford at her side. Mary Margaret and Annabell hurried to keep up. They made their way to Ravensford's reserved box and took their seats, Annabell, the Countess and Ravensford in the front. Mary Margaret sat in the back, positioned to see over the shoulders of the other two women.

The first play of the evening was nearly over. A Shakespearean tragedy that she watched with such absorption it was a shock when someone entered the box and moved in front of her.

The young man from outside had come to chat.

Ravensford rose and offered his chair, which the visitor accepted with alacrity.

'Would you care for refreshment?' Ravensford asked, startling Mary Margaret further.

'No, thank you,' she murmured, glad her voice sounded calm and uninterested.

'Always composed and in control,' he murmured.

She blinked and said nothing, no riposte coming to her rescue. He gave her a searching study, his face showing nothing.

'Andrew!'

The Countess's shrill voice broke whatever had caught Ravensford's attention. Mary Margaret was not sure whether to be happy or regretful. As uncomfortable as his interest was, she also found that she enjoyed it. In all, it was a very disturbing conundrum.

The Earl made an elaborate bow in the general direction of his parent and sauntered off. Mary Margaret felt the Countess's angry gaze on her and studiously avoided looking at the woman. It would do no good. The Countess would still make her life miserable.

A flash of gold caught her eye. She looked in the direction of the gallery, squinting to better see over the distance. Bucks and dandies milled about the area just in front of the stage, many calling to the actresses.

There was the golden glint again. She leaned forward in her seat. A tall, slim man lounged against the far corner. He was impeccably dressed in evening clothes tailored to his frame. His attention was on her.

No. It could not be. He would never come all this way. Never. But...

He waved in her direction. Thomas.

Mary Margaret blanched. He had followed her here. Where were Emily and Annie? Had he left them in Ireland?

'I took the liberty of getting you some punch,' Ravensford said, his baritone seeming to come from just behind her right ear.

Her pulse jumped. She glanced back at him, hoping her countenance did not betray her unease. Had he seen her looking at Thomas? Had he seen Thomas looking at her? Surely if he had he would think it nothing but two people exchanging interested glances. He did not know Thomas.

But the Countess did.

Mary Margaret shivered.

'Here,' Ravensford murmured, setting the punch down. 'Where is your cape?'

She stared at him. His words meant nothing.

'Where is your cape?' he repeated.

She shook her head. 'I don't have one.'

'Yes, you do. I gave you my mother's,' he said patiently as though talking to a child.

She shook her head again. 'I gave it back.'

What was Thomas doing here? Was he going to contact her? Was he going to tell her to steal the jewels now? She shut her eyes.

Ravensford's hand on her shoulder brought her back to the present situation. 'That cape was yours. When I give you something, I expect you to keep it.'

She stared blindly up at him. He was making such a fuss over something so trivial. 'It was not yours to give. You cannot take something from someone else and say it is yours to give where you wish.'

His fingers tightened on her shoulder. 'Is that a philosophy you live by? Or is it just for me and that blasted cape?'

She blinked and her mouth worked, but nothing came out. He spoke almost as though he knew, but he could not. No one knew, not even Emily.

'It is a philosophy I believe in.'

Instead of replying, he moved on to his mother and Annabell. She sagged. Surreptitiously she looked back where Thomas had been. He was gone.

She chewed her bottom lip. Perhaps she had

been mistaken. The lighting was not that good. It was ridiculous to think Thomas would come this far. In his mind as long as he had Emily and Annie that was more than enough to get her to do his bidding. That was it. She had been mistaken. A guilty conscience had tricked her.

She heard shuffling and noticed that the man who had occupied the Earl's seat the entire time had stood and was giving Ravensford back the chair.

'No need, Higgins,' Ravensford said. 'I am capable of standing.'

'Know you are, Ravensford, but must be moving on. Miss Annabell says I may pay m'respects tomorrow.' He bowed his way out without ever glancing in Mary Margaret's direction.

Instead of watching the young man leave, she concentrated on the activity starting on the stage. The Countess might treat her as though she did not matter, but being completely ignored was worse. She felt as though she did not exist. It was an awful sensation.

'Don't mind Higgins,' Ravensford drawled. 'He's never been known for his good manners.'

Against her better judgement, she gave the Earl a grateful smile. He always seemed to know how she felt. For a second warmth and security enveloped her, but only for a moment. Having her employer's son empathise with her was not a good thing. Especially when she had conspired with someone to rob that son's mother.

The rest of the evening passed agonisingly slowly for Mary Margaret.

Ravensford searched the gallery for the blond man who had waved at Mary Margaret. If he had not seen her blanch and look like she had been landed a facer, he would have thought the man a would-be swain. Instead he wondered if there was some connection to the man in Ireland who had been ordering her about. Far fetched, he knew, but someone had to be available for her to pass the stolen goods to.

He would have to keep an even closer eye on her. The knowledge did not make him feel better. Even knowing he was making a mistake, he had allowed himself to get involved with the woman. He had even imagined getting to know her very well.

He had been weak, something he would be careful not to be again.

Chapter Eleven

Several days later, Mary Margaret sat in the garden behind the house while the Countess and Annabell napped. She took advantage of the quiet time to read Jane Austen's *Pride and Prejudice*. A tidy smile twisted her mouth as she lived through Mr Darcy's internal war with himself. He was high in the instep and it nearly cost him the woman he loved. She set the finished book down and stared into space. Miss Austen's book was the perfect romance of two people from different levels of society.

She had heard that even the Prince of Wales read Miss Austen's books. Knowing that made her feel less guilty that the story had taken her out of her own problems.

Every day she woke, dreading the possibility that Thomas might call or contact her. So far, he had not. That strengthened her belief that she had been mistaken that evening at Drury Lane. The Thomas she knew would have forced her to meet with him by now. Even knowing that, she still worried.

'Miss, you are needed in the foyer.'

She jerked. She had been caught in her thoughts and not heard the footman. She pushed her fear of Thomas away and made herself smile.

'Goodness, Jeremy, you startled me.' She grabbed the book and rose.

'Pardon, miss.'

She smiled at him. His face radiated anticipation, making her wonder why he had come to fetch her.

'Why am I required in the foyer?'

He grinned, showing crooked front teeth. 'A surprise, miss.'

'Hmm.'

Minutes later, she stood in shock. Footmen carried large boxes through the front door while others carried more large boxes up the stairs. A veritable treasure trove was passing by her, all headed for her room.

'What is all this?' she gasped.

'What is the meaning of this outrage?' the Countess demanded at the same time, her voice rising above the bustle. The older woman stood at the top of the stairs, her robe caught at her throat with white knuckled hands. Her eyes blazed.

All movement ceased.

'Miss O'Brien's wardrobe has arrived,' Ravensford drawled, breaking the frozen silence.

He had come into the house unnoticed while everyone apprehensively watched his mother. With nonchalance, he handed his hat, gloves and cane to the butler before moving to the farthest wall.

He appeared to find nothing out of the ordinary. Mary Margaret knew he understood perfectly well what was going on. His bland look of interest did not fool her. Drat the man.

Both Mary Margaret and the Countess glared at him. He returned their angry looks with disregard, as though what he had done were not totally unacceptable.

'Andrew, come to my rooms immediately.' The Countess's gaze swept the assembled servants and came to rest on Mary Margaret. 'The rest of you clear this nonsense from the house. I won't have it. Return it to wherever it came from.'

Mary Margaret wanted to sink into the floor. She wanted to go up in a puff of smoke and regain consciousness in Ireland. She wished she had never succumbed to Thomas's threats and taken employment with the Countess. If only she had been stronger, but Emily had been at stake.

In spite of all that, she held her head high and met the Countess's furious look. 'I quite agree with you, my lady. None of this should be here.'

Ravensford pushed away from the wall and sauntered toward her. Mary Margaret stepped around a footman whose hands were full of boxes.

'This is my house, ladies,' he said gently, almost too gently. 'And I decide what goes on here. I also decide how members of my household will dress and present themselves to the world.' He looked at one and then the other. 'Do I make myself clear?'

Mary Margaret felt her mouth drop and quickly snapped it shut. She dared not look at the Countess. Everyone said the Earl rarely defied his mother, yet he was doing so now. Someone would pay for this and it would very likely be her.

The Countess said nothing more, turning on her heel and stalking off. There was a noticeable easing of tension.

'Continue what you were doing,' Ravensford stated. 'Miss O'Brien, come with me.'

Her hackles rose. 'I—' She stopped herself.

Everyone's attention had shifted to her. The last thing she wanted to do was make the situation worse, if that were possible, by defying Ravensford. With a supreme effort, she relaxed her rigid shoulders and followed behind him as he led the way to the library. She could feel the stares of all the servants. Her shoulders itched from tension.

Ravensford held the door for her, having gestured the butler away. She walked past him, head high, eyes focussed straight ahead. She kept moving until she had put the distance of the room between herself and the Earl's desk before stopping and turning back to face him. Somehow it did not feel far enough away.

'Feel safe?' He moved to his desk and poured a glass of the amber-coloured liquor he seemed to enjoy so much. He caught her watching him. 'Would you care for some? It will burn away whatever troubles you.'

She shook her head.

He downed it in one gulp. 'It is not every day I defy my mother,' he explained. 'Not that I am unwilling to do so, but it is generally easier not to. For everyone. She has a way of making someone pay the piper when she does not get her own way. Very likely you will suffer.'

Mary Margaret gaped at him. She had not realised he knew how his mother behaved. For some reason, she had thought him blind to the Countess's faults. Most people seemed not to see the uncomfortable in those they loved. Emily certainly could not see the evil in Thomas, or if she did she refused to admit it. Even when he hit her she made excuses. Ravensford made none for his mother.

He gave her a devilish smile that made her knees weaken. 'Please be seated, Miss O'Brien. I won't bite. I have never bitten an unwilling woman.'

She dropped into the nearest chair, shocked by what he had said. 'I hope not.'

He laughed wryly. 'What are you afraid of, Miss O'Brien? That I will ask you to be my mistress again? Don't worry. Even I understand no when it has been said to me twice.'

'You treat this with levity, but I am appalled at all you have bought. I said the one dress, not an entire wardrobe. What will people think?'

He poured himself another glass of liquor and downed it in one long swallow. Putting the empty glass down, he studied her with a reckless air. 'Who gives a damn, Miss O'Brien? Surely you don't.'

She sputtered. How could he think that? 'Just because I am not Quality does not mean I don't value my reputation. In truth, I need to be more careful than one of your station. If I become ruined, true or not, I will never be allowed to make my living. No one will have me in their household.'

'You are right as far as it goes,' he drawled. He poured another drink and downed it as quickly as he had the last. 'However, if I give you a letter of recommendation then you will get work.'

'Who made you all powerful?' she demanded, incensed by his arrogance. 'I very much doubt that a letter from the Prince Regent would negate the rumours that will fly about your buying me a complete wardrobe.'

He bowed to her. 'Then we shall put it to the test if need be.'

She gaped at him. 'You would get the Prince of Wales to write a letter about this? You are mad.'

He eyed her speculatively. 'There are moments when I have thought so. Particularly lately.'

His words nonplussed her. She had a strange feeling that he meant more than he said. It was time she was gone even if he had not dismissed her. She stood.

'I have not given you permission to leave, Miss O'Brien.' Keeping his gaze on her, he poured himself another drink and downed it just as quickly.

She frowned at him. 'I doubt you are capable, my lord. You are guzzling that vile stuff as though it were water.'

He poured another glass and saluted her with it. 'This is the finest Irish whiskey. You should be proud of your country. I brought this back when we came from my mother's. A friend first introduced me to this drink, only his is Scotch.'

He gulped the golden liquid down, his Adam's apple moving in rhythm with the whiskey. She winced. No wonder he was acting so strangely. He had to be the worse for drink.

'I will send back everything but the one dress.' She turned and made for the door. Enough was enough.

'Miss O'Brien,' he said, his voice a silky threat, 'I still have not dismissed you. Had you forgotten?'

She paused and looked back and gasped. He was right behind her; the sound of his movement had been muffled by the thick carpet. He grabbed her left wrist and held it tightly so that she could not get away without squirming. She stood like a statue.

'You are not yourself, my lord.' She hoped her voice sounded more firm to him than it did to her.

He grinned wolfishly. 'If you are implying that I am drunk, you are correct. However, I think...' he pulled her closer '...I am more myself than I have ever been around you.'

Before she realised it was happening, her body was flush to his. His face was scant inches above hers. And his mouth was a breath away from hers. Her eyes widened as his intention became clear.

'Adding insult to injury, my lord?' she managed to say before his lips found hers.

'Pleasure to inclination,' he murmured against her flesh. 'Close your eyes, Miss O'Brien.'

Too late. She had waited too long to struggle. His arms slid around her waist, trapping her hands against his chest. She pushed but to no avail. She was held tightly and expertly.

His mouth met hers in a rush of heat that left her feeling bewildered and delighted. She tingled from her lips to her toes. His tongue slid along her skin, tickling her into a gasp. He darted in, flicking against her teeth. In her surprise, she nearly bit him.

'Ouch,' he said, drawing out and looking down at her. 'You aren't supposed to do that.'

All she could do was stare at him.

'Let's try this again,' he murmured.

'I won't. That is—'

'Hush.'

His mouth moved against hers in seductive abandon. His tongue pressed for entry, then darted in and melded with hers. He tasted of heather and smoke and something infinitely sweet. Heat, then cold, then shivers raced through her body. She felt like she was falling into an abyss from which she would never be able to escape. Her entire world exploded and then came back together with him at the centre.

His mouth broke from hers only to nuzzle the

tender spot just below her ear. His hands roamed her back, stroking muscles that had tightened in delight. He moulded her to his desire. She moaned.

His lips returned to hers just as one of his hands slid to her breast and cupped it. The combination was too much. She arched into his caress. She returned his kiss as passionately as he gave it. She thought she would die if he quit. She purred.

When he broke away, she was stunned. He held her to him, but his hands dropped to her waist, his forehead rested on hers.

'I want you,' he murmured, his voice a husky rasp.

Bewilderment held her motionless in his arms. Her breathing was rapid and shallow. She felt bereft.

'Mary Margaret. Sweetheart,' he whispered against her cheek where he nuzzled her. 'You can't know how long I have wanted to do that.'

His hands shifted to rub up and down her back, fitting her against his enflamed body. She didn't know where she ended and he began. Her senses were in a daze of desire. The knowledge of his power over her was frightening, so much so that she snapped back to reality.

'Oh, no,' she moaned, appalled at what she had just done.

She pushed hard against him. This time he had

not been expecting resistance and his grip failed.
She stumbled from his embrace, panting as though
she had run up a flight of stairs. He moved to take
her back into his arms and she scrambled behind
the chair where she had so recently sat.

'No! We cannot, that is I cannot, that is—'

'Cannot kiss? Make love?' He watched her with
tender amusement. 'Why not?'

'You are drunk,' she gasped. 'How can you say
such things?'

He sighed and ran his fingers through his hair.
'Probably. Although not so much that I don't know
what I am doing.'

'What if someone came in and saw us? Especially after what you have already done.'

'Is that all you can think about—what other people will say? I have wanted to kiss and caress you
since the instant I first heard your throaty purr. You
excited me then and you excite me now.'

She fought back the delight his words created.
To know that he had been attracted to her from the
beginning was heady stuff. The interest she had felt
was not all one-sided. And yet, what did this really
mean? Nothing. He was treating her as he would
a mistress. The momentary madness ended.

'How could you?' she demanded, fighting back
the tears that threatened. He was attracted to her,

desired her, but that was all this was to him. A physical liaison that any woman could satisfy.

'I could because you wanted me to.'

She gasped. 'I am not a loose woman.'

His eyes narrowed. 'I never said you were.'

She put a hand to her chest, wishing her heartbeat would return to normal. 'But you are treating me as one. The dresses and…and the kiss and…'

He took a step toward her. 'Then marry me.'

She gasped. Shame engulfed her. 'How dare you insult me? You don't mean that. I won't play your game.'

He took another step forward and reached for her. She darted to the right, narrowly escaping him.

'You play the game, Miss O'Brien. Not I. Hot, then cold, but never consistent.'

Fury made her bold. 'I think not.'

Before he could try to catch her again, she bolted for the door and through into the hall. She didn't look back and didn't slow down until she was safe in her room.

Ravensford watched her flee. What had he done, proposing to her? It was the last thing he had intended when she entered the library. But the whiskey, his pent-up desire, her ardent response to his lovemaking…everything had conspired to make him act less than judiciously.

He twisted around and went to pour another drink. In for a penny, in for a pound. He downed two more glasses of the potent liquor until he was well and truly foxed.

A knock on the door was followed by the butler's discreet entrance. 'My lord, the Earl of Perth is here.'

Ravensford turned from his vacant study of the garden. 'Send him in.'

Seconds later Perth entered, one dark brow raised. 'You look the worse for wear, old man.'

'Have a drink?'

Perth grinned. 'Is that the cause or only the solution?'

Ravensford pointedly turned his back and poured two drinks. Facing his friend again, he handed Perth one glass.

'To lust in all its forms,' Ravensford said, toasting Perth.

Perth chuckled. 'A mistress or Miss O'Brien?'

Ravensford downed his drink. 'Oh, Miss O'Brien, who else? That woman has been the bane of my existence since I met her.'

'Following in Brabourne's footsteps?' Perth drank his whiskey more slowly, amusement lightening his swarthy complexion.

'Nothing of the sort. At least, not exactly.' Ravensford sank into a chair and motioned for

Perth to do the same. 'Brabourne married for love. I might do it for desire. Can't love a woman who is planning to steal from m'mother. No matter if m'mother deserves to have her jewels stolen or not.'

Perth laughed. 'Your speech is as disorganised as your mother's always is. I swear there are a few pieces of this puzzle missing.'

'Damn,' Ravensford said, appalled that he was slipping into his mother's habit. ''Tis a long story.'

'I have the time if you have more whiskey.'

'Right.'

Ravensford got the decanter and set it between them. In succinct sentences he told Perth everything.

'Don't you think marriage is a drastic solution?' Perth finally asked.

'Undoubtedly.' Ravensford tipped the decanter up only to see it was empty. 'Jones,' he bellowed.

The butler poked his head in. 'Yes, my lord?'

'More whiskey.'

Within minutes they were re-supplied.

'Blasted woman does things to my mind, not to mention my body,' Ravensford explained. 'The words were out of my mouth before I knew they were said.'

'And they cannot be taken back. You are a gentleman, unlike myself.'

Ravensford leaned over and poured Perth more whiskey, narrowly missing the table. 'You are too hard on yourself, Perth. Your code of honour is as well honed as anyone's. You just think it isn't.'

A dark look settled over Perth's features. 'So you say.' He gulped his drink. 'Come, White's beckons. I have an itch to gamble.'

Thankful to be gone from the turmoil he knew roiled upstairs, Ravensford called for his great coat, hat and cane. Neither man cared that it was only late afternoon as they strolled from the house and made their way to Bond Street.

Upstairs, Mary Margaret was stunned by the amount of clothing Ravensford had purchased. Boxes and dresses covered her bed, the two chairs and every other inch of space. Silks, cottons, taffetas, wools—every fabric imaginable, in all the colours of the rainbow, deluged her room. Then there were shoes and bonnets for every imaginable occasion. He had spent a fortune on her. She would never be able to repay him.

Why had he done this? Anger bubbled up in her.

'Ohh, Mary Margaret,' Annabell's light voice said in awe.

Mary Margaret turned around, tamping down on her fury. There was no reason to take her anger at

Ravensford out on Annabell. 'I didn't hear you enter.'

Annabell grinned. 'I knocked. When you didn't answer, I came in.' Her gaze skimmed the room. 'I can understand why you didn't hear me. If I had just received all of this, I would be oblivious to the world too.'

Mary Margaret frowned. 'It will all have to go back. I cannot afford it. I told the Earl I would take the one dress. Never this.'

'You cannot return all of this,' Annabell said, horrified. 'What will Ravensford say? What will the servants say if they see all these boxes going out?'

'What will they say if the boxes stay here?' Mary Margaret could not keep the bitterness from her words. 'I don't care what Ravensford thinks. He is too domineering by half.'

Annabell shrugged. 'He is a man and an Earl. He cannot help himself.'

'So true,' Mary Margaret said. 'So disgustingly true.'

Chapter Twelve

⁓⁓⁓⁓⁓

Mary Margaret sat demurely in one of her old dresses and watched as the Countess and Annabell entertained Mr Finch. The Countess poured tea and dispensed sandwiches with a blithe disregard for Mary Margaret. She was not surprised. For the last three days, the Countess had been doing everything in her power to make her miserable.

She wanted to burn every piece of clothing Ravensford had foisted on her. And she would when this farce was done. Right now she was only grateful that the hateful man had not come near her since his mockery of a proposal. His absence had nearly convinced her that he regretted making such game of her, for she never doubted that the offer was made in spite over her rejection of his previous overtures.

The Countess glanced her way with a malicious

smile. Mary Margaret turned her head to keep the older woman from seeing the anger and resentment in her eyes. Not even the serene beauty of the rose garden could ease her turbulent emotions. She was sorely tempted to ask permission to be excused even though she knew the Countess would refuse.

'My lady,' the butler intoned, 'the Reverend Mr Fox.'

Fear speared Mary Margaret, leaving her breathless and clammy. It *had* been him at the theatre, just as she had feared. He had come to London to spy on her, but why was he here? He could not talk to her in front of everyone, at least not about stealing the Countess's jewellery.

'Ah, Mr Fox,' the Countess said coolly. 'What brings you to London? I fear your flock will be lost without your guiding hand.'

He laughed as though at a great witticism and advanced into the room despite the lukewarm reception. 'You are always so droll, my lady. I found that I missed your intelligence and beauty.'

Mary Margaret watched in awe as the Countess began to visibly thaw. Thomas had that way with women. To her horror, Annabell gazed at her brother-in-law as though she beheld a god. Her stomach started churning.

From the corner of his eye, Thomas slid his blue

gaze over her. She knew that look well, and it boded no good. She had to do something.

Surging to her feet, she said, 'Oh, Thomas, have you brought me a message from Emily?'

He gloated at her. 'She sends her love and hopes you will return soon.'

'I miss her awfully.'

That was true and there was nothing else she could say. It would only inflame the Countess more if she professed to want to return home. But she knew that Thomas was telling her to get the job done.

Dismissing her, Thomas focussed his attention on Annabell. 'Miss Winston, I trust you are enjoying your stay in London.'

Annabell beamed up at him, the dimple in her right cheek peeking out. 'Immensely.'

He bowed over her extended hand. 'I never doubted it with the Countess showing you about.'

Mary Margaret's initial fear abated as she listened to Thomas's effusive charm. She wondered why the two women did not see through him. But then, she had not at first. She, like they, had been entranced by his spectacular good looks and easy way with words.

'Very prettily done,' Ravensford's baritone said from the doorway.

He had entered while all of them had been focussed on Thomas. His cynical gaze rested on her brother-in-law, and Mary Margaret's receding fear began to return. There was something about the way Ravensford held himself that spelled danger. Perhaps his broad shoulders were a bit too straight, or his square jaw too tight. She was not sure exactly what the change was, but she knew him well enough by now to know that he did not like Thomas.

Her initial unease was increased tenfold when Ravensford's glance passed over her. Dark circles intensified the colour of his eyes. He looked debauched and deadly, as she imaged a man would look who has reached the end of his tolerance. Surely Thomas's presence had not caused this condition. She devoutly hoped it had nothing to do with their confrontation in the library either.

'Ahem… I must be leaving,' Mr Finch said, breaking into the silence.

They had all forgotten him. Now everyone concentrated on his departure, using action to ease the discomfort caused by Ravensford's presence.

'I shall be sure and keep a dance for you,' Annabell said, referring to Finch's earlier request for a waltz at her coming-out ball.

He took her proffered hand and gushed, 'I shall hold my breath until then.'

It was all Mary Margaret could do not to laugh at his dramatisation.

'Then you will be in no shape for the dance,' Ravensford said drily.

Mr Finch looked like a balloon that the air had been let out of. 'Very practical, my lord.'

'Upon occasion I try to do the mundane.'

Mary Margaret listened to Ravensford in surprise. She had never seen him jab at someone before. Something was bothering him.

Mr Finch took his leave and hurried from the room. Ravensford settled himself comfortably in one of the chairs, his left leg over the right. His Hessians shone like mirrors.

'What brings you all the way to London, Mr Fox?'

Mary Margaret watched Thomas smile benignly at the Earl. 'My father is here for the Season and I am come to pay my respects.'

Ravensford quirked one brow.

The Countess asked point-blank, 'Is your father in trade, Mr Fox?'

Mary Margaret would have laughed if she could not see how furious Thomas was at the slight. His blue eyes were hard chips. His finely wrought mouth was a thin slash. Somehow, he managed to keep his tone level, even light.

'No, my lady. My father is Viscount Fox.' He

flashed a false smile around the room. 'I am a younger son.'

A considering light entered Ravensford's eyes, turning them to the bright colour of emerald with the sun shining through. 'And went into the clergy instead of the army.'

Thomas turned to face Ravensford directly. 'My middle brother is in the army.'

'Why, I didn't know you were related to old Fox,' the Countess said. 'How delightful. You must come to Annabell's ball this Thursday. I am sure we sent your father an invitation.' She turned her sharp gaze on Mary Margaret. 'Didn't we?'

She nodded, remembering the name. It had struck her that it was the same as Thomas's, but she had not considered that his father might be in London. What a very small world the aristocracy was.

'I—' Thomas said.

Ravensford spoke smoothly over Thomas. 'I am sure that a man of the cloth, as Mr Fox is, would find our entertaining too hedonistic.' The smile he turned on Thomas didn't reach his eyes. 'We would not want to make him uncomfortable.'

Mary Margaret enjoyed Ravensford's needling of Thomas, knowing her brother-in-law was too far from home to take his fury out on Emily. Still, part of her dreaded what he would do when he returned to Ireland. Or when he finally demanded a meeting with her.

Thomas gave Ravensford a bland look. 'I should be delighted to attend Miss Winston's ball. I am sure she will put every other young lady in the shade.' He gave the Countess and Annabell a brilliant smile.

Mary Margaret twisted away to look anywhere but at Thomas, but not before she saw the disgust Ravensford did nothing to hide. The Countess and Annabell, however, were enchanted.

'In that case,' Ravensford drawled, rising, 'we will expect you after dinner.'

Disappointment flashed across Thomas's face and Mary Margaret realised that he had been hoping for an invitation to dinner before the ball. She breathed a sigh of relief that Ravensford had prevented that. She did not want to see Thomas any more than she had to.

To add insult to injury, Ravensford added, 'Mother, aren't you and Annabell expected at Mrs Bridges' this afternoon?'

'Goodness, I had completely forgotten.' The Countess rose and motioned to Annabell. 'We must change and be on our way.' She held a hand out to Thomas, who took it and raised it to his lips. 'We shall expect you on Thursday.'

He bowed and took his leave without even glancing at Mary Margaret. She relaxed.

'Is he the curate who introduced you to my mother? The one who is married to your sister?'

She started. In her relief at having Thomas gone, she had forgotten how acute Ravensford was. Particularly when no one else was around and he could say what he wished.

'Yes.'

'Do you know him well?'

Apprehension and guilt made their way into her thoughts. Why was he asking these questions? What did it matter to him?

'Better than I would like.'

'And why is that?'

His eyes held hers. She wondered again how much he knew. Very likely more than she wished.

She chose her words carefully. 'He is not always as charming with women as he was this afternoon.'

'How is that?'

He evinced only mild curiosity, but Mary Margaret sensed something deeper. Her shoulders tightened.

'Oh, just…just that I have seen him lose his temper upon occasion. That is all.'

Disgust at herself twisted her mouth. Now she was being like Emily and evading the real question. Why did they protect Thomas?

'I see.'

She looked sharply at him. He watched her with narrowed eyes. She could almost think he did see.

'Does he visit London often?'

She licked dry lips. 'Not that I know of.'

'Does he visit his father's estate?'

'Is this an interrogation, my lord?' She was on the defensive and knew it. What did he want from her? 'I do not keep track of Thomas's comings and goings.'

He took out his pocket watch and checked the time. 'Perhaps he is here because of you?'

'I don't see why,' she answered without thinking.

'He must be concerned about your welfare. You are his wife's sister and he did find you employment with my mother, as awful as that is.'

'Well, perhaps,' she murmured, realising belatedly that he had given her a perfectly plausible reason for Thomas being in London. Along with his family being here.

'Then he will accept an invitation to accompany us to Astley's Amphitheatre tomorrow?'

'No. That is, I mean, he surely would, but we are not going there tomorrow. Annabell wants to see the wild animals in the Tower.'

His gaze on her was sardonic. 'Then Mr Fox

will join us for a tour of the Tower. I will have my secretary send him around an invitation.'

She gulped back a retort. The last thing she wanted was to have Thomas with them. But she had no control over who Ravensford invited. She could not even stop him from buying her a complete wardrobe.

'And about the clothes you bought for me, my lord. What do you suggest I wear to the Tower?'

His eyes narrowed at the sarcasm in her voice. She was even surprised by her daring to take him to task. The surprise was quickly followed by worry as she realised that in order to be comfortable enough to berate him, however so slightly, she must be *very* used to his company.

'Wear whatever you want, Miss O'Brien. Except for Annabell's ball. Then I want you to wear the pink dress Madame Bertrice altered for you.'

She made him a mock curtsy. 'And we both know that I will do as you bid, my lord. You schooled me in obeying orders before we ever left Ireland.'

His lips parted in a white slash of teeth. 'So you say, but your actions put the lie to your words.'

Before she could think of something else to say, he rose and sauntered from the room. He was the most infuriating man.

Well, she would get the better of him. Ravensford would find out nothing about her and Thomas because she did not intend to do as Thomas ordered. As for the clothes, she would go straight up to her room and continue folding and repacking them in the boxes she had not let the footmen return to Madame Bertrice.

Mary Margaret held up an afternoon dress of the finest white muslin trimmed with emerald ribbons. Crossing to the mirror, she held the frock up to her face and could not help but admire the picture. The garment was perfect for her.

She sighed and turned away. Temptation. She was not keeping these clothes no matter how beautiful they made her look. She was not so vain as to risk her reputation further.

A knock on her door was followed by Annabell's entrance. She and the Countess must have just returned from their afternoon visit to Mrs Bridges. The girl sat on the bed and watched Mary Margaret fold the afternoon dress.

'Ravensford will be furious,' Annabell said.

'Then he should not do something as disreputable as buying his mother's companion a complete wardrobe.' In a fit of pique, she stuffed the folded garment into too small a space.

Annabell giggled, then became suddenly silent. Mary Margaret frowned at the wadded-up gown before looking at her charge. A dreamy look transformed the girl's features.

'What did you think of Mr Fox?'

Unease crept down Mary Margaret's back. The look on Annabell's face screamed trouble.

'Annabell, Thomas is married to my younger sister, Emily.'

She hoped her tone had been pragmatic with just a hint of sympathy. It was so hard to tell how one really sounded, especially to a young woman who had just been smitten by a very handsome man.

'Oh,' Annabell said lightly. 'What are you doing to that beautiful dress?'

Mary Margaret scowled. 'I am trying to repack it.'

'I will send my maid in to help you,' Annabell said. 'It will take you hours to do this by yourself.'

'Thank you, but I can manage.'

Mary Margaret had no intention of getting anyone else into trouble with the Earl. When he started raving about the clothes being returned, she would be the only person responsible.

'As you wish,' Annabell said.

Mary Margaret gave the girl a considering look. Annabell was too docile. Normally she would have argued with Mary Margaret about the use of her personal maid.

The disquiet that had surfaced at Annabell's

mention of Thomas returned. Mary Margaret knew only too well how devastatingly attractive her brother-in-law was to women.

The next day Mary Margaret watched anxiously as Thomas took Annabell to see the lions, who numbered among the many wild animals housed at the Tower. The girl was smitten and Thomas was doing everything in his power to keep her that way. It did not help matters that the Countess had stayed home as usual. Had she come, Thomas would have been forced to divide his charms between the two women. As it was, he could focus completely on Annabell. She had to catch up with them.

Even worried as she was, she sensed Ravensford's presence before he spoke. Her skin tingled and her senses sharpened. He did that to her.

'Is something bothering you?'

'No. Should something be?' She immediately regretted the answer. She owed it to him and to Annabell to bring her concern into the open. 'That is not true.' She sighed. 'I am worried about Annabell. I think she is more interested in Thomas than is proper.'

'He is married to your sister.'

'Yes. That is why I am so concerned about Annabell.'

'I should have thought your sister would take first priority.'

What to tell him without telling him the truth? This was so hard. She shook her head. How could Emily stand the constant lying and subterfuge needed to protect Thomas's reputation? And yet, here she was hedging. She was not strong enough to tell anyone about the beating. Nor would most people care. Under the law, Emily was Thomas's to deal with as he pleased.

Instead she implied something else. 'My sister is used to Thomas's ways.'

Ravensford watched the couple disappear around one of the buildings. 'So theirs was not a love match.'

'It was for her,' Mary Margaret said in a tiny voice.

'Ahh. I am sorry for her.'

She searched his face for the truth of his feelings. 'I believe you really are. But aren't most marriages made for convenience?'

'Most. My parents' was a love match. It just so happened that both families approved.' He shrugged. 'And sometimes arranged marriages become ones of love.'

'But that does not protect Annabell from Thomas's charms.'

He rubbed the sapphire in his signet ring, a habit

she realised he had when he was troubled. 'You speak as though you expect Thomas to take advantage of her. Isn't that a rather harsh judgement to make against anyone and particularly a man of the cloth?'

Still more subterfuge, and yet Thomas did flirt with women. She was never sure if he went further.

She shrugged. 'Perhaps. I just don't want to see Annabell hurt.'

'Then we had best catch up with them.'

She sighed in relief.

Ravensford was now positive that Thomas had been the man threatening Mary Margaret, and his power had to do with her sister, Emily. He watched her as they searched for the other couple. There was a worried crease in her broad forehead and a pinched look around her mouth. She truly was concerned.

He saw Thomas's blond hair before he saw Annabell. Instead of going to the lions, the two had stopped to look at the ravens. It was said that if the ravens ever left the Tower, the monarchy would fall. A nice legend. He was more interested in the fact that Annabell clung to Thomas, her face radiant as she laughed at something he was saying. He began to understand why Mary Margaret did not like this situation.

Mary Margaret picked up speed and he put out

a hand to slow her. When she looked back at him, an irritated frown replacing the worry, he shook his head. He forced her to saunter up with him as though they had no care in the world.

'I thought you two were going to the lions?' he drawled.

Annabell beamed. 'We are, but Thomas was just entertaining me with stories of his parish. He is so droll.'

The man could even look modest, Ravensford saw in disgust. 'How interesting.'

Thomas gave Ravensford a challenging smile. 'Miss Winston has invited me to go to Astley's Amphitheatre tomorrow, Ravensford. I hope that will be all right with you and the Countess.'

Ravensford returned the smile. 'Of course. Perth is going so we shall be a party.' Perth did not know he was going.

For the rest of the afternoon, Ravensford kept with the couple. He had not liked Thomas Fox the first time he had seen him. There was something about the man that offended. The feeling was strengthened by the knowledge that, although Mary Margaret was careful about what she said, he knew she felt the same way. And Thomas had ordered her to steal from his mother. It would be his very great pleasure to catch the scoundrel. The problem would be to keep Mary Margaret from being implicated.

He glanced at her. She watched Thomas with an anxious look in her eyes that made him want to gather her close and tell her everything would be fine. He would protect her.

He shook his head. First he had asked her to be his mistress, then his wife. He was not in the market for either. If his luck held, she would continue to refuse him on both offers. Or so he told himself.

Chapter Thirteen

Descending the stairs, Mary Margaret saw that Perth had already arrived and Annabell was champing at the bit to be off. The girl had been in a dither all day, picking first one gown and then discarding it in favour of another. She acted as though she were meeting a lover. The idea was enough to make Mary Margaret's blood run cold.

'I am sorry I am late.'

She did not explain that there had been a stain on her best gown so she had been forced to change at the last moment. She might not have nice clothes, but she had clean ones.

Ravensford scowled at her. She returned his look with a bland one. She knew without his saying a word that he was irritated that she was not wearing one of Madame Bertrice's gowns. Well, let him stew in his juices. She tossed her head,

realising belatedly that the movement lost most of
its defiance when there was no hair to swing. As
usual, her hair was in a tight chignon.

'We had best be going,' Perth said, 'before Annabell here wears a hole in her slippers with all the
shuffling she is doing.' He grinned mockingly at
her. 'I did not know that beautiful women riding
bareback on trained horses excited you.' He cast a
wicked glance at Ravensford. 'I would not have
been surprised if Ravensford was the one dancing
about. He has always had a penchant for exotic
women.'

From the way Ravensford ignored his friend's
barb, Mary Margaret decided the taunt had gone
wide of the Earl only to hit her square in the heart.
Just the thought of Ravensford looking longingly
at another woman was enough to make her chest
tighten painfully. Now it seemed she was going to
have to actually see him desiring other women. She
felt sick.

If she did not have to go along as Annabell's
chaperon, she would plead a headache or anything
to get out of this excursion. As it was, the Countess
had already beaten her to the excuse.

The ride to Westminster Bridge Road, where the
theatre was, seemed to last forever. She said little
as Perth continued to tease Annabell and tried to

goad Ravensford. Annabell rose magnificently to the occasion, while Ravensford remained a stoic.

'You are in rare form tonight, Perth,' Ravensford said. 'Is there something about this outing that you have failed to tell me?'

A gleam entered Perth's dark eyes but his voice was noncommittal. 'A mild diversion, nothing more. You shall see.'

The carriage halted and the gentlemen exited. This time Perth helped Mary Margaret out. She put her hand in his, not surprised when she felt nothing but the strength of his fingers. She refused to let herself feel disappointment that Ravensford had helped Annabell. The less interaction she had with him the better for her peace of mind and body.

Thomas waited for them at the door.

As before, he was impeccably dressed. Mary Margaret marvelled that her brother-in-law could dress in the height of male fashion, yet live in a cottage no better than that of a prosperous farmer. Viscount Fox must be supplying his son.

The five of them exchanged greetings and entered the theatre. Mary Margaret had known the place would be large, but this was magnificent. Boxes went up four stories on three sides. The fourth side contained a stage and the orchestra. A huge chandelier cast enough light to make it possible to see across the rink where a scantily clad woman was standing on the back of a prancing horse and playing a tambourine.

She must have gaped for Ravensford said drily, 'It can be overwhelming the first time.'

All she could do was nod.

Ravensford led them to a box he had reserved while Perth made his way around the perimeter. Mary Margaret was entranced before they even sat down. She marvelled at the acts of equestrian daring. Beside her, Annabell clapped and joined the crowd in showing their appreciation.

'So,' Ravensford murmured under his breath.

Mary Margaret was so attuned to him that she heard even though she knew he had not meant her to. Turning to him, she saw he had a knowing smile and his attention was not on the performance, but intent on someone in a booth across the rink.

Perth—and a woman. He bowed over her hand as she smiled up at him. Even from this distance, Mary Margaret could make out hair the colour of spun silver. And she had to be wearing a king's ransom in jewels for she sparkled like the chandelier.

'Who is she?' she asked softly.

'Lady de Lisle, one of Perth's old flirts.' He frowned as Perth left the woman's side. 'What is he up to now? She broke with him many years ago and married another man. He has never forgiven her.'

'He seems to have forgiven her quite well,' Mary Margaret said with only a hint of sarcasm.

'He is up to something.'

'Perhaps he still cares for her.'

'I think not. He did not take kindly to being left at the altar while she ran away with another man.'

Mary Margaret gasped and waited for him to elaborate, but he did not. Not even when Perth joined them and sat down on the other side of Annabell. She did note that periodically Lady de Lisle glanced their way. Perth did not return the look.

At the intermission, Thomas rose and said, 'Mary Margaret, come with me for a breath of air. I have news from home.' He bowed to the others. 'If you will excuse us, this is of a personal nature.'

Apprehension made her shudder. He was going to tell her that her time was up. She rose, feeling like a prisoner going to her execution, and followed him from the theatre.

Outside he dropped the pose of solicitous brother-in-law and his voice turned hard. 'Have you got the jewels yet? I warn you, my patience is not endless.'

Her hands felt like ice even in the gloves she wore. Thank goodness he was here and Emily was in Ireland. Knowing that her sister was safe gave her the bravado she needed.

'I must have more time. Just until Annabell's ball.' She took a deep breath and rushed on. 'While everyone is busy I will sneak up to the Countess's room and steal the jewels. No one will expect it.'

His fingers tightened cruelly on her arm. 'Be sure that you do so. I will expect you to pass them to me that night.'

'Oh, no, someone might see. 'Twould be better to meet you the next day.'

But she would not do so. The day of the ball was quarter's day and she would have her pay. She would be off for Ireland. How, she did not know, but she would manage. She knew the way Ravensford had travelled. She would take the coach and the ferry.

'Don't try to trick me, Mary Margaret. I will make you sorry if you do.'

His grip was so tight she knew she would have bruises the next day. They would be worth it for the knowledge that she had outsmarted him.

'This appears to be a very serious discussion,' Ravensford said, walking toward them.

Mary Margaret jumped, wrenching her arm painfully when Thomas did not release her. Thomas stood calmly.

He smiled smoothly. 'We are just finished, Ravensford. I fear my news was not all good. Mary Margaret's sister has an inflammation of the lungs. Fortunately, the vicar's good wife is caring for her in my absence. Still, it is never comforting to know your loved ones are in danger.'

Mary Margaret heard the implied threat, but there was nothing she could say.

'I am sorry to hear that,' Ravensford said. He took Mary Margaret's unresisting hand and pulled her from Thomas's grip. 'Would you like me to arrange for my mother's doctor to see her?'

Mary Margaret looked into his eyes and saw a strange light in them, as though he waited expectantly for her to say something to him that he already knew. She shook herself at the fancifulness. He was being kind.

'Thank you, my lord.'

'That won't be necessary, Ravensford,' Thomas said curtly. 'My wife is well cared for.'

Ravensford gave the other man a cutting look. 'I did not ask you, Fox.'

Mary Margaret cringed and wished herself anywhere but between these two men. She did not think Emily was sick, or hoped that if she truly was Thomas would have told her before Ravensford's arrival. But then, neither of them had expected the Earl.

Concern for Emily grew. She glanced at

Thomas's furious face. To defy him would only make matters worse, and yet Emily must be her first concern. While the vicar's wife was a good woman, she was not a doctor. She would ask Ravensford to send his physician when they were away from Thomas.

'Thomas is probably right, my lord. The vicar's wife is very good with the sick.'

Ravensford gave her a look of disgust. 'As you wish, Miss O'Brien.'

She wanted to cringe from his disapproval but knew that would only make him despise her cowardice more. Meekly, she allowed him to lead her back inside the theatre.

She studiously avoided looking at Ravensford for the remainder of their stay. Even after Thomas made his farewells, she kept as far from the Earl as Annabell and Perth's presence allowed. At the town house, she kept her head down and mumbled a 'thank you' when Perth helped her out of the carriage.

'My pleasure,' he murmured sardonically.

She gave him a sharp glance but said nothing. As soon as Annabell was safely tucked away she would search out Ravensford and ask him to send the doctor to Emily. In the meantime he would have to continue thinking badly of her.

Ravensford watched Mary Margaret enter the

foyer behind Annabell, disgusted with the way she had let Thomas dictate to her.

'If the sky looked like your face,' Perth observed drily, 'we would be in for the storm of the century. Come to White's and tell me on the way what Miss O'Brien has done this time.'

'Good idea,' he muttered, pivoting sharply and re-entering the carriage. Inside he succinctly told Perth about the incident with Thomas and the doctor.

'Come along, old man,' Perth said as they reached White's. 'You need diversion.'

As they entered the exclusive men's club a silence fell on the room. Ravensford looked around, noting the familiar faces. Most occupants nodded; a few would not meet his gaze. A single man rose and came toward him.

'Wondered when word would reach you, Ravensford,' the lone man said. Tall and thin, he moved gracefully. Full grey hair swept back from a high forehead and black brows. Ebony eyes calmly studied Ravensford, as though the man searched for signs of agitation.

Ravensford raised one brow. 'What word was that, Chillings?'

Chillings looked at Perth. 'Do you know?'

Perth shook his head. 'We just came from Astley's Amphitheatre. Needed some normality.'

A tiny, feral smile revealed Viscount Chillings's teeth. 'Seems someone has it in for you, Ravensford. I wonder if it is the same person who wrote in the betting book about Brabourne.'

Ravensford stiffened. His and Perth's friend, the Duke of Brabourne, had found a damaging remark in White's famous betting book about the woman he was now married to. The comment had precipitated Brabourne's proposal. For the Duke it had been the best thing. He and his wife had a love match.

Without a word, Ravensford strode to where the book was kept. He opened it to the last page and read: What Earl, known for his prowess with the fairer sex, has bought his mother's companion an entire wardrobe? Beneath the damaging words was a record of the bets placed on when the companion would be leaving the Countess and moving into her own establishment, paid for by the Earl.

He had not expected this. He had told Madame Bertrice that if she valued his patronage no word would get out of who had paid for Mary Margaret's clothes. As far as the world was concerned, his mother had been the provider. This put paid to all his careful planning.

Mary Margaret was ruined, just as she had feared. With this circulating, she would not be allowed into the homes of any woman of the *ton*. Her use as a chaperon for Annabell was over.

'Easy, old man,' Perth murmured, putting a firm hand on Ravensford's stiff shoulder. 'Seems someone is out to get you the same way Brabourne was got. Although it didn't do him any harm,' he ended with a wicked smile. 'Much the contrary.'

'Brabourne was in love. I am not,' Ravensford hissed for Perth's ears only.

Chillings, his task done, rejoined his group. For a moment Ravensford wondered if the Viscount had written the damaging words. He as quickly dismissed them. He barely knew Chillings and there was no bad blood between them.

Ravensford looked slowly around the room, meeting gazes when possible. The fury that rode him abated enough that he could contemplate murder calmly. Whoever had done this would pay.

They left without a word to anyone. Outside, Ravensford pounded his cane against the ground.

'Blast it to hell! Whoever did this will pay.'

'Just as he did when this was done to Brabourne?'

Ravensford scowled at Perth. 'Brabourne never found the scoundrel, but working together he and I will now.'

They continued walking, having waved off the

carriage. The cool air helped Ravensford's temper, but did not erase it.

'In the meantime,' Perth drawled, 'there are several things you can do.'

'Such as?'

'Send the chit back to Ireland or set her up in her own establishment as the mysterious writer suggests.'

'She is not my mistress,' Ravensford said through clenched teeth.

'But not for lack of interest on your part,' Perth said.

There was no answer so he gave none.

Perth left him at his town house door. 'Tell your mother that I will be at Annabell's ball tomorrow, will you? I forgot to send my acceptance.'

'You are the most irresponsible scoundrel,' Ravensford said without malice. 'Yet you are invited everywhere.'

'It must be my charm,' Perth drawled sardonically. 'It cannot be because of my title and wealth.'

'Absolutely not. Especially with Lady de Lisle. She was an heiress in her own right and old de Lisle left her very nicely provided for.' He gave his friend a knowing look which Perth ignored.

'I believe I will call in on an establishment we both know,' Perth said with an air of mild interest. 'Care to join me?'

He was fleetingly tempted. But then a face formed in his mind's eye: green eyes, ebony hair and lips he had tasted twice and wanted to taste more. No, until he was through this attraction to Mary Margaret O'Brien, no other woman interested him in the slightest. Probably he would not even be able to perform. That would make the betting book and then things would be a thousand times worse than the mess they already were.

'No,' he told Perth. 'I have much to do tomorrow. Some of us have responsibilities.'

Perth chuckled as he sauntered away.

Ravensford climbed the steps and took his key out. The door opened. Timothy, the youngest footman, stood carefully erect but his eyes were red and half-shut.

Ravensford sighed in exasperation. 'How many times must I tell Jones not to have you wait up for me? Go to bed.'

Timothy, his face now as red as his eyes, bowed before hurrying off. Ravensford instantly regretted his harsh words. He needed to speak with Jones again, not berate Timothy. The lad only did as ordered.

He took off his beaver hat and gloves, tossed them on the side table, and then propped his cane against the wall. He was exhausted and frustrated.

Something had to be done about Mary Margaret, and he did not like any of his choices.

Mounting the stairs, he did not see the shadow on the second floor landing until he was upon her.

'What the—?'

'My lord. Ravensford,' Mary Margaret whispered. 'I need to speak with you.'

Her face was a luminescent oval in the golden light from the single candle he carried. Her eyes were dark pools. She still wore the dowdy dress she had worn earlier. The sight of it increased his irritation.

'My room is two doors down,' he said coldly, wondering if she would go there.

She nodded. Whatever she needed to tell him must be important. He followed her, curious in spite of himself. She slipped in ahead of him.

He closed the door and stood his ground. When she did not speak for long moments, he said, 'Well?'

Her hands clasped tightly together she said in a tiny voice, 'Will you arrange for your mother's doctor to attend my sister?'

That was the last thing he had expected. 'Braver now that Fox isn't around?'

His voice was harsh as he had meant it to be, but when she took a step back as though he had slapped her he regretted letting his anger come out.

He was not in the habit of intentionally hurting others.

'What could I say? He is her husband.'

'A valid point. Does he often put your sister in jeopardy?'

He watched her closely, hoping she would trust him enough now to tell him the truth. Emotions warred across her face. She looked pinched.

'Sometimes,' she said, her voice a painful rasp.

'Is there something I can help with?'

He took a step toward her. The urge was strong to gather her close and tell her he would protect her and her loved ones from the world. He resisted, even when hope flared briefly in her eyes before dying.

'You still don't trust me,' he said bitterly.

She turned her back to him and he thought he heard a sob. He put the candle down on the nearest table and went to her.

Putting his hands gently on her shoulders, he said, 'Mary Margaret, sweetheart, look at me.'

He felt her stiffen under his touch. She sniffed and raised her head. Hope flared in him.

In a voice that shook only slightly, she said, 'Please let me go. I have told you everything.'

Disappointment speared him, followed by anger. He twirled her around. 'I am fed up with you hedging. The truth is that your brother-in-law does not treat your sister well. He may even beat her and you are afraid for her and of him. I have offered my help. Do you think that I am powerless?'

Her eyes were wide and her mouth an 'O'. 'I... Do you know how hard it is to admit that your sister is beaten whenever her husband is angry? I know it happens, but that does not make it nice.'

He pulled her to him and cupped her head to his chest. Gently he stroked her as he would a cat that had been hurt. He continued, whispering meaningless words until he felt her relax against him.

'I will take care of it,' he promised.

She wriggled her head free and looked up at him. Bewilderment knitted her brows together. 'Why? She is nothing to you. I am nothing to you.'

'How wrong you are,' he murmured. 'How very wrong.'

His kiss was gentle, as though he cherished her above all else. Mary Margaret felt her heart expand with gladness. Perhaps he did care. Perhaps he even loved her. It was a small hope that grew as he tenderly cupped her head and tasted her mouth.

She melted into him, her hands braced against his chest. She felt his heart beat through her fingers, noted that it speeded up as his kiss deepened. She sighed with pleasure.

When one of his hands covered her breast it felt

natural and right. She arched her back to give him better access.

His mouth skimmed over her face and down the side of her neck to the top of her bodice. He licked lightly along the edge of material while he continued to stroke her breast. A sensation of heat and fever started in her abdomen and spread out to every part of her body.

'Turn around,' he murmured, his voice a dark, rich honey.

When she did nothing, just lying in his embrace, he shifted her himself so that the back of her hips were flush to his side. He switched his ministrations to the nape of her neck while his fingers deftly undid the many buttons that held her gown on. A rush of cold hit her as his palms skimmed down her arms, pushing the fabric down.

Slowly, so slowly that she nearly moaned in anticipation, he turned her back around. His eyes held hers captive as his hands slipped inside the bodice of her gown and slid it slowly down her bosom. His flesh burned through her chemise. Her nipples contracted into aching points.

He slid the dress further down. His palms smoothed down her hips and flanks until the gown fell to the floor. She shivered.

His gaze moved to her heaving bosom and lower. 'You are beautiful. Since you fell off the boat, I have wanted to do this. I don't know how I kept from doing this then.' A smile tugged at his lips. 'I am going to make up for all the lost time.'

She heard his words, their meaning penetrating the fog of desire he so easily created in her. This time she did not care. This time she wanted him. She thought he truly wanted her, not just her body. She smiled and moved into his embrace.

He groaned.

He lifted her and carried her to his bed where he carefully laid her on the downy comforter. Her hair had come loose and lay in ebony strands among the pillows.

The light of the candle barely reached them, but he could still see the curves and dark hollows of her body. His own responded with aching quickness. In sure, deft movements, he stripped.

The innocent in Mary Margaret told her to close her eyes. The woman in her kept her gaze focussed on him.

He took her breath away. His shoulders were broad and muscled. Auburn hair curled down his abdomen until it became a nest for the most masculine part of him. He was ready. His thighs and calves were well shaped and powerful. He was perfect in every way.

When he lay beside her, it was all she could do not to stroke and explore his body. Everything about his hard angles and dark shadows enticed her.

He undid the strings of her chemise and pantaloons, his tongue following his fingers. Delight caught her unawares and tossed her high. Contented sounds escaped her.

He chuckled deep in his chest. 'I wondered if you would purr.' He nuzzled her neck and then lower until his mouth took her breast. 'Now I know.'

He sucked and nipped. She made little gasping sounds.

Her hands circled him and her nails dug into his back. She was oblivious to everything but his mouth on her and where his fingers were going. They glided along her flesh, past her stomach and lower. She gasped in surprise when he first touched her. Her loins clenched pleasurably. His mouth returned to hers and the kiss he gave her was so deep she thought he would devour her.

Her nails raked his back as he gave her more pleasure than she had ever thought possible. When he broke from her lips, she whimpered and tried to force him back.

He laughed. 'No, sweetings. I want to watch you.'

She was beyond embarrassment. The things he

was doing to her created sensations that made her body spasm and twist.

He watched her face as his hands moved gently, but firmly against and in her flesh, dipping and stroking and exciting. She strained against him. It was too much.

'Open your legs,' he murmured, his voice so husky it was more a growl than words.

She opened slumberous eyes to see him poised above her. She did as she was told. He fit between her thighs as though he belonged there. She sighed with delight as he settled himself.

'Wrap your legs around me.'

Another order, but she was happy to do as he directed. He was hot and hard against her swollen flesh. She did not know what came next, but she moved her hips against his and felt the evidence of his desire.

He gathered her to him, kissing her deeply. Her breasts pressed like hot brands against his chest. He groaned and plunged into her.

Pain lashed Mary Margaret. Her eyes started open.

He stroked the hair from her face, his eyes catching hers. 'It is all right, sweetings. The pain will go away. I promise.'

For long minutes he did not move other than to kiss her gently and stroke her breasts and flanks.

She began to relax only to have her body start vibrating. He filled her to overflowing.

Slowly, he began to move. Sensations flowed over Mary Margaret with each thrust of his body. He stroked her and stoked her. A fire built in the pit of her loins. She felt tense beyond belief.

She shifted her hands to his hips and her nails dug into his flesh, urging him to greater speed and deeper penetration. With a groan, he obliged.

She twisted under him and pushed her hips higher. Whatever she sought was just over the next crest.

He pounded into her. She whimpered in need and pleasure—then exploded.

She gasped before a shout escaped her. His mouth fastened on hers and swallowed her sounds of release.

Seconds later, he groaned. His back arched and then he collapsed on her.

For long moments they lay, limbs tangled, breathing hard. When he finally rolled to her side, he pulled her to him. His hand cupped the back of her head and brought her to him for a tender kiss.

'Thank you,' he said softly.

She gazed at him, her body relaxed as never before. His eyes were slumberous, and his mouth was a sensual slash against his swarthy skin.

It came to her with a tiny shock that they had

made love. She was his mistress. She loved him. Had loved him forever, or she would never have been carried away by his lovemaking.

He smiled at her. 'Are you ready for more?'

Unable to speak for fear she would tell him everything, she only nodded. She did not think she could ever get enough of this closeness.

He moved over her, only this time she knew what to do.

Chapter Fourteen

Mary Margaret overslept the next morning. She woke with a start when Annabell landed on her bed with a plop.

'Wake up, sleepyhead. I had hot chocolate and toast brought up and you cannot eat them unless you are awake.'

Dazed and still feeling Ravensford's impassioned kisses on her skin, Mary Margaret finger-combed her hair back and stretched like a satisfied cat. 'What time is it?'

'Going on eleven.' Annabell smirked. 'You must have stayed up late after we returned.'

Surely Annabell did not know about her time in the Earl's chambers. She cast a surreptitious glance at the girl, but Annabell had moved on to the breakfast tray sitting on a nearby table. By now she knew Annabell well enough to realise that if the girl really had known something she would have stayed right where she was until she had got the information out of Mary Margaret. It was with a great deal of relief that she put on her robe and joined her charge at the table.

They poured chocolate and ate several slices of toast before Annabell said archly, 'Oh, I forgot to tell you. Mr Fox is below stairs, waiting to meet with you.'

Mary Margaret choked on a piece of crust. 'Thomas is here to see me and you forgot?'

Annabell laughed. 'Someone must put your brother-in-law in his proper place. I swear the man thinks he is some sort of Greek god and that all women should swoon at his feet.'

Mary Margaret goggled even as infinite relief flowed through her like water. She took a sip of chocolate. 'I thought you were rather taken with him.'

Annabell had the grace to look slightly uncomfortable, but only for a minute. 'Oh,' she said lightly, flipping her hand as though she tossed something away. 'I was only practising my skills at flirting. After all, being married and the clergy, he should be safe.'

'Prac—' Mary Margaret put her cup down before she spilled the contents on herself. 'That is

abominable. A lady would never do such a thing.'
Her laugh ameliorated her words.

Annabell smiled contentedly. 'A lady certainly
would. What she would not do is admit it to anyone else unless she trusted that person implicitly.'

Mary Margaret sobered immediately. 'Thank
you so much, Annabell. I cannot tell you how
much that means to me.'

Annabell rose and dropped to her knees beside
Mary Margaret and threw her arms around her.
'Oh, I shall miss you so when this Season is over.
You have become like an older sister. The one I
never had.' She hugged Mary Margaret tightly and
kissed her on the cheek. 'I so wish you could stay
part of Godmother's family or come to mine.' Her
face lit up. 'That is it. I will beg Papa and Mama
to let you come live with us. I have a younger
sister who will need a chaperon. Unless I contract
an acceptable alliance. Then you shall come stay
with me.' She beamed with satisfaction.

Mary Margaret hugged Annabell back and
fought off the tears her declaration had caused.
'My dear, that is so wonderful of you.' She carefully released the younger woman. 'But I could not
live with you, your family or the Countess. Much
as I would like to stay with you, I have a sister
and niece who need me. I shall be returning to
them when I leave here.'

'You cannot mean that.' Annabell jumped to her feet. 'Your sister is married to Mr Fox. The way he treats you he cannot want you with his family.'

Every word was true, but she could not, would not tell Annabell that. The girl did not need to know the sometimes ugly part of life. Instead she used Thomas as an excuse to end their conversation. She hugged Annabell and shooed her from the room. Minutes later she entered the drawing room where Thomas waited.

He whirled around at the sound of the door. 'It took you long enough.'

It took all of Mary Margaret's self-control not to cringe from the fury in Thomas's face. Annabell's little game of come-uppance would make this meeting nasty.

'I thought you would call tomorrow. I was asleep when I heard you were here. I am sorry it took so long.'

His words lashed out. 'See that it does not happen again.'

She nodded. How she wished she was braver and could make herself stand up to his tyranny. Somehow she managed to defy Ravensford all the time, but not Thomas.

The best she could do was ask, 'Why are you here?'

The smile he gave her was not pleasant. 'Have

you heard the latest *on-dit* making the rounds of the *ton*?'

She shook her head, not liking this. He was going to tell her something awful. She could feel it.

'I thought not,' he said with satisfaction. 'You probably have not heard of White's betting book either, have you?'

Again she shook her head. She was having difficulty getting a deep breath and her fingers were starting to shake. He was enjoying this too much.

'It is a book that the premier men in London write bets in. Your name is not in it, but it mentions you.' He gloated. 'In fact, there is a bet on how long it will take Ravensford to set you up in your own establishment as his mistress. Everyone knows he bought you an entire wardrobe.'

She swayed and would have fallen but for the chair behind her. As it was, she hit the seat so hard she nearly sent it over backward.

She was ruined. Last night had been nothing to Ravensford but part of a bet.

Black spots swam before her eyes.

'An interesting bit of information, don't you think?' Thomas asked cruelly.

She could not even nod. She could barely sit upright. Her heart was slowly crumbling to pieces.

She stared at nothing. Last night had been magical and magic did not last. She knew that. But, oh, how she had wanted it to.

And did this really make any difference? Ravensford had offered her marriage—again. She had all but said yes. So what if he did not love her and was only doing it to prevent a scandal? The aristocracy did not wed for love. That was something else she knew. But she loved him.

She closed her eyes.

'What are you doing here?'

Ravensford's cold voice penetrated the haze of pain surrounding her. She had not heard him enter. She had even forgotten that Thomas was here. It was strange how her world had gone from the crystal clarity of love to the dull blur of a heart wound.

'I came to speak with my sister-in-law,' Thomas answered, his voice equally chill.

'She does not seem interested in what you have to say.'

'Oh, she was. Believe me, she was.'

Thomas's voice was slick as oil on water. Mary Margaret wanted to jump up and slap him for destroying all her dreams, however far-fetched they had been. He was the one who had put her in the position to meet Ravensford and he was the one who had told her the truth and ruined everything.

She opened her eyes and looked directly at her brother-in-law. 'Go away, Thomas.'

He looked at her as though she had grown a second head. She nearly giggled, but it was too much effort. She felt a mild sense of wonder at her bravery, quickly gone.

'I will see you tonight at the ball,' Thomas said with heavy meaning.

She ignored him. Her emotions were too battered. *Ravensford had never said he loved her.* She had been too caught up in the wonder of what they were doing and his promise to care for her and hers that she had not realised that at the time.

He came and kneeled in front or her. Taking both her hands in his, he asked, 'What did he do to make you look this way?'

'He told me about the bet.'

'Ahh.' He leaned back on his heels. 'It was stupid of me to think you would not hear about it, but I had hoped.'

'For all your knowledge of the *ton* and politics, you are not very well versed in human nature.'

He shrugged and stood. 'It does not make any difference.'

She rose and moved to the door. 'You are deluding yourself, Ravensford.'

She left before he could stop her. She needed privacy and time to sort through her feelings, time to become numb, and headed for the gazebo.

She sat quietly in the sylvan green. Roses

scented the air and a light breeze kept her from getting hot. She loved it here.

Love. What an overused word. She loved cherries. She loved roses. She loved this gazebo. Then what did she feel for Ravensford? She cared if he was happy or hurt or angry. He was the person she thought the most about and cared the most for. She liked the way he considered others and went out of his way to help them. She liked everything about him.

Well...maybe some things irritated her, but not enough to matter.

Yes, she *loved* him. Everything else was only a like.

But what to do? He did not love her. He desired her, lusted after her. That was physical while love was emotional and spiritual. A flush warmed her as memories of last night heated her body. Perhaps there was the physical in love as well.

Marrying him would solve all her problems. He had the money and power to protect Emily and Annie from Thomas. He could give them a good life. She would be with the only man she would ever love or want to love. She would have his children. But being married to him when he did not love her would be a bitter pill.

She jumped up and paced the tiny, enclosed space. She could become his mistress. He would still provide protection for Emily and Annie. She might still bear at least one of his children—a bastard.

She stopped and buried her face in her hands. She could not do that to any child of hers.

Nor would he want to marry her if he ever found out that Thomas had placed her with the Countess in order to steal from her. It would not matter that she never intended to carry out Thomas's plan. It would be enough that she had allowed herself to go along with Thomas. Ravensford would despise her if he ever learned that. She could not bear the thought of being married to him when he found out and seeing his contempt every time he looked at her.

If he loved her, truly loved her, he might forgive her.

No, it would be better to go to the Countess and ask for her salary. It would not provide what Ravensford would, but it would be better for all of them this way. That had always been her plan.

Her decision made, Mary Margaret wondered why she did not feel at least a little better. But she did not.

She found the Countess in her suite and waited patiently until the older woman would see her. She had plenty of time to marvel at her continued bravery. In the past two hours, she had put herself forward more than she had in her entire life—except when dealing with Ravensford. She pushed that painful memory aside. There was no time to wallow in misery as the Countess's maid, Jane, had just opened the door.

'Her ladyship will see you now.' She frowned fiercely at Mary Margaret and barely moved enough to allow the younger woman to get by.

'Thank you,' Mary Margaret said quietly.

Jane had never liked her. Having to pack her clothes for the trip from Ireland had only made the animosity worse.

'My lady.' Mary Margaret curtsied.

The Countess gave her a stony look. 'What do you want?'

Not a good start, Mary Margaret thought, but then there never was with this woman. It took all her willpower not to wring her hands. That would only give the Countess satisfaction.

'It is the end of the quarter.' Perhaps the woman would take a hint.

'So?' She looked back at the embroidery in her lap.

Mary Margaret was not surprised, but she was angry. 'My salary is due.'

The Countess turned back to Mary Margaret, her eyes hard as fine gems and her mouth a cruel line.

'Salary? You have no salary coming. It was all spent to replace my cape that you convinced my foolish son you needed.'

'What?' Mary Margaret felt as though she had taken a direct hit to the stomach. 'But I sent it back to you. It was in perfect shape. I made sure myself.'

The Countess made a tiny, derisive snort. 'Do you really think I would wear something after you had? And there are all the clothes Andrew purchased for you. You will be a long time repaying those.'

Worse and worse. Panic rose its ugly head, and it was all Mary Margaret could do to make herself breathe. This was beyond reasonable.

'Why are you doing this?' Her voice was a deep rasp of anguish. 'I have never done anything to you. All I have ever wanted was to be a good servant and companion.'

The Countess sneered, her lovely face marred by hate. 'You have seduced my only child. Do you think I don't know what has been going on? You blanch, as you should. You are no better than the sluts who ply their wares in Covent Garden.'

Mary Margaret felt light-headed and wondered if she would further disgrace herself by fainting. She swayed but managed to stay upright.

'I have done nothing of the kind,' she said, but even to her, her voice sounded weak and false.

He had seduced her. Surely that made a difference. Didn't it? Not to this woman. Not to anyone but her.

A sly look replaced the previous fury on the Countess's countenance. 'I want you out of this house immediately. I will provide you with money to return to Ireland. If you do this, I will forget about everything else. But do not ever come near my son again.'

Blow on blow. She could get back to Ireland, but once there would have nothing to live on, let alone provide for Emily and Annie.

The small rebellious and brave part of her that seemed to be growing by the hour wanted to defy the Countess. That part wanted to marry Ravensford and be damned to the consequences. It gave her courage now.

'I need more than passage home. I need money to live on.'

She trembled at her temerity. Just days or even hours ago she would not have been able to say those things. But it was done. She kept her gaze on the other woman instead of looking away as she longed to do.

The Countess drew herself up. 'You are a bold piece. How much do you want?'

'What is due me for this last quarter worked.'

'Done,' the Countess said. 'Now get out of my sight.'

Mary Margaret did so with alacrity. She rushed out of the room, the door slamming behind her, and right into Ravensford's arms.

'Where are you going in such a hurry?'

'Home.'

The word was out of her mouth before she had time to even think. Her nerves were jangling and her mind was numb.

His face showed no emotion. 'Ireland?'

She nodded.

'Because of my mother or because of the bet?' His voice was dangerously quiet, but Mary Margaret had been through too much in the last twenty-four hours to care.

'Both.'

'I think not,' he said softly, too softly.

Before she knew what was happening, he dragged her back into his mother's room. 'Out,' he ordered Jane who stood her ground until the Countess nodded.

'You have overstepped yourself this time, Mother,' he said.

She glared down her aristocratic nose at him even though she remained seated and he towered over her. 'I am only trying to protect you from your own folly. She is nothing but an adventuress. I should have never brought her into my household.'

Ravensford still held her so Mary Margaret could not flee. She had to listen to them discuss her as though she was not present. The tiny core of rebellion growing inside her flared to life.

'I am not an object for the two of you to bicker over.'

'Keep quiet,' the Countess ordered.

'I am a human being with feelings.'

The Countess gave her a contemptuous look. 'You are little better than—'

'Mother,' Ravensford said. 'I warn you. Mary Margaret is going to marry me. What you say to her now will impact on what happens to you after we are wed.'

The Countess paled, her translucent skin looking like a ghost. Her eyes were bright flames. 'I will not allow you to do such a thing, Andrew.'

Mary Margaret twisted in his hold, but he tightened his grip. 'I did not agree,' she said softly, wondering why even now she contradicted him.

Because she wanted to marry him for love. Nor would he want to marry her if he ever found out that she had been sent here to steal from his mother.

He gazed down at her. 'Oh, you agreed. You agreed very willingly.'

She saw the fire and hunger leap into his eyes and knew exactly what he meant. By giving herself to him last night, she had, in his mind, committed to him. He was right, she had at the time.

'Things have changed,' she said, her voice deep and raspy with remembered pain. 'For me.'

'But not for me.'

'Andrew.' The Countess's tone demanded attention. 'I won't have it. If you marry her, I will do everything in my power to see that she is ostracised by Society.'

Compassion softened the angles of his face. 'That does not matter, Mother. Not everyone cares about being accepted by the *ton*. I don't. I am sure Mary Margaret does not. And we all know that Lady Holland does not. Nor has her lack of acceptance impacted on Lord Holland's political career,' he ended with a meaningful look.

The Countess huffed. 'I was not about to suggest that Lady Holland's scandalous past has hurt Lord Holland in the least. But no decent woman will go to their house.'

Ravensford shook his head. 'I doubt it matters to them, Mother.'

'Well, it should. Just as it should matter to you.' She cast a venomous look at Mary Margaret. 'You will be sorry if you defy me. She won't make you happy.' Suddenly, like the sun peaking through clouds, a wistfulness entered her eyes. 'Not like your father and I were.'

'She is right,' Mary Margaret said. 'Ours would be a marriage of convenience. You would grow tired of me.'

A strange light turned his eyes a deeper green. 'I am going to announce our engagement tonight during the ball.'

Both women gasped.

'No,' the Countess ordered.

'You cannot,' Mary Margaret whispered, horrified.

'I can and I will.'

Chapter Fifteen

Ravensford turned from the fire in time to see Mary Margaret framed in the drawing-room doorway. Fierce pride filled him.

After him, she was the first one down. Jones bowed himself out, leaving the two of them alone.

Madame Bertrice's gown accomplished everything he had wished for. The deep pink brought colour to her face, giving her the famous cream-and-roses complexion. Her tilted eyes glowed like green brilliants. Even the demure, almost harsh, line of her chignon appeared elegant, as though it had been specially designed to show off the gown's plunging neckline.

Mary Margaret's bosom swelled above the fine silk, drawing his eye to the dark valley that he longed to explore. Once had not been enough. He was not sure a lifetime would be enough. From the first moment he had heard the sultry purr of her voice he had desired her. Tonight she was his. Or would be, he thought ironically, seeing the coldness in her face, once he had convinced her that marriage was best.

'You are beautiful,' he said. He picked the jewellery box up from the table beside him and opened it. 'These will complement your dress.' He took out the grey pearls.

Her gaze flicked to the necklace and back to him. 'They are not appropriate.'

There was no bending in her. 'You have gained strength since I first met you.'

'I have had to.' Her voice was lightly tinged with bitterness. 'Is your mother down?' Only now did her tone hold a hint of discomfort.

'My mother has nothing to do with this, Mary Margaret.' When she did not respond, he added, 'She will be going back to Ireland soon. You and I will stay here. Your sister and niece are being brought here.'

Mary Margaret listened to his words and wondered why he was doing all these things. He did not love her, yet he would not let her go.

After leaving his mother's suites earlier, he had told her that no matter what the Countess had said or offered to pay her, she was not leaving. Since that time, she had been a virtual prisoner in the house. The only thing that had brought her down for the evening was his vow that he had already sent for her sister. She owed him her presence that he seemed so insistent on having.

'I will not marry you,' she said yet again. 'Your mother is right.'

But how she longed to do so. If he only loved her she would take the risk. Even now, it hurt just to tell him no when she wanted so badly to tell him yes. But it would take more than lust for him to tolerate her if he ever found out that she had been sent by Thomas to rob his mother and she had not told Thomas no.

'Turn around,' he said, more gently. 'I am determined that you will wear these.'

She sighed. How much longer could she keep fighting him? She did not know. For the moment it was easier to acquiesce. After all, he had already bought her an entire wardrobe, and although she did not wear any of the clothes, the entire world knew about them. They were still packed in boxes in her room. She turned.

His fingers brushed the nape of her neck and his warm breath fanned her skin. She clenched her hands into fists to keep from turning and wrapping them into his hair. He made her blood sing and her heart thrill.

'Please hurry,' she rasped.

'Am I bothering you?' His voice was as rich as cream and as potent as the liquor he drank.

'No.'

He chuckled low in his throat. 'I'm almost done. Then there are the ear bobs and the bracelets.'

She nearly groaned. This was torture, and drat the man, he knew it. No matter how she tried, her body and soul responded to him. No matter how she strove to hide her reaction he knew.

His hands shifted to her shoulders and he turned her unresisting body so that she faced him. 'Say yes.'

She caught back a moan. How she wanted to accept him. She wanted that more than anything. If only she could. If only they could somehow make it work. If only he loved her then she would take the chance. Romantic fool that she was, she believed that love could make anything work.

She knew he watched her but she studiously looked away. The last thing she wanted was to see the hunger in his eyes that he did nothing to hide. She wanted his love, not just his passion. He didn't love her and, foolish woman that she was, she wanted love.

'I cannot,' she whispered. 'I must not. Believe me, this is for the best.'

'Then look at me when you refuse and convince me that you speak the truth.' Anger tinged his words now and his eyes, when she looked back at him, flared.

Before she could say anything, and she did not know what to say, the door opened and Jones announced, 'The Countess of Ravensford and Miss Winston. Mr Fox.'

Mary Margaret broke from Ravensford's hold. The expression on the Countess's face as she watched them made Mary Margaret feel as though she had been caught doing something despicable. In the Countess's opinion, she had.

Thomas subjected her to a narrowed scrutiny. 'Cosy, aren't we,' he said sarcastically.

She arched one brow. 'I thought you were not invited until after dinner?' It was a low hit, but it gave her satisfaction.

He smirked. 'Your delightful charge invited me. I considered her wishes to take precedence over Ravensford's.'

Annabell came up to them and beamed. 'I see you two have finally worked everything out. I am so glad.' She hugged Mary Margaret. 'It will be wonderful having you in the family.'

Mary Margaret returned the girl's hug. 'You are so impetuous, Annabell,' she chided gently. 'The Earl and I have no agreement and nothing to arrange.'

Annabell stepped back and gave the two of them

an arch look. 'I did not fall off the turnip wagon yesterday.' She laughed and moved away.

It was just as well. Jones announced more arrivals. Dinner would consume the near future. Then the ball. Mary Margaret knew the entire evening would be a crush of bodies.

And she still had to tell Thomas that she was not going to steal the Countess's jewellery tonight. Discomfort was a condition she was becoming depressingly familiar with.

'Nice pearls,' Thomas hissed. 'Make sure you take them with you.'

She jumped, not having heard him come up behind her. 'Be careful. Someone could overhear.'

He laughed. It was not a pleasant sound. She moved quickly away only to find herself caught up by Ravensford. Before she knew what he was doing, she was being introduced to everyone.

Ravensford smiled at each person as he presented her, but his eyes were hard chips until the introduction was graciously accepted. Mary Margaret realised that he was trying to present her to his Society and force them to accept her regardless of the rumours flying.

After an eternity, they went into dinner. Mary Margaret nearly fled the room when she realised she was to be seated beside Ravensford. Everyone looked at her and she did her best not to blush.

The only saving grace with the arrangement was that the Countess was at the opposite end of the table.

The woman across the table eyed Mary Margaret through her lorgnette. 'Where did you say you are from, Miss O'Brien?'

'Ireland, my lady.' Old habits die hard and it was not until the form of address was out that Mary Margaret realised it was inappropriate for her current situation.

'She is from Cashel, Ireland, Lady Steele,' Ravensford cut in. 'Near my mother's estate.' He gave the woman a feral smile. 'Would you care for more turtle soup?'

'Please,' Lady Steele said, turning her attention to the gentleman on her left.

Mary Margaret's dinner partner to her right, Mr Atworthy, asked, 'How long will you be staying in Town, Miss O'Brien?'

'Quite some time,' Ravensford said smoothly before she could answer.

Mr Atworthy looked from her to the Earl, his interest obviously piqued. 'Really? Are you by any chance Miss Winston's chaperon, Miss O'Brien?'

A direct question with only one answer. 'Yes,' she said firmly before Ravensford could reply.

She was grateful that her voice had not wavered. They would dine on her like a shark on a minnow if she faltered. Ravensford gave her an approving smile.

'She was, Atworthy. No more.'

Atworthy raised one brow. 'How intriguing.'

The next course arrived and while the bowls and plates were removed Mary Margaret tried to marshal her thoughts. If she could get through dinner, she could escape while everyone was going to the ballroom and the rest of the guests were arriving. She just had to grit her teeth and bear the next hour or so.

She was nearly ready to plead sickness when the Countess stood, indicating that the ladies were to withdraw. She stood with alacrity even though she knew she had to wait for the other women to precede her from the room. All the gentlemen's gazes turned to her, watching as though she were an exotic animal and they did not know what she might do next.

A month ago she would have done her best to pretend they were not there. Even an hour ago she would have done so. But now she was tired and irritable. With a courage she had never thought she possessed, she stared each man down. The only one who refused to look away was Perth. He silently toasted her with the last of his dinner wine.

She finally swept from the room, buoyed up by Perth's silent support. Her joy was short-lived.

Two women she had previously met stood together, heads close. The first sniffed haughtily. 'So that is Ravensford's lightskirt. She isn't much. However, he has gone too far introducing her to polite society. I, for one, will never invite her anywhere.'

There it was. Even if she let herself weaken and marry Ravensford, it would be miserable. Not that she cared what the old biddy thought, but despite his earlier words, Ravensford might. And what would he and they think if they knew about Thomas's plan? It did not bear dwelling on.

Rather than continue to subject herself to such treatment, Mary Margaret decided it was time to go to her room. Later, after the dancing had started, she would come back down and seek out Thomas.

With weary relief, she entered her room and closed the door behind her. She would lie down for a few minutes and try to regain her strength.

She set the candle on the table and snuffed the flame. She stretched out on her bed with a weary sigh, careful to smooth her dress so as not to wrinkle it any more than necessary. The last thing she wanted was to get a maid to help her undress and then dress again.

Mary Margaret woke with a start. The room was too dark to see anything clearly, but she sensed she was not alone.

She sat up and swung her legs over the side of the bed until her feet touched the floor. 'Who is there?' she asked in a voice that just kept from trembling.

'Not Ravensford,' Thomas said nastily.

A kind of relief slumped her shoulders. Thomas was not someone she wanted in her bedchamber, but he would not hurt her. Or had not done so yet.

She lit the candle by the bed and carried it over to the chair beside Thomas. She sat down and placed the candle on the table.

'Why are you here?'

He snorted in disgust. 'Don't be any more stupid than you have to be. Why do you think I am here? Where are the jewels?'

The single light threw his handsome face into harsh relief. His eyes were dark sockets. Mary Margaret found that she was suddenly tense. Still, there was no sense in prolonging the inevitable.

She licked dry lips. 'I assume they are in the Countess's room. Or the Earl's safe.'

'When do you intend to get them?' he asked softly, his voice silky smooth.

She decided to get closer to the door. She stood and walked casually away, hoping he would think she was moving from nervousness caused by contemplating the theft.

'Where do you think you are going?'

He moved too fast. She broke for the door. He caught her, his fingers gripping her wrist cruelly.

'I asked you a question,' he said, tightening his hold.

Her heart beat like a drum. It was all she could do to keep herself from shouting for help. She told herself she was being silly. He might be hurting her, but still this was only Thomas. He could not reach Emily and Annie. He had no hold over her.

She took a deep breath and stared up at him. She was barely able to make out his features, but she sensed he was tense.

'I was leaving…but not to get the jewels.' She twisted her arm in a vain attempt to get free. 'I am not going to steal from the Countess.'

He tossed her against the wall. The force of contact knocked the air out of her lungs. She gasped.

'Tell me that again,' he threatened.

She forced herself to straighten up even though her chest hurt badly. She told herself she knew he would not seriously injure her, but she still feared the pain he could cause.

'Who's in there?' Ravensford's voice said from outside.

Relief flooded Mary Margaret only to be followed by dread. He would keep Thomas from doing anything more to her, but she had no doubt that Thomas would see that she paid for refusing to help him. She sighed and slumped against the wall.

'Come in,' Thomas said.

Ravensford entered and closed the door behind himself. He carried a candelabra with five candles. Light radiated out in a circle, so bright it hurt Mary Margaret's eyes after the dimness of seconds before.

'What are you doing here?' Ravensford's baritone was deep and dangerous.

Thomas smirked. 'Perhaps you should ask your *chère amie*.' He gave Mary Margaret a sly look. 'Or have you already told him?'

She knew she looked guilty when Thomas laughed.

'No, you have not.' Contempt dripped from every word. 'I swear you have no spine. Just like your sister. You sleep with the man but cannot find the courage to tell him the truth about why you are working for his mother.'

Shame burned through Mary Margaret. Thomas was a cad, but he said only the truth right now.

She could not make herself look at Ravensford. She looked at a spot near his shoulder. She did not want to see the disgust on his face when she told him. She could not stand to see his eyes fill with the same contempt that shone in Thomas's.

'Tell him,' Thomas said, 'or I will.'

She cast her brother-in-law a venomous look.

'I was supposed to steal your mother's jewellery tonight. That is why Thomas is here, to pick up the gems.'

There. The awful truth was out. It was over. Now he would hate her. He would be thankful she had refused his offer of marriage. He would throw her out when he threw out Thomas.

A single tear escaped her control. Not only would she never see him again, but he would always remember her this way—as a thief and cheat and coward.

Pain such as she had never imagined possible welled up inside her. So much pain, quickly followed by anger—at herself, at Thomas.

Without thinking, propelled by the mingled pain and anger, she launched herself at Thomas's sneering face. She balled her fist and let loose. She connected and Thomas rocked back on his heels.

She glared at him. 'I hate you for what you are and what you have done to my sister and what you tried to make me do.' Tears started down her cheeks in earnest and she twisted away from his shocked face. 'But most of all I hate myself for not being strong enough to tell you no right from the start.'

She heard scuffling and the heavy thud of someone hitting the floor. Thomas sprawled on the rug, one hand on his red jaw. Ravensford towered over him.

'Get up and get out. Leave England if you know what is good for you. Don't return to Ireland. With Mary Margaret's confession I can have the magistrate waiting for you there. Once word is out about what you planned, you will be ruined. No one wants a curate like you. And don't try to find your wife and daughter. If I catch you near them, I will have you horsewhipped like the cur you are.'

Shivers raced up Mary Margaret's spine. She hoped never to see Ravensford this deadly angry again. Her heart twisted. She did not have to worry. She would never see him again at all.

Thomas turned bitter eyes on Mary Margaret. 'Don't worry about your precious sister. I never wanted her. She got pregnant and I had to marry her because of my position. All I ever wanted in life was what I deserved, what I was born to. Your refusal to steal has only delayed that. I'll find someone else with more guts than a worm.'

He strode away, pausing inches from Ravensford. 'She's not worth whatever she will cost you.

Nor is her mealy-mouthed sister. You are welcome to the lot.'

Anger burned away Mary Margaret's tears. 'How dare you? How dare you speak of them like that? If Emily was pregnant before you wed, it was because you seduced her and she loved you too much to say no. You are despicable.'

'Get out now,' Ravensford said, 'before I thrash you to within an inch of your life.'

Thomas left without another word. Silence filled the room like dirt in a grave. Mary Margaret felt like her life was finished. From now on she would merely exist. But at least Emily was free of Thomas.

'Mary Margaret,' Ravensford said softly, 'come here. Please.'

She looked at him, expecting to see contempt or dislike and instead saw compassion and another emotion she did not dare name. 'I think it would be better if I left now.'

He shook his head. 'What have I been saying to you all this time?'

She stood mute. There was nothing left she could say. He knew everything about her and she knew he could not still want to marry her. He had not wanted to marry her in the first place. Only his honour had made him propose.

'Mary Margaret, if I have to come and get you I will make sure you don't get away.'

'Why?' Agony twisted her soul. 'You don't want me. You never wanted me—except in your bed. Then when the bet was made you were too much the gentleman not to propose.' She gulped air, trying to ease some of the tension tearing her apart. 'Please, Ravensford, don't do this. I can be gone immediately. You have done enough just by getting Thomas out of my sister's life. And I thank you from my heart.'

A tiny smile tugged at his mouth. 'I don't want your thanks from the heart, Mary Margaret.' He moved slowly toward her. 'I want more than that.'

She tilted back her head to see his face. His eyes were dark, his cheeks sharp lines. If she did not know it was impossible, she would say he wanted her—still.

'I have given you everything I have,' she whispered.

He stopped when only inches separated them. 'Have you?' A fierce predatory gleam lit his face. 'Then tell me.'

'Don't do this,' she pleaded. 'It is not fair that I love you and you don't feel the same about me.' She buried her face in her hands. 'There, I have told you. Once more I was not strong enough to walk from here without doing as you bid.'

With exultation he grabbed her and cradled her against his chest. One hand angled her reluctant head up so that he looked down at her. The other hand burrowed into her thick hair.

'Foolish, love. You are the strongest woman I know. You have cared for your sister, worked for my mother and stood up to Fox—not to mention me.'

Love. He had called her love.

Hope flared, only to die. 'I am weak or I would have never agreed to Thomas's plan.'

He kissed her gently. 'You had no choice. I heard him threaten you that day in my mother's library.'

'What?' She went rigid, both hands pressing against his chest in an effort to get free. He held her closer. 'You have known all along?'

He nodded. 'I knew you did not want to do as he said, but that you feared for Emily. Later I learned Emily is your sister.'

'But why did you let the charade go on? Why have you treated me so well?' Confusion now held her still in his embrace. She did not know what to think.

He grinned ruefully. 'I was intrigued by you, by everything about you.' He stroked one finger down her jaw to her chin where the cleft was. 'I still am. I think I always will be.'

'But I am nothing.'

'Stop that.' He shook her. 'You are kind and caring. You were willing to do anything to help your sister. And Annabell adores you. The servants like and respect you.'

She was dazed. 'But you don't love me. You cannot. We are from different worlds and I have lived a lie in your home.' Every word hurt, but they had to be said. 'And I want love when I marry.'

'Ah, Mary Margaret.' He stroked her hair back from her face. 'Have I been so good at hiding my feelings? Don't you know that I love you? Can't you sense it when I touch you, when I kiss you? And when we made love, didn't you feel me worship you with my body?'

Stunned, she would have slid to the floor if he had not been holding her. 'I know you desire me. But that is not love.'

'You have so much to learn about men, my love. Making love to you is a form of loving you. Just as caring for you and caring for your sister. Men show their love through deeds, not through words.' He paused as though gathering his courage. 'Mary Margaret, I love you. I want to marry you.'

Hope began to fill her heart. Perhaps there was a chance for them. Perhaps he truly did love her.

She tried her last argument. 'What about your mother?'

'She can go to Ireland or she can accept you and stay around and watch our children grow.' He gazed lovingly at her. 'Because now that I have found you and made you admit that you love me, I am not letting you get away.'

The hope that had started filled her to overflowing. She could no longer refuse him or herself. She loved him too much to let him go now.

'Then we will have to make this work.'

'Yes, my love, we will.'

Epilogue

⁂

One year later…

Mary Margaret stood in the doorway to the nursery and silently watched her mother-in-law. The Countess held the future Earl of Ravensford, cooing at the infant like the besotted grandmother she was.

A large, warm hand twined around hers and pulled her away. Ravensford, her husband, smiled down at her as he guided her along the hall.

'My mother will take good care of our son, sweetings.'

She snuggled into his side. 'I know. I just like to watch the two of them together. It reassures me that there is a gentle, caring side to your mother.'

He tenderly smoothed a strand of hair from her

brow. 'I know she still is not always nice to you. I am sorry for that. More than I can say.'

She went on tiptoe and kissed him lightly. 'I know. Things are better and with time—who knows? She and I might become bosom friends.'

He shook his head in wonder. 'Your continual ability to look at the positive always amazes me.'

He caught her lips with his, deepening the kiss until she leaned against his chest in complete surrender. He was her entire world.

'Aunt,' a young, feminine voice said in shocked tones. 'You and Uncle Andrew are going to scandalise the servants.'

Another woman's warm laugh filled the area. 'Annie, leave your aunt and uncle alone. Theirs is a love match.'

Mary Margaret grinned at her niece and sister. 'I am so glad you decided to come stay with us.'

'As am I,' Ravensford seconded. 'Not only do you provide additional family for my love, but you are safer from Fox if he should decide my threat is hollow.'

All three females gazed adoringly at him, but his wife hugged him. 'Thomas would never doubt you. He ran from my room that night like a fox fleeing the hounds.'

'And just what was he doing in your room?' the Countess demanded, having come up on the group without their noticing. Baby Andrew cooed contentedly in his grandmother's arms.

Mary Margaret reached for her son. 'It is time for his feeding,' she murmured, having decided to nurse her child instead of having a wet-nurse. She cast a mischievous glance at her husband as she left him to deal with his mother.

But Ravensford was not going to be deserted. 'Excuse me, ladies. I will explain everything to you later, Mother. Right now a father's place is with his wife and son.'

Mary Margaret chuckled as she sat down in the rocker and put her baby to her breast. Baby Andrew had just settled in when Ravensford closed the nursery door. He looked at his wife and child, the boy's mouth sucking avidly at one milky-white breast.

'Your bosom is larger than before,' Ravensford murmured, taking a seat beside them.

She intended to only glance at him, but the desire he made no effort to hide caught her. A flush mounted her skin, starting where her child suckled and rising to her cheeks.

'Ravensford,' she murmured in slight protest. 'This is not the time.'

'I know,' he muttered, his voice a husk. 'But after our son has his fill I insist on having mine.

He needs a little sister and I've a mind to do my best to provide him with one.'

Excitement curled in Mary Margaret's stomach. 'And I've a mind to help you, my lord.'

Ravensford leaned over and kissed her. 'I love you.'

'And I you,' she replied, meaning it with all her heart and soul.

* * * * *

THE STEEPWOOD

Scandals

*Regency drama, intrigue, mischief...
and marriage*

VOLUME ONE

Lord Ravensden's Marriage by Anne Herries

As everyone wonders at the truth behind the
disappearance of the Marchioness of Sywell, Beatrice's
beautiful younger sister is forced to return from London
– hotly pursued by Harry, Lord Ravensden!

✑

An Innocent Miss by Elizabeth Bailey

Believing his strong feelings for her to be returned,
George, Viscount Wyndham is amazed, then angered at
having his marriage proposal turned down. Has Serena
transferred her affections?

On sale 3rd November 2006

*Available at WHSmith, ASDA, Tesco
and all good bookshops*

M&B

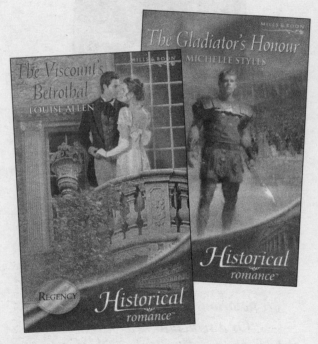

MILLS & BOON®

Live the emotion

*H*istorical
romance™

A LADY OF RARE QUALITY
by *Anne Ashley*

REGENCY

They have never seen Viscount Greythorpe listen so
intently when a lady speaks. To have caught the eye of
this esteemed gentleman, Miss Annis Milbank must
be a lady of rare quality indeed. Innocent to the world,
the question of who the beautiful Annis will marry has
never been foremost in her mind... However, Viscount
Greythorpe is confident she will soon be his...

THE NORMAN'S BRIDE
by *Terri Brisbin*

Recalling nothing of her own identity, Isabel was
sure her rescuer, Royce, had once been a knight, for
he expressed a chivalry that his simple way of life
could not hide. William Royce de Severin could not quell
his desire for this intriguing woman. Unbroken in spirit,
she made him hunger for the impossible – a life free of
dark secrets, with Isabel by his side.

On sale 3rd November 2006

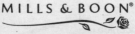